Blood Singer Trilogy Omnibus

Blood Singer
Blood Queen
Blood Origins
Blood Equinox
Willow Asteria

Content Warning

Please be advised that this book may not be suitable for all audiences.

This book contains sexual content, anxiety with panic attacks, degradation, narcissism, kidnapping, bondage, death, blood, dub-con, cheating, abusive father, and other topics some readers may not find suitable.

For anyone that has ever
wanted to take a bath with
a hot vampire prince...

This one is for you.

Blood Singer

Willow Asteria

The Vampire Prince

Part 1

Prologue

A forest surrounds my small village. We have always been told never to enter, under any circumstance. The village has everything we could ever need.

Ever since I turned eighteen something deep within the forest called to me, drawing me in. One night I just couldn't resist any longer. I slipped out of bed, still in my nightclothes. I snuck out of the group home and walked into the forest. I could feel the crunch of leaves under my bare feet.

I wandered in a trance-like state deep into the dark and dense forest. Everything around me was in a haze and I couldn't tell what direction was which. I followed the call until I found a cottage in a clearing. That is where the call was coming from. It was a sweet melody in the back of my mind. As I approached, the door opened.

"H...Hello?" I called out as I walked inside. The door slammed behind me. I spun to see what had caused it to shut. No one was there. It must have been the wind.

I turned back around to see the most beautiful man I had ever seen. Something about him made my heart flutter. Everything about him drew me in. He stood there towering over me, shirtless, his muscles on display. His long dark hair was down, a bit disheveled. He looked down at me, his eyes red as blood.

"Hello, doll." He gave a smirk, his fangs on display. His voice was like a melody that melted me away. He slammed me into the wall. I begged for him to let me go as he sank his fangs into my neck.

Everything went fuzzy and faded to black.

One

I jolted awake and looked at the time. 12:01 AM on my eighteenth birthday. A cold sweat dripped down my body from the nightmares I had just had. Nightmares I had experienced my whole life. This time I knew them not to be nightmares, but memories. Memories from all my past lives.

I knew two things to be true. First, is that I had lived and died more times than I could count. All before I turned nineteen. Second, is that the same man had killed me each time. The Crown Prince of the Vampires, Darius Dragomeir. Thinking his name sent a shiver down my spine.

Humans and vampires used to live in peace. No one was sure what changed that. We humans were second-class citizens to the vampires. They forced us to live in separate sections of cities. Many of us lived out in the countryside to avoid vampires altogether. However, outside of the city was a brutal wasteland and densely forested mountains. Though they didn't have to deal with vampires, their lives were not easy.

The city I lived in, Titus, was one of the worst to live in as a human. It was the capital city in our kingdom that shares its name. The Royal Palace was on the far side of the city, in the Golden Circle. Vampires lived in most sections of the city. Few places were safe for humans. Even in human areas, it was not uncommon for vampires to come in and take what they wanted. The human sections were very run down. Some humans ended up homeless because of the rundown buildings. Those humans ended up food or pets for a vampire. Sometimes it was just easier that way.

I always thought about moving to one of the villages where just humans lived, but something always prevented me from doing so. A sinking feeling grew within my chest thinking, "Now may be the best time for me to head to one of those villages." If I went, would I be safe there? Would I even be able to leave or will some strange force in the universe that had stopped me several times before stop me again? There was always a voice in the back of my head that pulled me back into the city. I had attributed it to my fear of the unknown, but maybe there was something else at play.

I laid back down, looking up at the ceiling, and then back at the clock. 12:02 AM. All my worries would not make the time go any faster. Would my final days be slow and painful, or will they flash before my eyes until all I see is the black abyss? I took a deep breath and closed my eyes. My heart pounded in my chest as the images from my memories played back in my head. I tried to force them out, to think of anything else. Absolutely anything else. All I could think of was what painful death awaited me.

"Sabrina!" A shrill voice yelled from behind my bedroom door accompanied by three hard poundings. My eyes stayed shut and gave a small yawn. "I'll be down in a moment!" I called out in response. After a moment of staring at the ceiling, I sat up and got out of bed. I thought after my revelation last night that today would feel different, but it didn't. I put on my dark denim jeans and a forest green sweater and sat at my vanity. As I applied my makeup, I got lost in my reflection. My long dark hair was a frizzy mess until I applied some product and brushed it through. I hated the thought of looking unpresentable.

My door burst open. "Gosh, you are slow in the morning," my best friend, Isabella, and I have lived together for years. She came in and sat on the end of the bed. The King took her parents when she was just a kid. She had lived on her own for a while when we met. I was so grateful when she let me stay with her. I finished applying my makeup and smiled at her.

"Sorry, I didn't sleep too well last night."

"Are you having your nightmares again?"

I nodded. She would think I was crazy if I told her everything. I mean, it sounded crazy. The fact that I reincarnated just to have the Vampire Prince kill me over and over? Maybe my brain just made that up. Maybe it was just a part of the nightmare.

"We need to be careful today. I just saw on the news the Prince is in another frenzy. A hundred humans have already died in the Golden Circle." Isa said. I felt my heart drop. Darius was a killer, and now he was after me.

"That's terrible. I'm glad we live on the other side of the city." I said, looking away.

The city was split into five districts. The Golden Circle, where the Royal Palace and many nobles resided. They named the Golden Circle after the flecks of gold embedded into the pavement. Etincea, our tech district. Titus was a technological city. From the stories I had heard of the countryside, this was vastly different from the rest of the kingdom. Kaedorr's Institute of Higher Learning is where many scholars from around the continent gather to obtain more knowledge. Only vampires were allowed to attend. Veneration Square was where all the best markets were held. If you needed something, The Square had it. Most of the shops were vampire-only, but humans had one or two good shops and farmer's markets. Elysium Court is where I lived, and most of the humans did as well. Nothing of its name held. Elysium was the scourge of this city. However, I was as far away from the Golden Circle as possible.

I stood, finally ready for the day. "It's about time," she told me. She always teased me for being girly. She was never interested in appearance. Few humans did anymore. It was the one thing I wouldn't let the vampires take from me. My interest in beauty and fashion was something that made me feel human, not just a number as many of us were.

We headed out of our apartment and down the stairs. Isa told me to be careful as a few of the steps had been broken when she returned home from work yesterday. The human sections of the city were not well taken care of. We had a few humans on the city council to represent us, but our needs barely received any funding. Just a way to keep us in the hands of the vampires for our every need and whim.

As we reached the ground floor, we heard crying from outside. A mother pleading with someone not to take away her daughter. As we stepped outside, we saw a car speeding off. A woman was in the middle of the road begging them to come back. Unfortunately, this was a normal sight. If a vampire wanted someone, no one could stop them from taking what they wanted. At any moment, that could be any of us if we came across the wrong vampire. Isa grabbed my arm and gave a little tug. I was just standing there, staring at the woman without even realizing it.

I followed Isa's guidance as we headed a few blocks over to a small farmers' market. It wasn't much, but it did supply fresh food. That was fairly scarce these days in the city. Just another reason those villages sounded better. Many of them had their own farms and produced so much food that some of it made its way into the city. We went our separate ways as we checked out the stalls and purchased what we needed for the week.

I noticed something odd about one stall. It was set away from the others; the table was also bare, and an older man sat on the other side. Something from within me was telling me I needed to speak with the man. As I approached, his mouth widened into a grin.

"Ah, welcome! And Happy Birthday." I looked at him in shock. No one knew when my birthday was, not even Isa. I never liked to celebrate it.

"How do you know it is my birthday?" I said to him with concern.

"Because you have a look of clarity, Blood Singer." His eyes went dark. As he called me a Blood Singer, my heart sank. I had never heard this term, yet it felt familiar.

"I do not know what you are talking about."

"Oh, but you do. And you will. He is already on his way. As soon as the clock struck midnight, your blood sang to him." I took a step back. I felt as if there was a knot in my chest. Everything felt a bit fuzzy. I heard Isa call my name from behind me and everything snapped back. The man, the booth, it was all gone. I turned back to Isa.

"We need to head home, there's something I need to tell you."

Two

Isa stares at me blankly from across our kitchen table. The light above us gives a small flicker as she finally blinks. After a long moment of silence, she finally opens her mouth to speak. "Did you hit your head or something?"

Of course, she didn't believe me. I mean would I have even believed myself?

"No, I didn't hit my head. I am being one hundred percent serious."

"Have you met the Prince? How do you know these nightmares are memories?"

Of course, I had never met him. Any human that had met him died shortly after. His thirst for humans was unlike anything else. That man, if you could call him that, was terrifying. Rumor says he feasts on at least fifty humans a day. His hunger cannot be satisfied. But yet, he was enthralling. Everything inside me screamed at me and pulled for me to find him. I couldn't get the image of him out of my mind.

As for her second question, it was just a feeling in my gut. I knew for a fact that those are all things that have happened to me before. Before last night, these nightmares were hazy. I knew someone was being murdered by a vampire, but the figures were always dark and in the shadows. Last night, it was as clear as day. It was him and I, and over and over he ripped out my throat with his fangs.

"I think you need to relax. Maybe you should see someone about the nightmares you have been having. Maybe talking to a professional will help you figure out what is happening in your brain." Isa was right, maybe it was time I talked to someone. There were tons of counselors around the city that specialized in trauma caused by vampires. She recommended the person she spoke with after her parents were taken. I took the piece of paper with their information, folded it up, and put it in my pocket.

"Promise me you will talk to them?" She said in a concerned voice. I gave a small nod. Isa stood, told me that she had to get ready for work, and headed into her room. I leaned back into my chair and sighed. I would talk to someone about my nightmare, just not that day. I couldn't get the words the old man told me out of my brain. "Blood Singer." What could that even mean?

"Hey, while you're out I'm going to head to the library!" I called out to Isa as I grabbed my purse. She stuck her head out of her bedroom and gave a concerned look.

"At this time of the day? Are you sure you can make it back before dark?" The library was on the other side of the city. It was pretty close to vampire-only territory, but it wouldn't take too long to get back in time. Humans had a self-imposed curfew. Nothing good could happen after dark. I told Isa that it should be fine and headed out the door.

I rushed to the library, and after about a forty-minute walk, I finally arrived. I had plenty of time to find anything that could have the information that I was looking for. As I walked in, a cool burst of air hit me. Places like this always had their AC on even though the days had gotten cooler and the leaves had changed.

I approached the desk where a small older woman sat. She looked like one of the librarians that you would see in one of those older movies. As if she was plucked and groomed for this job her whole life.

"Um...Excuse me. I have a quick question." I whispered, giving a warm smile. She looked up from her book to acknowledge my presence. "I was wondering if you had any books on the royal family and a Blood Singer?"

"A...Blood Singer?" She questioned.

"Um, yes. I heard a man mention it today at the market and I wish to learn more."

"Are you one of those blood whores? They aren't welcome here." She said coldly. Even though most humans hated vampires, there were a few who worshiped them as gods. They called themselves "Children of the Shadows", but most people didn't treat them with kindness. "Blood whore" was just one term they were referred to as, but there were many others.

"No! Absolutely not, I would never willingly give myself to those monsters." She stood and motioned for me to follow her. She took me to a small section of books in the back of the library. Many of them looked ancient.

"Now, I've never heard of a Blood Singer, but this is all the information we have on the royal family. Good Luck." She spoke to me as she headed back to her post. I looked through the books. None of the titles seemed to stick out to me. I wasn't sure what exactly I was expecting. "Blood Singers 101?" I chuckled at my joke. No better place to start than the top, I guess. I grabbed a stool and stood on it to reach the top shelf. Still out of my reach, I went up on my tippy toes to grab the book. I finally reached it and pulled the book out as the stool wobbled a bit. As I finally got the book unstuck and pulled it out, the stool broke from beneath me, causing me to fall.

Before I knew it, I was in someone's arms. I looked up and saw a man with short blonde hair, blue eyes, and a jawline that could cut someone.

"Better be careful there. Wouldn't want you to bust your ass." He said as he set me down.

"Thank you..." I said, a bit dazed. "Where did you come from? I didn't see you here before." He turned to leave and looked back at me with a smirk.

"You should be more aware of your surroundings." He said as he walked off. While thankful that he caught me, that situation was bizarre. When I got on the stool, I was alone in this section of the library. I didn't have time to worry about that. I had a lot of books to read in a tiny amount of time before it got dark. I sat down at the table and flipped through the book I had grabbed.

There was absolutely nothing in this book I could find useful, so I grabbed another. Then another. Eventually, I had gone through about ten books, and I noticed something interesting. Many of these books contained missing pages. Many were torn out, some blacked out. It was as if there was information someone didn't want anyone to know. I looked at the time. Crap. It was almost dark. I put the books back and grabbed a few new ones to take home with me. I headed to the front desk and checked them out.

As I left, the librarian told me to hurry home and be safe. About 10 minutes into the walk home, darkness set in. I walked faster. I needed to make it home and fast. Isa was going to kill me. The blonde man from before stepped out from an alleyway, blocking my path.

"Now, where do you think you are going, pretty lady?" He said as he stepped towards me.

"Going to mind my business, as you should be." I snapped back. He laughed.

"Oh, I think a delicious thing like you is my business." He stepped under a street lamp, and that was when I saw them. Fangs. My heart dropped. There was no way I was going to be faster than him if I tried to run.

"Oh, there's no use in running. Come to me." In a split-second decision, I decided to run down another alleyway to my right, hoping that would be a way to somehow escape him. Many of the alleys in this section of the city were maze-like. I hoped to use that to my advantage. My short legs rushed, avoiding the trash that littered the alley. My heart felt as if it were going to explode at any moment.

Unfortunately, I miscalculated and found myself at a dead end.

"I told you there was no use in running. Now come here, and I will be gentle." He growled at me as he walked down the alley. I turned to face him, my eyes filling with tears. He reached out to grab me and slammed me into the wall. He ran his tongue up my cheek.

"Oh...You're going to be delicious." His eyes turned red as he went to bite my neck. I shut my eyes tight, not wanting to watch. Just as his fangs grazed my skin, I heard a gurgling sound and then he released me. I then heard a loud thud. I opened my eyes and saw a tall man, his features shrouded by the shadows in the alley and the hood on his head. I looked down, my attacker lying there dead, a silver stake in his back. The man reached down with a gloved hand and pulled it out.

"No need to be afraid," he said, "from this point forward, no one is going to hurt you."

Three

"Who are you?" I asked, my voice still shaking. The man reached his hand out to me.

"Come, we should get you home before anything else happens. Do not worry, no one will try anything if you are with me." I looked the man up and down.

"That didn't answer my question," I said with a growl. He laughed and commented how I never change, no matter how many lives I have been through. My eyes widened.

"Who. The. Hell. Are. You?" I said coldly. The man finally lowered his hood. Another vampire. Why would a vampire kill one of his kind? Why would he try to protect me? It must be a trick.

"My name is Andrei. I am a friend of the Prince. He sent me to protect you." I looked at him and all I could do was blink. The Prince? The man that had murdered me one hundred times over? This had to be some kind of trick. I looked back down at the dead vampire at my feet.

"This was a lovely time, but I need to head home. I prefer to go by myself," I said as I walked out of the alley. Andrei followed me, not saying a word. After a few moments, I stopped and turned to him. I asked him to please stop following me.

"I cannot do that," he said simply. "It is my job to protect you." I noticed he was still clutching the blood-covered stake. He stood uncomfortably straight on high alert. I rolled my eyes and continued to head home. What was I going to tell Isa? There was no way I could let a vampire into our apartment.

"You are quieter compared to your last life. Last time you tried to stab me with a stake," he chuckled, "I am glad you did not, and I am happy to serve by your side once again. Hopefully, this time we will not fail."

"I don't know what you're talking about," I told him as I walked down the street. I could see people watching us through their windows. It was a strange sight. A small human being followed by a six-foot-tall vampire grasping a stake in his hand. We continued to walk in silence for a while.

"Oh no, I cannot allow you to live here. This place is horrendous," he said as we approached the apartment building. I stopped at the front door.

"I am not moving anywhere with you. You are not coming inside. When I walk through these doors, you will leave and not come back."

"Incorrect," he said as he just stood there, looking down at me. Was that all he could say? Was I not even worthy of a response? I had my limit of vampiric interactions. I glared up at him.

"Fuck you," I said as I turned away and went to reach for the door. Before I knew it, he was in front of me, holding the door open for me.

"After you," he said with a smile. I rolled my eyes and headed inside. He followed me as I headed up the stairs to my apartment.

"You know I will not invite you inside, so you can stand out here forever, or you can go home."

"I don't need an invitation, that's a myth," he said, finally putting away the stake that he had held so tightly our entire walk. As I approached the apartment door, it flew open and Isa rushed out and hugged me, squeezing me tight.

"You made me worried sick!! I told you not to be home so late!" She said with a sigh of relief. I could feel her head lift as she let out a shout. She pushed me behind her.

"You are not welcome here, leech!" She screeched. "Can you explain why a vampire followed you home?" She said to me, not looking away from Andrei. As she spoke, he pushed past both of us and entered the apartment. Isabella's eyes followed him as he entered. Her jaw drops. "No one invited you inside!" She said as she entered the apartment.

"Just a myth," he said nonchalantly as he examined every window and exit we had. I explained to Isa what had happened since leaving the library. How Andrei was supposed to be my protection, even though deep down I did not trust it. However, it was not as if either of us could stop him.

"How much do you remember?" He said after sitting down on our couch. His dark blue-black eyes almost pierced my soul. "And don't play the '*I don't know what you are talking about*' crap like you did earlier."

Isa shot me a look as she leaned against the kitchen table. "You mean to tell me what she told me this morning was true?"

"That all depends on what she told you," he said looking back at me. His fingertips tapped on the arm of the sofa after an awkward moment of silence. "Well, Princess? Just because I'm immortal doesn't mean I have all day."

"The Prince is going to kill me, as he has done many times. That's all I know. So, I am confused about why he sent you to protect me if all he's going to do is rip out my throat." Andrei looked away from me, finally breaking eye contact. A somber look took over his face.

"You say that as if you think he enjoys it" he sighed.

"Doesn't he? We have all heard about how bloodthirsty the Prince is. He would drain every single human on this earth if he could," Isa spat in response.

"As soon as he smelt your blood at the stroke of midnight, he had me lock him up in silver chains in his dungeon. He then sent me to find you to be your personal bodyguard. Does that sound like a man who enjoys killing you?" He stood, coming over to me.

"But why?" I said nervously, taking a step back.

"That is not my story to tell. Now this place is not safe for you. Pack your things and let's go." Isa stepped between him and me, a silver knife in her hand. We always had one hidden under the kitchen table for emergencies.

"She's not going anywhere with you," she growled. He gave a small chuckle. In the blink of an eye, he had her wrist in one hand and the knife in his other.

"Oh, I like you. You're feisty. You can come as well," he said as he released her wrist. Isa took a step back, clearly flustered by how quickly he had disarmed her.

"Fine, but we go in the morning when it is safer for humans to be outside." Andrei looked her up and down, then nodded in agreement.

Four

The next morning, we were packed and headed to an unknown destination. Whenever either Isabella or I asked where we were going Andrei would change the subject fairly quickly. However, it didn't take us too long to realize that we were headed out of the city. It would be my first time out of Titus. As we got farther and farther away, I looked back as I drowned out the sounds of Andrei and Isa bickering in the front seat. So many times I tried to leave but could not. Why was this time different?

"Lady Sabrina," Andrei said. My focus snapped back and away from the city. I looked up towards the front seat, Andrei looking back at me through the rearview mirror.

"We have a long drive ahead. Why don't both of you take a nap?" He said as he focused back on the road ahead, one finger tapping the steering wheel.

"No way am I taking a nap this close to you. Even last night with you on my couch I slept with one eye open and a knife in hand," Isa snarled. I barely got any sleep either. Not because of Andrei being in the apartment, but just the whirling thoughts I couldn't get out of my head about everything that had happened in just one day. Before I could even respond, I saw Andrei smirk from the rearview.

"My apologies, I did phrase that as a question. However, I didn't mean to give you any other option." A warm feeling took over my body and my eyes grew heavy. I could hear Isa give a small yawn from the front seat. It took so much effort to look up and see she was now fast asleep. I couldn't hold it back any longer and allowed it to take me.

I stood in the center of infinite darkness. No matter which direction I walked, all I could see was nothingness. My voice echoed as I called out for anyone to hear me. It seemed as if I had wandered the vast empty space of an eternity before I saw a light far off in the distance. And like a moth drawn to flames, I ran towards the light. The darkness twisted and conformed. I found myself in a clearing of a sunflower field, the warm sun shining down and giving my skin a soft glow. The darkness was completely gone. I walked to the edge of the clearing, admiring the tall sunflowers that lined the small circle of clover that I stood in.

"Beautiful, aren't they? I hope they are still your favorite." A deep masculine voice purred behind me. I turned around, and there he stood in black jeans and a crimson red tee shirt. His dark hair was up in a loose bun. A short strand dangled in his sculpted face against his pale skin.

The man who was after me. The man who had murdered me countless times. My body froze. My brain screamed for me to run, but my muscles seized up, refusing to move an inch as he stepped closer.

"Don't worry. None of this is real. I won't hurt you here." The back of his fingertips gently stroked my cheek. His emerald green eyes were misty as he looked down at me. "I can smell your fear. No matter how many times we have had this interaction, my heart still breaks," he said lowering his hand. My heart was pounding in my chest.

Words jammed in my throat. They couldn't find a way out of my mouth. So many things I wanted to ask him. How I wanted to smack his hand away as he touched my face and tell him to go fuck himself and find someone else to torture. All I could do was look up at him. No wonder he was able to kill me so many times. Had I frozen this way each time?

"That's alright. We will have eternity to fix everything once we break the curse," he said as everything faded to black.

My eyes softly opened to the sound of songbirds and the gentle morning sun shining through the window. The warm and comfortable sheets cradled my body. A scent of fresh pine and cinnamon filled my nose. I hadn't ever experienced this comfort in my entire life. I sat up and stretched. This was also the first time in a long time I had felt well-rested.

I looked around the room and my jaw dropped. The left wall had a large window that looked out to a beautiful mountain range. The trees were all colored for fall. It looked like one of those photos that were always a wallpaper preset. The actual room was just as beautiful. The bed was massive and had soft cream-colored bedding. The wall in front of me had a set of French doors that led to a bathroom. I couldn't see much from the bed, but what I could see was the most amazing tub I had ever seen.

After my initial awe of the room before me, my thoughts clicked back to the situation at hand. Where the heck was I? Where was Isa or Andrei? Why had he put us to sleep for the journey? I jumped out of bed and headed to the door on the right wall. Yanking it open, I found myself in an open hallway that overlooked a room on the first floor. The railing was black with gold accents. I walked to the balcony and looked below. There were two staircases on each side of the room that connected both floors. I rounded the corner and headed down the stairs.

"Hello? Is anyone here?" I called out. From the hallway on the left, I heard both Isa and Andrei respond in unison. I followed the sound of their voices that led to a living space. This room was even more magnificent than my bedroom. The back wall was one of those giant windows that could slide open to allow full access to the deck outside that had an amazing view of the mountain. A grand fireplace was centered on the right wall, and outside was a large fire pit surrounded by comfy-looking furniture.

"I was wondering how long it would take you to wake up," Andrei said with a smile.

"You have been asleep for 3 days. I was beginning to think Andrei had put you into a coma," Isa said, giving Andrei the side eye. Three days? That was insane. No wonder why I felt so well-rested. Was it due to whatever Andrei had done that had kept me asleep that long? Or was it my encounter in the sunflower field that had kept my unconscious mind occupied?

I heard steps from behind me. I jumped as I heard them, spinning around as a woman approached. She was about four feet tall with short dark curly locks. Her eyes were a golden amber. "My Lady, you must be starving after being asleep that long. I can prepare whatever it is you wish. Please, just say the word," her voice was soft.

"I am a bit hungry," my stomach growled with intensity. "Surprise me?" I said with a smile. She nodded and ran off.

"I can smell him. He visited you in your dreams, didn't he?" Andrei said as I turned back to face him.

"What do you mean you can smell him?" I asked as I sat across from him. Isa, who was sitting next to Andrei, nearly in his lap, got up and came to sit next to me. I had to ask her about that another time. The last thing I remembered was that it made her skin crawl to even be in a car with him.

Andrei explained that vampires' magic had a specific scent. Some are more recognizable than others, and the more powerful the magic, the stronger the scent.

"My Lord's scent is not one that I could miss or mistake for something else. It has strong earthy and spice notes."

"Like...Pine and cinnamon?" He nodded in response. Isa reached over and touched my shoulder.

"Yes, I met him. I have had little time to process what happened, or what he said."

"Well, that is one of my purposes here. What did he say? Allow me to shed light on it," Andrei said, stiffening up. The small woman came back into the room with a tray. On the tray were two plates with the most perfectly folded crepes I had ever seen. She sat one in front of me and front of Isa.

"Pardon the interruption," she said as she explained the various toppings she provided with the crepes. She smiled at me as she specifically put the chocolate hazelnut spread and bananas in front of me as if she had known those were my favorite. She handed Andrei an opaque glass. He took a sip, leaving his lips with a slight red hint. Though I could not see in the glass, it was obvious what was in it.

"The Prince was nothing like I expected," I said looking down, twiddling my thumbs. I was terrified during our interaction, but now thinking back it made my heart flutter. I could feel his soft caress still on my cheek. "He said something about a curse, but really explained nothing." I heard an annoyed huff escape Andrei's mouth.

"Of course he didn't, he always left the hard things to me. Did he tell you anything useful? Or did he just fawn over you for the three days you were asleep?" He took another sip from his glass. I finally took a bite of my breakfast. For the first time in my life, my taste buds sang. I looked over at Isa, who rarely ate much, and half of her plate was already gone. Andrei stood and walked over to the edge of the open balcony, looking off into the mountainside.

"The curse he mentioned is what causes him to kill you. It doomed the two of you to live in the loop of your own personal Hell. The nightmares of your previous lives shall torture you and die by your nineteenth birthday. He shall be driven mad and sent into a frenzy by the scent of your blood once you turn eighteen and be compelled to tear into your throat and drain you dry. Only to realize what he had done once it was too late," he said with a somber tone.

"Is that where his reputation comes from?" I questioned as I put down my fork. The small woman brought me a mug of coffee.

"No. The man you met in your sleep and the man you hear about are two sides of the same coin. He only lets his guard down for you, but he is the cruel Prince you hear of. He was like that long before the curse was in place." Every part of me hoped it was the curse that provided his evil nature. The fluttering in my chest from earlier was long gone. Andrei turned back to face us and address the woman. "Daphne, can you please refill my glass? All this serious talk dries my throat." She nodded, taking his glass and leaving the room.

"He spoke of breaking the curse, do we know how to do that?"

"If we did, we wouldn't be here."

"And where exactly are we?" I asked, feeling my eyebrows raise.

In a flash Andrei was on the other side of the room, meeting Daphne and taking his drink from her. He took a long sip and looked over towards me as he did. He lowered the cup from his lips. With a deep breath, he explained we were located in a secluded spot deep within the mountains west of the city. A magical barrier surrounded the house, keeping us hidden. He also said that no one could pass through the barrier. No one could get in.

And no one could get out.

He informed us that we were free to roam the grounds around the house, but the barrier wouldn't allow us to get too far. The house was free rein. Except for the basement. Under no circumstances were we allowed to enter. Isa questioned him on this. Andrei quickly snapped back. The house quivered from the boom of his voice.

"Do not enter the basement, or else."

Five

Days had passed with nothing happening. After our interaction about the basement, Isa had stayed in her room most of the time. Coming out for meals and then returning to her rooms. Whatever happened while I was asleep to make her comfortable enough to sit next to him now washed away. Andrei seemed to keep himself busy. I would notice him at the tree line looking into the woods for any potential threats several times throughout the day. I could hear his footsteps outside my door at night, pacing the halls.

Even though tension filled the air of the house, it was peaceful. I had not had a single nightmare. Darius had not entered my dreams either. For the first time I got to experience a good night's sleep. I spent my days either in my room or sitting in a hammock outside under the stars. Several times I had fallen asleep out there and was awoken by either Andrei or Daphne in the dead of night to have me return to my room.

One morning I awoke with a soft knock on the door, before I could respond the door opened. Isa slipped inside and shut the door behind her.

"We gotta figure out what's in that basement," she said as she sat at the foot of my bed. "It's driving me crazy. I can't stay here if there's some secret that's looming. It's hard enough as it is being in the same house and trapped with a vampire," her eyes widened. "Oh gods, I am so sorry," she sighed. "I can't even imagine what you are going through."

I sat up and stretched. She wasn't wrong, as much as I tried to push it out of my mind, I also had to know what was down there. I didn't even blame her for not mentioning my feelings at first either. With everything that had happened with her family, I knew this was hard on her.

"What happened when I was asleep?" Her face turned bright red as I asked. She questioned what I meant. I told her she seemed somewhat comfortable with Andrei when I found them together. Her face got more red. That told me everything I needed to know. "If he was human you would like him, wouldn't you?" I teased.

"This is not the time for this!" She stood. "This is my plan—every night at eight Andrei has gone outside on patrol. Once he is outside, we will head to the basement. Are you in?"

"I'm in."

That night came quickly. Isa and I sat on the couch around the fire pit, awaiting our time to move. Andrei came up to us with a smile.

"I am glad to see everyone out of their rooms. I wanted to apologize for the other day. My temper got out of hand. It shouldn't have. It's my job to keep you safe Sabrina," his gaze moved to Isa, "and anyone who is her friend, is a friend of mine. I will keep the both of you safe." He walked over to the edge of the deck, letting us know he was headed on patrol and would be back later. He jumped down. Isa and I both watched him as we waited for him to disappear into the woods.

"It's go time." Isa stood and quickly headed to the basement door. I followed her. My heart was pounding. My head was filled with ideas of what could be down there.

We got to the door, and both froze, staring at it.

We stood there for a few moments. I think both of us were a bit too afraid to make the first move. Eventually, Isa reached for the knob on the door. She twisted it, but it didn't open. She reached up into her ponytail and pulled out a pin, kneeling next to the knob.

Living on our own in the city had definitely given us some questionable skills, but we needed them to survive.

After a moment, I heard a click and the door opened. Isa stood and peered into the doorway. She looked back at me, gesturing for me to look. Past the door was a long flight of stairs that led into darkness. Isa reached into her pocket, pulled out her phone, and turned on the flashlight. She took the first step down.

"Shut the door behind you when you follow me in."

Six

As we descended the stairs a chill filled the air. It seemed as if we walked down the steps forever. Isa and I didn't dare speak a word. Eventually the stairs opened to a large circular room made of stone. Across from the stairway were three different hallways. The room had a faint glow that illuminated the space, but I couldn't pinpoint the light source. Something about this felt oddly familiar, but I couldn't place where I had seen it before. I couldn't explain it, but I felt a small tug pulling me towards the hall to the left.

I started down the hall saying nothing. After a moment I heard Isa call out for me to wait up. I heard her quick steps behind me. I didn't stop.

I couldn't stop.

The tug I felt had gotten stronger, pulling me down the hallway. With each step I took the path illuminated the way. I heard Isa saying something behind me, but I couldn't understand the words. Whatever she was saying was not as important as the tug I felt.

That's when the smell hit me. It was him; he was here. But this time, I wasn't afraid.

Isa eventually stepped in front of me grabed my shoulders, and gave me a small shake. The tug had stopped.

"Dude, are you alright?" She said with concern in her voice. "You look out of it and have not responded to me at all." I shut my eyes tight and reached up and rubbed them. A dull pain was left in my head. I told her I was fine, I tried to tell her about what I was feeling, but the words couldn't leave my mouth.

"Alright. Let's keep going, but slow down," she chuckled as she took my hand. We continued down the hall side by side. I wondered if she had smelt the fresh pine that wafted down the hall.

There was a sharp turn that led to the left. As soon as we turned the corner, we could see natural light coming from the far end of the hall. Isa and I rushed towards it. As we approached the light the hall widened. The carefully stacked stones gave way to a natural cave formation. There was about fifty feet from the man-made stone hall to the mouth of the cave.

"I was wondering how long it would take for you to find me." A rough voice said from the right. A voice I had never heard before. Isa and I both quickly turned.

Sitting with his back against the wall, silver chains wrapped around his wrists, ankles, and neck. His features sunken in, dark circles had settled beneath his red eyes. His dark shoulder-length hair was tossed about. Isa squeezed my hand tight, taking a step back. I didn't move. The tug returned, drawing me into him.

"Bri... Let's go back," I heard Isa whimper. I took a step forward. A smirk grew on his face.

Come closer, I won't bite. I heard him purr in my head.

With that I took another step, then another. Pulling away from Isa's grip on my hand, even as I felt it grow tighter. I could hear her pleading with me to return to the house. Again, I couldn't stop. I blinked and I was now directly in front of him.

Darius Dragomeir.

At this moment he looked completely different from the man I had met in my dream. He more matched my previous vision of the monster everyone described him. However, I found myself removing his chains.

"What are you doing?!" Isa screamed, running towards me trying to pull me away.

Do not stop. Release me. Be the good girl you are.

One by one, his chains fell to the floor. I could hear Isa sobbing, begging me to stop. I didn't care.

As the last chain fell, he stood letting out a deep chuckle. I blinked, and he was no longer standing in front of me.

Don't turn around.

I heard Isa scream. My heart pounded in my chest. My muscles refused to move. I heard a familiar thud behind me. A body hitting the floor. I then felt a heavy hand grip my shoulder.

"Come," he said. The roughness in his voice was half gone. I turned to face him. His eyes were now the dark green I was familiar with. The sunken features were now plump, the bags under his eyes gone. Isa's body lies on the ground behind him. I push him out of the way and kneel to her. Shaking her limp body. Begging her to wake up. Tears streamed down my face.

I could feel him standing behind me. Grabbing me by my shoulder again, yanking me up.

"It is time to go before Andrei realizes you came down here," he said with venom in his voice. He picked me up and threw me over his shoulder.

In an instant, we were out of the cave. Trees quickly flash by. I screamed and screamed, demanding for him to release me. After what seemed to be forever, he stopped and dropped me to the ground.

"Gods, you are so annoying," he spat. He kneeled, grabbed the back of my neck, and forced me to look him in his eyes. "Take a nap. I will tell you when you are allowed to wake."

With the last word, everything went black.

$\mathcal{S}$even

I awoke in a daze.

Everything around me seemed to be a blur. I sat up grabbing my head and squeezing my temples, hoping that would ease the pain I felt.

"Easy," a woman's voice. One that I had heard before. I looked over and saw Daphne standing at my bedside. Holding out a glass of water. I took a sip and everything came into focus.

I sat in a large canopy bed. The sheets were dark gray. The sheer red canopy tied to the posts to leave it open. I wore a crimson red silk nightgown with black lace trim. My skin crawled thinking of how it had gotten on me. The walls are just as dark as the sheets. Detail trimmed into the wall giving the room character. While I examined the intricate design, I noticed what was missing.

Windows.

"Where are we?" I took another sip of water "Where is he?" Daphne looked down at me. The same look Isa had given me when she had found me on the streets. It was a pity. I could feel my heart tearing as I realized I would never get that look from Isa again, or any look.

"Just rest now. Take another sip of water. The Prince said he would return shortly to visit you." She headed towards the door. "Please call for me if you need anything."

"Wait! You didn't answer my first question."

"It is not for me to answer," she said as she walked out the door. I heard the click of the lock as she shut the door behind her. Immediately I jumped out of bed rushed to the door tried to open it. It wouldn't budge. I banged on the door, begging to be let out.

My pleas were met with silence.

My throat was raw from the screaming. It felt like I had been locked in this room for eternity. I had pleaded for the door to open until it hurt to speak. I sat with my back against the wall next to the door. Hours of silence had passed. So many thoughts had been running through my head as I sat alone.

I couldn't get the image of Isa's dead body out of my head. The blood dripped from the side of Darius's mouth. I had to get out of here, or I would be next and would have to do this all over again.

A chill ran through my body. How many of these atrocities had I experienced? All I could remember was the end. The final moments before he had drained me. How much had he tortured me beyond that final act? How many friends had he killed? How many times had I been locked away?

My breath grew quick. My heart felt as if it was going to explode. My vision narrowed. I could barely focus on what I was looking at. My fist clenched so tight I could feel my nails dig into my palm.

Relax. I am trying to work and your panicking is very distracting.

I heard his voice in my head. It didn't help. How the hell could I relax? I pulled my knees to my chest, burying my head into them. I heard the door next to me fly open. It had to be some trick. I couldn't bear to look.

"Look at me." I heard his voice, but this time not in my head. From in front of me. "Please," his voice was soft, not like it was before. I took a deep breath and looked up. He was kneeling in front of me. He reached up towards my face, wiping away the tears from both sides. I flinched at his touch.

"Look, I'm sorry. I was starving, and I couldn't feed off of you. You mean too much to me for that." What a half-assed apology. One that I would never accept. He stood, taking my hand and gently guiding me to my feet. "As for locking you in here, I had company. They have left so you are free to roam the house. Welcome home, doll."

"This is not my home. Isa was my home, and you took that away from me!"

He sucked his teeth in response.

"I said I was sorry, get over it. Humans die every day." He stood in the doorway.

"Dinner is at 6 PM. You will meet me for dinner in the dining room." He snapped his fingers and that familiar scent filled my nose. A second and third door had appeared in the bedroom, as well as a large wall clock. It read 1:30 PM

"That is your bathroom and closet. We will discuss the rules of the house at dinner." With his last words, he vanished. I looked out the door down the hall. He was nowhere to be seen.

Daphne then appeared. Carrying several bags and boxes headed toward my room. I retreated into my room as she approached. Free to roam, but I think I was too afraid to see what was beyond that hallway.

"These are all gifts from the Prince." She sat the bags and boxes on the end of my bed. "I am to show you each one, then put it away for you. Please sit." I didn't protest; I was too worn out to fight. My body collapsed on the bed. I didn't think it was possible, but this was much more comfortable compared to the one at the mountain house. Rolling to my side to face Daphne, I gave her a nod to go ahead.

One by one she opened each bag and box filled with unique pieces of clothing. A variety of jewelry, and more makeup and perfume that I knew what to do with. To be honest, everything filled me with so much joy, that for a moment I had forgotten the situation. I had forgotten that he killed my best friend, that he held me as his prisoner.

I couldn't let myself forget. However, it was something about him that fogged my mind. I wanted to hate him. However, something deep inside me prevented me from doing so.

Daphne hung a silk dress on the back of the closet door. Informing me that Darius requested I wore it to dinner. The dress is a deep green with thin straps and a high slit. I guess when he referred to me as his doll, he meant it. Disgusting.

Once Daphne finished putting everything away, she checked to see if I needed anything. I told her no, and with that, she left the room. Leaving my door open this time. I laid in bed for quite some time. I hated being here. I hated what happened to Isa. I hated that it was my fault. My thoughts were blank as if my brain had turned off. After a while, I lifted my head to look at the clock.

4:30 PM

I stood with a sigh, heading to the bathroom. A dark marble shower awaited me with the best water pressure I had ever experienced. With a single press of a button, the shower was at the perfect temperature. The room filled with the scent of lavender and eucalyptus. Standing under the running water, I could feel all my troubles going down the drain. I could have stayed in that shower forever.

I dried my hair and applied my makeup. I stood wrapped in the towel eyeing the dress that hung on the closet door. It was absolutely beautiful. I wanted to hate it, but I couldn't. I got dressed and walked out the bedroom door. Daphne stood outside the door. She informed me she would lead me to the dining room.

We walked through several long hallways before we entered a massive dining room. The room was lit by a massive fireplace and several candles that sat along the massive table. Darius sat at the head of the table with the fireplace to his back. Another servant carefully put two place settings on the table. One in front of Darius, and one directly next to him. The thought of sitting that close made me want to rip my skin off. His glass was already filled with a deep red liquid. He took a sip. His eyes pierced my soul as he gave me a look up and down.

"Welcome, glad to see you arrive on time. Please sit, we have lots to discuss."

Eight

The food was amazing. The meal started with a cup of creamy seafood soup served with the softest breadstick I have ever had. The next course was a perfectly cooked filet mignon served with a butter garlic sauce and mushrooms. The last course was a decadent crème brûlée. Everything I ate made my taste buds squeal in delight.

Darius tried to start a normal conversation with me several times while we ate. He told me how wonderful my blue eyes looked in the green dress he chose. He asked several times about my life prior to my most recent birthday. He asked about my family. I answered him with glares and silence.

Daphne brought me a latte after I finished my dessert. Darius had gone through five glasses of the red liquid through dinner. I knew what the liquid was, but it made my skin crawl to think about it. He did not eat a single bite of food, they brought nothing out to him except for his refills. He took a long heavy gulp, then slammed down the glass. It shattered on impact.

"You will answer me when I speak to you! That will be the most important rule of this house," he snarled. I sat straight up in my chair, nervous about his temper.

"The second," he started, his voice calmer. "You will do everything you are told. This will be important for your safety." He stood walking towards the fireplace. Hands behind his back.

"Third. You will not ask or attempt to leave. You belong to me." I tried to interject. He faced me. "You will not interrupt me." his voice boomed as he bared his fangs.

"Finally, you will forgive me for what I have done to you. In this life, and your pasts." He sat back down. Elbows on the table, his fingers intertwined, his nose sitting atop them.

"I have worked very hard these past two decades to control my hunger for you. I have a good feeling about this life. We will break the curse. The fact that I can be in the same room as you is a wonderful development." He snapped his fingers twice and the male servant brought him another glass. He swallowed it all quickly.

"You may speak. I'm sure you have questions." He leaned back in his chair. I did. I had so many questions I didn't even know where to begin. Tension filled the room.

"What's a Blood Singer, and am I one?" My question took him back. He looked away. His fingertips tapped the table. This head sat in the palm of his other hand.

"Where did you hear that term?" he says coldly. I explained to him the old man that I had met in the market. His eyes filled with rage and threw his glass into the fireplace. He looked back at me. The green in his eyes gave way to blood red. I think he then realized the fear that ran through me. As soon as we made eye contact, his eyes went back to green, and he apologized as he sat back down.

"A Blood Singer is someone whose blood calls out to a specific vampire. No matter how far away, the vampire can always smell the blood of their Singer. The vampire craves their blood more than anything, and many have a thirst that cannot be satisfied if they can smell their Singer," he took a deep breath. "Yes, you are my Blood Singer."

"Is that the curse you mentioned?" I broke the extended silence between us. He nodded.

"Half of it, yes. The other half is your constant reincarnation and us having to live in this nightmare for eternity." He stood again, this time heading for the door.

"For our first night together, I think this has gone well. Best not to push our luck. Good night, doll." And with that, he was gone. The male servant cleaned off the table. Daphne came by my side, motioning for me to follow her.

"I don't want to go back to my room. I hate feeling trapped."

"Come along, I have something that may help with that." She gave me a warm smile that put me at ease.

I followed her to a spiral staircase. As we walked up, she told me this was my favorite part of the castle in the past. When I questioned her on that she changed the subject.

Had I lived here before? Nothing seemed familiar. I couldn't match anything that I had seen so far to the nightmares that I had.

We finally reached the top of the steps. "Oh. My. Gods," I said as we entered a large circular room. A glass dome made the walls and ceiling. From here we got a view of the entire castle and the mountains that surrounded us. Daphne smiled, offering me another latte. I agreed. Heading over to a wicker hanging chair. I curled up in the seat, amazed at the view. After a few moments, Daphne returned with the latte in hand. She also brought me a few books.

"Stay up here as long as you wish. Call for me when you are ready to head back to your room. I will guide you back."

I sat for some time enjoying the peace and quiet. Taking in the view of the mountains as I sipped my latte. I looked over a few of the books Daphne had brought up. Most of them were fantasy stories, but there were a few about the history of the Kingdom of Titus and how the Dragomeir family rose to power. Like the books from the library, many pages were ripped out.

As I read, I heard footsteps from behind me.

"Beautiful view," I heard Darius say. I didn't turn to look at him. He came and sat at my side. A pained expression on his face.

"Go away," I said not looking up from my book.

"Please don't push me away. I am tired of not being able to be with you."

"You should have thought about that before you killed my friend," I shut my book. "I will never forgive you. I hope you know that." I turned to look at him. He was staring off at the mountains. A crow flying over the window, landing in a tree, still close enough for us to see. He stayed silent. I stood up slamming down my book on the side table.

"I can't stand being around you. I agreed to dinner, not to spend my free time with you."

"Sit down. You're being annoying again, let's just enjoy the view. We used to sit here for hours watching the sunset. Sometimes we would still be up here when it rose." A faint smile appeared on his face. His gaze was still out towards the mountains.

"I'm leaving." I went to turn away, and as I did Darius appeared before me. That smile was gone.

"Remember the rules, doll." He grabbed my wrist tight, pulling me into him. "I don't want to punish you on your first day." He wrapped an arm around me, pressing my body into his. I could feel my cheeks burned as he smirked down at me. "Now, be a good girl and come sit with me for a bit longer. I enjoy your company when that bratty mouth of yours isn't running." I gave a small nod and he guided me over to the wicker chair. He sat down and pulled me into his lap.

His hand on my thigh caused my skin to slightly burn. I hated it as he gently rubbed his thumb on my inner thigh. My body screamed at me to push away his hand, but instead, I leaned back.

"Good girl," he purred.

A few days had passed since our encounter in the observatory. I could still feel his touch on my thigh, his breath in my ear causing a chill to run down my spine. We had sat there for hours as we sat in silence and watched the scenery.

Something about that moment gave me a feeling of deja vu. I had a feeling it wasn't the first time we had sat like that. I wonder if previously it was under duress like it was this time.

I decided it would be better if I stayed in my room. I only left for my meals. Luckily for me, Darius had not been around. Daphne had informed me he needed to spend a few days away from here after being so close to me.

It made me wonder how many days I had left before he snapped.

Darius and I had dinner together about a week after the moment in the observatory. As I walked into the dining room his head snapped to look at me. He stood from his seat and pulled my chair out for me, pushing it in once I sat down. He sat back at the head of the table and Daphne and the male servant, I had learned his name was Liam, served us.

"You have been hiding from me." His stare went right through me. "Stop that."

"I enjoy my solitude. So, I will have to pass," I said taking a bite of my pasta. You would have thought I just told him I was going to chop off his dick and feed it to hell-hounds by the look he gave me.

"This is not a request." He took a sip from his glass, not breaking eye contact as he drank it all in one go. "Liam, refill." He sat down his glass. Liam quickly refilled his glass, just as quickly as Darius had devoured it once again. Darius had four more refills back-to-back before speaking another word to me.

"During the day you will be out and about the castle. I expect you to be out of your room by 10 AM. You shall not retreat to your room until 10 p.m. Do I make myself clear?"

"Go to hell," I responded. Darius' eyes filled with rage. In a blink, the table had been thrown across the room. The dishes smashed into pieces on the floor. Out of shock, I jumped from my seat. "What the hell is wrong with you?!" I yelled. Darius quickly moved to me, pinning me against the wall with a hard grip on my neck.

"You will be out of your room from 10 AM until I give you permission to go back. Keep up with that smart mouth of yours, and I will take the little bit of freedom in this house you have left. Do you understand me, Sabrina?"

"I don't have any freedom! I have nothing left for you to take!" I could feel myself tearing up.

"Oh," his free hand traveled down my body, gripping my inner thigh once again. My body quivered as he squeezed. "I think I have plenty left to take. Next, I will take away these beautiful dresses." He leaned in close, his breath hot in my ear. "I would love to see you walk around in a little silk nightgown, or better yet, nothing at all. After that, I will take away your own room. I would love to have you keep my bed warm." His hand moved up my thigh, inching closer to the most intimate part of me. A tear fell down my cheek. His tongue traced its path. My heart raced. No matter how much my mind told me how much I hated his touch, I craved more of it.

"Last chance, do you understand?"

"I...I understand," I whimpered. He finally released me. I slid down the wall and sat on the floor. He looked down at me and his eyes returned to green. As if he had a moment of clarity, he took a few steps back. He left without another word.

I spent my free time in the observatory for the next few weeks. I had dinner with Darius twice a week. He said he couldn't stand to be around me more than that. Once a week I would wake to my door being locked. It would be unlocked before dinner. I was told on those days that there was company that couldn't know I was there. Whenever I asked about it, they immediately changed the subject.

Dinners with Darius were always extravagant, and awkward. I never knew which Darius I would see that day. It was like there were two of him trapped in one body. Luckily there were no more explosions.

Some days he would ask about what I had been up to that week, asked about the books I would be reading. Those days he seemed concerned about me. He even apologized several times for the arrangement we found ourselves in. No matter how many times he had begged for my forgiveness, I refused to give it.

Other days he was cold and filled with anger. Asking him anything would set him into a fit of rage. Those were mostly silent dinners. That's when it was the most awkward.

No matter which Darius was at dinner, if I asked about the curse, the topic was changed. I wanted to know more. Who cursed us, and why? What was his plan to end this curse? Those questions were always unanswered.

I always knew when I would have dinner with Darius. Daphne would always bring me a new dress to wear. Tonight it was a beautiful light blue tulle dress. Silver stars were embroidered into the skirt of the dress. Daphne waited outside my room while I got ready. When I came out, she greeted me with a smile and escorted me to the dining room.

Dinner was silent. Darius didn't say a single word. I would not make any effort to have a conversation with him. He just stared at me while I ate. Daphne and Liam, stood near the door, awaiting our requests.

"I have to go away on business for a few weeks," the silence finally broke. "Daphne and Liam will take care of your needs while I am away. Don't do anything stupid, I will know." With that, he stood and vanished.

For the first time since I had been here, I felt relieved.

Nine

Darius had been away for a few days. The castle had been quiet. I found myself sitting up in the observatory most of the day and sometimes falling asleep in the wicker chair. I had even wished I had Darius sitting in that chair with me so I could lean against him and steal his warmth. I hated myself for those thoughts. I watched the sunset and found my consciousness slipping away as the sun faded. I tried to stay away, but something was pulling me into a deep sleep.

When I opened my eyes, I found myself back in the eternal darkness, a gentle melody playing, guiding my way through it.

"Darius," I called out to the darkness. "Is that you?" The melody got louder as it called to me. Eventually it led me to a bright light. As I walked towards the light it led me to a study with a large window looking over Titus. Against the wall was a piano, Darius sat in front of it. He was playing that melody that had guided me here. I stood there for some time listening to him play. I didn't realize he had any talents other than being a psychopath. He wore a dark-colored suit. The sleeves rolled up to show off his tattoos. He stopped playing. He laced his fingers together and stretched outward, still facing the piano.

"That was a beautiful song," I said softly.

"Thank you, I wrote it for you," he turned to face me. His undereyes were a bit red, as if he had been crying. "Look, I called you here because I needed to apologize." He took a deep breath. "I know I am a monster. I am a bad guy. That man that had you pinned to the wall in the dining room, that's not the man I want to be for you."

"How you treated me was awful." We stared at each other in silence for a moment. "What you have done to my best friend was even worse. I don't think I will ever forgive you."

Darius stood taking a few steps over to me. He swallowed hard as he gently took my hands in his.

"I will do better. I will be better. You don't understand how hard it is for me. This curse is eating away at me. All I want is to pin you to a wall and drink every last drop when I am next to you. I hate that. I just want to live with you, laugh with you, love you. I need you to forgive me."

I didn't respond right away. I pulled my hands away from his. I stayed in silence for a moment.

"Why? Why is me forgiving you so important? You say we have all this history, but you are a stranger to me Darius. Please shed some light on this for me."

I watched as he tried to stop tears from filling his eyes. I could see the heartbreak all over his face as I told him he was a stranger.

"Sabrina, the reason we were cursed was because there are people who don't want us to be together. What we had scared them. It scares me to think I won't ever feel your love again. Please. Give me a chance. I won't be an ass anymore." He got on his knees as he begged for my forgiveness. "I will do whatever it takes to make it up to you. I promise."

"Stand up! You look ridiculous."

"Sabrina, please," he begged once again

"Fine! I will try to forgive you if you get up and stop looking so pathetic." He stood and gave a big smile.

"Wonderful. I'm glad you are able to look past what a horrible monster I am! Once I get home, you and I are going to have so much fun!" He pulled me into a kiss. His hand pressed tightly into my back to keep me in place. His lips were so soft and warm. I was surprised at how gentle it was. It wasn't the kiss of a horny predator, but that of a kind lover.

I slid my hands up his chest and gently pushed him away. A moment later he pulled away with a smile.

"Pump the brakes, I said I would try to forgive you. I did not agree to let you kiss me."

"My apologies, I just got a little too far ahead of myself. You are just too irresistible, curse or not." He took a step back, a goofy grin on his face. "Enjoy the rest of your alone time. Please explore the castle. There are a few hidden gems you will love."

My eyes opened wide as I was back in the observatory. The gentle tingle could still be felt on my lips. I couldn't help but to smile.

I felt more comfortable to explore while he was away. I kept humming the song he played as I wandered the halls. It was buried deep in my mind.

I found a library with more books than I could ever read in a lifetime. It was obvious no one had entered the library in many years as everything was covered in dust and spider webs. Daphne had found me one day looking over the shelves, asking if I had any interest in the library. I told her I was excited to see such a collection. The next time I returned, it was spotless.

I had several books taken from the library to the observatory. I had read so many books about far-off lands, worlds where magic and vampires don't exist, distant kingdoms where vampires and humans lived together, and so much more. I had gotten caught up in several books about a kingdom to the south filled with Fae. Learning about their queen was fascinating to me. She ruled her kingdom alone, there had not been a King of the Fae kingdom in centuries. A woman in a seat of power would never happen here.

I had also discovered a square courtyard. A large sundial sat in the center. Around it were the phases of the moon made of opal. The garden beds are filled with a variety of flowers. Exotic butterflies rested on them and then flew around me as I stepped closer to watch them. An enchanting feeling hung in the air.

This has become my second favorite place in the castle. I found myself visiting just after dinner just to watch the stars come out. During the night of the full moon the opals filled the courtyard with the most beautiful glow I had ever seen.

I let myself get lost in the castle's beauty for about a week. I tried so hard to forget about what had happened before my arrival, but nothing could push that out of my mind.

Though the castle had become more peaceful while I was awake, my dreams had intensified. The night Darius left I had a new dream. Isa and I go into the cabin's basement, finding Darius and freeing him. I freed him. I allowed him to kill my friend. My only friend. I experienced this dream almost every night for three weeks.

The night before Darius' return it seemed to be the worst, and the most vivid. I could hear him drain her, hear him in my mind to be a good girl and not turn around, and the thud of her dead body hitting the ground. I shook her, begging for her to wake up. I could barely see from the tears streaming down my face.

This time she did.

Her eyes opened. She looked up at me and smiled. I hugged her tight. Her head nestled in my shoulder. She hugged me back, squeezing so tight it hurt.

"I can't believe you let him kill me," venom hung on her words. "Payback time, bitch!" I felt a sharp pain in my neck.

Ten

I was shaken awake. My eyes flew open. Darius was on top of me with a worried expression.

"It's ok, you are here," he whispered to me. "No one is going to hurt you." I sat up, as did he. Emotion overwhelmed me and I just couldn't hold it back any longer. I let out a large wail and tears flowed. Darius grabbed me, pulling my head into his chest. His large hand gently gripped the back of my head, his other arm wrapped around me hugging me tight. His voice was soft, not like how I had heard it before.

He apologized over and over. I swear I could feel something wet hit the top of my head. His body was hard and warm as he pressed me into him. After a while, I tried to pull away. He held me tighter.

"Just a moment longer," he pleaded. The hand holding my head releasing, I could feel it move towards his face. I didn't fight him. Instead, I leaned my body against him and closed my eyes. I could have stayed like this forever.

His dark green eyes looked down on me with a softness that matched his voice. "Don't tell anyone about this," he chuckled, wiping his eyes.

"No promises, I need to have a weapon against you," I smirked up at him.

"Oh, you have my heart, isn't that weapon enough?" He gently stroked my hair.

"I have your heart?" I finally pulled away from him.

"Always and forever. The only one who ever has, and whoever will," he promised as he stood. As he looked down at me, I realized where his gaze was.

"You're such a pervert! Get out!" I yanked up the blanket covering my body. I was wearing a thin silk nightgown, it left nothing to the imagination.

He turned towards the door. "Meet me for breakfast in an hour. Also, stop covering yourself all the time, I enjoy looking at your gorgeous body." And with that, He was gone.

I took a deep breath, and fell back onto the bed looking up. How close was I in that moment to being devoured? My heart ached in my chest as I reminded myself who the enemy was. Had he known what my dream was about? Or, did he think I dreamt of him ending me? I laid there for some time, not wanting to get up.

Daphne then entered my room.

"Good morning," she said in a sing-songy voice. The room brightened as if natural sunlight had been let in. I let out a groan. She came by my side, removing the blanket from my body. I heard her try to stifle a laugh. I looked over at her as she picked up a golden button.

"I see feelings for the Prince have changed?" she teased, showing me the button.

"No, they have not." I finally got out of bed. Daphne followed me as I headed to my closet. I wasn't sure that was the truth. Something felt different about him, about the way I felt about him. Was this my own free will, or his vampiric charm?

"I don't let men I do not like into my bed. Is that a human thing?" I rolled my eyes. I informed her that he was in my room when I woke up. She gave me a knowing glance as she looked through the rack of clothes. She pulled out a knee-length green sundress, showing it to me, and awaited my approval.

I took it from her and put on the dress. Once I was ready Daphne and I headed to the dining room together. Something inside me was happy that Darius was back. Even though I thought I had enjoyed his time away, I did miss him. I hated myself for it. I had all of these feelings that I couldn't explain. I was at constant war with myself.

Just before we entered, Daphne's body stiffened. She grabbed my wrist pulling me away from the door. Before I could question her, she covered my mouth.

"Am I not allowed to visit my only son? You haven't been to the main castle in the city since her birthday. I wanted to check to see how my curse was coming along," an older man's voice sneered.

"Because I can't Stand to be around you, father. The gaps in between I can forget and forgive, but not when I can smell her. I am here because I can't smell her as much. As long as she remains in the city, she is safe from me," Darius' voice filled with disgust.

The two went back and forth for some time. I couldn't believe what I was hearing. Was it his own father who had cursed us? One question was finally answered, but it had led to more. Daphne pulled on my arm, motioning for us to leave. I followed her to the garden. Once inside she let out a sigh of relief.

"The King is the one who cursed us?" I asked, sitting next to her on a bench.

"Yes, and I hope he doesn't plan on staying long. Dimitri is terrifying." I couldn't have agreed more. Just hearing his voice had filled me with an overwhelming sense of dread. I looked over at Daphne, and before I could say a word she started.

"It is not my place to tell you, maybe the Prince will tell you more once the King leaves." As if on command Darius came charging into the garden. He grabbed my arm, yanking me up from my seat. His eyes filled with fiery rage.

I tried to pull away from him as he yanked on me. His grip was so tight his knuckles were white.

"Daphne, please have you and Liam pack our things and meet us back at the cottage." He looked me in my eyes. A chill ran down my body. "We're leaving now."

Eleven

Before I knew it we were in his car, speeding down the mountain range. I could still feel the rough touch on my arm. I leaned my body against the car door and watched the trees blur by. The mountain roads were curvy and dense fog hung in the air, but that didn't stop him from driving what felt like one hundred miles per hour.

After about an hour the red from his eyes faded back to green. He slowed down, just a bit. I still thought we were going way too fast. He relaxed back into the driver's seat, putting one hand on my thigh. I pulled it away. He let out a huff and put his hand back on the wheel.

"We will be at the cabin in about two hours," he glanced over at me. "Sorry for being rough, I had to get you out of there before my father saw you."

"Because he's the one who cursed us?" Darius gripped the wheel tighter and nodded. "Why? Please fill in some gaps, I am drowning over here."

Silence. Darius' mouth tightened. After a moment I asked again.

"Because my love for you got in the way of being the monster he wants me to be." My jaw dropped. I stared at him and blinked hard. "Bri, I know you want answers. However, I am not ready to talk about it. This is equally as traumatic for me as it is for you. On top of that, I need to put every ounce of energy and control I have to not tear into your flesh. Once we are settled in the cabin and after I feed, then I will answer all your questions. I promise."

The rest of the ride was silent.

We finally made it to the cabin. The same one Andrei had brought me to. As we pulled into the driveway, I saw two people standing on the porch. One was clearly Andrei. No one could mistake his tall and perfectly straight stature. I sat up straight, trying to focus my eyes to see who the second person was. As we got closer, her features came into view.

Isabella.

Twelve

As soon as the car stopped, I jumped out of the car. I could hear Darius yell at me telling me to wait until he put the car in park, but I ignored him. I ran towards Isa, as she did to me. She got to me faster than I could blink. We embraced each other as we sobbed. We spoke in unison about how we thought the other was dead.

Darius was next to Andrei in a second. Their voices were quiet, I couldn't hear what they were saying. However, I could tell that it was about us. They never looked away from Isa or me. We finally released and headed towards the porch.

"I saw you die. I held your dead body, how are you alive?" I managed to say. Isa looked at Andrei nervously, he gave a nod as if he was giving her the go-ahead.

"Sabrina... I am not as I was when you left. I did indeed die, but..." She trailed off. Andrei was then by her side, holding her hand, and telling her to take a deep breath.

"Andrei saved me. He found me in the basement right after you left. I am a vampire. I hope you don't hate me," tears welled in her eyes. Andrei rubbed her back telling her that it was ok.

"Isa! I could never hate you." I hugged her tight. "I just hope you don't hate me for letting it happen. "

"When Andrei found me, I was barely breathing. He said if he found me a moment later it would have been too late." She hugged me back and chuckled. "No, I don't blame you. I blame him." She growled on that last word. I turned to Darius, who was sitting on the porch swing, looking up at the sky, pretending not to pay attention. Andrei made a not-so-subtle cough.

Darius looked back at us. "Welp, we might as well get inside. I'm starving, and we have a lot to discuss about how we are going to defeat my father and break the curse." Both Andrei and Isa gave him a look that screamed 'Are you serious?'.

Awkward tension hung in the air. Darius threw up his arms. "Gods be damned. When you are wrapped in silver and are starving, you will understand why I did what I did. I am sorry you are now an immortal being with power who now gets to spend eternity with the man you love. And don't deny it, this house reeks of sex and passion." Andrei and Isa both looked away. "I am going to feed. Daphne and Liam should be here soon." With that, he was gone.

I turned back to the two of them "Wait, are you two a thing?" Isa giggled and it was now Andrei who looked up at the sky. That was all the answer I needed.

Daphne and Liam showed up shortly after Darius left. We all waited hours for Darius to return. It was dark when he jumped up on the back patio, causing the fire in the pit to dance.

"It's about time you showed back up," Andrei said to him as he leaned back into his seat, wrapping his arm around Isa.

Darius sat across from me, the fire illuminating his face.

"I have a hunger that can't be satisfied, of course, I would be gone for a long time," he chuckled. I didn't find that to be funny, but the others did. Or maybe they laughed because he was their Prince? I was surrounded by people I could trust, but at this moment, I felt alone. The only human amongst them, other than Liam who barely spoke a word.

As if he had a direct link to my mind, Darius stood and sat next to me, wrapping his arm around me, and pulled me close to him. I wanted to pull away, I wanted to hate this, but I couldn't. His body felt warm and safe. I allowed myself to lean against him.

Good girl, rest. You deserve it. I heard him purr in my head. Andrei finally asked the question that was on everyone's mind.

"How is she not dead?" He watched me closely. Darius grinned.

"Oh, I am glad you asked, brother." He let me go and stood up, removing his shirt. His back facing me, I saw it before he was able to turn to show the others. Symbols branded into his skin down his spine, flecks of silver throughout the brand. As he faced me, he flexed his muscles and winked at me.

"Is that..." Andrei asked approaching Darius to get a closer look.

"Fae magic? Absolutely it is. Thanks to Daphne I can be around my wife. I still have to focus on not killing her, but it is somewhat manageable. Some days are harder than others."

"I'm sorry, did you just call me your wife?" Confusion and anger filled my voice.

"The day we were cursed, the first time I killed you was our wedding day. We didn't get to say our vows, but yes. You are my wife." I think I'm going to be sick. No way would I ever marry him! I knew for a fact that was a forced marriage.

Sabrina Dragomeir did have a nice ring to it though.

"This is not important right now Bri, we will continue this later," he growled as he put his shirt back on. Turning his attention towards Andrei. "To end the curse, we need to kill my father. We have tried so many things in the past and failed, this is the only solution."

"That means you will be King, are you ready for that?" Liam asked from across the hall.

"Absolutely, if that will free us from this nightmare. We can continue what we started once he is gone."

"The humans have grown to hate you for what you have become, you know. It won't be easy to reinstate peace," Andrei warned.

"I know, but once the curse is broken, Bri will be free. People will remember who she is, and I think it will be alright in the end." Was there more to the curse than this? What did he mean to remember who I am? I wanted to ask but couldn't get a word in from the boys going back and forth.

Too much was happening at once. Not too long ago Isa and I were normal girls. I was now entangled with the deadly Prince. Isa, now a vampire. I couldn't recognize my life anymore. To be honest, I didn't recognize myself at this point. I could feel the change happening within me that started on my birthday. Ever since, nothing had felt right. I could feel it again. The crushing feeling in my chest, my vision blurred and narrowed.

Everything snapped back as I heard Darius let out a laugh. His joy pulled me out of whatever I had let myself sink into, but he didn't notice. I felt a light tap on my shoulder. I turned to see Daphne standing there.

"Shall I ask Isa to come with us to the kitchen to get coffee?" Her smile filled me with comfort. Something about her was so familiar and comforting. Even if she did work for the vampires, something told me she was on my side. I nodded in response.

"So, you're fae?" Isa asked as Daphne handed her a cup of coffee. We all sat around the kitchen table.

"Correct, I am originally from Serafina." She set out the cream and sugar to add to our coffee, however, she did not allow me to put any in mine. She did it for me.

Serafina was the fae land I had read about in many books from the castle library. Serafina was a beautiful, enchanted forest. It was home to many fae creatures. Our lands had not had contact with them in centuries. Even the book I had read was dated from hundreds of years ago. Daphne was the only fae I had ever met to my knowledge. It was very rare to see one here. Little was known about their people.

"So how is it being a vampire?" I asked Isa.

"I was terrified at first. I thought I would hate being a vampire, but something about it just feels right. As much as I hated it at first it feels as if it was meant to be. Once I was turned, something inside Andrei and I snapped into place. We were fated to be together. I couldn't imagine life any other way."

I was happy for her, but a bit jealous. Would I ever feel this love and joy from Darius? To him, was I just a plaything? Again, so many questions filled my head. I wonder why we were getting married so many years ago, were we truly in love, or was I his captive bride?

"Earth to Bri... Helloooo?!" I heard Isa. Our eyes met. "You good? You looked like you were spacing out." I chuckled and apologized. Letting her know the thoughts in my head. That's when Daphne chimed in.

"Your love brought Aphrodite and Eros to their knees. Your love was the most beautiful and genuine thing I had ever seen. When it was over, the world wept for twenty years. So many cities were lost due to the never-ending rain. The rain stopped when you were reborn, but the damage to the world could not be undone." It was like Daphne was reading my every thought.

Isa and I just stared at her. Was that true? Was it the curse that caused the storms and floods we had read of in history books?

"Those who remember are waiting for the world to return to how it was when Darius and Sabrina were in love." She looked up towards the kitchen door.

"Enough, we have scared her enough for one day," Darius said from behind me.

I turned to face him. Both Darius and Andrei stood in the doorway, Liam not too far behind them.

"If we have any chance of winning, we need to prepare. Starting tomorrow at sunrise everyone meet out front. Our training will begin then" Andrei said.

Thirteen

"The number one rule of training is no complaining," Andrei said. Darius stood at his side as he looked over us. Several silver weapons lie in the grass in front of us. Both Darius, Andrei, and Isa wore gloves that matched the ones Andrei had when we first met. "Any complaints will be answered with fifty laps around the cabin." His eyes fell on me. "That includes you, my Lady." He paced behind the weapons.

"Here are the weapons that will be available as the training goes on. At the end of training each day you will spend an hour with a different weapon. Eventually, you will choose the one you are most comfortable with." He stopped in the center, again looking towards us. "We will start with endurance training. Right now your best plan is not to go on offense, you need to know how to run if things get sticky." He approached me and grabbed my wrist pulling my hand to him. His eyes were apologetic as he sliced into my palm. Both Darius and Isa's head snapped to me.

"Run," Andrei commanded, and I did. I ran into the forest as fast as I could. I could hear Darius screaming at Andrei, asking him if he was out of his mind. His voice caused the trees to shake. I ended up tripping on a clump of roots. My body slammed into the ground.

When I looked up, I was back at the house. Isa reached down a hand to help me up. Andrei looked at me with disappointment.

"We have a lot of work to do if you can't even make it fifty yards before falling on your face." Why weren't Darius and Isa trying to get me? I looked down at my hand and there was no evidence of the cut he had made. "If that was real, you would have been dead, fifty laps. For everyone."

I was the last to finish. The air felt dense as I tried to breathe. My legs gave out under me. This time I didn't hit the ground. I was in Darius' arms. "Andrei, she's human, shouldn't you go a little easy on her?" Andrei's gaze snapped towards Darius.

"Fifty laps carrying her on your back," he snarled.

"What? You can't be serious?"

"One Hundred." With that, Darius flung me over his shoulder and began his laps. How did I get roped into his punishment? After his laps, he gently sat me on the ground. With a heavy breath, hands on his knees, he glared up at Andrei. Andrei reached down, picked up one of the weapons off the ground, and tossed it to Darius. He caught it with no problem. "Rapier for you, my Lord?" Darius smirked.

"You know it," he responded. Liam and Daphne were looking over the weapons, not sure what to take. Darius went over and picked up a bow and offered it to me. I stood and took it from him. Once my hand grasped the bow something felt right. As if at some point in my past lives I had used one before. I wonder if I had skill back then. I wonder if any of that has been transferred into this life.

It did not. I missed every shot. Many arrows fell to my feet as I released the bow. After many failed attempts Darius stepped behind me.

"I don't need your help," I growled at him.

He disregarded my words and gently guided my hands into the correct position.

Release. I did and hit the target straight on. It was the only one that struck all day.

Once he was done helping me, he went back to sparring with Liam, teaching him how to wield the longsword that he held in his hands. I was thankful that I wasn't the only fawn in this arena. Liam's legs wobbled; the sword was knocked out of his hands several times. Daphne stood next to them awaiting her turn with a katana in hand.

Isa and Andrei stood off to the side. He had several daggers strapped to his waist. He was teaching Isa to use the twin blade she now wielded.

That night something had changed in the air that filled the cabin. We all seemed closer. The tension and anger Isa and Darius felt seemed to have melted away. Even at dinner, when I was the only one who ate, I didn't feel alone. I felt surrounded by family.

Daphne drew me a hot bath that night filled with bubbles, telling me to call out to her if I needed anything. I soaked for hours in the tub, feeling truly relaxed as I looked out the window and watched the night sky twinkle. When the water turned cold, I dried off and slipped on a green silk nightgown. I laid down to close my eyes. I didn't open them when I heard my door open and felt Darius slip into bed beside me, pulling me close to him. My back pressed against his warm chest.

I had the best night's sleep.

The endurance training was just as intense as it had been the day before. However, this time we all ran through the forest, having to evade several obstacles throughout. Those who got caught in an obstacle were declared 'dead' and removed from that round. To no surprise, Darius survived every round. I barely survived the last round.

No one changed weapons. Daphne and Liam sparred with dull versions of their chosen swords with each other. Liam barely ever spoke, I wonder if he was like Daphne, or if he was something else entirely. I never see him drink blood, nor go hunting with Darius and Andrei.

Isa somehow within this short time had become a master with her twin blade. Maybe in the time I was away, she had already had some practice. Again, I felt envy. I struggled with every shot I took. It wasn't until I heard the rustling of trees that my instincts kicked in. I quickly turned and landed an arrow in between the eyes of a stag who stepped out from the forest.

53

Fourteen

Cheers erupted behind me. I heard Andrei telling me 'nice shot' as I fell to my knees. Nothing I had to deal with back in the city could have prepared me for this feeling. I looked up at the deer. It broke me.

I let out a loud wail as tears flew down my face. My first kill and it was someone who didn't deserve it. The air around me grew cold; the winds had picked up, swirling around me. It was Daphne who appeared by my side, sitting cross-legged. Her hand was on my shoulder. A calm washed over me; the winds died down.

"His sacrifice won't be wasted," she whispered. I looked over to her. Something about her smile always made me feel better. Daphne was the most comforting person I knew. Just being in her presence aided me in ways I did not understand. I looked back at the deer. It was gone.

Andrei now stood in front of me, his hand extended down. I took it and he assisted me up. As I stood, he wrapped me in a hug. In the softest tone, he told me he was proud. He said it so quietly that I was sure only I could hear him. He patted the top of my head and released me.

I looked around for Darius. He was nowhere to be seen. Andrei smirked down at me. He knew who I wanted to speak to the most.

"He is taking care of the deer. He's making sure none of it will be wasted. That man is very skilled with a blade." A chill ran down my spine with the last sentence. So many times growing up I had heard the tales of Darius Dragomeir and how he enjoyed torturing his victims. Death by one thousand cuts was one of his favorite techniques.

Or so the rumors go.

Andrei picked my bow up off the ground. "Training is done for today. Good job guys. All of you are learning fast."

Liam went off to find Darius to assist him with the deer. Andrei and Isa went off together into the woods for an afternoon hunt. Isa refused to drink human blood. She said the idea of her hurting another was too much for her to handle. She said she mostly drank from deer she would find in the forest. She said she drank from a bear once, but the taste was a bit 'gamey'. She said fox was her favorite, but those creatures were masters at hiding, so it was a rare treat.

Daphne stayed by my side, asking if she wanted her to run me a hot bath. Absolutely, I did. My muscles were still sore from yesterday. I barely made it through today's endurance training. Bodies like mine were not made for running. I was only 5'; my legs were short. As I ran my thighs rubbed together causing them to burn. My chest nearly assaulted me with every exercise. Every girl wants large breasts until they have them. They're not as glamorous as the magazines made them out to be.

The bath was just as relaxing as the day before. The warm soapy water melted all my troubles away. Daphne had left me a latte and some books on the side table next to the tub. I took a sip of the latte, looking over the books, wondering which I wanted to read. I sank back in the tub, my head going underwater. I stayed there for a few seconds. Clearing my thoughts. My eyes shut, my body submerged, and I felt at peace.

As I emerged from the bubbles that inner peace left my body. Darius sat on the edge of the tub smirking down at me, shirtless. I thanked the gods Daphne had put in so many bubbles. I needed them to hide my body.

"You were under for some time, I was worried you were trying to drown yourself," he teased me.

"Get out! Can't you see I am trying to relax," I demanded.

"Oh yes, I see it all," he stood and unbuttoned his pants. I could feel my cheeks burn. "I've come to help."

"I don't want your help. You're most of the reason I am stressed." He chuckled under his breath as he removed his pants. I looked away.

"Will you stop it? Get dressed and get out!" I felt him slip into the tub behind me, positioning himself with a leg on each side of me. He gently rubbed my shoulders, pulling me back to lean against him.

"You're so tense," a predatory growl in my ear. "Just relax. I won't touch anywhere you won't enjoy" He rubbed down my arms, then back to my shoulders.

"I do not want you touching me at all," I snarled.

Liar purred in my head.

I wonder if he knew my every thought, or if his messages were a one-way street. Part of me wanted his hands to stray. The other half was screaming at me to try to drown him for his audacity. I closed my eyes, allowing him to massage my shoulders. Leaning back to rest against him. We sat like this for some time. He eventually let go of my shoulders and relaxed himself. He let out a deep sigh.

"What?" I sat up looking back at him. His head was tilted back, his eyes on the ceiling.

"I just, never thought we would have a moment like this ever again. I am... soaking it in," He laughed, as did I. What a stupid pun. For someone so terrifying, he was absolutely a joyous idiot at times. He lifted his head. His eyes met mine. He quickly grabbed at my waist, spun my body around, sitting me on his lap. My legs wrapped around his waist. My bare chest pressed against his. One arm wrapped around me, keeping me pressed against him. The other gently stroked my cheek.

"You are breathtaking." I noticed his fangs were on display, I tried to pull away, but he pulled me in closer. His free hand guided my chin up to look up at him. In an instant, his mouth slammed against mine. The motion caused some of the water to form a wave and spill out of the back of the tub. His kiss was rough, full of hunger. His hands explored my body. He roughly pawed at my breasts and toyed with my nipples between his fingertips. I let out a soft moan into his mouth as he played with me. He pulled away from the kiss. His eyes now that deep red that I had feared.

"Tell me, am I the first man who's touched you?" His voice was deep and sensual. I nodded. I felt his hands slide down to my body gripping my thighs. "Good," he responded. He lifted me up and slowly lowered me onto him. I let out a moan as he entered me. I felt my body give in to him. I had never felt so complete until he was deep inside me. He guided my hips to slowly bounce up and down onto him. As I rode him, he told me what a good girl I was. Each time he pushed his considerable length deep inside me.

His mouth found its way to my neck. His tongue slid across it before he began to suck. I could feel his fangs scrape against my skin.

"Is... that... safe?" I managed to ask in between moans. To be honest, I didn't care. It felt so good I did not want him to stop. He growled, standing up from the tub, my legs wrapped around him tighter. He walked us over to the bed, pulled me off him, and tossed me down. Before I knew it, I was on my stomach, and he had mounted me from behind. His hand was firmly pressed against my mouth.

"I'm tired of hearing you speak. The only thing I should hear are your screams." He rammed into me once again. This time much rougher. My whole body trembled from pleasure as I moaned into his hand. He thrusted in and out of me, leaning down and pressing his chest into my back.

"What a good girl you are. Go on, cum on my cock." He growled, his breath tickling my ear. I felt my own body explode from the pleasure. As I came, he flipped me onto my back. Never once pulling out as he did. His hand reached around my throat squeezing tightly. I arched my back, begging him for more. His free hand roughly groped my breasts. He began to thrust even harder inside of me, causing me to let out a scream. His hand slid up from my throat, covering my mouth. Pounding harder and faster inside of me like a wild beast.

"Who owns you?" He growled. His hands found their way to the back of my thighs, folding me over and pinning me down by them as he continued to thrust inside me.

"Y...you do!" I moaned. He bent over once again, this time taking my sensitive nipple in his mouth, flicking his tongue against it. I could feel his fangs scrape against my breast. All I wanted was for him to sink his teeth into me. I wanted to give him all of me. I squealed as I found myself once again exploding from the pleasure.

Darius grunted as he pressed harder inside me. I felt him release. It was so hot and deep inside me. I craved more. He pulled out, slapping me on my ass. I could feel it drip out.

"Let's get you cleaned up, then we can relax until dinner."

He gently picked me up and carried me back into the bathroom, sitting me on the counter. He drained the tub and began to run the water in the shower, letting it heat up. He looked over at me concerned.

"Are... you alright?" He came over to me, taking my hand in his. " Did I fuck up? Should I have asked?" Worry filled his voice. I looked up at him.

"That... was wonderful." The worry melted off his face as he smiled. "Though... I have to admit... I feel like a slut for enjoying it so much. I am supposed to hate you," Darius smirked, kissing me gently.

"Well, you can be my slut any time. Stop putting so much energy into hating me. It would be so easy to let me own you. You know you want to be mine. " He went back to check the water and said it was perfectly warm. He helped me off the counter and guided me into the shower.

We spent the entire shower intertwined with one another. He pressed me into the shower wall. Kissing me hard. His fingers explored my body. After some time, he pulled away. Teasing me about how we should hurry and get ready before the others realize we both are missing.

Once we got out of the shower, I finally looked in the mirror and saw the hickey on my neck. I glared at Darius.

"How is everyone supposed to know you belong to me if I don't mark you?" He chuckled as he pulled his pants back on. "Wear something green for dinner. I think you are the most beautiful in green." With that final comment, he was gone.

Fifteen

I wore a forest green tee shirt and dark blue jeans to dinner. As soon as I walked into the dining room, eyes were on me. Darius had not yet made it downstairs, leaving me alone with the wolves. I sat down across from Isa, her eyes glued to my neck. It was silent.

"I know that I am show-stopping, but please continue the conversations you were having before I entered the room." I broke the silence. Andrei nearly spit out his drink as he busted out laughing. Isa was not amused. Darius finally came down to dinner. He stepped one foot into the dining room when Isa threw a glass at him.

"Have you lost your mind?! What if you lost control?! What if you killed her!?" Isa screamed now standing from her seat. Andrei was no longer laughing. He said something quietly to her, too quiet. I wasn't sure what was said, but whatever it was it set her off even more. Darius was in front of her in a blink of an eye. His hands gripped her shoulders. He said something equally as quiet as Andrei. Whatever he said seemed to calm her down somewhat.

"Yes, what I did was risky. However, I knew what I was doing. I wouldn't have done it if I didn't think I could handle it. Trust me, I don't want to lose her again." He released her. Daphne walked into the room informing us that dinner would be ready in a few minutes. Everyone got situated at the table. Darius sat next to me, his hand on my thigh under the table. Daphne and Liam came out shortly after with dinner. As they set it on the table Darius raised his glass.

"I just wanted to thank everyone. I know more than anyone what a total ass I can be. Having you guys by my side, I know we can end this curse." Andrei raised his glass to meet Darius'. Everyone followed shortly. Our glasses clicked together, letting off a rhythmic chime. With that, everyone drank, and I ate.

Tonight's meal was a delicious pasta served with crushed tomatoes and garlic. Liam went around filling up the trio's glasses with blood.

"I thought garlic was bad for vampires to be around?" I asked, taking a bite.

"Just a myth," Darius and Andrei said in unison.

The next two months were long. We spent most of our time training with one another. Trying to prepare for our next steps. Winter had come to the Kikaro Mountains. This made training for me very difficult. My human body couldn't withstand the cold. It seemed like it didn't affect the others at all. If it did, they never showed it.

We had grown so close in our time together. It broke my heart knowing that soon it may come to an end. Darius had gone back to the city for a few weeks. He said the best plan was to act as if everything was normal. When he returned, he said that his father suspected nothing.

I hated to admit that I missed him while he was away. Part of me felt empty without him. I craved his touch, but I couldn't let him know that. The night he returned to the cabin, I wanted nothing more for him to come into my room and take me once again. Unfortunately, he did not.

Darius disappearing from his duties was not that uncommon. He lived by the beat of his own drum. That's how he said his mother put it when she was still alive. That was the only time I heard him talk about his mother. It seemed like a sore spot, so I didn't want to question further. Something in my gut told me that his father was involved with her death.

I had taken a break from today's training. I sat inside, watching Andrei and Darius spar from the window. I enjoyed a delicious mushroom bisque that warmed my freezing bones from the inside out. Isa had just come inside. She shook the snow off her hat as she removed it. I had just watched Liam tackle her into the snow. She prepared herself some soup and came and sat by my side.

"I heard the boys thinking we will make our move next month." She said taking her first bite. I removed my gaze from the window, and then to her.

"Already? Do you think we are ready?" Nervousness radiated from my voice. Isa gave a subtle nod.

"As ready as we'll ever be. Dimitri will be distracted next month, apparently, they are having some festival, and in preparation for that many palace guards have stationed themselves throughout the city. Making his protection much lighter than normal."

As we spoke, we heard a commotion from outside, apart from the norm from their sparing. Darius' face and hair were covered in snow. Andrei stood across from him laughing. Darius reached down, forming a snowball of his own. Launching it at Andrei however, it had missed and hit Daphne in her back. She pivoted quickly and a snowball fight had broken out between the three of them. Liam joined shortly after it began.

Isa gave a little giggle; asking me if we were going to let them have fun without us. No way. We snuck out the back door. We prepared our snowballs as we approached the front. We threw ours in unison. Each of our snowballs hit our targets. Both Darius and Andrei looked around, confused about where the assault had come from. We couldn't control ourselves as we busted out laughing, launching another towards them.

It wasn't long until we were in the front yard tossing snowballs at each other. I think this was the first time I had seen everyone have fun together. The past few months Andrei was very serious regarding training and had kept Isa and Liam on that same path.

Darius had gone back and forth. Some days he was wonderful to be around, others I wanted nothing to do with him and his bad attitude. Daphne would tell me on those days that he had a lot on his plate, and to not be so hard on him. We all had a lot on our plate, but he was the only one who would take it out on others. On his bad days, I would place a silver chain on the doorknob before going to sleep. I got a tiny bit of joy having him sneer in pain trying to open the door. He always tried, never learning his lesson from the time before.

Today was one of the good days. On those days I tried to forget the cruel words he had said to all of us. A snowball smacked me in the back of my head. I quickly spun around to see him chuckling. He made a smart-ass comment about me paying attention and not be so lost in thought. I glared at him and threw a snowball at him, slamming into his face. He wiped away the snow and gave me a predatory glare. My back slammed against a tree, his hand around my throat, my feet dangling above the ground. I tried to push him away. Everyone went still. His eyes turned red; his fangs bared.

"Dar... We were just having fun, let go, you're hurting me," I managed to say as he squeezed tighter. He didn't say a word. We stood there for what seemed like an eternity. A deep hunger in his eyes. Could this be the moment we all feared? He finally let me go. I slid down the tree, landing on my ass. He also fell to his knees screaming in pain. All I could do was sit there, wide-eyed, as if I was frozen to the ground. Andrei was quickly by my side, swooping me up. I blinked and we were inside. He sat me down on the couch. Daphne had met us inside. She said something to Andrei, but I couldn't hear their words from the ringing in my ears. But I could see the panicked expressions on their faces. Andrei left, leaving Daphne and me alone in the living room. She wrapped me in a blanket and placed a hand on my back.

After a while, the ringing in my ears had stopped. I noticed then that everyone sat with me in the living room. Watching me in silence. Everyone, except for Darius. I sat up straight, looking around for him, but he was nowhere to be seen. Andrei finally spoke, breaking the silence. Letting me know that Darius had left. He would not be returning.

"He left?! No, he can't leave! Tell him to come back!" That panicked feeling returned.

"Sabrina, it is no longer safe. Without that seal that Daphne put on his back, you would be dead right now." The seal. The one that had controlled his hunger for me, could it have done so much more? "He will meet us at the castle when it is time."

I spent the next week in bed. I didn't want to talk or see anyone. I was not able to fully process what had happened during the snowball fight. What had set him off? Why was it that moment that set off his kill switch? We had spent so much time together leading up to that. After our rendezvous in the bathtub, we were inseparable.

Even though I didn't want company, Daphne and Isa would visit me every night, brought me my dinner, and forced me to eat it. Every bite I took made me want to be sick. They would tell me how training went that day.

On the morning of my eighth day in bed, Andrei entered my room. He did not knock. Once inside he entered my closet, he wasn't in there very long. Pulling my blanket off the bed he tossed my training clothes on the bed.

"Vacation's over. Time to get back to training. We don't have much time left."

Sixteen

The morning of our move to the city came quicker than I wanted it to. I put my hair into a loose braid. Slipping on my jeans and the green shirt that Darius loved to see me wear. I had hoped that once we got into the city, maybe I would be able to see him shortly after. I threw my backpack over my shoulders. Andrei said to only pack the essentials, but I managed to fit my favorite mascara and lip gloss in. I was thankful they took up no space at all. He hoped that we would not be spending too much time in the city.

I met everyone downstairs. Everything was already loaded into the two cars we would take into the city. Isa, Daphne, and I would take one, and Andrei and Liam would take the other. Andrei gave his final instructions to everyone before allowing us to get into the cars and make the long drive back to the city. He told us the route to take, what to say to anyone who stopped us, and where we would all meet up once we arrived. Andrei and Liam were the first to leave. Daphne said she needed to finish a few more things before she was ready to go. She went back upstairs, leaving Isa and I waiting in the living room.

"Hey," she whispered. "I just wanted to say, just in case this goes bad." I cut her off. Telling her this was going to go as planned, and not to think that way. What a hypocrite I was. My thoughts were the same as hers. I couldn't bear the thought of losing any one of them. Even if it was my own life that was lost, I knew it wouldn't be long until I was reborn. I just hoped they would find me if that happened.

Daphne came back down with a big smile on her face. "Alright! All ready." She headed out the door and we followed her. Daphne drove as Isa and I both sat in the back seat. It would be a two-day drive to reach the city. The plan was to drive straight through, only stopping to swap places. Isa and I began to talk about what we would do once the curse was broken. Isa said she wanted to travel and visit places with Andrei she couldn't have imagined visiting before this all happened. She asked Daphne what her plans were.

"I hope I am able to go home." A deep somber filled her voice. Isa asked what she meant, asking why she couldn't return now. "Serafina was my home, after the curse. Dimitri built a wall, blocking off access to the fae lands. I am hoping once the curse is broken, I can return home."

"Is that why you have limited access to your magic? The wall?" Isa questioned. Daphne nodded, keeping her eyes on the road. We all quickly changed the subject. It was evident that it pained Daphne to talk about Serafina.

We could finally see the city skyline off in the distance. We switched seats so that Isa was driving. Daphne and I sat in the back. We thought it would be the best idea to allow the vampire to drive into the city. We were hoping that it wouldn't seem as suspicious.

We entered a part of the city I had never visited before. This was one of the sections that the vampires had complete control over. No human, with their free will, would live here. I sunk into my seat, wanting to stay hidden. The moon was high and the streets were filled. I could hear the commotion of the city just beyond the car door. We pulled into a parking garage, and the hustle and bustle from the city quieted down.

Before we left it was agreed that we would park on level B5, the lowest level of the garage. I sat back up in my seat as we descended. Isa gripped the wheel so tight I could see the veins in her hand. Daphne looked down at her book, refusing to look up. She sat on the same page for some time. I don't believe she was reading but using it as an excuse to not investigate the city. None of us said a word. It was a vast change from the rest of the car ride. We all had been full of laughter, save for when one or more of us was asleep.

Isa finally pulled into a spot and put the car into park. Her body was still tense. Daphne finally looked up from her book.

"Did you see Andrei's car?" She whispered. Isa turned back to us, unbuckling her seatbelt.

"Yeah, I didn't see them, but I did see their car. It's parked three spaces over. They must have already gone upstairs." I could see her eyes scanning the view from the back window. "You two wait here, I'll make sure the coast is clear." Daphne and I nodded. Isa stepped out of the car, locking the door behind her. We saw her walk around the car and begin to look around the garage level. She was shortly out of view.

Moments later she came back, knocking on the trunk to get our attention, letting us know we were good to go. As Daphne and I got out of the car, Isa popped the trunk and began to get our bags out. We gathered them quickly and headed to the elevator.

As the doors of the elevator began to shut, we saw two cars back-to-back begin to park on the same level. I reached over quickly mashing the 'Close Door' button, hoping it would close faster. Thankfully it shut fully before they could get out of their car.

"To the top," Isa said. A sigh of relief escaped her mouth.

"To the top," Daphne and I said together. The elevator gave a small chime as we reached each level. It wasn't long before it reached the penthouse way above the parking garage.

"Please enter passcode," a robotic feminine voice said as the elevator came to a stop. I reached up to the pin pad and entered the code 102520. "Welcome home," the robotic voice chimed as the doors opened.

There Darius stood in the doorway. He wore a dark button-up shirt, with the sleeves rolled up, exposing the dark tribal dragon tattoo on his left forearm. His hair was just as it was in the flower field in my dreams. A neat top bun, with a few loose pieces to frame his face. He had the biggest grin on his face.

"Welcome home, indeed." he purred as I threw myself into his open arms.

Seventeen

His arms wrapped around my body, squeezing me tight. We stood there in each other's embrace for some time. We didn't say a word to each other. The conversations of the others sounded like buzzing in my ears. At this moment I couldn't care less about what anyone else had to say. Being in his arms made something in me feel complete.

I saw a hand grip Darius' shoulder. I looked up and met Andrei's gaze.

"Alright, break it up, we don't want a repeat of what happened during the snowball fight," he said sternly. With that, Darius released me. Setting me down on the hardwood floor. He turned to face everyone and welcomed us all to his city penthouse.

He gave us a tour of the penthouse before we talked business. The center room has an open-concept kitchen and living space. A breakfast bar separated the two. The back wall has a large window to overlook the city. The building we were in, The Rune Spire, was one of the tallest in the whole city. To the left of the kitchen was a small hall that led to Darius' office and three spare rooms. These rooms are where Daphne, Liam, Andrei, and Isa would stay during our time here. Each room was perfectly furnished and had a beautiful city view of their own.

To the right of the living room was a staircase that led up to the loft area that overlooked the kitchen and living space. This is where a beautiful black and gold set of French doors sat. While the others got situated in their rooms Darius led me up the stairs and stopped at the French doors.

"Go ahead and open them," he teased from behind me. "Don't you want to sneak away into our bedroom?" I turned to face him.

"Our?" My mind raced, would that even be safe? Did I even care? Darius nodded motioning to the door.

"Well, don't keep me waiting." I turned back to the doors and opened them. A large bedroom waited behind the doors with the biggest bed I had ever seen. The other three walls and ceiling are all glass, giving an almost 360 view of the city. As if he could read my mind, he pressed a button on the wall next to the door. The glass then became opaque, blocking the view of the city. With another press it began to glimmer, mimicking the night sky.

"You thought the bed at the castle was comfortable, I can't wait for you to lay in this." He sat on the edge of the bed smirking up at me. "Take your clothes off, that way you can enjoy these sheets," he growled.

"I will not be taking my clothes off," I sneered in response. However, it made my body tingle. An image pushed into my brain of him pinning down my wrists, my exposed body underneath his as he made me his once again. I could feel my body burning. I tried to push it out of my head, but it wouldn't budge.

If you won't let me fuck you now, I'll do it in your mind. His voice embedded into my mind.

"You're a pervert!" I exclaimed. Sitting my bag down on the bed next to him. "I need to unpack my things. Are you going to help or just watch?"

"Oh, I plan on just watching, the left side of the closet has been cleared out for your things. There are built-in drawers for you to use." He laid down on the bed. I went into the closet and began to put away my things. All I could think about was how this was a far cry from the tiny apartment Isa and I had lived in just on the other side of the city.

"I hope you packed that little red silk nightgown with the black lace. You are smoking when you wear that," he called out from the bedroom. I rolled my eyes not saying a word. Some things never change, I guess. Human or vampire men only have one thing on their minds.

It was not long before I felt him behind me, his body pressed into mine. He wrapped his arms around me, pulling me in closer. He took in a deep breath, and his body shuttered.

"I'm sorry, doll. I have to have you now," he purred in my ear. He lifted me and quickly tossed me to the bed.

"Darius!" I squealed. Before I could finish my thought, his hand was on my mouth. His eyes were blood red, and he had that predatory smile across his face.

"Before you say anything," He licked his lips. "The only things I want to hear out of your mouth are your sweet little moans, my name, and begging for more. Do you understand?" He pushed me backward, so that I layed on my back. His gaze was always even with mine. Everything about me at that moment melted. I simply nodded as I surrendered to him.

"Such a good girl," he purred as he uncovered my mouth and tore off my jeans. He used my sweatshirt to tie my wrists together and to the headboard. It all happened so fast, there was no chance for me to stop him before I was naked and bound. He quickly pulled my legs apart and held them down. I was completely at his mercy, and I didn't mind it. No, my body craved it. The wetness between my legs grew as he teased me.

He lowered his head in between my legs and licked his way up my thigh. His eyes are on mine. He then grazed his fangs down my thigh. A gasp escaped my lips. I could see the hunger in his eyes. How he wanted nothing more than to bite down. Just as I thought he was going to let his intrusive thoughts win, he licked his way back up my thigh and to the most intimate parts of me.

"Oh, doll. You are so delicious," he purred as he feasted on me. I didn't want this to end.

No, I needed more.

"Darius, please don't stop," I pleaded. His tongue explored deeper within me. My whole body quivered. I was so close to climaxing. I was right at the edge, I just needed a moment more, as he pulled away.

He looked at me through his brow, licking his lips.

"Not yet, doll." He got up on his knees and began to unzip his jeans. "Not until I give you permission." He pulled out his cock and leaned in. He gently petted my entrance with it. It was agonizingly torturous. I needed him inside me. I craved that feeling of completion.

"Beg," he demanded.

"Please Dar. I need you inside me!"

"Oh, you need me inside you?" He slowly put in just the tip.

"Please! I need all of you!" I begged. It was true. I needed him deep inside me.

He obliged. He quickly thrusted into me over and over. I arched my back. Moaning loudly for him, begging for him not to stop. His rough hands found my throat and squeezed.

"Such a good fuck doll you are for me," he purred, "cum for me, doll." I did. I couldn't hold it in any longer. My entire body exploded from the pleasure.

He pulled out and smirked down at me. Not saying anything for a moment. His hand traveled down from my throat to my breasts.

"Mine." He growled. "You are mine." He roughly grabbed my hips, flipping me to my stomach. One hand was firmly planted in the middle of my back while he rammed inside me once again. Loud moans escaped my lips to the rhythm of his thrusts. I pressed back into him, craving even more.

I felt him release inside me, deeper than before. He leaned down without pulling out.

"Mine." He growled once again. "Say it."

"I am yours." I moaned softly as I felt myself still quivering against his girth.

"Good girl." He pulled out. Gods, I wanted him inside me forever. Unfortunately, time was not on our side.

Darius freed me from the headboard. I sat up and my eyes met his.

"You are the most beautiful creature I have ever seen," he said as he leaned in and gave me a gentle kiss on my lips.

"Get dressed and finish putting your things away, I can hear the others waiting for us downstairs."

I stood and finished putting away my things, got dressed, and went back into the bedroom. Darius was nowhere to be seen however the bedroom doors were open. I headed out the doors and back downstairs where everyone gathered in the living room. Isa sat on Andrei's lap in a large armchair. Daphne and Liam sat across from them on a loveseat. Darius stood behind them, looking out the window, hands clasped behind his back. His gaze towards the castle on the far end of the city. I sat on the sectional in between the chair and loveseat. We all watched Darius as we awaited his words. You could feel the tension building. You could cut it with a knife.

"What's the plan boss?" Andrei finally broke the silence. Darius looked back towards us, taking a few steps in our direction.

"Tonight, we will rest and enjoy each other's company. For it may be the last night we all spend together. At dawn, I will sneak us all into the castle through the tunnels under the city."

"There are tunnels?" Isa questioned. She and I have lived here our whole lives and never heard of any tunnels.

"Yes, they are used in case of emergency to evacuate the Royal Family. Once we are in the tunnels and in the castle, we will have to plan our moves in the moment. I couldn't get the guard layout for the castle, without arousing my father's suspicions." He came and sat by my side, wrapping his arm around me, and pulling me in close. "For this to work, we will need to stay in teams. No matter what, stay with your partner. Bri and I will be one team. Daphne and Liam, you will be together. Andrei, you will have Isa on your team. Try not to get too distracted," he teased. Andrei rolled his eyes.

"You either, my Lord" Andrei teased back. Daphne stood; she was holding a small box in her hand.

"If I may...," she started softly. "I would like to perform a protection ritual. Something that may help us during this journey. It won't be much since I have limited access to my magic, but it will be something." Darius gave a nod.

Daphne set the box on the coffee table and opened it. She pulled out six black candles, lighting them one by one. Something was engraved on each one, but there were symbols that I didn't understand. Once they were all lit, she gave us each a small stone. Each had an engraving that matched one of the candles she had lit. She instructed us to close our eyes and grasp the stone tightly in our hands. She chanted in a language I didn't understand.

The stone grew warm in my hand sending a tingle through my body. Dancing lights began to form a vision in my head. I tried to focus, trying to understand what I was being shown. It was still so unclear. However, I could make out some of it. Darius and I stood in the center of a dark, twisted forest. It seemed I was using magic to clear the way. We spoke, but the words were a jumble. Eventually, we exited the forest together, hand in hand. A corrupt castle in the distance.

Before I could get any more information on the vision it was gone. Daphne instructed us to open our eyes.

Eighteen

I told no one about the vision. I didn't want to add anything else on everyone's plate, not when we had so much on the line currently. The next morning, we all gathered our weapons, putting on our black leather armor. Andrei said he had gotten it from an enchantress outside the city. She had claimed that it would help us blend into the shadows. It would also mute our heart beats. We would be completely silent as we snuck around the castle. I hoped she was right.

We crept through alleyways. Hoping we wouldn't be seen. Darius led us through the labyrinth of the city's alley way. Eventually the building gave way to a gated cemetery. The Dragomeir crest twisted in the iron bars of the gate. Darius approached the gate as he pressed his thumb into his fang causing him to bleed. He smeared it on the crest and the gates opened.

He explained that it was blood magic that kept this place sealed for only the Royal family to enter. The cemetery was larger than it appeared to the outside. Darius walked us to the center of the cemetery to a tall black obelisk.

"Wait here," he said, wandering down a set of steps to the right.

After about five minutes I looked down in the direction that he had just headed, he was nowhere to be seen. I was about to take a step down as I felt someone grab my wrist. It was Andrei.

"Give him time. This is his family cemetery after all." A somber tone escaped his lips as he released me. "Five more minutes, then you can go check." He gave me a soft smile. We all waited around the Obelisk. The sun was peeking through the sky-high buildings around us casting a gentle glow. After a few moments, Andrei slid me a knowing glance and a nod in the direction Darius had gone. Quickly and quietly, I headed down the steps following his path. After a moment I saw Darius.

He was on a small island that housed a single grave. A cherry tree in full bloom shaded the island. A single gold bridge is the only way to cross the soft blue waters. Darius was kneeling in front of the grave, his head bowed. As I approached from behind, he lifted his head and wiped his eyes.

"I told you to wait," he snarled.

"You have been gone for about ten minutes. We were worried about you." I gently placed a hand on his shoulder. He grabbed it tightly as he stood pulling me into him. Squeezing my wrist so tightly that it felt as if he was going to crush bone. I let out a scream.

A look of terror filled his eyes as he realized what he had done. He released me. His mouth tightened as he took a step back.

The grave was now fully in view. My chest tightened. I felt as if I was going to vomit. I looked over at Darius, his eyes refused to meet mine.

"This is why I wanted you to wait," his voice shook. "I hope you like it... This cherry tree was from your homeland... It was the last thing to cross into our land from yours."

I fell to my knees. Looking back at the headstone. Sabrina Dragomeir. It was then his hand who gently sat on my shoulder. I could hear several footsteps behind us. The others must have heard my scream. I could hear them speaking to Darius, but I couldn't hear what they were saying. It all sounded like a jumbled mess. The only thing I could focus on was my grave. After a moment I looked up. All my friends are standing behind me. They all had this look on their face. None of them knew what to say to me. I couldn't blame them. If I was in their shoes, I wouldn't know what to say either.

"Are... there others?" Finally escaped my mouth. Darius shook his head, kneeling by my side. He told me my other bodies were cremated and added to the water that surrounded this island. I finally stood, telling the other I would unpack this later, we have a mission to complete. They all gave me a blank stare as I walked off the island and back to the obelisk.

Darius caught up to me as we headed back. Gently taking my hand in his.

"Is your wrist ok?" He whispered. I gave a nod to him. The pain I had felt still lingered, but it was now dull and would fade soon. We got back to the obelisk and Darius opened a hidden door in the back of it.

Darius led the way down into the tunnels. Followed by Daphne, Liam, myself, Isa, and Andrei in the back. Our weapons were ready, just in case a few guards were posted in the tunnels. They were a lot darker than I had hoped. Isa took my hand, guiding my way. It wasn't total darkness, I could make out general shapes, but it would be hard for me to attack, or defend myself if needed.

Darius said that this part of the tunnels was supposed to be darker, to confuse any attackers. He told us —me— not to worry as we should be in the lighted part shortly. After a few more twists and turns he was right. The tunnels were filled with dim light. This meant we were close to the castle. Off in the distance, we began to hear some footsteps and voices. Darius ushered us all to the left as we stuck to the shadows. Awaiting whoever was approaching to pass us. Darius held out two fingers. If there were only two of them, we should be fine in case anything happened. We heard their footsteps get closer.

"I despise being on tunnel duty," the woman said.

"It's not so bad, it gives us plenty of alone time." That voice belonged to a man.

Isa gripped my hand tighter. I could feel her shaking. I leaned against her. Hoping that would help calm her nerves. I was also on edge. I knew I wasn't ready for the actual battle. Even with the months of training, my soul wasn't ready. All I could think about was that poor deer. How could I do that to a person?

The footsteps grew closer. I prayed they would keep going straight, and not turn in our direction. Hopefully, they couldn't hear my heart nearly beating out of my chest. They finally passed us, not even looking in our direction.

Two guards. An older man and woman, wearing the Royal Guard light armor. Once they walked past Isa let go of my wrist and darted into the hall. Darius tried to reach for her, but she was too quick. She stood in the hall facing them as they turned to see what caused the commotion behind them.

"Mom... Dad..." she sniffled, "what are you doing here?" Her voice was broken.

The two guards looked at each other, then at her. "Isabella, is that really you?" They said in unison. Isa dropped her twin blade and ran to them, wrapping them in her embrace.

Darius looked back at us still in the hall motioning for us to stay put and watch how this would play out.

"You guys have been alive... this whole time?" Isa said, taking a step away from them.

"Yes, we have," the woman said coldly.

"What are you doing down in the tunnels?" Her father asked. Suspicion rooted in his voice. Isa froze.

"If you guys were alive... all this time... Why didn't you come find me?" I couldn't see Isa's face, but from the sound of her voice, I could tell she was crying. Her Father asked her again why she was in the tunnels. Ignoring her questions. His hand now gripping the dagger in his waistband.

"That's really all you're concerned about?! I haven't seen you in the past ten years! I thought you were dead! I mourned you! I visited your graves weekly! Have you been in the castle this whole time? Did you ever once worry about the child you left behind to fend for herself?" Rage had filled her voice.

"The King offered us a better life. So, we took it," Isa's mother spoke. "And in exchange, we are now a part of his guard. And ordered us to kill anyone who we find trespassing in these tunnels." Her voice was cold, with no emotion. My heart broke for Isa.

I thought about how every year on the anniversary of their 'death' Isa and I would make what she said were their favorite foods. We would celebrate the life they had. Each week Isa would go to the cemetery and give them fresh flowers on their graves. It had to be white lilies with yellow roses. Those were her parents' favorites. On the weeks they didn't have yellow roses she would get white and dye them herself. I thought about how Isa had to grow up alone. In a city where humans were hated and hunted. How she had to figure out the hard parts of life without her parents by her side.

What happened next happened too quickly for me to process. In between wiping away my tears, Liam was gone, no longer by my side. He now stood in front of Isa. Her father held a knife in his chest.

"You monsters, I won't let you hurt her any longer," he said as he gargled on his own blood.

Nineteen

"Pathetic," Isa's father tossed Liam's body to the ground.

"The rest of you can come out of hiding now." Her mother readied her sword. Darius was the first to step out of the shadows. Without a word he had the man pinned to the wall. Andrei followed behind him, attacking Isa's mother. Daphne and I quickly rushed to Liam's side, hoping something could be done.

"Arthur and Rose Valentine." Darius snarled. "You are released from your duties from the royal guard." I looked up at Darius at that moment to watch him rip the head off Isa's father. I heard her mother begin to scream. I was too in shock from what happened with Arthur to even look in her direction as the scream turned into a gargle, then silence. Darius released Arthur's body and then was beside me to check on Liam. Andrei had Isa wrapped in a hug so tight that we could barely hear her sobs.

Unfortunately for Liam, it was too late. Arthur's blade had dug too deep into his heart, and he had lost too much blood. We all knelt around his body hand in hand. Thanking him for his sacrifice. For what he had done had saved Isa's life. Daphne was the first to speak.

"I will take him to his final resting place, you four go on without me." Isa tried to protest, but Darius quickly cut her off telling Daphne to meet us back at the penthouse once she was done. Daphne nodded and took Liam's body and disappeared into the shadows of the tunnels.

"Are you alright?" I finally asked Isa. She nodded, wiping her eyes.

"Seems like we all will have a lot to unpack after this," she chuckled.

"That we will, let's get a move on before more guards come." Darius had already begun walking away from us. We all followed him. After a few more minutes we arrived at a large stone stairway. A set of dark red double doors sat at the top. That was it. The way into the castle that we had been looking for. Darius and I headed up the steps. Andrei and Isa waited at the bottom, keeping an eye out. About halfway up the stairs began to rumble. Darius grabbed me, throwing me over his shoulder. In a blink, we were standing in the open doorway as the stairs crumbled. Leaving us separated from the others.

"I know where the other entrance is," Andrei called up to us. "We will meet you there." He and Isa both were out of my sight in a blink. I hoped we would meet up again soon. Darius and I slipped fully through the door, shutting it behind us.

"Welcome to the main castle, It's a lot bigger than the one we stayed in in the mountains. Stick close so you don't get lost." We stood in an empty room about five feet by five feet. The walls were solid concrete. Darius walked over to the wall across from the door and pressed his foot down on one of the tiles next to it. I heard a click from within the wall. It slid open and revealed a massive library. Much larger than the one back in the mountains. However, this was just as dusty. Many of the shelves looked burned and many books were missing.

"My father's doing. There are things that have happened within our history he doesn't want to get out." His eyes darted around the room, looking for danger.

"Our history? About how it was before the curse?" He nodded but said nothing. I knew there were details still hidden even from me about the curse. I hoped he would tell me, but I doubt he would. Not until it was broken.

"Come," he said as he quickly navigated through the narrow bookshelves. I followed behind him. I asked him how far it was to the other tunnel entrance for us to meet up with the other.

"That would take too long. Hopefully, when Andrei gets there, we will figure that out and meet us where we are going." We finally were at the library entrance. Darius peeked out his head and then motioned for me to follow. We walked through the halls; I couldn't help but find myself in awe of the decorations around the palace. Darius grabbed my wrist.

"Look nervous. Don't say a word," he commanded as two young men rounded the corner. Greeting Darius with a smile. The one on the right was tall, and slender. He had a scar over his right eye. The man on the left was tall as well, but he was muscular. His eyes were as dark as the tunnels had been when we first entered. Darius gripped me tighter.

"Ah! Darius," the slender one said. "I was wondering if you would be home for the Blood Moon."

"And I see you brought a toy with you to celebrate." The muscular man licked his lips, looking me up and down. I took a step behind Darius. I didn't need to pretend to look nervous.

I was.

The three talked for some time about their plans for the Blood Moon. The other two made lewd remarks about how many women Darius would devour during the festival. The skinny one reached down, taking a piece of my hair in his hand.

"She smells delicious. Her scent reminds me of the Fae. Gods, they were delicious."

"Remove your hand from her, less you want it broken." Darius spat. The man released my hair.

"Come on, why are you like that? She's just some human."

"She is my human. Remember what happened to the last person who touched my things," he was nearly foaming at the mouth as he spoke. His eyes were blood red.

"My bad man." The slender one took a step back and looked towards the other. Darius grabbed his arm, twisting it until I heard a snap. I jumped back as I heard him scream.

"I am your Prince. You will address me as such." Darius released him with a shove. "It will serve you well to remember who you are speaking to." He then glared at me, pulling me with him into the next room as we walked away.

We traveled up a spiral staircase leading us to a large sitting room. Filled with many chairs and couches. Hung on the walls were some of the most beautiful artworks I had ever seen. Darius finally released me. My skin was left red from where his grip was.

"Who were they? Should we be worried they saw me?" I finally spoke as we approached an ornate door.

"Some sons of some stupid count, I don't remember their names. They are nobody worth remembering." He opened the door and led me into a bedroom. The dark walls matched the ones from the castle in the mountains. The same four-poster canopy bed sat in the middle of the room.

"Wait here. I need to make sure the coast is clear before moving forward, and you will only slow me down." Before I could say a word, he was gone. Leaving me alone.

I did not think that was the best idea. Who knows what could happen to me while he was away or who lurked in these halls?

I sat on the edge of the bed, my bow readied toward the door. I couldn't help but think about how everyone else was doing. I wonder if Andrei and Isa made it into the castle just fine. How Daphne was handling the loss of Liam.

I sat in solitude for some time. I wondered if everything was alright. I hope that Darius hasn't gotten into any trouble. As if my worries had been heard, the door opened.

However, it wasn't Darius who stepped into the room.

"It's... you?!" I stood aiming my bow. "Who are you!" I demanded as the man from the farmers market shut the door behind him.

"Woah, put the bow down. I am here to help you." He raised his hands in the air. The old man was hunched over, wearing a brown tunic and black pants. He walked with a simple wooden walking stick. He looked like a simple man who had lived a hard life. "If you want to break the curse, you will need my help."

"Answer my questions. Who are you and how did you know I was in here?" I didn't lower my weapon. Something inside me screamed for me to fire.

"Please, child. I am only here to help." He took a step forward. "The Prince sent me here. He told me where he put you. He is being hung up by some of the nobles he ran into while scouting. I am just a simple servant of this castle."

"Don't come any closer! Why were you at the market that day?"

"Darius sent me to find you. To make sure you were ok. I had to leave when your friend appeared. I didn't mean to scare you. Please, we must move before the guards come this way during their rounds. My name is Clive."

I finally lowered my bow. "Fine, let's go." He nodded and headed out the door.

I followed him for some time. We went through many flights of steps and down many hallways. This place seemed more like a maze than a castle. We arrived at a large courtyard. It was lined with cherry trees like I had seen back at my grave. A koi pond sat in the middle of the courtyard. Surrounded by several benches. A gazebo was off in the north corner.

Clive motioned for me to sit on one of the benches. He let me know that this is where Darius said he would meet us, and he should be here any moment. We sat in silence for just a moment. It was calm before the storm of Darius's screaming could be heard. Several guards were dragging him into the courtyard on his knees. He was wrapped in silver chains, just like the ones from the basement. He was covered in blood, and I couldn't tell if it was his or someone else's.

"Get away from her you miserable son of a bitch!" he wailed towards Clive. Clive clicked his tongue, taking a step towards Darius. An evil smirk grew on his face. "And show yourself, don't be a fucking coward!" Darius hissed. One of the guards kicked him on that last word. That frozen feeling came over me once again.

Run. Find Isa and Andrei. Get out of here. He screamed in my head, but I couldn't move.

Guards were blocking every exit I had. I looked over at Darius, tears in my eyes. I raised my bow, before I could let off a shot at Clive a guard had knocked the bow from my hand, wrapping me in his arms. His forearm pressed into my throat. His other hand was holding my hands together behind my back. Darius was screaming for me to be released.

"Oh no, neither of you are going anywhere," Clive chuckled. Before my eyes, he transformed. He was now tall, slender build. He had long dark hair and bright green eyes that matched Darius. His simple walking stick is now black with a gold dragon holding a red orb.

"Father please, let her go. She doesn't need to die again."

<h1 style="text-align:center">Twenty</h1>

The man who stood before us was the man we came to kill. I couldn't believe it. I was so close in the bedroom to firing an arrow. I should have trusted my gut. We should have done a lot of things. It was now too late for what-ifs.

Darius and I were taken to the dungeon and locked together in a single cell enforced with silver bars. There was no way we were going to be able to break our way out. Dimitri stood on the other side. A smug look on his face.

"I hope you enjoy your final moments together. Neither of you is coming out until the other is dead," with that he was gone. Leaving Darius and me alone in the dimly lit dungeon. The chains still wrapped around his body. He sat on the floor, looking out of the bars. A look of pain on his face. I approached him, wanting to take off the chains to alleviate his pain.

"Stay far away from me. The chains are staying on" he snarled. I took a few steps back. "Hopefully Andrei and Isa will find us soon. We need to regroup.

Three days passed. A guard came down once a day with a small bowl of cold soup for me. Just enough to keep me alive. Nothing was brought for Darius. Bloodlust lived within his eyes. He still refused to even look at me. The chains left burns on his skin.

There was no sign of Andrei or Isa. I prayed that they made it out and that they were with Daphne. Trying to figure out how to free Darius and me. I tried to think of anything but the worst outcome for them. I knew they would be here for us soon.

I awoke on day five with Darius inches away from my face. A quiet predatory stare into my soul. After a moment he backed away to his side of the cell.

"S-sorry," he winced. "I thought if I just smelled you the hunger would subside." His eyes never looked away from me. I recognized that look from my nightmares.

"Well, I am surprised to see that you both are still alive," Dimitri sneered as he walked down the steps. "How... disappointing."

He approached the bars near Darius. Whispering something. I couldn't hear what was said. Whatever it was threw Darius into a rage. He flew to the bars, reaching for his father. Roaring in pain as the chains dug into his skin.

"I will KILL you!" He screamed over and over. Dimitri took a step back just in time to escape Darius' grasp. The chains had made him slow.

"Only after you kill your *true love*." Venom dripped from those last two words.

Two more days have passed. The pain from my hunger was impossible to ignore. It kept me awake. I hadn't slept well. Darius refused to speak to me this past week. The hunger in his eyes got worse. His fangs had been out for the past several days.

I let the intrusive thoughts of what could have happened to Andrei and Isa begin to slip into my mind. They were dead. I was sure of it. Otherwise, they would have come for us.

Come to me. A purr in the back of my mind, one similar to our first encounter under the basement.

"No," I said aloud.

Free me. Be a good girl and free me. His control was slipping if not already gone. The only thing protecting me were those chains.

"You stupid bitch! Unchain me!" His roar shook the silver bars of the cage. I could feel the tears fill my eyes.

"Darius, stop. You are scaring me. Just hold in a little longer. Someone will come save us," I whimpered. I blinked and he was now in front of me. He towered over me as I cowered under him. His eyes were cold. Deadly.

He knelt looking me in my eyes, wiping away a tear.

"Please," a whimper of his own escaped his lips. His eyes returned to that beautiful emerald.

I obliged.

Everything inside of me begged me to stop, but just as before I couldn't. I was no longer in control of my own body.

As the final chain hit the floor, Darius slammed me into the wall. Before I could scream, he sunk his fangs into my neck. A burning sensation filled my body. His venom filled my veins.

Everything slipped to black.

I stood again once in unending darkness. All the pain I had experienced was washed away from me. I was certain I was dead and that the light that had appeared before me now was the other side.

I walked towards the light and found myself in a large throne room. The room was open. Natural light from the full moon and stars filtered in. Vines filled with flowers wrapped around the columns. A single throne sat on a dais. The throne was also twisted in those beautiful floral vines. It sang to me. I approached the throne, sitting in it.

As I sat, ghostly figures filled the throne room. All dressed as if this was a masquerade, dancing with one another. I looked down, my dirty leather armor gone. I now wore a shimmering green dress with long bell sleeves.

"Don't forget who you are." I heard Daphne's voice from behind me.

Darius now stood before me. He wore a black tux with a bright green tie that matched his eyes. A golden mask covering the top half of his face. He smirked down at me on the throne as he extended his hand. As I took his hand everything fades away. One by one the people, the flowers, the building. Darius was the last to fade into the darkness.

Images from this last life flashed before my eyes. Starting with the day I had met Isa.

Everything went black once again.

Part 2

Twenty-One

I t was a snowy day in the village. It was snowing way too hard for us to go out to play today. All of us children had been sent to our rooms as a special visitor was supposed to arrive tonight. Madam Valdon said if anyone was caught out during the visit we would be punished severely.

"Who do you think is getting adopted this week?" Maxine said from across the bedroom in a whisper. "I hope it's me." She was wrapped up in her wool blanket smiling at me as she squeezed her stuffed bunny tight.

"No way! It's going to be me next. I am the oldest!" Sarah said.

Whenever we had a visitor one of us was always adopted the same day. It was always the same. A visitor would come, and we would all be locked in our rooms. Eventually, the house mother would come and take a few of us to meet the visitor. Those children were always adopted by the visitor.

It wasn't long before the house mother came upstairs and called three girls down to meet the visitor, Maxine being one of them.

"I'm so jealous," Sarah sighed as she crossed her arms. She was nearly thirteen and was yet to be adopted. She was older than all of us.

"I'm sure you will be adopted soon." I smiled at her. We all longed for a family that would love and care for us. However, I knew that would never be the case for me. Madam Valdon always told me I was too weird to be adopted. I wasn't worth the trouble. She hated me for the nightmares that had kept me up at night. She thought I had made them up to spite her.

I looked over and saw that Maxine's bunny was still on her bed. I knew she would miss her bunny if she left without it. She took him everywhere with her. I got out of bed and walked over to grab the bunny.

"What are you doing?" Sarah asked.

"I can't let Maxine leave without Mr. Wiggles! I'll just sneak down and give it to her. Madam Valdon will never see me."

"You are on your own with that one! You're going to get caught and get into sooooo much trouble! You saw what happened to Alex when he got caught sneaking out when there was a visitor." Poor Alex, had his mouth taped shut for two weeks. He wasn't allowed to be around any of the other children. He had been locked in the basement, forced to watch us all play through a tiny, barred window to the outside. When he came out from the basement, he was a different kid. He never spoke and would scratch his skin until he was covered in his own blood. He was transferred to a different home in the middle of the night shortly after.

"I'm not going to get caught. Just stay here you scaredy cat." I quietly slipped out of our room and tiptoed down the stairs.

"My my..." I heard a woman say from the dining room. Her voice was like nails to a chalkboard. "These children look wonderful... better than the photos." I peered into the room and saw the three girls standing in front of the woman in a daze. Their eyes glassed over. Madam Valdon sitting at the table counting money.

"Well... it is all here. These girls now belong to you," Madam Valdon said. The woman gave a wide toothy grin. Her fangs on display.

"Wonderful! I can't wait! I must have one now! This one!" She grabbed Maxine lifting her. Maxine hung there like a ragdoll as the woman sank her fangs into Maxine.

I stood there completely frozen and watched as all the color left her body. I dropped Mr. Wiggles in shock at what I just saw. No... This must be a dream.

"Please do not make a mess," Madam Valdon spoke. "I just had these carpets cleaned." The woman finally pulled away from Maxine, tossing her over her shoulder.

"My apologies. I couldn't help myself. That girl's blood sang to me, I just had to have her. Come along children," she said to the other who followed her. I quickly ran up the stairs and slid into the bedroom. I shut the door behind me. My breathing was heavy.

"You were gone for a bit. I was worried you got caught," Sarah said from her bed.

"No... I didn't make it in time..." My eyes filled with tears. Is that what happened to all those other children... What was that monster?

"Where is Mr. Wiggles then?" Oh no. I must have left him once I dropped him.

"I... must have dropped him..."

"Well get in bed before Madam Valdon comes up here and figures out it was you who went down!"

I got into bed, pulling the blanket up over my head. Closing my eyes tight, trying to go to sleep. All I could see was that woman biting Maxine. After a long period of silence, the door opened.

"Well, all those girls found homes," Madam Valdon said as she opened the curtains. It was now sunrise, and I didn't sleep a wink. "Poor Maxine dropped her bunny before she left. I will have to mail it off to her! Now everyone hurry up get dressed and come down for breakfast. We have a busy day ahead of us!"

After that, I never looked at anything in this house the same. I cried every time a visitor came and kids were selected. Everyone always thought it was because I wasn't getting adopted. That's what I let them believe. I had stopped playing outside with the other kids. What was the point if we were all to be killed?

I was passing by Madam Valdon's office and I could hear her talking behind the door.

"Are you sure? That child is riddled with nightmares. I'm sure they have tainted her blood." She had to be talking about me. "Well, if you are sure, you may come to collect her tonight. Bring cash." My heart sank. I knew that I would meet the fate Maxine had.

I stared out the window. Our village was nestled deep within the Kikaro mountains, with nothing around for miles except a castle you could see way off in the distance. I had always pretended that I lived there and was a princess. There was nowhere for me to run. Some wild animals would surely find me and turn me into their meal if the cold and hunger didn't reach me first. Madam Valdon's door opened; she smiled down at me.

"What a wonderful tenth birthday present! Someone is coming to adopt you tonight! Go on and pack your things, Sabrina!"

After dinner, Madam Valdon sent everyone but me upstairs. She sat me down on the couch in the foyer.

"It shouldn't be long before your new mother arrives!" It made me sick as a smile grew on her face. How could she be so happy about sending children to their deaths?

"Please... I don't want to die," I whimpered.

"Ahh... So, it was you who dropped the bunny." She knelt so we were at eye level with each other. "Don't worry, I'm sure if it's like Maxine's death it will be quick and painless." I sobbed as there was a knock at the door. Madam Valdon stood and went to open the door.

"Welcome, please come in from out of the cold." She greeted them, stepping out of the way. A short woman with dark curly hair stepped inside. She whipped the shaw off her peacoat. She gave me a warm smile as our eyes locked.

"Daphne..." I shuttered. Memories flooded into my brain. Everything was still a bit fuzzy, but I knew I was safe.

"You remember." She came to me and hugged me. She then stood and looked at Madam Valdor. "I think you are done here," she growled.

"Excuse me?" Madam Valdon hissed.

"Your days of selling children are over." As Daphne spoke a dagger came out of the darkness, piercing Madam Valdon in the throat. She fell to her knees, choking on her own blood. Andrei stepped out of the darkness with a woman I didn't recognize.

"Daphne, take Sabrina back to the castle. I will clean up and set Lacey up as the new house mother."

Twenty-Two

It was a cold day in Titus. The winters here were always brutal. I sat in an alleyway in Titus' market district. Shivering from the cold, still in my summer dress. I had awaited near the dumpster hoping that one of the merchants would have overstock they needed to toss. I was so hungry back then, so cold, That I did not care what was being tossed, I could put it to use.

I heard yelling coming from the market. I stood up, peeking down the alley to see what was happening. A girl, a bit older than me, came racing down the alley with a sack over her shoulder. A hood over her head, so I couldn't get a good look at her. As she passed me, she grabbed my hand, pulling me with her.

"Let me go! Where are you taking me?" I called out as we ran.

"Just keep running before they catch us! I just stole a crap ton of food from the market," she huffed. We ran for some time, eventually crawling through a hole in the side of an abandoned building.

The girl dropped the bag, and a variety of food spilled out. She put down her hood and smiled at me.

"We are going to eat good tonight."

That was the first time I had met Isa. The memory came flooding into my brain as we were reunited at the castle. As soon as I stepped out of the car Isa had picked me up and held me tight.

"I missed you so much!!!" She sobbed, squeezing me tighter.

"I... I missed you too" I whispered, hugging her back. I looked over at Daphne. "I... I missed all of you. I don't know how... But I remember. A lot is really fuzzy, but I remember." Tears filled my eyes. Isa put me down and wiped her own tears away.

"Let's get you inside and warmed up. We have a lot to talk about once you are settled in and Andrei returns," Daphne said as she guided me inside.

A few hours later Andrei returned to the castle. I had already changed my clothes and got settled into my old room. I used to think these walls were a prison cell. Now something felt warm and comforting inside them. Daphne had prepared me a hearty mushroom soup that filled me with warmth and chased away the horrors that Madam Valdon had brought.

The three of them sat and watched me eat. I used a warm slice of bread to mop up the rest of the soup. I hadn't realized how much I had missed Daphne's cooking.

"Tell me," Andrei started. "What exactly do you remember?"

"I remember you three... and Liam." My heart broke as Liam's memory returned. I never got to say a proper goodbye. I wonder where his final resting place was. "I remember being locked in a cage right before I died..." I paused. Someone else was in that cage with me. A man? A beast? I could not recall, but I remember whatever it was, it was my undoing. "And I remember a masquerade. A beautiful open ballroom that was lit by the moon. The walls were filled with vines and flowers."

Andrei dropped his glass causing it to shatter. Daphne gave me a shocking glance.

"A masquerade?" Isa questioned looking confused.

"The Masquerade of the Vernal Equinox." Daphne and Andrei said in unison. Isa then gave them a look.

"How do you know that with such little detail?" Isa asked.

"It was where this whole thing began. The day Darius and Sabrina met," Andrei said. He rested his head in his hand as his elbow sat on the table.

Once Darius's name left Andrei's lips, I felt a sharp pain in the back of my mind as his memories forced their way out of whatever part of my subconscious they were hidden in.

Flashes from the ball and a wedding. Those memories and the ones in between were too fast to pick out any details. I remembered what happened in the cabin basement, our first dinner back at the castle, our moment in the bathtub, and that final moment in the cage. I could feel his touch between my thighs, his fangs in my neck. I could hear his piano melody playing in the background as the memories played in my head.

"Where is he? Where is Darius?" I finally spoke. The room fell silent. They all looked at each other rather than to me.

"He is still locked in that cage. He has been for the last one hundred years." Andrei said somberly.

"I'm sorry...Did you just say..." The words jammed in my throat

"Yes, it has been one hundred years since you died last. We were worried that you were never going to return. Dimitri has kept Darius locked away as punishment for defying him. He plans to let Darius out once you turn eighteen."

"Let me guess, Dimitri has been letting him starve," I whimpered. "So that when he's let out...we won't be able to conspire against him again?"

"That would be correct. However, we have someone on the inside, who has been secretly feeding him. Unfortunately, it's not enough to satisfy him, but enough to not make him turn completely mad." Isa said as she nervously twiddled her thumbs

"If we have people on the inside, how come you haven't gotten him out? We can't just leave him there to rot!"

"After Isa and I barely escaped the tunnels with our lives, Dimitri shut down the city. No one goes in, no one goes out. We tried to sneak in a few times, but it was too dangerous. With you, it would be even worse. Humans no longer are welcome in the city unless they are food. The human sections were infiltrated, and most humans were killed instantly. Others were taken to blood dens." Andrei stood, coming to stand by my side. "We have eight years to prepare for Darius' release. Once he's released, he will come here instantly. The plan is to capture him and rehabilitate him. Once his craze is calmed, we will plan our next move."

My heart was pounding in my chest, feeling like it was going to burst. I couldn't begin to imagine the torture that he felt after a hundred years of barely being fed. He barely was holding on when we were captured together.

"This is a lot to dump on you on your first day back. Did you want to relax? Did you have any questions?" Daphne spoke up, she had been cleaning the glass shards off the floor.

"How...did you guys find me? Why do I remember so much this time?" I asked softly. Daphne stood digging in her pockets, pulling out a stone. It was the same one that I had held during the protection ritual she performed. It now gave off a soft pink glow.

"I held on to this all those years. One night I awoke and saw it glowing on my night-stand. When I held it, it told me where to find you." She put the stone back in her pocket and smiled. "The magic of Serafina blessed us that day."

Twenty-Three

The day I had dreaded had arrived. It was now the eve of my 18th birthday. We had spent the past eight years training and honing my skills. No matter how well I did with a bow, they all looked at me as if they expected more. I had begged them to turn me, that way we would all be on equal playing fields, but they always refused. They claimed that it was not in my best interest and that I did not need the vampiric kiss to be on the same playing field. I was now a master with my bow, Shimmerthorne. The bow and I moved as one. We were able to hit any target head on.

"We are ready as we ever will be," Andrei said to me as I paced back and forth in the observatory. "You will be totally safe. We won't let him touch you."

"Are you ready to see him?" Isa said as she laid down on a bench looking up at the stars.

"I am not sure how I feel." I stopped standing at her feet. "Part of me is terrified of dying again," I trailed off and began pacing again.

"But...?" Isa sat up

"I think I miss him," I said as Daphne came up the stairs with a pot of tea and a cake. "What is this? What are you doing?" I stopped and watched her setting the cake down. With a flick of her fingers the eighteen candles were set ablaze.

"I made your favorite! Strawberry with cream cheese icing!" She smiled wide. "Go on, blow out the candles so we can give you your gifts!"

"I don't think this is appropriate since we are about to be attacked by Darius who is in a blood craze."

"Well, it's only 11:30 so we have at least 30 minutes to celebrate before showtime!" She took my hand and guided me to sit in front of the cake. I looked up at her in protest.

"You have 30 seconds to blow them out yourself or we are going to sing."

"Oh gods, please not again. I don't think my eardrums ever recovered from Andrei's performance from my last birthday." I chuckled. Last year Andrei put on a one-man show for me. He sang and danced, neither of which was he was good at. I blew out the candles and they all yelled Happy Birthday in unison as they went to pull out some presents from various hiding spots. I opened each one and appreciated each of the gifts that my friends had given me.

"Thank you, guys. These are wonderful!" I smiled up at them as I tried on the bracelet that Daphne had gotten me. Rose gold wire had wrapped around pink stones forming little roses. Isa and Andrei had gotten me several different types of make-up and a few exotic perfumes they had imported.

"We wanted you to have at least one more happy moment before shit hit the fan," Isa laughed.

The clock chimed. It was midnight. Happy birthday to me. The laughter that filled the observatory went silent. The smiles from everyone's face faded. Andrei walked over to the glass and stared towards the direction of the city. We watched him and waited.

"How long until he gets here?" I finally got the courage to ask.

"A few hours. We are way away from the city, but with how fast he is, how hungry he is, I'm sure he isn't wasting any time," he responded, not taking his eyes off the horizon. "Why don't you wait in your room? Isa, will you stand guard while she rests?" Isa stood and nodded.

"How can I rest at a time like this?"

"You will need it, so go," he said coldly.

Isa and I headed down the steps and made our way to my room.

"You know it's going to be ok right?" Isa said quietly. I wanted to believe her. Darius was a powerful vampire. He was stronger, faster, and deadlier than any of us could imagine, and that was before he was in a blood craze. I couldn't imagine how the four of us planned on stopping him from getting what he wanted most.

"That's what I keep telling myself," I sighed as we stopped in front of my door. Isa looked around, making sure we were alone.

"There is one more birthday present for you. Under your bed. It is from Daphne and me. Andrei cannot know about it. Promise me you won't tell him." Urgency filled her voice. She looked down at me with worry.

"I won't tell him. What is it?" I raised my brow.

"I will stand outside the door. Go rest now. If anything happens, I will call for you to run. You will know what to do." She avoided answering my question.

I sighed and walked into my room, shutting the door behind me. I peeked under my bed and saw a small wooden box under it. I pulled it out and sat it on top of the bed. In the wood was an engraving of cherry blossoms and a sun.

I opened the box and found a note and a few items wrapped in pink silk. I unfolded the note and read it.

Sabrina

I may be putting all of us in danger by telling you this, but you are more than what you appear to be. You are more powerful than your mind is allowing you to be. You are not human.

You are fae.

We were worried if we told you before the curse was broken, that you wouldn't be able to handle it and your powers would spin out of control. With Darius approaching we need to be on an even playing field to win.

In this box, you will find everything you need to survive the night. Please don't ask questions, answers will come in time.

No one can know that you know the truth.

Daphne

My head began to pound. There was no way I was fae. I couldn't feel magic flowing through my veins. I felt no connection to nature or the elements as they did. Daphne would have no reason to make this up, but it was something beyond my mental grasp.

Then I remember the incident with the deer from my previous life. The swirl of wind that surrounded me while I was in a panic over what I had done, and how it had calmed as I did.

I unwrapped the silk from the items in the box.

The first was a silver stake, which I assumed was for emergency use only.

The second was a second bracelet that mimicked the one Daphne had given me. This one however the silver wire was twisted into moons around opals. I had put it on the opposite wrist.

The final item was a photograph, the edges tattered and torn. On the back was written in Darius' handwriting.

Vernal Equinox D+S 1st anniversary. The day I proposed to the love of my life.

I flipped it over to see Daphne, Darius, Andrei, and me. We were all dressed for the masquerade, different attire than the one I remembered from my flashback. A huge opal ring on my finger. We all looked so happy together. I looked closer at the photo and realized I was wearing the same bracelets but on the opposite wrists.

I swapped the bracelets on my wrists and felt something click inside me. It was faint, but I could feel it.

Magic.

Twenty-Four

I t wasn't much longer until I felt his roar cause the castle walls to tremble. I shot up from the bed and grabbed my bow and the stake.

"Bri! Go! He isn't alone!" Isa called out from the hallway with a grunt. I rushed out my door to see her fighting a strange man. She was too preoccupied to see the woman with a silver stake in her hand sneaking up behind her.

On instinct, I shot my bow. The arrow gave a golden shimmer as it flew and hit the woman in her chest. The silver tip of the arrow pierced her heart causing her to collapse on impact. The man Isa was fighting got distracted by my arrow as he watched his comrade fall to the ground, she slit his throat.

"How many are there?" I asked as I got another arrow ready.

"I'm not sure, but we must get you somewhere safer. Andrei said he would meet us in the library, so let's go."

"No," I paused. I could feel that familiar tug in the back of my mind. "Come with me. I know what we need to do!" I began to race down the hall. Isa leaped in front of me. Her twin blade sliced the head off a man who was rounding the corner.

"Where are you going?" She called out to me as I continued to race past her. Passing the decapitated body, trying not to look down at it as blood spilled on the stone. I didn't answer her. She continued to follow me.

"Sabrina! Last time you kept going without answering me I ended up a vampire. Tell me what your plan is?" She grabbed my wrist pulling me to a halt. I spun to face her.

"I'm going to the garden. That's where he wants us to meet."

"How do you know that? Also, we need to stick with the plan for your safety."

"I just know. Please, Isa, I'm not the weak girl I once was, trust me. This is what I need to do." She let go of my wrist and gave me a sweeping glance.

"Alright. If that's what you need to do, I am with you. Lead the way." I gave her a nod and continued down the hall. As we approached a set of stairs, I could hear murmured voices and footsteps. Isa and I waited quietly at the side of the stairs, keeping out of sight.

"He said this is the floor her room is on. She has to be close."

Three men stepped into the hall. As soon as the first came into view I shot my arrow into his heart. Isa had sliced through another. The third stepped back in shock. Isa quickly appeared before him.

"Oh no, you aren't going anywhere." She said as her blade went through him as well.

We were not the same women who went into the cabin basement. No, we were much more than that now. It was hard for me to imagine us being that helpless ever again. We rushed down the steps. Isa stayed in front, looking out for any more intruders.

As we approached the garden, my thoughts were on Andrei and Daphne. I wondered how they were fairing in all this. I hope they have made it to the library and were safe. They could hold their own, but a small part of me was still worried.

I quickly snapped back into focus as I heard Isa calling out to me.

"Watch out!" She called as she fought with three large men who appeared from the shadows. I aimed my bow, and before I could fire it was ripped from my hand.

"Ah, ah, ah. Not so fast." The man in front of me threw my bow to the ground, gripping my wrist tightly. I looked up at him and focused on the scar over his eye. It was the man whose arm Darius had broken for disrespecting him that night we broke into the castle. He lifted me, my feet dangling from the floor. A large smirk on his face. I squirmed in his arms. He blocked my view from Isa, but I could hear her struggling with the men she had been fighting.

"Let me go!" I demanded.

"Oh, absolutely not. Do you know how long I have waited for this?" He snarled in my face. I glanced over to the garden entrance. I had been so close. If I could break free somehow, slip through that door.

"Oh, no need to look over there, no one is coming to save you." He turned towards Isa and an evil smirk grew on his face. I could see her now, the three men had her wrapped in silver chains. She squirmed and wailed in pain as they dug into her skin.

"See. No one to save you." He turned back towards me, tossing me to the ground. I went to get up, trying to reach for my bow. Before I could blink, he was above me, pressing his foot into my chest to hold me in place. He knelt, digging his heel into me.

"He will kill you for hurting me," I whimpered.

"He is here to kill you, love. I doubt he will care if your arm is snapped. He is in such a frenzy I'm sure he will think he did it himself." He grabbed my arm and slowly began to bend it back as he laughed. My eyes filled with tears as I begged him to stop. He did.

"Oh, this is going to be fun, watching you beg and cry. I didn't realize how much I was going to enjoy it." He bent my arm again, just to the point before it snapped, and held it there as I screamed in pain. Calling out to Darius, begging him to find me, to save me. His calloused hands twisting my skin causing it to turn red.

"I took great pleasure in watching the Prince suffer these past one hundred years, you know? Watching him beg for blood. When he was released, he killed three hundred feeders in an instant before he locked on to your scent. Yet here you are, still hoping he's going to save you. Darius is a monster. We all are." He twisted my arm once again. The pain caused me to see stars. I let out a scream as I felt my arm break. In a swift motion, he finally bent my arm back so far that it snapped. He removed his foot from my chest. My ears began to ring. I couldn't understand the words he said to the three who had Isa. More men filled the halls.

I watched as they dragged Isa away. She still fought them, like a fish caught in a net. The chains rendered her helpless. I felt two heavy footsteps stop at the top of my head. I looked up.

There he stood in his ragged shirt, the front drenched in blood. He wiped the blood from his mouth as he looked down at me with disgust.

"Who did this?" He looked up at the crowd. His voice was quiet yet demanding. The ringing in my ears dissipated as Darius spoke. I felt him creep into my mind. My pain eased.

The crowd of men fell silent as they all turned towards Darius.

"Who did this?!" He roared. His eyes are as red as the stains on his shirt. The crowd parted, leaving the man with the scarred eye singled out. In a blink, Darius was in front of him.

"Did you hurt her?" He said rage filled his voice.

"She was trying to escape. I was trying to stop her for you."

"Every last one of you was under specific instructions not to harm her." Darius grabbed the man by his throat. "You have pissed me off for the last time." He snapped his neck and dropped his body onto the floor.

"Unchain her and take her to the library with the others." He barked at the men holding Isa. Darius then strode back over to me. He knelt at my side and picked me up.

"Please. Put me down!" I pleaded.

"Shut up. If I was going to hurt you, I would have done it by now." He walked us into the garden.

He sat me down in the center of the sundial. He twisted my arm back into place. He bit into his wrist causing himself to bleed and shoved his wrist into my mouth as I screamed in pain.

"Drink so your arm will heal." He pressed firmer. The moon overhead caused the opal moons on the sundial to shimmer. His blood filled my mouth. I forced myself to swallow it. He traced his fingers down my arm and stopped at my bracelet. He quickly picked up my other wrist and examined them. His mouth widened into a toothy grin.

"Oh, Daphne, you were always one step ahead of me," he chuckled as he pulled his wrist away. His bite was already healed. The pain from my own arm was gone. I lifted it and examined it.

"It...It's not broken anymore."

"You're welcome," he reached up and wiped his blood off my lip.

"How are you not trying to kill me right now?"

"Oh trust me. I want nothing more than to completely devour you." He leaned over and licked a tear off my cheek. "Promise me you won't ever take these bracelets off?"

"Why? What would happen If I did?" He leaned back for a moment, then pinned me to the cobblestone. His mouth to my neck, his teeth grazing my skin.

"Their magic is what is protecting you from me." He breathed into my neck and slid his tongue up my neck. My skin tingled from his touch. I arched my back letting out a soft moan.

"What do you say we get my father's men out of the castle?" He stood, pulling me up to my feet with him. "Once they're gone, we can pick up where we left off."

Twenty-Five

Darius and I quickly made our way to the library. I was able to grab my bow after we left the garden, but I didn't need to use it. Darius had quickly gotten rid of anyone who stood in our way. I tried to avoid looking as he snapped the necks of the guards who stood in our way. They couldn't even let out a scream. It was over for them before they could even realize what was happening.

We finally arrived at the library. Darius flung the doors open, and as soon as he did Andrei pounced on him, slamming Darius to the ground.

"What the fuck are you doing asshole?" Darius said as Andrei held him.

"Making sure you aren't going to hurt anyone!"

"For fuck's sake." In a quick motion, Darius flipped Andrei off of him and was now sitting on Andrei's Chest. "When are you going to learn you are no match for me?" He said, calmly looking around. "Where are the guards I sent here?"

"They have been taken care of," Andrei heaved. "Get off my chest I can't breathe."

Darius stood, reaching a hand down to help Andrei stand. The two gave each other a simple nod. Daphne and Isa finally came out of wherever they had been hiding.

"Your arm. It's healed." Isa approached me, looking at my arm in confusion. Andrei's attention then snapped to me. He was before me in an instant grabbing my wrists and examining them. He then gave Daphne a glare.

"How," it wasn't a question. It was a demand for answers. "How did you get these back?"

"I had been searching for them ever since they went missing before the wedding. I was finally able to locate them about fifty years ago."

"Fifty years ago?" Darius questioned. "Isn't that when you came to visit me in Titus?"

"Indeed. I had suspected that your father had these bracelets hidden within the walls of his castle. I was correct." Daphne sat down on top of the table looking at Andrei in his eyes. "I will not apologize for telling her what she is and giving her something that is her birthright."

"We agreed that we wouldn't tell her," Darius said.

"You agreed. I will always put her best interests first."

"The fact is all of you hid things from me." I interrupted their bickering. "I think knowing that I am fae is a pretty important bit of knowledge. Think about if I had known this when we tried to kill Dimitri?"

"It wouldn't have done you any good to know then," Darius said coldly. "Magic in this region has been blocked. My father hates the fae and wants to make life difficult for them. It's another part of the curse."

"Why? I think it's about time you tell me everything." I demanded. The four of them looked at each other nervously. Daphne took a deep breath.

"Your name is Sabrina Alexandra Saison, High Queen of Serafina," she said as she got down off the table. My jaw dropped.

"I'm sorry, what did you just say?" I stared at her, giving a heavy blink. Daphne had to be on some drugs. There is no way I was Queen of Serafina.

"I was your advisor and was from the moment you were born. In Serafina, there are six types of fae magic: fire, water, earth, air, light, and dark. The queen can use all six types of magic. Only one person at a time has all six types. And when one dies, another is born. I have been the advisor to the Queen since the birth of our first Queen." My vision narrowed on her as she spoke. Darius gently pressed his hand on my lower back for support. He guided me to a chair and helped me sat as Daphne continued.

"Every year Serafina held a masquerade ball, to celebrate the coming of Spring, and to celebrate you, as it was your birthday as well. As Titus grew into its kingdom, they would always send an emissary to the ball. One year you said to the emissary to not return. That if the royals of Titus could not bother to appear it was not worth a relationship with them." She paused looking at Darius. "The next year Darius and Andrei came to the ball, and I still hold the belief that that was the worst thing to ever happen to you, to our kingdom."

"Rude," Darius and Andrei said in unison. Daphne rolled her eyes and continued.

"The two of you immediately fell in love. From what your court could tell, it was a perfect match."

"It was my father who was the problem," Darius began. "He didn't even want me to go to the masquerade to begin with. He was offended by what you had told the emissary. I had heard about the powerful and beautiful Fae Queen, and I had to see you for myself. Everything I had ever heard about you was a lie. You were more beautiful than I could have imagined. Your powers were beyond my own. To be honest, I was afraid of the power I could sense from you. When I had spoken to my father upon my return and informed him of what I had learned, he wanted you taken down before you could destroy us. So, he sent me in as a double agent." He paused, his jaw clenched, and he let out a sigh. "I never wanted to be a double agent. I wanted to be close to you. I was over the moon when I found out you felt the same. So, I told you of my father's intentions. We were together for a year plotting behind my father's back before I asked you to marry me." He walked over to the window, looking out. "It was supposed to be a secret. I was going to defect from Titus and live in Serafina with you. I awoke the morning of our wedding with incredible hunger. Everything from that day seems to be in a blur. I just remember holding your dead body, and my hunger was gone." He choked on his words. It was then prolonged silence as he composed himself. "That night a letter had been sent to me from my father. Telling that this is what happens when he is disobeyed and disrespected and that I should come home before Serafina fell into ruin."

"And it did. A new queen was not born. Everyone panicked. It wasn't until two years later I felt another queen was born. A few members of the court who had been trying to maintain Serafina came with me to Titus to greet the new queen. They were all slaughtered upon crossing the border. I barely escaped. When I found you, you were human, not fae. I watched as a human family raised you. I watched you and your parents die on your eighteenth birthday. Over and over. And during the early years of the curse. The wall was built and I felt my magic fade away. I was stuck here in Titus. Andrei eventually found me and told me what Dimitri had done."

"We had tried so many times to stop the cycle. We had never gotten close," Andrei finally spoke up. "We tried hiding you, turning you, once we even took you to a territory up north. I wouldn't recommend going there ever again."

"Daphne and Andrei told me all this the day you were captured by Dimitri," Isa finally spoke. She had been so quiet before, almost hiding. "I wanted to tell you right away, but they said it could send you into shock."

I sat there in silence. Looking at all of them. Taking in the history, my history. I understood why they had hidden this from me. If they had told me in my previous life, I would have ran. Ran deep into those woods and never looked back. I would have been eaten by a mountain lion.

"Are you ok?" Darius asked, kneeling by my side. My eyes met his and I nodded.

"This..." I took a deep breath. "...is a lot to process, but I am ok." He leaned forward and gently kissed the top of my forehead.

"We will figure this out, together. Take as much time as you need." He stood looking at Andrei. " Come with me, let's get the rest of these assholes cleared out, and figure out what to do next."

Twenty-Six

I laid on my back in bed looking up at the ceiling. I toyed with the bracelets on my wrists, examining them as Isa and Daphne sat on the edge of my bed talking to each other. I was too enthralled by my own thoughts to hear what they were talking about.

"Tell me about the bracelets?" I asked.

"You used them to help control and funnel your magic. You had a lot of issues controlling your powers. They were always too much for you to control. You were the most powerful queen we had in centuries. The bracelets were gifts from a Fae kingdom across the ocean. I'm not sure of their exact origins. It seems that they also have some protective properties as well. Darius doesn't seem to want to kill you as badly as we thought he would."

"You never told me how your arm was healed after that guy snapped it," Isa questioned.

"Darius fed me his blood, causing it to heal," I said as I continued to look at the bracelets.

"Well, that was... kind... of him," Isa responded.

As we spoke there was a gentle knock on the door.

"Come in," I called out and the door opened. Darius took one step into my room and looked at Isa and Daphne.

"Excuse me, do you mind if we could have a moment in private?" He formed it as a question, but we all knew it wasn't. Daphne and Isa looked towards me and I gave them a nod. They slipped out, shutting the door behind them. Darius stood near the door in silence for some time, tension building between us.

"Is everything okay?" I asked. He stood there, sorrow in his eyes. He didn't move, he didn't say a word. I sat up and tilted my head. "Hey, what's wrong?"

"I am sorry for using my powers to manipulate you into removing the chains. I should have held on. I shouldn't have killed you," he choked on his words as they came rushing out of his mouth.

"I forgive you. You were starving. I know it wasn't an easy time for you." In a blink he was before me, knees on the bed, my cheeks in his hands.

"I don't deserve your forgiveness." His green eyes shimmered.

"I will be the judge of that, Darius Dragomeir." I pressed my lips into his and his arms wrapped around me. He collapsed backward, gently holding me in his arms on top of him as we kissed. After a long moment, our lips parted. I hung my lips just above his as we shared the same air.

"Please continue to judge me," he smirked.

"Oh, I think the trial is over. I think it's time for my ruling," I giggled

"Can I say one more thing to the court?"

"I will allow it." He quickly flipped us. I now lay on my back under him. His hands are on the bed on the sides of my shoulders. His hair hung down in his face, a predatory grin on his face as his tongue slid over his top lip. One of his hands slid down my body and gripped the bottom of my shirt. He toyed with the fabric for a moment before ripping my shirt off my body.

"That's better." He leaned down and gently kissed my stomach, working his way up to my chest. Squeezing my breasts in his hands as he slid his tongue on my nipples. I moaned, arching my back.

"Do you trust me?" He looked up at me, the grin on his face widening.

"Y...yess..." I moaned gently. He kissed his way up to my neck, and as he did, he gripped my wrists pinning me down to the bed. "Darius...what are you doing?" I scrunched my shoulders a bit, denying him access to my neck.

"Hush, doll," he purred. "Show me that pretty little neck of yours." I relaxed, tilting my head to give him better access. He ran his tongue up my neck. His breath on my neck sent a tingle down my spine.

His hands moved my wrists above my head. He used one of his hands to hold them in place as the other slid down my body and began to remove my bottoms. His fangs grazed against my skin as his hand found its way in between my legs, toying with the most delicate part of me. I felt my wetness grow.

"What a good girl you are for me." He pulled away from my neck and smirked down at me. I could feel my cheeks burning as he gently slid in two fingers. "Tell me. Who do you belong to, doll?"

"You. I belong to you," I moaned. He began to piston his fingers roughly in and out of me.

"Good girl." He licked his lips. "Don't move. Do you understand?"

"Yes, I understand." He knelt once again, his mouth against my neck. I felt him hesitate, and then I felt his fangs scrape against my skin once again. His fingers became gentler inside me.

"No...please don't be gentle," I pleaded. I wanted him to destroy me.

"Don't be gentle?" He purred in my ear. "You want me to be rough with you? Beg."

"Please. Please be rough with me. I need you to be rough with me," I begged. He held me down tighter and began to use his fingers even more roughly than before.

Then I felt it.

His fangs sank into my neck.

It wasn't like before. This was gentle. There was no burning running through my veins as it had done in the dungeon. No, a different feeling now ran through me.

"Darius! What are you doing?" I moaned. Pure euphoria rushed through my body. I immediately gave in to the pleasure, orgasming all over his fingers.

He pulled his mouth away. A little blood dripped from the side of his mouth. He bit his bottom lip, his fingers still deep inside me.

"It appears these bracelets of yours solve all our problems." He finally released my wrists and wiped his lips. He pulled his fingers out. "Don't tell anyone about this. Understood?" He formed it as a question, but I could feel his control in my mind. I gave a nod.

"What a good girl you are. Shall we take a bath?" He smirked

I finally sat up. I gave him a gentle push off of me.

"How are you so calm about what you just did? You could have killed me, Dar!" The weight of it all finally hit me as the euphoria from the bite faded.

"You are alive, and you loved it. I loved it. Fuck, you taste so sweet. It was a win-win. I am not sure why you are mad." He got up off the bed and stood to the side.

"I am mad because you are cursed to crave my blood and drain me! You just bit me without even asking Darius."

"This time feels different. Those bracelets are helping me. They have given you some sort of protection against the curse. I was hungry. Did you want me to go to the closest village and slaughter them instead?" He growled.

"Get out," I softly demanded

"What?" He looked at me in shock

"Get out!" I screamed at him. He stood there for a moment, a blank expression on his face.

"Fine." He was gone in an instant. Slamming the door so hard behind it that it caused the photos on the wall to fall and shatter on the floor.

Twenty-Seven

A few hours passed. I laid in my bed sobbing. No one came to check on me during that time. I'm sure they just wanted to give me some space. I was also sure that Darius had either gone to his room to brood, or he was downstairs bad-mouthing me to Andrei.

I reached down and fiddled with my bracelets. Thankful for their protection. However, what he had done had seriously crossed the line. No matter how good it felt, I couldn't let him do that ever again. I could still feel his mouth on my neck and his fangs sinking into me. I thought about how different it felt from the time in the dungeon or any of my memories.

I had a lot of questions about what was going to happen next, but I knew one thing for certain. I could not stay here.

I stood up and put on some new clothes. I quietly opened the door and made my way to the observatory. Andrei, Isa, and Daphne sat there, speaking in hushed tones. Once I entered, they stopped talking and turned to me.

"Trouble in paradise?" Andrei teased.

"Have you spoken to him?" I questioned.

"No, after he left your room, he left the castle. All he said was he would be back later. What happened?"

"This is what happened." I took a deep breath and stepped towards them, lowering my shirt collar and tilting my neck.

Andrei and Isa were before me in an instant, Daphne right behind them as they examined my neck. I could see the anger growing in their faces.

"How are you alive? What happened?" Andrei took a step back, giving me some space.

"He stopped himself. He said the bracelets gave him control. I didn't tell him he could, he just did." I looked over at Daphne and then to Isa. "I am sorry, but I can't stay here with him."

"You can't leave," Andrei said. "If you leave, there's no telling what could happen to you. I'm sure Dimitri's men are hiding in those woods waiting for you to be vulnerable."

"If she wants to leave, she will leave. I will go with her. You cannot keep her here," Daphne chimed in. An anger in her voice I had not heard before. "I know somewhere we can go, where she will be safe."

"Darius gave strict instructions for her not to leave! That we do not leave until the time is right," Andrei snapped back.

"He is your Prince. She is my Queen. Neither you nor him have any say in what she or I do!"

"Daphne. Be reasonable," Isa finally spoke. "It's better if we all stay together." I could almost feel my heart break. Is she taking Darius' side?

"No, it's better for him to keep her close so he has an easy meal. I will not allow it. We are so close to breaking this curse. If he kills her again, I will never forgive him. She took too long to come back last time. You don't understand what's at stake!"

Andrei looked to Isa, then headed downstairs. Leaving the three of us alone.

"You're right Daph, we are close, and you two leaving will set us back. We need to stick together." Isa said softly.

"Why are you taking his side?" I demanded. "He hurt me, Isa. He tricked me into putting my guard down, and he hurt me. Why is that ok for you?"

"It's not! I am very angry with him, but he is my Prince," she sighed. "I don't have a lot of choice here."

"Bullshit! You always have a choice!" I yelled. My eyes filled with tears. "Daphne and I are leaving. You can come with us, or you can stay."

She paused, looking at me. I could tell she was holding back tears. Daphne came over to me and took my hand.

"Let's go get you packed," she said to me in a calming voice. She then glared at Isa. "You have an hour to decide." Daphne gave my hand a slight squeeze and guided me towards the stairs. Isa said nothing as we walked away. She had already made up her mind but was too much of a coward to say it aloud.

"Thank you," I said as we finally got to my room.

"I will always pick your side. No matter what." She smiled back. She pulled out a suitcase from my closet and packed it. "Sit, I will handle everything."

"Where are we going to go?" I said as I sat on the edge of the bed.

"A small village near the wall. It will be safe for you there. Plus, there is someone you should meet."

"Who?"

"All will be revealed in good time."

Daphne had finished packing my back and went to her room to pack hers. I sat on the bed, waiting for her to come back so we could leave. There was a firm knock on the door, and before I could answer it swung open.

"You cannot leave," Andrei said, Isa, standing behind him.

"I am leaving Andrei, I'm sorry."

"No, I am sorry," he said in a stern voice. I blinked and he was directly in front of me. He grabbed my wrists and pulled me close to him. A shimmer overtook his eyes that drew me in.

"You are not leaving," his words were like a melody. "When Darius comes back you will no longer be mad at him." His words stroked the back of my mind, commanding me to obey.

"Andrei," I said in a low tone. I could feel my inner magic fighting his control. "You have two seconds to let me go."

"What is going on here?" I heard Daphne from the doorway.

"Daphne, fuck off. She isn't leaving. If you want to, you will go on your own," Andrei snarled.

"Andrei, calm down please," Isa said nervously. Her voice was shaking. He didn't let go, he squeezed harder.

"Darius gave me an order. To keep you here. To keep you safe. I will not fail him."

"This is your last chance. Let go," I growled. Daphne and Isa were both screaming at him to release me. Andrei yelled back at them to be quiet.

"I'm sorry. I hate that I have to do this. If you agree to stay, I will let go," he said in a much calmer tone. I could feel the buildup of emotions and magic fill me. Screaming for release.

"I'm sorry too," I said coldly. I took a deep breath and Andrei let out a scream letting go of my wrists. He jumped away from me and lifted his hands which were on fire. I grabbed my bag that sat on the bed and ran to the door. Daphne nodded. She knew we needed to go now. Isa stood there frozen in shock. She looked at us, then to Andrei, then back to us. She was then by Andrei's side helping put out the fire. She had made her choice.

Daphne grabbed my hand and we ran to the front door. We quickly got in one of the cars and sped down the driveway. I slumped into the passenger seat and sobbed.

"We have a long drive. Get it all out. We can talk if you want, or we can sit in silence while you cry. Just whatever you do, don't hold it in."

Twenty-Eight

We drove for days before reaching a small mining village nestled between the wall and mountains. Daphne refused to answer any of my questions about the village, or the people we were going to meet there. She pulled into the driveway of a large house near the village center and put the car in park.

"Are you ready?" She smiled.

"Hard to be ready for something when I don't know what to be ready for."

"To meet more of us," she said as she got out of the car and headed to the front door. I got out of the car and ran to catch up to her.

"More of us?"

She just gave a simple nod in response then knocked on the front door.

"Found them about twenty years ago," she said as the door finally opened. An old man opened the door. He was in a simple brown tunic and pants. He was hunched over, tightly gripping a simple walking stick. He looked at Daphne and gave a warm smile.

"Ah, welcome back. Always a pleasure," he said to her, he then looked at me and we locked eyes. "Is this.."

"Yes, it is. She has finally returned." The man dropped his walking stick fell to his knees and bowed before me.

"My Queen. Thank you for gracing me with your presence. Please come in and make yourself at home."

"Please stand!" I rushed to him, grabbing his walking stick and helping him up. His body trembled as he stood.

"Thank you, my Queen. You are truly a gift to this world," he smiled. I gave Daphne a nervous glance.

I assume this is what she was referring to when she asked if I was ready. The answer was, no. I was not ready at all to watch anyone bow before me or to have them call me their queen. It was shocking to say the least.

We entered the home and were greeted by a few young children and a middle-aged woman. All of them bowed when greeting me. Though the home was the largest in the village, it was not large at all. The kitchen and living area were essentially one room. A fireplace sat on the far wall. There was a staircase that led upstairs near the front entrance, I assumed that is where the bedrooms were.

"The Queen requests to see Xander," Daphne said. Everyone went silent. The woman had dropped the glass of water she was about to offer me, and it shattered all over the floor.

"Xander is dangerous," the old man said.

"We understand that, but she needs to speak with him urgently. He is locked away, is he not? It should be safe for her to speak with him."

The old man sat on a stool and looked at Daphne, then at me.

"Yes, we can take you there this evening. Ron will guide you." He gestured to the oldest of the boys. He was maybe fifteen.

"Thank you, Silas," Daphne said as she looked around. Her eyes stopped at a worn painting on the wall. It was over a forest filled with color and light. "Hopefully we can all go home soon."

"Hopefully. The tunnels are nearly complete," he coughed. As he did a black dust came from his lungs. He continued to hack as the middle-aged woman rushed to him, getting him water. She must have noticed the concerned look on my face as she turned to me.

"We have been trying to mine under the wall for centuries. Most of the men here spent their entire lives in the mines. Unfortunately, it has come at a cost."

"I am sorry to hear that," I said softly.

"Please...If you could do anything to heal my father." She looked up at me with pleading eyes. Daphne took my hand.

"Unfortunately, due to the curse and the wall the Queen has very limited access to her powers. At this time, she cannot help."

The woman gave a defeated look. I felt terrible. As their queen, I should be able to help them. Not only to cure Silas of his aliment, but to also provide better living conditions for them.

"I understand," she said somberly. "Ron, please take the Queen and her advisor to the guest house." The boy jumped up from his spot and motioned for us to follow him.

He led us out the back door and through a small grove of cherry trees. We found ourselves at a small house. It looked like one of those cute little cottages you would see in fairy tales. The front was cobblestone that had vines and moss growing on it. The front door was a deep red and had a rounded shape.

"I will come back just before dark to take you to meet with Xander," he said as he bowed to me.

"Please, you don't need to bow," I said softly. Ron stood, staring me in my eyes.

"You may not feel like it, you may not remember, you may not know how. You are our Queen. We will show you that respect." He smiled and walked away disappearing into the trees.

"He's right, you know," Daphne said as she entered the cottage. "They don't expect you to know how to be queen."

"The look that woman gave me, she expected something. I wanted nothing more than to help her." I followed her inside. We entered a small living space with a fireplace. To each side of the living room was a bedroom. One for each of us.

"Lesson number one: Everyone will want something from you. Lesson number two: You cannot help everyone," Daphne sighed. "There are some things we need to prepare before we meet with Xander."

"Yeah, who the hell is that? And why did you not tell me any of this in the car?"

"I did not wish to overwhelm you. Now Xander is a very powerful fae. Somehow, he has held on to a lot of his magic, even with the wall. I hope that he will tell you how you can access yours as well."

"Why is he locked away?"

"He may, or may not, have murdered some people."

"Some people?"

"Ok, like fifty people, but you will be safe! If he can help you gain access to your magic, interaction with him will be worth it."

As darkness set in there was a knock on the door. It was Ron with three lanterns.

"Ready to go?" He questioned as he handed us the lanterns. We both nodded and followed him to the edge of the village and into one of the mining tunnels.

"He's down here?" I questioned as we entered the pitch-black tunnel.

"Indeed. This section of the tunnels has been shut off for years. It is only used to house him." The dim light from our lanterns illuminated our way.

As we walked, I remembered what Daphne had told me. Don't look him in the eyes. Do not let him touch me. Only ask direct questions, never leave them open-ended, or we will never get an answer.

As we walked deeper into the tunnel loud banging could be heard. Three in a row.

A dark twisted voice could then be heard.

"One. Two. Three. Coming to me." Followed by a cackle. Daphne looked over at me, she could sense my hesitation as we heard his voice.

"We are about halfway there," Ron said back to us. His eyes were now filled with darkness. I froze.

"Are you ok?" I questioned. Daphne and Ron stopped and turned to me.

"I am a dark fae. That's why they sent me down here. I can't be twisted by his mind games, and I am not afraid of the dark," he said matter-of-factly.

"Sorry, I didn't mean to be rude."

"You weren't. You didn't know. You couldn't have." He turned back and we walked through the tunnels again. I examined the walls made of dark stone, the deeper we went the more the stone glittered. Colorful flecks showed through the dark stone.

Three more bangs. Louder than before.

"One. Two. Three." A pause. "Coming to me." That same voice as before.

"One of Darkness." Bang.

"Two of Light." Bang.

"Three a Queen." Bang

"Coming for me." The cackle began again. It didn't stop as we entered a large room.

It was round, a few torches were on the wall. Ron went around to light them with his lantern. On the far side of the wall was a cell made of stalagmites and stalactites. Like sharp black teeth. They wove in and out of each other creating a barrier between us and the man inside it.

Sitting in a chair on the other side of the cell was a man shrouded in darkness. The shadows clung to his olive skin. His eyes were deep voids. He stood and approached the cell wall. He reached out his arm and pointed to me, then gave a come here motion with his long bony finger.

"The Queen has come to me," he smirked at me revealing two rows of sharp teeth.

Twenty-Nine

"Come now, Queeny. Tell me why you have come," Xander teased.

"Show her with respect," Daphne demanded.

"Of course, of course." He held on to that last syllable like a snake. "Besides, I know why you are here. I have been waiting for you."

"Waiting for me?" I said a bit nervously.

"Oh yes." Again, he held that 'S' sound. "I had a vision of this exact moment, eons ago" He paced the cell wall. Running this hand across the rock formations. "Go on, Queeny, do not be afraid."

"I am not afraid of you, or anyone else." I stood my ground.

"Oh, come now, that is not true. If it was you would not be here. How does your neck feel?" He stopped pacing and slid is black fingernails down his neck. "What a shame, the High Queen of Serafina turned into a blood whore." Venom dripped on those last words.

"Enough!" Daphne declared. "Tell us, how do you still have your magic after the wall?"

Xander broke out into insane laughter. His hand moved up to his face then slowly pulling it down, causing his skin to tug. He stopped his laughter and then looked at Daphne with a serious expression on his face.

"It's still inside me. I can feel it pulsing through my veins. Hard and THROBBING!" He laughed again. "Throb. Throb. Throb!"

The shadows that had clung to his body spread across the walls. One by one the torches went out, and then it was our lanterns. Leaving us in total darkness.

"I can feel it throbbing inside you too, Queeny," his voice directly in my ear from behind. I quickly spun around and punched the air.

"Don't be so on edge. So confrontational!" I heard again from behind me. Again, I spun around to hit the open air.

"Xander, enough. Turn the lights back on," Ron commanded.

"Oh no. I will not. You know Darkness will never bring light. If you wish the light to return, she will have to bring it."

"I can't,." I whimpered. The darkness around me was almost suffocating.

"Feel it build. Feel it throb," Xander teased.

"Sabrina just take a deep breath it's going to be ok," Daphne whispered to me.

"Silence!" Xander shrieked "Queeny must do it herself. Don't you feel it? Connect to it."

I took a deep breath. I could feel my magic buzzing through my veins. It was chaotic and disorganized. I tried to focus it, and channel that feeling into my hands.

I tried to remember that feeling of release when I had set Andrei on fire. That whole moment now felt like a blur. I could hear his scream in the back of my mind. I felt terrible. I wish I could apologize to him. I hope that it isn't too late to do so.

I felt the palms of my hands grow hot. A tiny spark flashed between them, then disappeared as well as the warmth I had felt.

"Now, now," Xander huffed. "Is that all you have? Pathetic. You used to be the most powerful of us all."

"How dare you speak to me that way," I said in a roar. "You think this is easy? I just found out I was fae a few days ago. Yes, I can feel the magic inside me. I can feel it almost bursting out of my skin. It wants out so bad. Not only do I have that going on, but I hurt two of the only people to ever care about me! The person I want to care about me more than anything only cares about two things!" I could feel the heat again. This time over my whole body. "I finally met my people. And this is the condition they are in? They live in shit holes and are dying trying to get home. It is my fault they cannot go home. I am useless! I can't help them. I can't even help myself." The heat was becoming unbearable. "So sorry that I wasn't what you expected."

On that last word, A flash of bright blinding light filled the room. The intense heat left my body. As the light faded every torch was lit. The shadows that filled the room and clung to Xander were gone.

"Now we are getting somewhere." He gave a toothy grin. "Have you only ever used your magic when your emotions are out of control?"

"Yes. I have only been able to use it two times before now." I answered.

"You have a mental block. Come here Queeny, closer. Let me touch you to release it."

"Absolutely not!" Daphne said. She moved herself to stand in front of me. "You will not touch her."

"Come now, sister. Do you not trust me?"

"After what you did? Never again." She snarled.

"Wait, are you two related?" I questioned.

"Twins," they said in unison. "We both awoke side by side. Long ago. Before the first of the fae arrived here. One of Light. One of Dark. To maintain the balance."

"Dear sister. Do you want me to help her, or not? I will not hurt her. I understand more than anyone else what is at stake here."

Daphne looked at Xander, and then at me. She let out a huff of breath.

"Fine, but I am staying by her side."

"Of course. I would not expect anything less. Now step forward."

"Are you sure that's the best decision?" Ron questioned us from behind. Daphne turned to face him and gave a nod. She guided me to the cell wall. The shadows returned to Xander clinging to his pale skin.

"This is going to hurt, Queeny." He quickly reached out and placed my forehead in the palm of his hand. The shadows crept up his arm and laced through his fingers. I let out a wail. My knees buckled and I grabbed one of the stalagmites. I squeezed it tightly.

I could hear Daphne yelling at him, but I couldn't understand the words that she was saying. The pain had completely taken over my mind. It felt like something was stabbing my brain over and over. I could hear Xander's twisted crackle. My vision blurred. I gripped on the cool damp rock harder. I swear I could feel it crack from my grip.

Xander released my head. The stabbing pain became a dull ache.

"Well, well, well. It seems you can handle more than I thought you could. I honestly expected you to pass out," he smirked.

"How dare you hurt her! What did you do?"

"I did what I said I was going to do. I never said it was a painless process. Come back in three days. You should have full access to your powers by then. I want to make sure it is going as planned."

Daphne let out a low growl glaring at him.

"By the way, dear sister. You owe me."

Thirty

After the encounter with Xander, we returned to the cottage. My brain felt fried. All I wanted to do was go to sleep. I had so many questions for Daphne. I wanted to try to get some answers before I had forgotten my questions.

Daphne helped me lay down on the couch and she sat in a chair across from me.

"Why didn't you tell me about your brother?"

"It wasn't important that he is my brother. Besides, after all, he has done. It's hard to think of him that way," she sighed and looked away.

"How did he know all that stuff about me?"

"He is a Seer. They are rare, but they can see things past, present, and future." She put the tip of her thumb against her mouth and rested her fist against the bottom of her nose. "Get some rest. You need it. Do you want help to your room?"

I shook my head and stood slowly.

"No, I got it," I said as I made my way to my room and collapsed on the bed.

I opened my eyes to endless darkness once again. I gripped my temples and screamed.

"I don't want to see you! Go away." I yelled into the darkness. Silence answered back. I wandered through the darkness. In search of any light that would guide my way.

"Darius. I mean it. I do not want to see you. So let me wake up." Again, there was no response.

"Are you even listening to me?" Who was I kidding? Did he ever listen to me? This time three loud bangs answered back. Like the ones I had heard in the tunnels. I jumped and began walking faster in the darkness as the stabbing pain returned to my head.

Was it possible that somehow Xander was doing this to torment me?

Finally, a light appeared. It looked different than it did in the past. Six different colors swirled and mixed. Red, Blue, Green, White, Yellow and Black. I followed the light and it opened to the large room from my memories of the Masquerade. I stared at myself sitting on the throne.

I wore a shimmering pink gown. A bow sat next to the throne and hung on a stand. Not just any bow, my bow Shimmerthorne. I was absolutely radiant. My dark hair was braided to the side. A rose gold crown adorned with gems that matched the colors of the light I had just seen. This other me finally made eye contact and smiled.

"Well, it is about time you and I come face to face." My smile was warm and welcoming.

"Darius is out in the darkness looking for you, but I think we needed to have a little chat." She stood and walked towards me. I say walked, but it was more of an effortless elegant glide.

"What do we need to talk about?" I asked myself. This was so weird having a conversation with a different version of me. A version of me that I knew could easily crush me, and the world. I could feel the power radiating off her.

"First, forgive him. Yes, it is hard. He tries his best. Also, let's not lie to ourselves. We love his fangs inside us. Next time have him bite our inner thigh. It is truly blissful," she giggled.

An image flashed into my mind. No, more than an image. It was an intense memory. I laid upon a canopy bed that was draped with flowers. My bare skin against soft silk. Darius was in between my legs, his eyes locked on mine. He gave me a wink and sunk his fangs into the subtle skin of my thigh. I let out a moan as pure euphoria ran through my veins. He pulled away from my thigh, licking the blood from his lips. He then feasted on the most intimate parts of me. My back arched, my hand on top of his head, begging for more.

I then snapped back to the conversation at hand.

"That man is desperate for us. He will do anything we ask. If we don't like something, simply smile and ask him to change. He will. That smile will cause him to melt."

"No, he won't. He only cares about himself and his own needs," I retorted.

"Give it a try. You will see that I am correct. Now onto the more important matter." She extended her perfectly manicured hand out to me. "Take my hand."

I did. She gently wrapped my hand in hers and gave a little squeeze. As she did, my mind began racing. Images flashed through my mind, too quickly for me to process. Flashes of fire, water, earth, air, light and dark.

When they stopped, I was back in the darkness, alone. I looked around in confusion.

"Sabrina?!" I heard a familiar dark voice call out. "Sabrina!" I could tell he was worried.

"I'm here, Dar. I am here." In an instant, my bedroom from the castle appeared around me. Darius sat on the edge of my bed, his head in his hands.

"Come home. Where are you?" He said without looking up at me.

"I'm not ready to come home yet." I sighed.

"Please?" He looked up at me. He had dark circles under his eyes.

"When was the last time you fed?" I questioned him.

"I went into a frenzy after our fight. I haven't had a drop since. I feel terrible about how I treated you. You're correct. I am an asshole. I shouldn't do anything to you without asking you first. Please come home. No one is mad at you. We are worried about you."

I paused, not responding to him right away. I looked him up and down and moved closer to him. I took his hands into mine.

"I can't come home yet. I am safe, but I need to stay gone a little while longer."

He gently pulled me into his lap and tucked a piece of hair behind my ear.

"Why do you have to stay gone?" He whispered.

"I need a little bit of self-discovery every once in a while. How are Andrei's hands?"

"Good as new, they healed almost instantly," he chuckled under his breath. "Proud of you for using your magic, we all are."

"Thank you, tell Andrei I feel terrible and that I'm sorry."

"I will pass along the message. Promise me you're safe?"

"I promise. Will you do me a favor? Go feed before you go crazy."

"I will." He looked up at me, nervousness filled his face. "You forgive me?"

"This time, yes. Don't let it happen again." I leaned in and gently kissed him. His arms wrapped around me and held me in a tight embrace. He pulled back after a moment and gently cupped my chin. He lifted it slightly so I matched his gaze.

"Come home soon. I miss you, doll."

"I miss you, too."

Everything faded to darkness.

Thirty-One

"Sabrina? Are you ok?" I heard Daphne's voice and felt her gently shake.

"So... sleepy..." I yawned, still not opening my eyes. "Let me sleep a little more."

"You have been asleep for thirty-six hours. I think it's time to get up." Her voice was a bit stern. My eyes jolted open and I sat straight up.

"That long?" I questioned. My stomach let out a long growl. Daphne giggled.

"Come on, Silas and his family are about to have breakfast. They invited us to join them."

"That sounds wonderful." I smiled up at her and stood. "Give me about fifteen minutes to get ready and I'll meet you outside."

Daphne nodded. She left and shut the door behind her to give me some privacy. I opened the window to let some fresh air in and got ready. I fashioned my hair into a similar braid that the dream version of me had. I slipped on a green long-sleeved sweater and some black pants. A few cherry blossoms flew into the room from the opened window and danced around me.

I took a deep breath. The air around me felt different. I gently flicked my hand upward and the petals danced in the direction I had motioned. I smiled. Not only did I feel more connected to my magic, but it was in my control.

Once I was ready, I went out to meet Daphne. She was standing outside. She wore a delicate yellow blouse and black pants similar to mine. She was admiring the cherry trees closest to the cottage.

"Back home, there were tons of cherry trees. They were your favorite, so you had thousands planted throughout the forest," she said as I approached her. "The magic within Serafina kept them in constant bloom. When you died, the first time, so did they." She sighed and turned to me. "Ready for breakfast? I bet you are starving."

"Yeah, I am. Can I ask you something?" I questioned as we headed towards Silas' house.

"Of course. Ask anything you wish."

"You and Xander were here before the fae?"

"Correct." Her face scrunched at the mention of his name.

"Are you fae then? Or something else?"

"We aren't sure. I smelt pine and cinnamon when I entered your room this morning."

"That you did." I looked away. I didn't want to talk about him yet. I needed time to myself. So much has been thrown at me these past few days. I needed to know who I was without Darius.

"How are they?" She asked softly.

"Andrei's hands have healed. They just wish for our return. They aren't mad."

"Darius and Andrei are not mad. I am not sure Isa feels the same way," she said sternly.

"What do you mean?" I stopped. I tilted my head slightly as I asked the question.

"She chose her mate over her best friend. You set him on fire. I am not sure she will forgive easily." She turned to face me. "I would be careful with that one."

"You think so?" I sighed. I knew she was right. Isa was different from when we had first met. I was too.

"I know so. Now let's hurry along."

Daphne and I finished the short walk to Silas'. His daughter stood outside awaiting our arrival. She bowed to me and gave me a small smile.

"Please stand. You never told me your name." I smiled back at her.

"Cora, my name is Cora." She stood up straight.

"Thank you for opening your home to us Cora, it is truly a pleasure."

"The pleasure is mine, Your Majesty." She guided us into the home and to the dining room where Silas and the children already sat. Ron was getting some of the younger ones something to drink, as well as trying to rein in some others to the table. He looked up at me and smiled.

"My Queen, you seem to have recovered well after the tunnels."

"Indeed, I have. I needed lots of rest after that encounter." I sat down at the table in between Daphne and Silas.

"Welcome to family breakfast, Your Grace," he said as he took a sip of water. As he swallowed, he coughed. This time stronger than before and more black dust was coming out with each cough. The room went cold. Cora ran to her father's side and offered him more water. He drank an entire glass, but it didn't seem to help. The children cried. I heard one of them praying to the gods under their breath.

I grabbed the glass and Cora looked up at me. I took a deep breath and focused. I felt something within me begging to be released. Everyone looked at me as the glass filled with a glittery gold liquid.

"Here, drink this," I said softly.

Cora took the glass and gave it to her father. He struggled to take a sip, but once he did it went into his mouth with ease. His coughing stopped.

"My lungs. They haven't felt this good in three hundred years," Silas said in shock.

Everyone looked at me with wide eyes. They all stood, pushing away their chairs, and kneeled to me.

"All hail Sabrina, High Queen of Serafina. We are grateful for your blessing," They said in unison.

We spent the rest of the day in the village. We visited the small shops around the village center. People bowed as we passed them, as they greeted us, as they bid us a good day. It was exhausting.

I was happy to heal Silas. It was the least I could do for him. The kneeling, the bowing, and the way people spoke to me was overstimulating. I'm not sure if I will ever get used to this. Daphne and I entered a small shop filled with many different jams, pickles, and other canned goods. The shop owner bowed as we entered.

"Welcome to my shop, Your Grace. All the items here in my shop are made by me from the produce from my garden. Please let me know if there is anything you wish to try."

I smiled and gave her a nod. We had gone through almost every shop in town and bought a few things in each, paying much more than what the shopkeepers had asked. Another way I thought of helping this poor village. I planned to give the items purchased to Silas' family for their hospitality.

I examined the shelf looking through the various jams they had on display. I was truly surprised by the variety of options available.

"You should try the peach. It's a big favorite." the shop owner said from behind me. I turned around and she had prepared a small plate of different breads and spreads for me to try.

"Thank you. Which is the peach?" I smiled. The shopkeeper pointed to a pale orange spread. I took a slice of the bread and spread some of the peach jam on it. As I bit into it the flavors melted on my tongue.

"Wow. You're right this is amazing." I blinked and when I opened my eyes I was no longer standing in the shop with Daphne.

I now stood in a peach orchard in the middle of summer. A gentle breeze was the only thing that gave mercy as the sun blazed down on my pale skin. A castle was in the distance, made of light gray and green stone. I was wearing a green summer dress with gold embellishments.

"Have you ever had a peach this fresh?" I giggled. Darius had come out from behind one of the trees. He wore a dark suit with the top two buttons undone.

"Unfortunately, Titus does not have anything like this." He reached up to pick a peach from the tree and took a large bite. The juices dripped down his chin.

I blinked again and I was back in the shop with Daphne and the shopkeeper looking at me concerned.

"Everything ok? You kind of spaced out," Daphne said, coming to my side.

"Yeah, sorry. I think I just had a memory of my first past life." I looked down at the piece of bread that I still had in my hand. "We will take ten jars of this jam," I said looking back at the shopkeeper with a smile.

Thirty-Two

As promised, we headed back to the tunnels three days after our first meeting with Xander. As we walked through the tunnels everything felt different. The darkness that lurked in the shadows seemed to dissipate as I approached them. The chill that filled the air was now a soft warm breeze. There was no banging. No laughter.

We finally got to the chamber where Xander was held. He stood in the center of the cage, completely shrouded by darkness. It seems that he had pulled all the chill and darkness into this cage with him. As we entered, he lifted his head to look at us.

"Welcome back," he grinned, showing off his sharp teeth. Daphne extended her arm towards me, motioning for me to stay back. It was then I noticed the rock formation that I held on to did indeed crack and left an opening out of his cage. Daphne stepped forward.

"What did you do?" She growled at him.

"Oh, I didn't do anything. The Queen and I made a bargain. We both fulfilled our ends by the look of it."

"I made no bargain with you," I told him.

"Oh, but you did. I helped you. You helped me," he smirked then motioned to the damaged rock. "Now all you need to do is say the word, and I am free."

"You will never be free," Daphne snarled. "You betrayed us. You sold us out to Dimitri. You gave him the power to enact the curse."

My jaw dropped. What did she just say? Xander was the reason that we are here in the first place?

"I helped him with an issue he was having with his son. He told me no harm would come of the Queen." He stepped toward the edge of his cage. "If I had known what he truly intended, I would have denied him."

"Liar! You only say that now because he didn't provide you what he promised." Daphne stepped forward reaching through the hole the damaged rock had left and grabbed his arm. The shadows that surrounded Xander now rushed up Daphne's arm and turned to light. Xander wailed in pain and fell to his knees. "I should have killed you then and there, but I felt sorry for you." Her voice filled with a rage I hadn't heard from her before.

"Please! Stop! I will tell you how to break the curse!"

"You said there wasn't a way when I asked before. Another lie to save your own ass," she said with disgust.

"No! There is a way! I was a coward before. I will tell you, please!" He wailed.

"Enough. Release his arm," I said calmly. Daphne's head jerked towards me. "That's an order." Daphne released his arm and took a step back. Light now radiated from of her. The sight of her was almost angelic. It scratched a deep memory from within my mind. Was this Daphne's true appearance unaltered by the curse?

Xander quickly moved back to the far wall out of her reach. I approached the stone bars and glared at him, looking him in the eyes.

"Well? I don't like to be kept waiting," I demanded answers.

"His cane. The red orb that sits atop it. Smash it. The wall will crumble, and his hunger will vanish. Everything will be as it once was," The words quickly rushed from his lips. His voice was broken. I stepped towards the damaged piece of rock and grasped it.

"Thank you for freeing me," another soft broken sentence escaped his lips. I looked up at him, a blank expression on my face. The rock formation grew. Slowly closing the cracks.

"No!" He stood rushing back towards the stone bars as they closed. I let go and the stone continued to grow. He begged and pleaded for me to stop. He deserved eternal darkness. A solid stone wall now faced me. A pounding could be heard from the other side. I looked over at Daphne.

"Let's go," I walked back to the entrance.

Thirty-Three

We agreed to stay in the village for a few more days. Tomorrow was the full moon, and it was important we stayed until the moon waned. Every full moon they have a bonfire and celebration. According to Daphne, this was a practice that was widespread back home in Serafina. This was a time to recharge and cleanse ourselves of anything that no longer served us. After the party, we would return to the castle.

A part of me was sad to leave the village. I would miss my people. We didn't know each other long, but I felt a deep connection with every single one of them. This village will always be near and dear to me. I was reborn here.

I couldn't wait to get home. I missed Darius more than I ever expected to. I found myself lying in bed at night wishing he was by my side. Hoping he would visit me in my dreams. Unfortunately, he had not. I wondered if he missed me as much as I missed him.

I laid on the bed, looking up at the ceiling. I wondered if there was a way for me to reach out to him. I shut my eyes tight and tried to focus on contacting Darius. Trying to force myself into the space in our minds where we had met before. I sat there for some time, trying, but nothing came out of it. I let out a huff. When I saw him again, I would need to ask him how he does that. I rolled over to my side. I needed to get to sleep, my thoughts had kept me up long enough.

As I laid there in the silence I heard deep from the back of my mind.

No need to call for me so loud, doll. I am here.

My eyes jolted open and I sat up straight looking around. I was no longer in the cottage's bedroom. No, I was now back in the castle bedroom. I was entangled in the red sheets. I was no longer wearing the pajamas I was wearing, instead a tiny silk nightgown clung to my skin. The room felt cold and dark. Darius leaned against the door. His shirt was half unbuttoned; a few loose hairs hung in his face.

"I am getting impatient," he growled at me. "When are you returning?"

"I will come back when I am ready. There are a few more things I need to do."

"The only thing you need to do is come back. If you are not back tomorrow, I will hunt you down and make sure you never see daylight again. Do you understand?"

"Excuse me?" I stood up from the bed. Darius was before me in an instant. He grabbed my throat and sat me down on the bed.

"You are excused," he growled as he grabbed my chin and had me look up at him. "I cannot have you running free. It is too dangerous, so if you do not come home, I will come get you."

"You have two seconds to release me. Remember what happened to Andrei when he wouldn't let me go?" I said to him.

"That was a fluke and you know it," he smirked down at me.

"Oh, was it?" I smirked back, grabbing the wrist that held me. He simply nodded. I shifted my focus to the lights that hung on the wall. I could hear the electricity buzz in my ear. I took a deep breath and on my exhale they all popped and shattered one by one. Darius released me, looking around in shock.

"How did you do that?" He demanded.

"Oh, it's just a dream world. Can't I do as I please?"

"No, this world has the same laws as the real world. So, spill it." He leaned back against the wall, keeping some distance between us.

"Worried I would hurt you?" I teased him.

"After everything I have done, I deserve it. Yes, actually. You have before. In some weird, twisted way it was what made me fall in love with you." He said the last sentence almost under his breath. We stared at each other for some time in silence after that.

"I met with Xander."

"The Xander?" He questioned, his eyes going wide. "Is Daphne insane?"

"He removed the block that was inside of me. I have access to my powers. He told me how to end the curse. Before that, I need to spend more time with my people."

"You found more fae? How is that possible? All the fae in Titus were executed after your death."

"Some of my people survived and have settled near the wall. I will be home soon. I will leave here after the full moon."

Darius gave a huff and then came to sit by my side. He took my hand in his as I looked up to meet his gaze.

"Do you have all your memories back?" He questioned in a whisper.

"No, not at all. Though I did have a little vision of us in a peach orchard."

Darius broke out into a chuckle. "Oh, you did? Well, what did you see?"

"Not much, just you making a mess of yourself from a peach."

"Well, Serafina did have some of the best fruit in the region. And the royal orchards were known to be the best of the best. You invited me to tour them after months of me begging to come see you again." He reached up and gently stroked my cheek with the back of his hand. "After all of this is over, I will take you back myself. We can experience it all over again." He leaned in gently brushing his lips against mine. He ran his fingers through my hair. "You have two days after the full moon to get back home, or I will come hunt you down."

"I will come back after the full moon. I promise."

Thirty-Four

The full moon festival was nothing like I had ever seen before. A huge bonfire sat in the center of the party. The fire danced to the rhythm of the music that was being played by a few of the locals. The villagers were around the fire, drinking and dancing. None of them had a care in the world. A few of the food vendors from the village had set up stands to feed the people of the party.

Honestly, after everything with Xander, I was happy to have a moment of relaxation and a time when I could let my guard down. Daphne had gotten to the party way before I did. She stood in the center of a group of people with a cup in hand filled with a dark pink liquid. She was dancing like a crazy person. I had never seen her so free or loose before.

She locked eyes with me and ran to me.

"Bri! You are finally here!" She smiled wide, slurring her words a bit.

"Whoa there. Having too much fun already?" I giggled.

"I forgot how strong Fae wine is," she giggled, grabbed my wrist, and pulled me towards the stand where a man and woman were serving the wine. "Two please!" She asked the man as she disposed of the empty cup she already had. He smiled back at her and handed her two cups. She immediately handed one to me as she thanked him.

"Based on how you are, I am not sure I should drink this," I questioned her.

"No, no. It's fine! Just take it easy since it's your first time." She took a sip from her cup and motioned for me to follow her. She ran back closer to the bonfire and danced like no one was watching. I followed her. It was nice to see her so carefree. I took a sip of the pink liquid. It was so sweet and refreshing. Without realizing it I had drunk the entire cup. Daphne looked up at me and laughed.

"I said take it slow, silly!" She grabbed my hands and spun me around. The world did not stop spinning after that.

"I couldn't help it! It was absolutely delicious!" I smiled and followed Daphne's movements. "You know, I didn't ever expect you to be a bad influence."

"Sometimes we all need a break from being on the straight and narrow. The full moon is a perfect time to relax and recharge! I forgot how fun these parties could be! Wait here, I'm going to get us another drink, and maybe some of the food too!" She skipped away.

I now noticed how all eyes were on me as I danced to the beat of the music. I was definitely too drunk to care. I watched the band as they played, I was focused on the violinist's bow. I watched it go back and forth for much longer than I would like to admit. Silas and Cora approached me, which finally broke my fixation on the bow.

"Glad to see you enjoying yourself, Your Majesty," Cora smiled at me.

"It is a wonderful party," I replied, my vision finally steadying a bit.

"The full moon is a lot more than just having a good time," Silas began. "It's about recharging and reconnecting with our inner magic. Soon, we will begin our ritual. I would love for you to lead it with me."

"I have never led any sort of ritual," I said, a bit nervous.

"Well, now that your powers are back, it is important you learn. Especially if you ever plan to return us to our home." Silas sneered a bit at the last sentence. He was right. As Queen, it was important to know these rituals. I also needed to figure out a plan to get everyone back to Serafina. I hadn't put too much thought into that at all. I had been so focused on breaking the curse that I had no idea what the plan for Serafina would be. Would they even remember me as their Queen? Or had they moved on with time?

"I would love to join you. I will sober up and be ready when you need me."

"Wonderful, please meet me here in about thirty minutes," He smiled. They both bowed and took their leave.

Daphne should have been back by now. I looked around and couldn't see her through the crowd of drunk and dancing fae. I made my way back to the drink stand. I wondered if she ended up drinking even more before she had gotten back to me. When I arrived, I found the stand unattended.

"Excuse me, have you guys seen a short woman with curly hair come through?" I questioned a group that was standing near the stand. Each had a drink in hand.

"Nope. This stand has been unattended for a while now, Your Majesty," One of the guys answered.

"Instead of looking for your friend, want to sneak off and get lost with me?" Another said. The group looked at him in shock. Like a group of frat boys who had just scored the queen bee. Unfortunately for him, he would not be scoring anything, but a damaged ego. I looked him up and down.

"Not my type. Also, that is no way to speak to your Queen." His smile vanished; however, the rest of the group broke out into laughter.

"Gotcha, I don't have fangs. I get it." He coughed and heard him under his breath. *Blood whore.*

I wasn't sure if he was just bad at hiding his insults, or if he wanted to make sure I heard him. Before I could respond the ground rumbled. Darkness crept up his body and funneled into his mouth. He choked and gagged on it as it slithered down his throat. Everyone in his group jumped back. The music had stopped and all eyes were in our direction.

As the group cleared, I saw Ron. His eyes were pitch black, shadows clinging to his hands.

"She is our Queen. She is a lady. You will respect her," he growled. Cora and Silas came running towards him. Cora grabbed his wrist and the darkness vanished. The man now gasped for air.

"Apologize to her," Ron said coldly. The man looked over at Ron, not responding to him. He was still trying to catch his breath. "I said apologize, or next time I won't stop," he growled.

The man looked over at me. He took a deep breath.

"I apologize, Your Majesty. It will not happen again." A chill wind flew through the air with his words. Cora was now dragging Ron away by his wrist. She was scolding him for making a scene, but I couldn't hear her exact words, but I heard his.

"I will defend our Queen with my life."

Silas, who now stood alone in the space where Ron just was called out for everyone's attention.

"Well, this has been an eventful full moon. Our Queen has returned, and her powers have returned as well. It seems my grandson has gotten a grasp on his magic as well. For the first time in generations our magic is returning to us," he waved me over to him. I approached him as he continued to speak. I glared at the man who spoke ill towards me as I passed him. Silas took my hand. "Please everyone join us around the bonfire as we begin our ritual." He guided me to the bonfire, and everyone gathered around in a circle. I looked around, still trying to look for Daphne. I didn't see her anywhere. My heart pounded harder as Silas spoke words in a language I had never heard but somehow understood every word.

"Tonight, we gather under the full moon. Tonight, we give thanks to the earth, the wind, the water, the fire, the light, and the dark that run through our veins. We ask the Moon Goddess, Hinaki, to restore us to our glory and guide our paths." He looked over towards me. "Sabrina Alexandra Saison, we ask that you follow your path and guide us home. We ask that the Goddess guides you through your journey." As he spoke the fire flared, and he smiled.

He knelt on one knee. As did everyone else. My hand still in his, he looked up at me.

"You are close to glory. All hail Queen Sabrina," he said looking up to me.

"All hail Queen Sabrina," everyone else said in unison.

A slow clap came from behind us in the darkness from the tree line. He all looked in the direction of the sound.

Out of the darkness, Dimitri stepped into the fire's light.

"Seems like I am interrupting," he gave a predatory grin. Behind him stood too many of his soldiers to count.

Thirty-Five

The crowd erupted into screams, most running off. Only a few of us stayed at the fire to face Dimitri.

"You are interrupting, nor were you invited. It would be best for you to take your leave," I growled at him. He clicked his tongue in response.

"What a shame. My worthless son can't do anything right. Even in a frenzy, I see he failed to eliminate you." My focus was set on the red orb that sat atop his cane. He looked down at it and smirked. "No worries. A little girl like you will be no issue for me."

"I am no longer a little girl. This is your last chance to leave before it gets ugly for you," I stepped forward. Any remaining feelings from the fae wine quickly vanished as adrenaline pumped through my veins.

"Oh yes, I had heard you had gotten your powers back. No worries. I made sure that wouldn't be an issue," he chuckled. "I also disposed of the Ancient One. Can't have her getting in our way."

"Where is Daphne? What did you do to her?" I demanded an answer. Dimitri took a few steps forward. The light of the flames danced on his pale skin. I imagined those flames encompassing his entire body. It was then I realized I could no longer feel the magic through my veins. My eyes went wide. "What did you do?" I growled at him.

"Oh, the wine you were drinking. That was from my special reserve. One of the main ingredients is morning glory."

"Used to bind our magic, render us defenseless," Silas said from behind me. My stomach went into a knot.

"Now, I am a reasonable man," he stepped closer to me. "Come with me, and the people of the village will not be harmed. Fight me, and I will kill every last one." His green eyes stared directly through me.

"If I come with you, will you leave them alone?" I said after a moment.

"Yes. I will," he said sternly.

"Promise. Promise me you will never harm them, you will leave them be, and I will come with you."

"I knew you were a smart girl," he extended his hand out to me. "I promise no harm will come to the people of this village."

I looked back at Silas. Tears threatened to fall, but I could not let them. "Take care of my people, as you always have. Thank you for everything you have done for me."

137

"Stay strong, Your Majesty. We will meet again someday," he whispered to me. I looked back at Dimitri and took his hand. He grabbed me tight and yanked me towards him.

"Good girl. Maybe my son wasn't so stupid to choose you after all. It seems you're a smart girl," he chuckled and began pulling me away. As we walked through the crowd of his soldiers, he stopped for just a second. Without even looking at them he commanded them.

"Burn every building to the ground, but make sure no one is hurt in the flames." He continued to walk, gripping me tighter.

"You promised!" I cried out to him.

"I said I wouldn't hurt them. Buildings aren't people. Maybe you aren't as smart as I thought." He pulled me close to him. He grabbed my chin tightly forcing me to look into his eyes. "Sleep," he commanded. I felt his command deep in my mind, and I couldn't help but to oblige.

I awoke with a throbbing headache, blurred vision, and a stinging pain in my arm. I sat up and felt a tight pull around my neck. I reached up trying to pull whatever was around my neck off but was met with cold metal.

My vision finally cleared a bit and I got my first look at the room around me. I sat in an almost bare bead. No pillows, no blankets, only a top sheet to cover the mattress. The metal around my neck was on a short chain connected to the headboard. An IV dangled nearby and was filled with a bright pink liquid. It was going directly into my arm. I assumed it was more morning glory. The rest of the room was cold, dark and empty.

I tried to push past the throbbing, trying to put together a single thought, but the pain in my head was almost too much to bear. I needed to get out of here. I needed to find Daphne. The door swung open and the room filled with a bright light. A tall figure stood in the doorway.

"Good, you are finally awake," Dimitri said as he walked closer. "I hope you like your accommodations. You will be staying here for some time." He chuckled under his breath.

"What do you want from me? Just let me go," I growled up at him.

"I cannot let you do that. As long as you are around, you are a distraction," he paced by my bedside. " Unfortunately, I cannot kill you, you will just reincarnate. I need you completely removed from the game. You see, I have big plans for my son. Plans he cannot accomplish if he is constantly worried about you," he paused, standing at the foot of the bed. "When I leave here, your door is being walled off. No one will find you. No one will hear you. I hope that no one will smell you. I will be the last person that you ever see."

"Don't! You don't have to do this! Just send me over the wall! I won't speak to Darius again! Please."

He paused for a moment and chuckled.

"From what I heard. Serafina is a wasteland. No reason to return. It is uninhabitable. You would die, unfortunately, I can't have you die yet. Oh, and before you get your hopes up. I sent a group to that castle in the mountains," he chuckled. "Other than my son, who is on his way back in chains, there were no survivors. Daphne is being executed tomorrow night. No one is coming to save you." He laughed harder, his bright green eyes turning red. He turned and walked away. I fought against the chain, but I could barely move. He stopped as he got to the door frame. He spoke without even looking at me.

"When that IV runs out, you will die. Thanks to the morning glory, you won't reincarnate. Good riddance."

Thirty-Six

The hours that passed felt like days. My veins burned as more of the liquid dripped into me. I drifted in and out of consciousness. I could hear the thud of stones against the other side of the door. Everything I had gone through, everything we had fought for now meant nothing as my end approached.

Let sleep take you.

I heard a gentle purr in the back of my mind.

Trust me. I am here.

I shut my eyes. I tried to block out the sounds of the wall being built right outside the door. I heard a loud bang, which caused my eyes to open.

Darius now sat on the edge of the bed.

"Are...are you really here?" I questioned. The throbbing in my head now fading away.

"I wish, only in your mind, doll. Hang in there. I am coming for you. I arrived at the castle not too long ago. I already tricked my father into thinking I am on his side. I will find you."

"Where are the others?" I questioned. "How are you here with me? I thought the morning glory blocked my magic?"

"I don't know. Andrei and Isa fled when our castle was attacked. I instructed them to. I told them to meet us here, hopefully, they will arrive soon. Daphne is being held in the dungeons. I will get her out before anything bad happens, I promise. As for the morning glory, this magic that connects us. It is not mine. It is not yours." His green eyes filled with tears as he spoke. "The day you invited me to tour your orchards, we stayed out all night. We laid in the grass and watched the stars. A star fell from the sky that night, and landed on us. It didn't hurt us. But we were glowing from the stardust, that covered us. Ever since that night we had a bond that kept us connected. The curse has messed the signal up a bit, our connection used to be much stronger. The heavens want us to be together. Nothing will stop that. Not even my father." He leaned over and gently kissed me. "Just hang in there for a few more hours. I will find you. I have to go pretend to be on my father's team."

"Please hurry," I whimpered. He stared at me for a moment. I could tell he was fighting with himself to stay strong in front of me.

"Sabrina..." He said softly.

"Yes?"

"I love you." He vanished before I could respond.

The throbbing in my head returned at full force. I felt the entire castle shake. I could hear the stones on the other side of the door crumbled and grunted as if they had fallen on whoever was out there building the wall.

The throbbing in my head only got worse. I looked up at the IV bag. It was under half empty. There wasn't much time left. My eyes felt so heavy. I was so cold.

I closed my eyes for just a moment. When I opened them, I noticed a shadowy figure lurking in the corner of the room. I looked up at the bag and it barely had anything left in it. How long had I shut my eyes for?

"Who's.... There?" I whimpered; it was so hard to speak. The shadow figure didn't move, didn't say a word. I couldn't look away from it. It had no features. Just a cold dark shadow that clung to the corner of the room.

The throbbing in my head was even worse than before. I was too weak to even lift a single finger. I honestly doubted that anyone would come to my rescue. I closed my eyes once again. I just couldn't keep them open. With each throb I saw a vision.

The first was the first time meeting Darius at the Vernal Equinox Masquerade. He looked so handsome in his suit. The second was us in that orchard. He was so arrogant before... but now he seemed nervous. My heart beat faster as the visions continued. They were blurry and moved too quickly for me to understand what I was seeing. I wished I could remember more about our first time together.

A deep chill ran through me.

"Dar, what are you doing? You know it's bad luck to see the bride in her wedding dress before the wedding." I hid behind a changing screen. I didn't want him to see my tulle dress that was adorned with flowers. The bodice clung to my body with a sweetheart neckline.

He stood in the doorway silent. I could see his hands shaking. His eyes were a deep shade of red that I had never seen.

"Is everything okay?" I rushed towards him, taking his hands in mine. "Is it your father, is he here?" I questioned.

In a blink he had pounced on me, slamming me to the ground and pinning me. I squirmed under him. The struggle caused a side table to fall over, spilling the bright pink wine all over the white carpet.

"Darius, get off me! What are you doing?" I panicked. For the first time, I couldn't feel my magic. I was defenseless as he roughly grabbed my head and exposed my neck. Before I could scream for help his fangs were in my neck and he held me tightly as he drained me dry.

My eyes jolted open. My heart pounded in my chest; my mouth was dry. That shadowy figure now stood at my bedside. It looked down at me in silence for a moment. It reached down to me with its long, bony fingers and caressed my cheek.

"No... get... away..." I whimpered "I... I'm not... ready..."

"Sabrina." It called my name in a dark scruffy voice. It grabbed onto the collar around my neck.

"No!" I cried out. It yanked the collar. It crumbled and snapped in its hands.

"Sabrina! It's me," it said to me. Now taking the IV out of my arm. I cried out in pain as it was removed. "Shhh... I'm here. It's really me," his voice was now clearer.

"Darius..." I whimpered. The shadow around him faded as his features came into view. He sat at the edge of the bed by my side and nodded. He took his wrist to his mouth, biting into it, causing him to bleed. He gently lifted my head and firmly pressed his bleeding wrist to my mouth.

"Drink, doll. I've got you," he whispered. His blood flooded my mouth and forced its way down my throat. Warmth ran through my body. Darius' hands began to shake. He then dropped my head and flung back towards the opposite wall.

I sat up and watched as his eyes filled with hunger. It was then I realized my bracelets were gone. His breath was heavy and slow.

"Give me a minute," he growled. "I'm going to get you out of here. I just need to compose myself." He clenched his jaw.

"Take a deep breath. It's going to be ok."

"Shut up. I can't stand your voice!" He barked at me. I watched as he pressed his back into the wall and then slammed his fist into it. "It would be so easy. You're weak. You're mine," he growled.

I stood, my legs wobbling under me. I was still so weak from the morning glory. I had to find a way to calm him down.

He slammed me back down onto the bed, pinning me in place.

"Easy, prey. You aren't going anywhere," he purred into my ear. I could feel his breath on my neck. It sent a shiver down my spine.

"Dar, stop it. This isn't you," I pleaded with him as he ran his tongue up my neck.

He moved one of his hands over my mouth and pressed down firmly.

"I thought I told you to shut up," he growled deeper, then grazed his fangs over my neck. He paused. We stayed like that for what seemed like an eternity. He then released me, taking a step away. I felt life return to me as he did.

"Come on. We have to go get Daphne. She will help you get your bracelets back," he said coldly walking towards the door.

Thirty-Seven

Darius guided me through the secret passages to the dungeon. He stayed silent and his distance from me. Then tension between us hung in the air. I felt a lot better than I had before, however, I still felt weak and throbbing in my head.

"Stop," Darius said as he quickly turned towards me. "We need to go through a main section of the castle for a moment before we can get to the secret passage that leads directly to the dungeon." He took a step towards me and gave me a predatory glare. "Stay quiet and keep close."

I gave a small nod and he turned back to the wall. He pressed one of the stones and the door slid open. He waved for me to follow him into a small sitting room. I watched him release a deep breath.

"I'm sorry for how I am acting," he said just under his breath, never once looking at me.

"It's fine. I get it."

"No, you don't. You will never understand what it is like to have to kill the girl you love most over and over. You will never understand how insane you make me," he growled finally looking me in my eyes.

"How insane the curse made you," I corrected him. "Please don't act like you are the only one hurting from this."

His eyes widened and he took a step back.

"Do you really remember every time?" He whispered. I just nodded.

He clenched his jaw, and his lips formed a tight line, letting out another deep breath. He stood there for a moment, not saying a word. He then rushed towards me. I flinched, taking a step back. I figured this was it, he just couldn't resist anymore. Hopefully all the morning glory will be out of my system so that I will reincarnate. He wrapped his arms around me and pulled me in tight. I tried to push him away, but he was too strong.

"Stop squirming, I'm not going to hurt you," he embraced me tighter. I stopped fighting him and wrapped my arms around him. I closed my eyes. Pretend that we were anywhere else but here. His warm body pressed into mine. At this moment everything seemed to melt away.

"Never again," he said softly. His fingers ran through my hair. "I am stronger than the curse. We are stronger." He gently cupped my chin and lifted it to match his gaze.

"Never again," I smiled up at him. He softly ran his thumb down my lips. My stomach felt like it was doing nonstop somersaults and I felt heat rush to my cheeks.

"Come on. We have to get Daphne," he said after a moment of staring into my soul. He released me and headed into the hall. I followed close behind. The only sound was our footsteps echoing in the air. It seemed as if the hallway was endless until we reached a set of shut double doors. Darius pressed his ear to the door and stood there for a moment. He gave a nod and then opened it.

A large conference room greeted us. The back wall was a window that overlooked the city. The lights twinkled as if they were dancing in the night sky. I looked over at Dar, whose expression showed that he had gotten lost in the lights.

"After this is all over, I will be King," he sighed. "I will try to make up for the atrocities my father has committed." He looked over at me. "I hope to make you proud, be the King you want me to be."

"Well looks like we will have something in common." He raised his brow in response. "I don't know how to be Queen. I thought coming here, with your father, would save my people. Instead, it harmed them greatly. I have taken everything from my people. They have lost their homes, twice, because of me. I don't want to be the Queen you wish me to be. I want to be the Queen they need me to be."

He chuckled, shaking his head. "You always have been better than me." He walked over to one of the bookshelves and tilted a book causing the self to slide open revealing a secret passage. We quickly made our way into the secret passage and Dar slid the shelf closed. Unfortunately, that left us in total darkness.

"Take my hand. I will lead the way." I felt him tightly grip my hand and begin to lead me through the darkness.

All I could think of at that moment was Ron when he led us for the first time to meet Xander. His eyes were solid black. I wonder if I was able to do that as well. I could feel my power rumble from deep within me. It felt different than it ever had before. I could feel it, all of it. It pulsated throughout my being. At the same time, it felt distant, disconnected, and out of control. I needed to get my bracelets back before we faced Dimitri. I tried to focus my power. Begged the darkness to illuminate itself, but it refused. The darkness refused to budge.

I felt Darius give my hand a tight squeeze.

"Hang tight, we are almost there." He stopped and I felt his hands grip my waist and he lifted me over his shoulder. "We have to go down some stairs, I don't want you to fall and bust your neck." His hands held my hips tightly, his fingers dug into my skin. As he walked me down the steps, I heard him inhale deeply. After a silent moment, he spoke as we reached the bottom of the stairs and he set me down. "Your scent is intoxicating. You know that, doll?"

"You are so creepy. We can continue that conversation later, you know after we save Daphne and kill your father."

"Right." He huffed as he grabbed my wrist tightly and began guiding me once again through the darkness. "When this is all over. We will have much to discuss indeed. I would like to take you on an actual date. If you will allow me to." I heard him clear his throat. My heart skipped a beat, and I felt butterflies filled my stomach.

"That sounds nice. Ask me again when this is all over," I giggled. After we walked through the darkness for a bit longer, Darius finally came to a halt.

"Stay quiet. There shouldn't be anyone on the other side, but just in case, I don't want them to hear you," he whispered as one of the walls slid open, a dim light finally illuminating the darkness. Darius peaked out looking around. My wrist still held tightly in his grasp, and he moved forward, pulling me along with him.

The room was small. At one end was a tall staircase. On the other side of the room sat an empty desk and a large set of double doors behind it. Darius shut the entrance to the secret passageway as we heard footsteps coming from the staircase. Darius gripped me tighter and pulled me towards the doors.

"My Lord, what are you doing down here?" Both of our heads quickly turned towards the staircase. An older man in a guard uniform was approaching.

"I'm sorry," Darius growled. "I don't remember having to answer to you. Who are you? A nobody. Never question what I am doing." He dropped my wrist and stepped towards the guard. "As a matter of fact, why was no one at this post? What are you doing?"

The guard took a step back in surprise. "I meant no disrespect. My apologies, my Lord." He knelt in front of Darius. I looked down at the guard from across the room. He was trying to hide it, but even I could smell the fear from him.

"Turn around, doll," Darius said calmly, a darkness taking over her voice. My gaze shot to him. "I didn't stutter. Turn around." Anger filled his voice. I immediately obeyed him. I turned away facing the wall.

"My Lord, please forgive me," I heard the man whimper.

It wasn't long until I heard a crack and pop. My whole body tensed up and my ears rang. The walls closed in around me. My breathing got heavy.

I felt a tight grip on my shoulder. Darius then appeared by my side.

"Come on. Let's go get Daphne," he said sternly and opened the doors in front of us.

We entered a dimly lit hall. Each side was lined with cells. The sounds of moans and groans echoed through the hall. I kept my eyes on the floor. Based on the sounds I heard, I did not want to see the people who were kept here.

My heart pounded as we walked further into the dungeon. It almost stopped when I heard a familiar voice.

"Sabrina? Darius? Thank the gods," Daphne's voice was like music to my ears. I looked up and saw her rush to the cell bars. She reached out and grabbed my hand. "I thought you... I thought I would never see you again." Tears welled in her eyes. I gave her a weak smile, squeezing her hand in return.

"I know. I know," I said softly. I looked over at Darius. He pulled out a set of keys from his pocket and unlocked Daphne's cell. She rushed to the open doorway. She paused, looking up at Darius.

"Thank you," she said as Darius lifted his hand to stop her.

"No, none of that. We have to hate each other. It will make things weird if you start to be grateful towards me now," he chuckled. Daphne just rolled her eyes and then focused them on me. I watched as her eyes traveled me up and down, then back down, focusing on my wrists. She then looked at Darius once again.

"Don't start. I know what I did," he grumbled. "I need you to help her find them. I need to head back and distract my father for a while."

"Do you have any idea where they could be?" She asked him.

"If I did, I wouldn't be going through my own personal hell." His jaw clenched. "I know they are still in the castle. He made the mistake of last time not keeping them close. He won't make that same mistake. My tip to you is to stay in the shadows and use the hidden tunnels. Let no one see you." He took a step back. "When you find them, call for me. I will come and we will end this for good." I blinked and he was gone. Daphne then turned to me.

"Let the hunt begin," she smirked.

Thirty-Eight

Daphne and I spent the rest of the day slipping in and out of various secret passages throughout the castle. We had searched several rooms that looked as if they were used to stash treasures from across the lands. Unfortunately, we had no luck.

"This is hopeless. We can't just go through every room and just expect them to be sitting out. We have to move on without them," I huffed as I sat down on a red velvet chair in the study we were currently searching.

"We can't give up. You need them. You need them to break the curse, and you will need them afterward once the magic is back fully." She sat down the box she had in her hand and came to stand in front of me. "Take my hands and close your eyes."

I took a deep breath and grabbed her hands, closing my eyes. "What is this going to do?"

"Shush. Take slow deep breaths. Try to connect with your magic."

I could feel my left eye twitch a little as I tried to focus on my magic. I could sense it running from me as if we were in a game of hide and seek. I could feel myself catching up with it. I could taste it on my tongue, and feel it on my fingertips. Then it would vanish. I could feel Daphne's hand tighten against my own.

"Call to your bracelets. They will tell you where you need to look."

I tried again. I could feel my magic pulling away just as I could feel myself reaching out for it. It continued to taunt me for some time until it just stopped. I couldn't feel it at all anymore. I dug deeper within myself, hoping to connect once again.

I then felt a hard thrum within me. My ears filled with a high-pitched ring. My eyes jolted open. Everything looked crisp and more clear than it ever was. The ringing had faded into a whisper.

Come find me.

It teased in the back of my mind. I sprang up from my seat.

"Follow me. I can feel it," I said to Daphne heading to the door. A smile lit up across her face as she followed me.

The secret passage we needed to get to was on the other side of this floor. So far, we have been lucky to not come across anyone who got in our way. We snuck our way past a room that had a few men. I could hear them talking, but I didn't care what they were saying. Until something one of them said made my ears perk up.

"Two more days until the Prince gets married huh?"

My heart dropped. Daphne looked up at me confused.

"Apparently. Have you met his bride? She's terrible. She's a noble from Zentari."

Zentari was a small vampire territory from the north. They hated humans more than the vampires of Titus. Only a few places remained in Zentari where humans lived, and they were farms.

"Once they are married, Zentari is being annexed into our territory. The King informed me once the merge is complete, we are to eradicate the humans in the territory. I just sent three battalions to the south. They are awaiting the signal."

Daphne's and my eyes locked with one another, and we rushed to the secret passage. Once the door shut behind us Daphne and I spoke over top of one another. She put up her hand, allowing me to go first.

"We have to stop Dimitri before that happens. Darius didn't tell me anything about getting married." I could feel my blood starting to boil. As much as I hated to admit it, I didn't want anyone marrying Darius. He is mine.

"Probably because he knows it won't come to that. Relax. We will break the curse before Darius has to marry anyone and before he can get rid of the humans. You need to focus on the right now. Don't worry about any of that."

I huffed and rolled my eyes. She was right. I needed to focus on finding my bracelets. Everything else needed to come second to ending the curse.

Daphne and I continued to make our way through the secret tunnels. I honestly had no clue where I was going, I just followed the whisperings in my ear.

We exited the secret passage and found ourselves in an abandoned section of the castle. Dust and cobwebs gathered in corners and clung to the walls. Dingy sheets that were once white covered most of the furniture.

"Oh, this is gross. They really should send a maid up here every once in a while," Daphne said as she pulled off the sheets to inspect the room. Dust flung into the air. I waved my hand around to try to get it out of my face.

"I can feel them. They are close." I said to Daphne. I could sense a pulsing coming from somewhere nearby. My whole body ached for it. The whisperings in my ear grew louder.

Come, my Queen. Be whole once more.

I rushed towards the whisperings. I could hear Daphne's footsteps following me close behind. I could hear them; they were so close. I came to a large set of doors. They were boarded up. The pulsing was strong. The whispers had gotten so loud and jumbled. I knew this was where they were hidden.

I pulled and yanked on the board that held the door shut, but they wouldn't budge. It was not a moment after I heard Daphne yell to me to move out of the way. When I looked back at her she was charging the door with a metal sculpture. I quickly jumped out of the way as her war cry filled the room and she bashed the boards with the sculpture. The cracking of the wood filled my ears, almost silencing the whispers from the bracelets. Dust flew through the air and filled our lungs as she beat the door.

Daphne dropped the sculpture and put her hands on her knees.

"That was enough physical activity for one day," her breath was heavy. I chuckled as I pulled away the broken bits of board.

"Well, it got the job done that's for sure." I finally removed the last piece that was in the way of the door opening.

"Well, well, well. What do we have here? Did you two rats get lost?" A feminine voice arose from behind us. I quickly spun around and saw a tall woman. Her long dark hair was up in a high pony, and it wrapped around her shoulder. Leather clothes clung to her body, leaving nothing to the imagination. My eye met hers. They were bright red and filled with a hunger that I had looked into too many times. It was Daphne who spoke first as I watched her stand up straight. She gave the woman a quick up-and-down glance and then she looked to the left and the right.

"Rats? Plural? I only see one," she growled. The woman let out a puff of air in response. She took a step closer. Daphne did as well, putting her arm out to keep me behind her.

"You two are supposed to be dead. I believe the King will find it very interesting that you are out roaming the castle." A smirk grew across her face as her eyes locked with mine once again. "I just don't understand how. I hope my precious Darius didn't betray me." A chuckle escaped her lips. That's when it hit me. This was the woman that he was to marry. For a moment I felt my heart sink.

I hated to admit it, but I could honestly see them together. There was a lot I forgot about Darius. Too many lives to recall. Too many blurred memories. The one thing I knew for a fact was that he was not a good man. He killed. He lied. He enjoyed it. She had the look of someone who would happily do the same at his side.

I would never be that woman for him. Part of me knew he understood that and hoped he didn't resent me for it.

I don't.

I heard his deep voice overpower the whispers of the bracelet from deep in the back of my mind. I felt a smile grow on my face.

"What are you smiling at? Are you excited for death?" She sneered at me. I felt something rumble inside me.

"Excited for death?" I stepped forward. "I have died more times than I can count. Let me tell you a little something about death. It isn't warm. It isn't welcoming. It demands from you. Takes from you. Corrupts you until you have nothing left. When you experience it as many times as I have, you are not excited for death." My anger continued to rumble deep in my core. I could feel it building, crawling under my skin. It begged for release.

"Are you afraid then, rat?"

"I am death," I growled at her and allowed the anger that was building inside me to release. I let out a scream, and the mirrors and windows shattered around me. I watched as she covered her ears and fell to her knees. Daphne was completely unaffected by my surge of power. The woman let out a wail of her own. I grabbed a piece of wood and hurled it at her as she began to stand. The splintered piece of wood pierced her directly in the heart.

"I hope you are not afraid," I said to her as her body turned to ash. I turned back to the doors, pushing them open. Not saying a word to Daphne. She didn't say anything to me either. Her face said it all. She was just as shocked as I was at what had just happened. On the power I had unleashed, and the coldness I had gained with it in that moment.

We entered the room and a small box sat on a dusty table. I grabbed the box and ripped it open. I could still feel my magic trying to bust out of my skin. There they were—my bracelets. I quickly slipped them on and I immediately felt my magic begin to ebb and flow within me. It no longer felt as if I was going to explode at any moment.

I looked over at Daphne and gave her a soft smile.

"It's show time."

Thirty-Nine

We gathered back in Darius' room. Away from prying eyes. Daphne and I sat on the bed. Darius paced back and forth. His jaw clenched.

"Andrei and Isa should have been here by now, but we can't wait for them any longer," he said as he walked over to the window and looked out at the city below.

"Would have been a real shame if your best friend didn't attend your wedding," Daphne teased. He shot her a glare.

"I told you that wasn't my idea! I wasn't actually going to marry her." he huffed.

"She seemed to think so. You were her precious Darius," Daphne broke out into a laugh.

"Enough. Both of you." I said quietly. "We can give him a hard time about the rat after the curse is broken." I stood walking to Darius' side. "We need to come up with a plan. Without the other two."

"Is there a secret passage that leads into his room or his office?" Daphne questioned.

"There is, but to be honest with you I am not exactly sure how to get to it. That is a secret he's kept even from me."

"We need to bait him. Lure him somewhere where he thinks he will have the upper hand," I said calmly. Both of them looked at me with nervousness in their eyes. "I say we go to the courtyard where the execution was going to happen. Daphne, you will be the bait, tell him you want to change teams."

"He would never fall for that," Darius interrupted. "He knows that Daphne would never be on his side, not after all he has done to you."

"He might if..." Daphne trailed off. "No, it's too risky."

I looked at her and cocked my head. "What? Spill it."

"You know how the two of you have a mental connection? Xander and I have something similar, but more advanced. I can allow him access to control my body. If we allowed him to, he could be the bait for Dimitri."

"Absolutely not. He betrayed us before. He will betray us again," Darius said, his face filled with anger.

"I can take back my body before he did anything like that, our thoughts would be connected."

"After what I did to him, I am not so sure he would help us." I sat back down next to Daphne. "Otherwise, I would say it was a good idea."

"I already asked him about that. He said he's not mad, he understands why you did it. He also agreed to help, if you free him after."

"Absolutely not!" Darius interrupted once more. I lifted my gaze to meet his.

"We don't get the luxury of good options. Sometimes we just have to sort through the bad ones and make it work. Here's my plan. Let's run through it, see what you guys think, and make sure everyone is on the same page."

We didn't have much time after we hatched our plan to put it into action. Darius and I hid in the shadows of the courtyard across from each other. I looked over to the center of the courtyard. Daphne paced next to the stage that was set up in the center of the courtyard. A guillotine sat on top of it. It made my skin crawl thinking about her head rolling if Dimitri had his way.

This better work. I hear Darius' voice purr in the back of my mind.

It has to. We don't have a choice.

"Broke out from the dungeon to run to your death?" I heard Dimitri say. My head snapped up. I watched as he entered the courtyard, alone. The red orb on his walking stick glittered. It teased me, called me to destroy it. My heart pounded in my chest.

"I figured it was time for you and I had a little chat." It was Daphne's voice, but it was filled with darkness. She finally looked up and her eyes were blacked out. I watched as a predatory smile came across Dimitri's face.

"Ah, Xander. My old friend. I was wondering where you have been hiding all these years."

"Unfortunately, our alliance caused my people to turn against me. I am currently... indisposed. I am hoping you are open to making another deal."

"Oh? What are you offering?"

"You want the secret to gaining control of Serafina, and the power it holds?"

Dimitri's face lit up.

"Oh, are you willing to give me that information now? You were so against it before?"

NOW. Darius' voice boomed in the back of my mind. At that moment roots popped out of the ground. They wrapped around Dimitri's arms and neck, lifting him up slightly. A low growl escaped his lips.

"You will regret this, Xander."

"The only thing I regret is turning my back on my sister and the Queen."

Darius walked out of the shadows.

"Well father, it looks like I am able to accomplish something without you."

"Oh, don't count this as a win yet, son." Fire came out of the red orb, setting the vines to flame. I could feel the burn deep within myself like it was myself who was engulfed. I wailed out in pain and fell to my knees. I felt someone grab the back of my shirt and pull me out of the shadows.

"Well, well. I was wondering where you were hiding," Dimitri sneered in my direction. I was tossed to the ground. I looked up and saw three guards had now joined Dimitri, including the one who had pulled me from my hiding spot. The vines I had created were now nothing but ash. It hung in the air like snow. It wasn't long until I felt the guard grab me once again and press a blade to my throat. My arms are twisted and held behind my back.

Don't cry. Don't let him see you cry. This doesn't hurt. I am not afraid.

"Stop! Let her go," Darius commanded. The guard said nothing in response.

"Oh, son. I tried to tell you, over and over. This girl will bring nothing but heartbreak. I can't wait to see that realization when her throat is sliced right in front of you."

"If you hurt her. I will kill you all. I will burn this city to the fucking ground," Darius growled.

"Hm. Some King you will be. Killing your own people for some girl." Dimitri then turned his attention towards me. "Do it," he said firmly, but the guard did not move. "What are you waiting for? I gave you an order!" Dimitri's voice became more agitated with each word. It wasn't a moment later that the guard dropped me. He and the other guards put their daggers to their own throats. Blood sprayed everywhere as they cut into themselves. The courtyard then filled with a familiar maniacal laugh. Daphne's hands were covered in shadows. As soon as we locked eyes the darkness left her fully. Her eyes returned to normal. Her body swayed a bit, and just a second later she collapsed to the ground unconscious.

While Dimitri was distracted Darius rushed at him. Before he could succeed at his plan Dimitri pounded his staff to the ground. A ring of fire surrounded me, and at the same time I grabbed Darius by his throat lifting him. Dimitri's nails dug into Darius' skin. I swore I could see blood through the flames. The fire was close. I could feel it teasing my skin. The fire wanted nothing more than to overtake me.

"I am tired of these games. Since you refuse to be a good son, I will have to get rid of both of you." All I could do was watch as Dimitri Squeezed the life from Darius. I could see his claws dig into Darius' skin causing him to bleed. That familiar feeling sank deep into my chest once again. I was dizzy, everything was spinning and closing in around me. The hot air burned my lungs as I tried to catch my breath. I tried to focus on my magic. I felt the walls begin to cave in. Everything was out of focus.

"Sabrina! Heads up!" It was Andrei. His voice snatched me out of the darkness I was allowing myself to fall into. I looked up and saw my bow, Shimmerthorne, being tossed my way. I caught it, and all at once everything within me ignited. I stomped my foot once on the ground. The fire disappeared around me. I aimed my bow, and a shimmering arrow formed as I drew back. I released and the arrow soared through the air and pierced the orb, causing it to shatter. The earth shook.

As if the big bang had happened inside me, flashes of my previous lives passed through my head. They were crystal clear. I felt my magic become one with me. I could hear

Daphne let out a deep breath as she sprung up. She now glowed as if she was the sun herself.

"No! What have you done?!" Dimitri cried out. He had become too distracted as everything he had worked for now crumbled around him.

"What we should have done ages ago," Darius said as he kicked his father, knocking him down to his knees. Darius finally unsheathed his sword and quickly raised it above his head and sliced it down. Dimitri's head rolled across the courtyard. I finally released the breath I was holding. Darius fell to his knees. Andrei now appeared by his side. Isa was by Daphne, making sure she was alright.

I walked over to Darius and extended my hand down to him.

"Is it over?" He questioned. He took my hand and stood, pulling me into a firm embrace. For the first time in a long time, I felt whole.

"It's just begun," I said softly.

Forty

The month that followed Dimitri's death was hectic, off-limits to say the least. Darius was crowned King of Titus the next day. His first order of business was the collapsing of the wall. Andrei and Isa had been sent to oversee that progress and make sure everything was going according to plan. He also ordered for sections of the city to be off limits to vampires, allowing the humans sanctuary.

He cleared a wing of the castle for Daphne and me. Since Dimitri's death, the guards had been more welcoming and accepting towards us. The ones who weren't had been removed. Darius promised that once the wall was down, he would personally guide me home. I couldn't wait. Now that my memories were back, there was nothing I longed for more than being with my people. I missed my orchards and the beautiful landscape of Serafina.

Part of me was nervous about what I was going home to. No one had been to Serafina in centuries. Would they even welcome me back? Is there anyone left to even welcome me? As I laid in bed, these were the questions that filled my brain and kept me from sleeping.

One morning I awoke to a soft knock on the door. I sat up rubbing my eyes and yawned.

"Come in," I called out. A small woman had entered. She was one of the maids who had frequented this part of the castle.

"The King requests your presence in his office," she said meekly before rushing out of the room before I could respond. I rolled my eyes. Since his coronation, he had been too busy to see me. He still owes me the date that he promised. I got dressed, put on a dark green dress and braided my hair. I made my way to his office. As I did, people in the halls parted to clear the way and bowed. I got to his office and opened the door, not even knocking. He was sitting at his desk. The sun was shining through the window illuminating his pale skin. His phone was pressed to his face. Once I walked in, he stopped his conversation.

"I have to go. The most important person in my life just walked in," he said with a smile as he hung up.

"Oh, so important that you haven't spent any time with me?" I huffed, sitting on the edge of his desk.

"I know. I suck," he chuckled. "The transition was a lot harder on me than I thought it would be. I am going to be more present. I promise."

"You better. I kind of missed you," I smirked down at him. "If you don't give me attention, I would be really upset if I had to find it somewhere else."

Darius stood as his brow furrowed. He stood over me, grabbing my hips tightly.

"You're such a brat, you know that. Don't worry, doll. You are about to get more attention than you can handle," he growled into my ear. I arched my back and wrapped my legs around him.

"Promise?" I giggled. A knock at the door interrupted our moment.

"Go away!" Darius yelled out as he licked up my neck and pushed my dress up to expose me.

"My King, I have urgent news from the wall," someone called out from behind the door. Darius groaned and fixed my dress to cover me back up.

"Fine, come in," he commanded and the man quickly came inside. "What is it?"

"The wall, it's fully collapsed. The way to Serafina is now clear."

"Well, doll, are you ready to go home?" Darius smirked down at me.

"Ready as I'll ever be," I smiled up at him.

Blood Queen

Willow Asteria

The Fae Queen

One

E ven though Darius was driving as fast as he could, it still felt as if time has slowed to a crawl. Daphne sat in the back seat, staring out the window. With the curse broken and the wall down, I was finally able to return home. No longer were Darius and I trapped in a cycle of death that kept my true self secret and my memories locked away.

We all couldn't wait until we returned to Serafina. I couldn't wait to walk through the forest, have picnics in my orchard, sit on my throne, and be with my people. The people are who I missed the most. I missed the diversity of fae that filled my life. As my memories returned, my heart broke for all the people that I left behind.

My thoughts rushed to what could have happened to my land and my people. Dimitri's words rang through my head as I recalled what he had told me. *Serafina was a wasteland. No one was left. There was nothing to return to.* Was that the truth, or something he had said to make me lose all hope?

After hours of silence, Darius finally spoke.

"We are about twenty minutes from our destination. Why don't you get some sleep?" He said softly. How could I sleep at a time like this? My heart raced and adrenaline pumped through my veins.

"He is right, Sabrina. You need your rest for what is to come," Daphne finally spoke. Her voice was softer than I had ever heard it. I could tell that worry filled her head just as much as it did mine.

As I fiddled with my bracelets, Darius reached over, placed his hand on mine, and gave it a gentle squeeze. My gaze met Darius' and a warm smile filled his face. He had been different since we learned the wall was down. He was kinder and more supportive than I had known him to be in the months after we defeated Dimitri. A part of me thought he felt bad for how distant he had been during that time.

During the drive, Darius told me about all he had done in those three months. His main focus was removing any of Dimitri's men who would make his job as King harder. He wanted to bring a new era to Titus, an Era of peace. He wanted vampires, fae, and humans to live in harmony. He had some of the scholars at the Academy work to create synthetic blood to reduce the human death rate. That was still a work in progress.

I watched as those green eyes of his stayed focused on the long, desolate road ahead. Darius leaned back into his seat with one hand on the wheel, his other now on my thigh. He squeezed it gently and smirked.

Mine.

His voice purred in the back of my mind. Since the curse had been broken, he and I could communicate telepathically much easier than before. I finally allowed my body to relax and the scent of cinnamon and pine filled my nose. Maybe it wouldn't be such a bad idea to rest my eyes for a moment.

The sounds of cheers and clapping pulled me from my nap. I opened my eyes and looked out the window. We were pulling into the small fae village. Silas, Cora, Ron, and many others stood in a crowd. I was overjoyed to learn that they were safe. I had never stopped worrying about them after Dimitri's attack. They cheered louder as Darius put the car in park.

"Figured we should make a short detour before heading to the wall," Darius said.

I could not believe what I was seeing. The village was completely different from before. The buildings were brand new. They still had that cute charm that I remembered, but they now were more modern.

"My first day as King," Darius began, "I sent money and aid to help them rebuild after what my father had done."

"That was very kind of you," Daphne spoke up from the back seat. "I think I can get used to a version of you that helps people."

"Don't get used to it. I do not plan on being nice long term," he paused and then looked at me. "Only for *her* will I be nice."

Before I could even respond, he was out of the car in a flash and opened my door for me.

"After you, my Queen. Your people are waiting," he gave a small bow. Darius gave me a look through his brows and chuckled under his breath. The past three months had been all about him and his rise to the throne. The night before we left, he sat me down and told me moving forward, he was going to focus solely on returning me to my land and my people.

As I stepped out of the car, Cora ran to me and embraced me in a hug. Ron and Silas were not too far behind her. The village elder looked much healthier than he had the last time I had seen him, he no longer walked with a cane and he had not coughed at all.

"Oh," she gave an exacerbated sigh. "I was so worried when you were taken by Dimitri." She finally released me and took a step back.

"I was lucky to have Darius come to my rescue. Without him, I would be long gone, and the wall would still be up."

Daphne appeared by my side and took my hand. She gave it a small squeeze in support as we both took a step forward to address the crowd of fae who now stood before me.

The air felt different than it had before. It was charged with magic, and I could now see the magical auras of those who stood before me, like a faint glow that surrounded them. I took a deep breath, and that is when the crowd began to shout their questions at me.

They wanted to know everything about the state of Serafina. How will Serafina and Titus ally together? Was Serafina safe to return to? Are the villages still standing? Was there anyone in Serafina left to return to? The questions poured in, and Daphne took a step in front of me, raising her hand to the crowd to silence them.

"The Queen will answer all your questions in time," she looked back at me, and I stepped forward to stand by her side. Darius stayed behind me. His hand was on my shoulder in support.

"I wish I had the answers to all of your questions, and I wish that I could pacify your fears of the unknown. Unfortunately, that is what we are walking into - the unknown. No one has been to Serafina in centuries. At this point, it is unclear if it is safe to return. I will travel to Serafina and return with the answers you all seek. I will find out what is happening and make sure it is a place we can all call home once again. I promise this to be true."

Silas then came to my side and spoke to the crowd.

"Please all, return to your homes and businesses. Our Queen has had a long journey and we have much to discuss before she continues to the wall and into Serafina." The crowd began to disperse and went back to their daily routines.

"Come, let's all return to my home," Silas said to us and motioned for us to follow.

As we walked the village streets, I was in awe of how they rebuilt. Daphne and Cora talked the entire walk to Silas's home. I was so deep within my thoughts that I only heard the buzz of their voices.

"Well, here we are," Silas said as we approached a large and beautiful home. A porch wrapped around it. The kids had been awaiting our arrival and rushed to us from the porch as we arrived. Silas and Cora quickly instructed them to head to the playground until dinner time. They all ran down the street toward their destination.

Cora motioned for us to go up the porch steps and enter their home. As soon as I stepped over the threshold, I was hit with the scent of cloves and rosemary. Their new home was vastly different than their last. The entry room was large and filled with luxury furniture similar to what we had back at the palace. Cora guided us to a sitting room to the right of the entryway that was filled with red velvet upholstered furniture and a dark oak table. A fireplace was nestled in the far wall. This fire was alive — no, it was magic. It danced and sang out to me. I could hear the whispers of the flames praising my entrance as they grew larger.

Darius, Daphne, and I all sat together on the couch, with me in the middle. Darius' hand was firmly gripping my thigh. Ron, Silas, and Cora sat across from us. All of us seemed to look around the room avoiding eye contact. Darius even made a small comment about an art piece that was on the wall. All of us wanted to ask the same questions, but none of us wanted to speak first. It was Ron who finally broke the silence.

"Take me with you," he said firmly. Cora looked at him in shock with a gasp. Silas didn't seem to be phased at all by Ron's exclamation.

"Absolutely not!" Cora stood from her seat. "We have no idea what the state of Serafina is! It is too dangerous."

"Ron can handle it," Silas said. "Cora, please sit. Do not make a scene in front of the Queen and her advisors." Cora paused and sat back down in her seat and a look of embarrassment washed over her face.

I looked over at Ron, who sat straight up in his seat. His eyes were on me with a determined look on his face. I will never forget what he did for me during the night of the full moon. He stood up for me when no one was watching, and when Daphne had vanished, Ron was still there by my side.

"It is dangerous. Cora is correct about that," I spoke in a soft, but stern tone. "However, you have proven your loyalty and strength to me. You may join us. The rest of you must remain here until we return. Please keep the people of the village safe until my absence."

"It is an honor for my grandson to be chosen to aid our Queen," Silas said standing from his chair. Cora shot him a glare. I could see the worry on her face.

"Cora," I said softly. "Ron is a strong fae. He will do us all proud in helping reclaim our homeland."

She nodded, but a look of sadness had taken over her face.

"Do you all plan on staying in the village for long?" Silas questioned.

"Only until sunrise," Darius said firmly.

"Well, it would be a pleasure for you all to stay here as our guests. Cora can show you to your rooms."

Silas was always so welcoming and kind. Once I reclaimed the throne of Serafina, I needed to make him an advisor at court. He had earned it.

Cora stood and motioned us to follow her up the stairs. "Will you need two or three rooms?" She asked.

"Two," Darius said, not a heartbeat later.

Two

I lay in bed on my side, staring out the window, with Darius completely passed out next to me. The covers were down around his waist, exposing his bare chest. I watched him for a while. The way he slept was amazing to me. Perfectly still and perfectly silent. The scent of pine and cinnamon filled my nose as I layed with him.

Once I was sure he would not wake, I slipped out of bed, quickly removed my tiny nightgown, and replaced it with black leather pants and a black sweater. I threw my hair up in a high pony and silently snuck out of the room. Hopefully, if he did wake, it would be long after I had completed my mission.

I tiptoed down the stairs and out of the house. Journeying just outside of the village. As I approached the entrance of the tunnels, a chilling wind came from them, sending a shiver down my spine. As I stepped into the darkness, the torches on the walls lit up with every step I took. I held my head high and chin up as I entered the chamber where Xander was held. Cold, solid stone greeted me.

I gave a small flick of my wrist, and the stone began to twist and contort back into the stalactites and stalagmites that acted as prison bars. Xander stood at the bars as if he was waiting for my return. His eyes were pure black, staring straight at me. We stood there for some time, another chilling wind hitting my face. I did not falter.

"We are going home tomorrow," I finally said, "thanks to you," I added.

Xander stood straight and tall, like months in total darkness and isolation had not affected him at all. He had been down here alone for so long, I wondered if closing his stone cage changed anything. How did he spend his time alone in the dark?

He didn't respond, but just stood there, staring at me. His eyes were still pure darkness. I waited a moment longer for him to say something, anything. But he never did. Maybe the darkness broke him. I turned to leave. I planned for this to be the last time I saw him, especially since he refused to respond to me. As soon as I took a step toward the exit, he spoke.

"Take me with you. There is something in Serafina you will need my help to defeat." His voice was a bit raspy.

I paused, then turned to face him. The void was now gone from his eyes, exposing his amber irises. I approached the stone bars, looking up, staring Xander directly into his soul, if he had one.

"What do you know?" I demanded.

"I felt the wall when it fell. My full power has returned. Ever since I have been having dreams of our homeland. It is twisted, covered in poison. I have seen many outcomes of what is to happen. If I do not come, you will die. Serafina will fall forever. Once you are gone, there will be nothing to stop the darkness. Darius will die. Titus will be swallowed by the darkness. Daphne will die. Andrei and Isa will die. Ron will die," Xander rambled on, and I saw the darkness creep into his eyes once again. He reached up, grabbing hold of one of the bars. His grip was so hard that I could hear the stone screaming as it cracked.

"What is the outcome if you do come with us?"

His eyes snapped back to mine. "Fully uncertain. You have a ten percent chance of reclaiming the throne and a one percent chance of death."

"The other eighty-nine percent?"

"Filled with so many outcomes, I cannot name them all. About sixty percent is a positive outcome."

"Well, it is better than zero percent. I am not sure if I can trust you. You not only betrayed me but all of Serafina."

"Let me make it up to you and our people. Helping kill Dimitri was only the first step in how I plan to redeem myself. I will be loyal to you until my last breath."

I clenched my jaw, took a step back, and looked Xander up and down. I was not sure if I could ever forgive him for what he had done. My people were suffering because of him.

Could I even believe what he was telling me now?

"You have one chance. If there is even a *hint* of you thinking about betraying me or my people, I will burn you alive and feed you to the hellhounds. Do you understand?" I growled. I could taste the venom dripping off my tongue.

"Yes, my Queen. I understand and give myself to you." He knelt before me.

"So, it's a deal?"

"It's a deal," he said softly with his head hung.

I took a deep breath, and on my exhale, the stone withered within itself, freeing Xander from his prison. I prayed to the gods that this was not a mistake. Xander stood, watching me, awaiting what I would do next.

"Don't say a word about your visions. Understand?"

"Yes, my Queen."

With that, we made our way out of the tunnels.

When we exited them, Darius and Daphne stood there, still in their pajamas, with angry looks on their faces.

"How dare you leave without telling anyone where you were going!" Darius screamed loud enough to cause the trees beside us to quiver. His eyes were blood red, and his face was twisted with rage. Daphne stood behind him with the look of a disappointed mother. Both of their faces went blank when their eyes met Xanders.

"What did you do?" Daphne said with a twinge of fear in her voice. Darius quickly grabbed my arm and pulled me behind him.

"What did you do to her!" He snarled. Xander said not a word, just motioned for me to speak.

"I freed him. We need him to come with us to Serafina," I said sternly. Darius whipped around to face me.

"Do you *not* remember what he did to us? He took you away from me!"

"He brought us back together. Without him, Dimitri would still be here, and I would be dead again," I held my tone and stood straight and tall. He may be the King of Titus, but I was the Queen of Serafina. These were my people and my decisions. I watched as Darius bit his tongue.

Are you sure this is what you want to do? He said to me through our bond. Our eyes locked. I nodded, and I saw the red shift to green. Darius took a deep breath and nodded back.

"Brother, I hope you plan to make up for all you have done," Daphne said as she stepped towards him.

"Indeed I do, sister. I will do anything to prove myself worthy of our Queen's forgiveness, as well as yours."

We all walked together back to the village. The sun was starting to rise and people were coming out of their homes. The sun shone on Xander's face and illuminated his sunken features. I could see the bags under his eyes, and how his skin was slightly sallow. Not even the sun's rays could penetrate the darkness in his eyes. Everyone stared at the four of us, and I noticed a few people rush inside as they saw Xander. He would certainly have lots of work to do to gain back the trust of our people.

Cora, Ron, and Silas were already on their porch waiting for us to return. I saw Cora's eyes widen and cheeks turn rosy as she saw the sun hitting Xander's face. A second later, she shook off the look and spun away, turning her attention to Ron.

"What is he doing out of the prison?" Silas questioned as we approached. His face was contorted with anger.

"I released him. He helped with taking down Dimitri and wants to help reclaim Serafina. I am giving him the chance for redemption."

Silas nodded. "Alright, if that is your wish, my Queen. However, until he does, he is not welcome inside my home."

"Understandable. I'm going inside to get dressed and gather our things. Sabrina can stay out here and babysit," Darius said as he walked up the porch steps and headed inside.

Daphne followed him. I turned back to Xander, who was watching Cora and Ron. His eyes were fixated on them. I coughed under my breath to get his attention, and his head snapped toward me.

"Sorry, I was... zoning out," he muttered. Silas' eyes narrowed as he went inside, motioning for Cora to follow him.

Ron rushed to be by my side, putting himself between Xander and me.

"I will not allow you to have the chance to hurt her ever again," he snarled.

Xander smirked. "I am happy to hear that, boy."

Three

Everyone was on edge for the remainder of the drive to the wall. Darius gripped the steering wheel so hard his knuckles turned white. Darius and I sat up front, and Xander, Daphne, and Ron sat in the back. Daphne sat in the middle between them. All of them were tense and avoided looking toward Xander. About halfway, Darius finally broke the silence.

"What is your plan for when we enter Serafina?"

My mind began to race. I had been so overwhelmed with all the ideas in my head about what could be happening, that I had not even thought of a plan.

"I want to go home," I said as I leaned my head against the window. My head filled with the sights of Serafina. The cherry blossoms, my orchard, my castle. I couldn't wait to see it all once again. I took a deep breath, and I could almost smell the forests around my castle.

It was different from the forests here in Titus. Though we shared a border, our climates were very different. Titus' forests were full of pines and firs, and the air was cooler most days, especially high in the mountains. Serafina was hot and humid, and the forest was dense and full of tropical plants. The colors of the wildflowers that grew on the trees were vivid and diverse. The trees were also much older and larger than the ones in Titus. Many people believed that Serafina was where life originated.

I found myself once again daydreaming about Serafina, and when I came back to reality, we were pulling into a huge encampment filled with industrial machines. The wall was now fully visible, and in ruins. People were rushing around looking very busy as they cleaned up the debris.

Darius parked the car and was opening my door before I could even reach for the handle. I stepped out and immediately heard Isa's voice. She was shouting for whoever was talking to get back to work.

I hadn't spoken to her since our battle with Dimitri. Tensions were still high between us. We never discussed what happened the night I left the castle, and I don't know if I would forgive her for choosing the boys over me. The one hundred years that passed changed her in ways that I did not understand.

Once everyone was out of the car, we followed the sound of Isa yelling to find her and Andrei overseeing a group that was organizing the stone from the wall into things that were destroyed or that could be repurposed.

"Seems like you guys have everything under control," Darius said as he slid his hands into his pockets.

"It is coming along," Andrei said as he approached. Isa stayed back a bit, still bossing around the men. "Come with me and we will give you the full report," he motioned for us to follow him to a large tent. Glancing over and noticing we were walking away, Isa turned and hurried to follow close behind Andrei.

We entered the tent and Andrei led us to a table with a map of the wall and the multiple camps that lined it. The wall was clearly marked on the map. The side where Serafina should be was blacked out. It was in harsh contrast to the Titus side of the map where the camps were marked and notes about their progress.

"This is the site with the clearest path into Serafina. However, the forest is very dense, and we are going to have to travel by horseback instead of car."

"I assumed as much. The last time I was in Serafina, cars did not exist," I chimed in, as we all circled the table, looking at the map. Isa stood directly across from me, but she refused to look in my direction. Andrei and Darius went back and forth, talking about the demolition of the wall. I stared down at the map and zoned out of the conversations around me. My heart pounded in my chest. It was so surreal that I was so close to going home. Once again, images flashed in my head of my homeland. It was Isa's voice that brought me back to the present.

"I don't think it is wise if we go to Serafina. The forest is too dense, and there is a purple haze that sometimes leaks from the trees. It's too dangerous. It is unclear what lies within that forest. We sent in scouts a week ago and they were due back three days ago. We have not heard a word from them. We should all just stay here."

"The fae have been wanting to go home for centuries. We owe it to them to allow them the chance to return home," Daphne said, a snarl in her voice.

"We owe them nothing," Isa said. There was a coldness in her voice I had never heard before.

"Enough!" Darius snapped. "It is our — my responsibility. I will do anything within my power to make sure Sabrina and her people have a safe land to return to. If anyone has a problem with it, they can get off my payroll," he growled towards Isa.

I watched as she shrunk inside herself and avoided Darius' gaze. Andrei cleared his throat.

"Lady Sabrina, what is the plan for reclaiming Serafina?" Andrei questioned. Lady was my title here in Titus. Though I was Queen of Serafina, I was not their queen. I did not expect them to address me as such, as I would never be a vampire queen. Darius insisted they refer to me as Lady out of respect to him.

"Well, I plan to return to the palace. I want to go to the heart of Serafina, show them their queen lives, and we shall go from there."

"That is where the Darkness is centered," Xander spoke, and I shot a look at him. "We will have a difficult time in Serafina. It will not be an easy journey home."

"How do you know this, and what is this Darkness?" Darius questioned.

"Because we are having visions about the state of Serafina. It is unclear at this time what the Darkness truly is. That purple haze is connected, but I am unsure of the source. It is not beyond saving, but we all must stick together to succeed," Daphne spoke up. Everyone turned to her.

I raised an eyebrow. "We? Are you telling me that you have had visions as well?"

"Yes, my Queen. I apologize for not bringing it up before. I did not want to give you another thing to stress over. The visions I have been having are of the castle. It is in ruins. Darkness surrounds it and has corrupted most of the forest."

I could hear the others begin to whisper to each other about what had been revealed. I swear I heard Isa comment how she was right about the danger. Darius quickly shut her up by telling her she has no place to decide. I looked over at him and I could see the worry in his eyes as his gaze met mine. I turned my attention back to Daphne.

"Please do not hide things from me. I can take it."

"My apologies. I meant no disrespect." Daphne said softly, but not weakly. I know she only had my best interest in mind. She always had. I could not be mad at her for that.

"I know. You just want to protect me. I appreciate it. I also appreciate open and honest communication."

Out of the corner of my eye, I could see Isa roll her eyes. I need to pull her aside later and talk to her. Why was she being so difficult?

Want me to handle it? I heard Darius' voice in my mind.

No. I will speak with her later.

Say the word, and I will take care of her.

A shiver went down my spine. I knew exactly what he meant by that. My mind flashed back to that day in the basement when I heard Isa's body hit the floor.

"We will be ready for whatever the gods have in store for us," Ron said confidently. I knew that no matter what happened, I had Ron in my corner.

After we talked business, Andrei guided us to a circle of tents where we would be spending the night. Daphne, Ron, and Xander each had their own tents, and Darius and I would share one. Inside the tent was nothing like I would have imagined. It was filled with lavish furniture and expensive furs. The bed was large enough to fit four people. I looked over at Darius, and before I could open my mouth, he spoke with a wide grin across his face.

"What? Did you honestly expect us to be roughing it? I am the King of Titus. You are the Queen of Serafina, have you forgotten? That aside, I wanted one last bit of luxury and comfort before we head into Serafina."

I giggled as he guided me to sit on the end of the bed. He stood before me, and his grin turned into a predatory smile.

"We have an hour before we meet everyone for dinner, correct?" I questioned as I looked up at him.

"Plenty of time for what I want to do to you, doll." His hand found its way around my throat and he gently forced me to lie back on the bed. It was only a second later Darius was on top of me and ripping away my clothes like a savage beast. I arched my back, pushing my body into his. He pulled away for just a moment to remove his clothes. I drank in the sight of him. He was truly handsome, and when naked he was completely irresistible.

Our eyes locked, and Darius licked his lips. "May I?"

"Oh, I see," I teased. "An old dog can learn new tricks."

"I won't ask again, doll," a low growl escaped his lips.

"Just make sure you don't take so much that I can't stand after."

"Oh doll, when I am done with you, you won't be walking anywhere." The hand around my neck slid down my body, and both of his hands found my wrists and pinned them to the bed. Darius wasted no time before his fangs found their way into my neck. He gently grazed them against my skin which sent a shiver down my spine.

I moaned softly as they sank into my skin and pleasure coursed through my body. I thought I was in heaven until I felt him thrust inside of me. This is what true euphoria felt like.

I was his. I craved nothing else.

Darius pulled away from my neck and his emerald green eyes met mine. "Absolutely delicious." He licked away my blood that clung to his lips. With lust in his eyes, he went back to my neck and ran his tongue over where he had just bitten. Never once did he stop thrusting into me, but instead his pace and force increased.

I moaned even louder. I knew it was at a volume that could be heard from outside the tent, but I didn't care. It had been so hectic the past few months, I had nearly forgotten how good it felt to have him inside of me.

Nearly.

I felt my whole body quiver in pleasure as he pounded me harder and deeper than I even thought he could go.

It wasn't long before I reached my climax. I quickly found it once again after Darius had gone for seconds on the other side of my neck, and bliss completely took me over.

I felt him release deep inside of me. He pulled away from my neck but kept me pinned under him. A single bead of sweat dripped down the side of his face. His hair dangled in the space between us as he hovered just above me.

"You are not a Queen. You are a Goddess."

<h1 style="text-align:center">Four</h1>

W e all were up before the sun could peak above the horizon. Our horses and gear are all ready to go. To my surprise, it was Isa who was double-checking everything to make sure we were prepared for what was ahead.

Five horses were ready and waiting for us to mount and ride into the dense forest of Serafina. Ron, Xander, and Daphne each had their own horse. Isa and Andrei shared one. Leaving one left for Darius and me to share. There was a time it would have made me cringe to get into a car with him. Now, it filled me with excitement to have to share a horse with him.

I saw Isa knelt to make sure we had arrows and daggers accounted for. I took a deep breath and made my way to her. It was now or never.

"Can I talk to you?" I said as I stood behind her. I hadn't been this nervous to talk to someone in one hundred lifetimes.

"Nothing to talk about," she responded coldly and abruptly.

"Nothing?" I questioned. I could feel my blood boil under my skin. She clearly was upset about something. She had given attitude the entire time we had been here. Isa was the queen of passive aggressiveness. I knew something was bothering her from the first time she rolled her eyes upon our arrival. "Come on. I don't want any issues between us during this journey. I need to know that I can trust you."

"That's funny," Isa said as she finally stood and turned towards me. Her voice was sharp as she spoke. Her brows furrowed as she continued. "I have *always* been there for you. I am not sure why you *wouldn't* trust me."

"When I needed you most, you chose them."

"I chose my people," she said firmly.

"I used to be your people," I looked her up and down. I could barely recognize the woman who stood before me. "As Queen, I will choose my people. If I ever hear you speak against my people again like you did last night, I will end you," I growled. Before she could respond, I turned and walked back to Darius. He was packing a few things into the saddlebags. The forest was too dense to bring a cart of supplies. We could only bring what we could carry.

"How long do we have until we leave?" I said, grabbing his wrists.

"About fifteen minutes. Why?" His eyebrow raised in concern.

"That's enough time. I need to blow off some steam."

I watched as his face turned into pure delight as we snuck back into one of the tents nearby. The tent was nothing like the one we were in last night. It had the bare essentials, only the beds, one small table, and a few weapons that were hung on a rack. Two metal frame single beds sat on each side. Two men were seated lacing up their boots for the day. Their faces turned to pure shock and terror as we walked in. They all dropped what they were doing and knelt before Darius.

"My King," they all said in unison.

"Out," Darius said firmly. I watched as the men rushed to leave the tent, leaving us alone. As soon as the last man exited, Darius' body was pressed into me. His hand was under my chin as he lifted it and hungrily slammed his mouth to mine.

I reached down, quickly unfastened his pants, and pushed them down.

"Someone is extremely eager," Darius purred as he pulled away from our kiss.

"I need you. Now." I pushed him back onto one of the beds. Darius smirked and raised an eyebrow as he watched me undress. He took his cock in his hand and slowly stroked it. My excitement doubled as I watched how it grew for me. I quickly mounted him, and he grabbed onto my hips, slamming me down onto him.

I let out a moan as he stretched me. He kept his hands on my hips and guided me up and down slowly. My body was overwhelmed with pleasure. I put my hands on his chest and forced his body down onto the bed. My pace quickened as I rode him.

"Oh, you think you're in charge just because you're on top?"

I ignored him as I circled my hips with him buried deep inside me. Darius let out a groan as he tilted his head back, and his cock twitched inside me. I bounced faster, taking him in and out of me. I needed more of him. There was nothing I craved more than him.

He sat up and wrapped his arms around me tight.

"Playtime is over, doll," he said as he pounded into me harder than I could imagine. I arched my back and pressed my body into his, moans escaping my mouth in rhythm with his thrusts.

"You are mine, Sabrina. Mine to hold. Mine to fuck," he purred in my ear. "Tell me, doll. Tell me how much you love it when I fuck you." His voice was pure ecstasy in my ear. He slowed down his movements, pulled almost all the way out, and then slammed me back down. Darius repeated this over and over. My body gave into the pleasure as I begged him for more.

"I love it when you fuck me! Please don't stop," I pleaded as I clenched around his cock.

He flipped us over and pinned me under him. Relentlessly, he plowed into me. The bed collapsed under us, but that did not stop him from pounding. My eyes rolled into the back of my head, and everything around us melted away as he exploded inside me and groaned with pleasure.

We had been traveling for three hours and were all on high alert as we made our way through the dark and overgrown forest. It was completely different from what I remembered. The paths were filled with thorny vines that made it difficult to travel. Many times it was so thick we had to clear it away. The forest was so dry I didn't want to use my fire magic. I could have easily set the whole forest ablaze. Luckily Darius and Andrei had brought a machete and hatchet. Thorns twisted around every tree, the canopy was so dense with twisted vines and branches that no sunlight was visible, and the beautiful flowers that once thrived in Serafina were now wilted, dried, and black.

A purple haze hung from the trees like nothing I had ever seen before. It was translucent and snaked through the trees. I could feel magic vibrate from it as a shiver ran down my spine. Something about the feeling told me that this was evil magic at play. Even my years around Xander did not prepare men for the dark feeling that the haze provided. Whatever magic this was, it was meant to destroy Serafina.

"Lady Sabrina, If I may," Andrei said from behind me. "I believe we have passed this tree seven times."

I didn't want to admit it, but with how overgrown the forest was, I had no idea where I was going. I recognized nothing. My gaze fell to the tree in question. It had a huge hole in the center of it as if fire blasted through it.

"You're correct. Unfortunately, with how dense and dark it is hard to navigate."

"Navigating the darkness is my specialty. Let me ahead." Xander and his horse rushed to be ahead of us. I had previously been leading. I thought I knew my forest, but the centuries I had been gone changed everything.

I leaned back against Darius and heard as much as felt him chuckle under his breath. I looked up and saw that smirk that I was so familiar with.

It didn't take long for Xander to get us past the tree that we had been circling for hours. I wondered how close we were to the castle at this point. How many more hours would we have of traveling through the dark until we found some sort of light?

The journey thus far had been eerily silent. Too quiet. The lack of wildlife and even the lack of breeze had us on edge. Everyone stopped in their tracks when the bushes rustled around us. Wordlessly, we all readied our weapons and searched the darkness for the source of the sound. It had been so long since I had Shimmerthorne in my hands. The time after Dimitri's death had been full of work in the castle. Though I was not Queen of Titus, Darius made sure everyone treated me as such. I had spent time working with the human council members to make sure the humans were being taken care of. The last time I had used it was to destroy the orb that had kept us cursed.

One by one, masked fae jumped out and surrounded us. They were short, all with different shades of green skin, and each wielded a spear. Each of their elaborately carved wooden masks represented a different animal. There were eight of them in total. We all pulled our horses to a stop. As the ones in front of us pointed their spears at us.

"Who are you? We have not had anyone in this section of the forest in centuries!" The one in the wolf mask demanded.

"I am Sabrina Alexandra Saison, Queen of Serafina. I have returned to reclaim my throne and restore this land," I announced.

"Lies!" they all yelled.

"Queen Sabrina was murdered a millennium ago!" The lion-masked one exclaimed. I could feel Darius as he winced at the word murdered.

"It is true," Daphne and Xander spoke in unison. I turned to look at them.

Daphne's eyes filled with light as Xander's filled with darkness. The shadows around Xander flared and Daphne had a golden glow. "Queen Sabrina has returned. Are you to be the first to stand in her way and fall before her?"

All of the masked fae fell to their knees as they spoke.

"Ancient Ones! Please do not harm us! We mean no disrespect!" They pleaded.

Daphne and Xander's eyes returned to normal.

"I am glad to hear there will be no issue," Daphne said triumphantly.

"I would have ended the issue before it even began," Xander smirked.

The one with the bear mask stood, removing his mask. His blue hair fell to his shoulders as his mask was fully removed.

"My name is Tamir. I am the son of the elder of the earth fae. Please allow me to guide you back to our village. I am sure you are in need of rest."

"That would be lovely. Thank you, Tamir. Please, lead the way," I smiled down at him.

Five

The village was nestled in a clearing in the forest, and I rejoiced to feel the sun on my skin. The houses and buildings were constructed with sticks and leaves. It was a very small village with about ten buildings in total. Tamir took us to the stables, where we dismounted and housed our horses for our visit. There was one field and a small pasture. It looked as if it had seen better days. The crops were bare, and the livestock scarce.

Tamir had informed us that all the fae villages were now separated from each other and no communication or trade happened between any of them. The major cities no longer stood. They were now overgrown and corrupted by the purple mist. In many of those places, there was no sign a city had existed at all.

We were taken to the largest of the buildings in the center of the village. A large fire pit sat in the middle of the room. An older male with long, silver hair and pale green skin, aged with wrinkles, sat behind the fire with a long pipe in hand.

"Tamir. Do my old eyes fool me, or have you brought me our Queen and the Ancient Ones?"

"I have, father," Tamir said as we approached the fire. "We found them while on patrol. They have returned to restore Serafina."

"We have been awaiting your return, Queen Sabrina. Our lands are quite dark without you."

"I am glad to be back. I apologize for all that has fallen onto our lands."

"It is not you who needs to apologize, my Queen." The old man's eyes glared at Darius.

"I see you have brought the murderer," he paused, then looked towards Andrei and Isa, "and his peons."

A low growl escape Darius' mouth, and I gently squeezed his hand to try to relax him.

"Unfortunately, he was cursed and not in control of his thoughts or actions when he . . . when I was killed. That is also the reason it took me so long to return," I said.

"Cursed?" The elder raised his eyebrow.

"By my father. He cursed me to go into a blood frenzy for centuries. I craved Sabrina's blood more than air. I couldn't stop myself." Darius's voice cracked slightly as he spoke. The elder raised his hand to stop Darius from speaking more.

"That can be put behind us. I am glad you all have returned. I knew this day would come. A prophecy that has been passed down for generations telling of it." The elder sat his pipe down on the table next to him. "Serafina has been taken over by darkness. I am

179

sure you have seen the purple mist. It corrupts and makes the forest unlivable. Most of the forest is now filled with dead trees. The castle has been leaking this mist since shortly after the Queen's death. We call the area around the castle the Circle of Death. That is where it started, and it has slowly been spreading across the forest."

The elder stood and walked toward us, stopping before us.

"The Ancient Ones will fix everything and restore peace to Serafina. It has been prophesied."

"We will do our best," Xander and Daphne said in unison.

"Please, will you join us tonight as we celebrate your return?" The elder questioned.

"We would be honored," I smiled at him.

"The honor is ours, my Queen."

When they said celebrate, they truly meant it. Glowing orbs of lights danced in the air to illuminate the village. There were several bonfires around with people dancing and telling stories. Several people had carts outside their homes, passing out a variety of foods and beverages.

Daphne and I were a bit leery of trying any of it based on our last experience. However, that did not stop Darius or Andrei from having the time of their lives. I am pretty sure that they were already seven glasses deep between the two of them. Thoughts of the vernal equinox masquerade that I used to hold, and of the first time I met Darius came to my mind. It was clear that he was already drunk when he arrived. I had him removed before the ball had even ended.

Who would have thought that the two of us would have ended up with each other?

Daphne, Ron, and Xander were mingling with the fae native to this village. Ron was so excited to finally meet fae from the homeland. Everything was so new to him. He was truly in awe of it all.

To no one's surprise, Isa was nowhere to be found. I am sure she was inside somewhere.

"I hope you are enjoying the celebration," Tamir said from behind me, and I turned to face him.

"I am. You guys truly know how to throw a party."

"Your friends seem to be enjoying themselves as well." He motioned towards Darius and Andrei. They were now having a push-up competition with some of the warriors we had met earlier today. I chuckled and rolled my eyes as I heard Darius call out.

"Oh, this is nothing! Let's do it one-handed!" He put one arm behind his back and continued to do the push-ups.

Show off.

Do I impress you?

Always.

I turned back to Tamir. "Yes, it seems they are."

"Not everyone will be happy with your return, my Queen. Please make sure you tread carefully once you leave here," he said in a hushed tone.

"Thank you for the advice. I am sure we have a difficult road ahead."

"Indeed. After what happened, no one will be welcoming of your vampiric companions. Please keep that in mind as you travel. They may cause you more difficulties."

Xander, Ron, and the Elder then joined our conversation.

"The Elder said that he had some information that would be useful to us," Xander said as they merged into our circle.

"Indeed. I recommend that you travel south to Lake Kikami. There are rumors that a water fae lives there in solitude. He may know more about the darkness that has corrupted our lands."

"Do you know anything about this water fae?" Ron chimed in.

"Unfortunately no. I can tell you that the journey to the lake will take several days from here. Please take as much time as you need to rest before heading to your next destination."

Are you hearing this? I hope you aren't so drunk you aren't paying attention.

I am hearing every word. We will leave tomorrow night. Andrei and I will not be prepared to travel in the morning.

Darius was correct.

They were not out of bed until well past noon. Xander and Ron had to drag them out. Daphne, Ron, Xander, and I had spent that time with the villagers. Learning their stories. They had been so grateful that The Ancient Ones had returned. It was well known in Serafina that Daphne and Xander had been around long before the first Queen. They were highly respected.

Tamir and his warriors guided us for about an hour into the journey. They claimed it was a part of their patrol route. I was thankful that they accompanied us. It was nice to know that the people of Serafina were still kind, even after centuries of darkness and isolation.

"Continue south. After about another hour of travel, you will enter the Circle of Death. Waste no time there. Though the forest is dead, there are still monstrosities that thrive. You will need to travel several days through the Circle before you arrive to the lake."

"What kind of monstrosities?" Daphne questioned.

"Many kinds. Serafina is not as it was when you were last here. Many of us are too afraid to leave the village to see what is truly out there. The things I have seen still haunt my nightmares." Tamir looked up at me. "Be on your guard, all of you. For the Circle will claim you if you are not."

"Thank you again for all your help and assistance." I dismounted my horse and kneeled before Tamir to be at eye level with him. I took his hand in mine and a golden glow surrounded us. "Please use this magic to fertilize your lands. Your crops and livestock should forever have bountiful harvests."

"Thank you, my Queen. We are forever grateful for you." The warriors all bowed as I stood. I looked around and the section of the forest we stood in was now filled with life. Fae lights danced between the bright green leaves, and beautiful flowers bloomed all around. The twisted thorns had all vanished from sight.

"It looks like the restoration has begun," Darius said as he helped me back onto the horse.

A smile crossed my face as I took in the first of many steps to take back the land that was mine.

Six

Once we entered the Circle of Death, the air changed. It was stagnant. The trees were petrified, and the ground was bare, except for the purple haze that clung to it before creeping up to the branches of the trees.

We all rode in complete silence. The farther we traveled, the more my body tingled with anticipation. Darius's body behind me was also tense as he tightly gripped the reins.

Xander led the way through the Circle of Death, with Ron by his side. The two of them had seemed to grow closer since the journey began. Shadows emanated from them as they continued forward.

The wind shifted and put me even more on edge. Something wasn't right. I felt the hair on the back of my neck rise and goose bumps overtook my body. Before I could say anything, Ron's horse bucked, tossing him to the ground. All of our horses went crazy from the chaos. We all steered our horses away to not trample Ron, who was scrambling to stand. The ground started vibrating, and I realized what set off his horse. The tremor worsened as a giant wyrm erupted from the ground a few feet ahead of us.

It had red-brown scales, almost like rusted metal. There were no eyes, but as it roared into the sky, we got a front-row view of its many rows of serrated teeth. Xander rushed and scooped Ron up off the ground, throwing him on the back of his horse as the wyrm dove towards him. It barely missed them as its face slammed into the ground.

Darius quickly regained control of the horse as I aimed my bow and released an arrow imbued with fire. As the wyrm lifted its body, the arrow struck into its chest. A roar filled the air as it writhed in pain. Shortly after my arrow struck, I saw missiles of light strike. Daphne dashed ahead of us and I watched as light left her hand and impaled the wyrm. They ripped and tore into the wyrm's scales. Its black blood sprayed over us as it took hit after hit.

The monster again slammed into the ground, almost hitting Isa and Andrei. Isa jumped off the horse and onto its head, her twinblade already in hand. Before the wyrm could rise from the ground, Isa impaled it with her blade atop its head. The wyrm thrashed as it tried to knock her off. Isa's face was cold and collected as she drove the blade deeper, not stopping until it moved no longer.

"Is everyone alright?" Darius called out.

Everyone took stock of each other. Other than our adrenaline rushing, we were all ok. Ron's horse was nowhere to be found, but we did not want to risk going off our path to find it. He and Xander agreed to ride together.

"What the fuck was that?" Isa questioned as she slid her twinblade into its sheath that was attached to her back.

"Nothing like that had ever lived in Serafina during my rule, or a hundred rules before mine.," I responded. I remember reading a book long ago about how wyrms roamed this land before the first Queen, but she made it her mission to hunt them to extinction so her people would be safe.

"They did once live here," Xander said as he looked back, his shadows still on high alert. They whirled and flared around him, as if ready to strike. "Many years before the fae roamed Serafina, it was filled with creatures like the wyrm. It seems in your absence that they have returned."

"We should be mindful of what else has returned to these lands." Daphne's voice shook as she spoke.

"Indeed," we all said in unison.

We continued after our encounter with the wyrm. We wanted to make sure we got through the Circle as fast as possible. Unfortunately for Ron, we never found his horse. After all the warnings and the encounter with the wyrm, I wondered if Isa was right. Should we have stayed in Titus for our safety?

The Terrain had been flat so far during the journey. It was nothing like the mountainous terrain of Titus. The past few miles of our trek had been different. The incline had continuously gotten steeper. There was one peak in all of Serafina, and of course, we had to pass over it. It was the fastest way to the lake. We did not want to waste any time going around it.

It was always told that the gods had cut off the peak for it once touched the sky and pierced their home. The top was now a wide plateau.

We finally got to the plateau and decided we needed to take a rest. Nightfall was upon us. The last of the sun's light kissed the sky, casting a red glow on the clouds. From the plateau, you could see all of Serafina. Once what was covered in treetops and fae lights was now a gray forest of petrified wood and that damned purple mist.

I slipped off the horse once it came to a stop and took a deep breath. I could feel my heart pounding in my chest as I looked to the east. My heart plummeted into my stomach.

Ruins.

My home was in ruins.

What once was a beautiful limestone two-story palace, adorned with gold accents and greenery, was now ruins. Only about half of my home remained standing. The gold was now tarnished, twisted vines weaved throughout the stone, and that purple haze leaked from every crack and window.

It felt surreal. As if this was all some terrible nightmare that I would soon wake from. Though there were few trees on the plateau, I felt as if the branches reached around me. Everything closed in. My vision tunneled onto the castle. Everything else was in a blur. My legs wobbled under me. I was no longer in control of my own body. A sharp ringing filled my ears. A numbing pain washed over me. I fell to my knees from the weight of everything stacked on my shoulders.

This was my fault.

I am the reason Serafina was corrupted by this darkness.

A heavy hand gripped my shoulder, sending a shock through me, causing all of my emotions to freeze briefly. I looked up and Darius was standing behind me. His green eyes were misted. He tried to hide the pain, but he couldn't hide it from me.

I am sorry.

Calm washed over me as I heard his voice in my mind. Darius walked around to the front of me, kneeled, and gently lifted my chin. He put his forehead to mine, and our eyes locked. Those green eyes that I loved so much. Somehow, he made everything around us disappear.

It was just us. The ringing in my ears subsided.

Focus on me, doll. Eyes on me.

The numbing pain faded as I heard his words. My body fell into his, and all at once the pressure broke me. I collapsed into his chest and sobbed for what felt like hours. Darius held me in a tight embrace. His hand gently stroked my back.

I then felt another set of arms wrap around me, and then another. I looked up from Darius' chest. Isa and Daphne joined in, trying to comfort me. The nothingness that surrounded Darius and me had now faded back into the scenery at the plateau.

"We are here for you," Daphne said softly.

"We will fix this," Isa was the first to stand and take a step back, "together." She gave me a warm smile, something I had not seen in ages from her.

"Together," I said back to her—to all of them. Darius released me as I stood. A smoky scent now filled my nostrils. I looked around and in a perfect ring around me was scorched earth, puddles of water, and jagged rocks. I looked down at Darius, who was still knelt in front of me.

I had lost control. I knew I had. The surrounding scene left all the evidence I needed to tell me my power exploded as I fell into despair. Yet, here he was, knelt in front of me. Somehow, he was able to avoid the power and bring me back.

That man walked through flames to save me.

My eyes stayed locked with his as he stood.

"Well, now that that's over, let us set up camp for the night."

"I will take the first watch," Ron said.

Seven

I opened my eyes and purple filled my vision, and when I sat up from my bed and looked around, everyone was gone. The purple haze was so dense that I could barely see five feet in front of me. I saw a tall male silhouette through the haze and I stood.

"Darius? Is that you?" I called out to the figure. It just stood there with no response.

"Andrei?" I called out once more. The figure again was still unresponsive. It was too tall to be Xander or Ron. I began to walk toward the figure, and it vanished.

"Hello? Who's there?" I called out once again. The purple haze grew thicker, and I heard a deep chuckle from behind me. Spinning around, I once again saw the figure in the distance.

"As the Queen of Serafina, I demand you announce yourself!"

Again, I was met with silence. I rushed towards the taunting shadow, and again it vanished.

Over and over, it would reappear and I would chase it. I was never able to catch up to the silhouette.

An overwhelming sense of despair filled my body as I pursued the figure. Where was everyone? Where was I? Would I ever be able to catch up to the being and find my way out of this mist?

"There is no escape. Serafina is mine. I will destroy you and your friends, just as I did your home." The voice was dark and rich, like cold velvet to my ears.

My eyes went wide as the morning sun began to light the sky with soft yellows and oranges intertwined with the clouds. I looked over and saw the others almost done packing up camp. I sat up and stretched my arms above my head as I yawned.

"Why didn't you guys wake me? I could have helped pack up."

"We thought it best we let you sleep, my lady," Andrei said as he handed me a bowl with some berries. My eyes lit up at the sight of them. I popped one in my mouth and the flavor burst on my tongue as the sweet juices slid down my throat.

Darius came and sat by my side as I finished eating. He clenched his jaw and looked up as if in thought. I looked over at him and raised an eyebrow.

"Seems like you did not sleep well," his voice was nonchalant.

"No, I did not," I said closing the conversation. I was not ready to talk about the nightmare I had. I felt his presence in my mind, ready to ask more questions, but I quickly shut him out.

Eight

Kikami Lake was once the most beautiful lake in all of Serafina. The shimmering aquamarine water was one of our greatest natural wonders. Not only was the water always perfectly warm, but the lake also healed most who submerged in it. Fae would travel long distances to the lake to take advantage of its healing properties if they had any kind of ailment.

The story of the lake's creation was one of the most told stories in all of Serafina.

Long before Serafina was Serafina, a small tribe of water fae had traveled there in search of a better life. They had been told that there was a beautiful lake there that would bring their people to glory. When they arrived, all they found was a small puddle. Without more water, the tribe would not last. Their priestess told them to stay and pray, and that the lake would come to them.

That is just what they did.

They prayed for three days and two nights with no answer. On the third night, they finally were sent what they so desperately needed.

The god Tempuno sent down heavy rains that expanded the puddle into a great lake. The goddess Stelini sent down shooting stars that landed in the lake to give the lake its mystical shimmer. The tribe rejoiced and named the lake after their priestess, Kikami. For thousands of years, Kikami Lake brought prosperity to that water tribe.

Now, the lake was nothing but a memory. Dry and cracked land stretched before us, completely barren of any life. It was very evident no one had been here in many years.

"This can't be all there is," Isa said as she looked around.

"I wonder how old the elder's information was," Darius grumbled. "Seems like he had no idea what he was talking about."

I watched as Daphne dismounted her horse and began to examine the ground. She walked towards the center of the lake. Daphne looked as if she was searching for something. Daphne's gaze focused on the ground.

"Daphne, what is it?" I called out to her. She raised a finger into the air to tell me to wait, but Ron dismounted his horse and began to follow her on foot. We all watched in silence as they examined the ground. Once they were about fifty feet from us, I watched as they both sunk into the ground, completely vanishing. Xander screamed out to them as I watched him sprint past us on his horse.

"Ron? Daphne? Come back!" He cried out in total panic.

We all followed after him, stopping right before where they sunk into the ground.

"No! No, no, no, no! I can't lose you," Xander was in total panic as he dismounted, dove into the ground, and vanished. I heard Darius let out an exacerbated sigh from behind me.

"Well, I guess we will go next," Andrei chuckled as he dismounted and helped Isa off their horse.

"I did not plan on going mud diving today. Do you think it will ruin my good hair day?" Darius chuckled as he dismounted.

"Guys this is no time for jokes!" I said as Darius helped me down. Darius rolled his eyes and Isa came by my side, extending her hand.

"All together?"

"All together," I took her hand. We stepped forward in unison and quickly sank through the mud. This was one of the worst things I have ever experienced. I felt the slimy and gritty mud coat my body. We passed through the mud for only about thirty seconds before we fell into a cave. All of us hit the ground hard. The other three were there waiting for us. Xander was standing next to Ron, hovering over him asking him a million times if he was alright. He was. Thank the gods we all were. I watched as Darius roughly wiped his hands over his body, trying to remove the mud that coated him.

"This shit is absolutely disgusting," he mumbled and groaned as he tried to get clean. I focused hard on my magic as I pulled the humidity from the air, forming a small cloud above us. Rain fell from the cloud and washed away the mud on us. Once all the mud was gone, I dispersed the cloud.

"You look like a wet dog," Xander said in Darius' direction.

"Watch it," Darius growled back at him. His hair clung to his skin. He shook his hair to get rid of the excess water.

I finally looked around at where we were. The cave forked into two directions. Glowing crystals were nestled into the walls. They were the only light source, but they did the job well enough.

"Well, which way should we go?" Ron questioned as he looked towards me. My eyes darted back and forth, trying to decide where to go.

"This way." I had no rhyme or reason for picking this direction. Hopefully, it took us somewhere we wanted to go. We traveled for a short time. The only sound was water droplets falling to the cave floor. The tunnel never split off into any more paths.

Eventually, the tunnel widened and led us to a large, open room. As I looked around, I noticed several tables scattered around the room. Some were tipped over, but the ones still upright were filled with books, journals, and what looked like alchemical ingredients.

I walked further into the room to get a better look and saw that some of the books and journals, both on the tables and scattered across the floor, had pages torn out or were marred with burn marks and singed pages.

Ron walked over and picked up a few.

"This is the writing of a madman," he said as he looked over the papers in his hand.

"What does it say?" I walked over to him and picked up some of the sheets. Absolute gibberish was scribbled all over the pages. Front and back, they were covered in symbols that I did not recognize. The group was now all picking up papers of their own.

I saw Daphne and Xander lock eyes. A look of shock and realization appeared on their faces.

"What is that look about?" Darius questioned as I watched him try to read one of the papers. Xander raised an eyebrow toward Darius.

"That's upside down," Xander said with a chuckle under his breath. Darius quickly turned the page the correct way.

"I knew that! I just wanted to see if anyone else knew." Darius' eyes darted around. He then turned away to examine one of the tables.

"It's ok. We all know you are the smartest vampire in Titus," Xander gave a wink to Andrei, who was trying to hide his smile.

I was glad to see everyone get along, even if it was just for this brief moment.

"This is an ancient language that I have not seen in thousands of years," Daphne began in a serious tone. All eyes fell toward her as she gathered more pages.

"So far, what I have seen is about time travel and resurrection," Xander said as he flipped through the pages in his hand. "What about you, dear sister?"

"Theories on how to summon The Ancient Ones and the gods, potions to be made, and a list of ingredients." Daphne studied one of the pages in her hand, a confused look on her face. "This is a recipe for beef stew."

"This page is titled 'Unfortunate Souls from Realms Beyond' and lists fae, humans, sunflowers, thorns, betrayal, and revenge." Xander looked toward me as if somehow I could make sense of it. I looked at the mess all around us, wondering who did this and why.

"Ah ha!" Darius exclaimed from the other side of the room. "Mushrooms! That explains how crazy this is!"

Glancing over, I smiled and shook my head when I saw what he found. Darius was right. The mushrooms that grew in Serafina had a psychedelic effect. The amount varied on the species, but all of them had that effect to some degree.

"So, most of this is complete nonsense?" Isa said as she sat atop one of the tables.

"Appears so," Darius said as he opened a small red box. As he did, a red mist poured out of it and filled the room. My lungs stung as I inhaled it. It dissipated as quickly as it appeared. I tried to speak to see if everyone was alright, but I couldn't.

I couldn't move at all. We all were perfect statues, and we stood there for what seemed like hours. Who knows how much time had passed before I heard an unfamiliar raspy voice.

"Who are you? How did you get in here?" A tall, lanky man stepped into my view. His skin was a pale blue, and a cold void filled his gray eyes as they locked with mine. His long white hair was the only sign of his age. Most water fae had blue or green hair, even though I had heard of one rare occasion of scarlet red. I felt the muscles in my face relax as they were freed from whatever magic had the rest of me, and the others, paralyzed.

"I am Sabrina Saison, rightful Queen of Serafina. These are my traveling companions. I'm sure you recognize Daphne and Xander, especially how much of your notes have to do with summoning them. We were sent here by an earth fae elder. He told us you may have information on what is causing the darkness in Serafina, and perhaps how to stop it?"

The man looked me up and down before walking out of my line of sight. He was completely silent for some time. I then heard him exhale deeply.

"My name is Carlow. I am the last water fae that was native to Lake Kikami. I am a direct descendant of the Priestess Kikami. Her powers of premonition flow through my blood." Carlow walked back into my sight. "It is an honor to have you visit, Queen Sabrina."

I felt my body fully release from the magic, and when I looked around, I saw Ron, Daphne, and Xander also in motion.

"Thank you. The pleasure is mine, truly." I gave him a warm smile. Darius, Andrei, and Isa had yet to move. A look of concern grew on my face.

"I am sorry. I have kept them frozen for my safety. I am sure you understand. For what Darius did to you, he should be executed."

I am sure many of the citizens of Serafina thought that way. Once we reclaimed our home, I would need to do damage control. I needed to find a way for my people to accept Darius. That may be more difficult than reclaiming Serafina.

"I understand. We are in your space. Thank you for your help."

Carlow nodded, walked over to one table, and removed one of the books from a pile. He opened it and his eyes scanned the page.

"I have been studying this for centuries and have been experimenting to find ways to restore the forest. Unfortunately, I have been unsuccessful in any restoration. However, I have learned more regarding what caused this darkness."

"Please, tell us more," I heard Xander say from behind me.

"The Darkness is seeded deep within the castle. I have seen him."

"Him?" We all said in unison.

"Oh, yes. Him," Carlow said in a mysterious tone. "He is tall, with skin as dark as night. Everything about him will draw you in. Early after your passing, he brought many fae into the castle, and they were never seen again. Even more maddening, the man hasn't been seen since the purple mist appeared."

Carlow sat down the book, gathered a few things that I could not see, then headed toward Darius. Before I could process what was happening, Carlow had taken a silver dagger, gave Darius a small cut, and collected the blood in a vial.

Fuck! That burns! Will you have him unfreeze me now? I am sick of this!

Darius' voice pounded in the back of my mind.

What are you waiting for?

Shush! Let me get the information I need first. Clearly, he isn't comfortable with you here. Just be patient.

A low snarl vibrated against my spine. I glared at Darius and shut him out of my head.

"Vampire blood is a great alchemical ingredient. It is the least he could do." Carlow corked the vial and quickly labeled it before putting it on one of the tables. It seemed as if everything had a specific home, even though to me everything was utter chaos. "I recommend you all head east. There is a dark fae village a several-day journey away. Rumor is that is where the man came from. They may be able to provide more information."

"Thank you. The information you've provided has been extremely helpful," Daphne spoke as she came to my side.

"Your glow is more magnificent than I ever imagined," Carlow said with a smile as he look at her in awe. Daphne gave a girlish giggle as her cheeks turned rosy. I had never seen her react to a compliment as she had just now. She was always so poised and put together. In the years she was by my side during my rule, she never had given anyone any attention in that way. If only I could read her mind at this moment.

"They have been attacked several times due to the rumor that is where the Darkness originated. They won't be the most welcoming. Keep that in mind as you approach them. I did find some horses up above. I assume they belong to you?"

"Yes, they do."

"Wonderful. Follow this path, and once it splits, go left. It will lead you to my stable. I housed your horses there when I found them." Carlow waved his hand toward the vampires.

"Finally!" Darius exclaimed. All eyes shot to him. "I was beginning to worry that we would be frozen forever." Carlow's gaze went back to me.

"My Queen, while it was wonderful to have you here, your leech companions are not welcome to stay."

"I understand. We will be on our way. Thank you for the information." Before Darius could say anything else, I shot him a glare.

Say a single word. I dare you to disrespect him and not feel my wrath.

Darius put his hands up in surrender.

We all left the tunnel together, with Carlow guiding us out. I'm sure he just wanted to keep a close eye on the vampires to make sure they weren't going to go snooping anywhere.

Once at the stable, we mounted our horses and rode out. Carlow reminded us of the directions to the dark fae village. As I gave him my final thanks, thunder rolled, and lightning cracked across the sky. Heavy rains began to fall, and it wasn't long before the dry lake began to refill with water. We barely made it to the lake's edge before we were swept away by the large amount of water.

We all watched in amazement as the area around us came back to life. Willows quickly grew around the lake, and lily pads and lotus flowers sprang up from the waters. In a matter of moments, the lake was filled.

The sky cleared and the moon's reflection appeared in the water. Carlow turned to me with a look of awe and excitement on his face.

"The lakebed has been dry for centuries. I don't know what you did, but thank you."

Darius gently elbowed me and pointed to the sky. The clouds had cleared and revealed a meteor shower. Stardust danced around us as a few of the stars fell into the lake. The lake's water gave a soft glow as the water started to shimmer.

<h1 style="text-align:center">Nine</h1>

The trip to the dark fae village was even longer than our previous journey. We had been traveling already for two days and still had several days ahead of us. I was relieved to not have any more of those purple haze nightmares. I had assumed that they were just a product of my anxiety. We had set up camp for the night. I could tell everyone was exhausted. We did not get much time for rest. We traveled from sunup to sundown, only taking one short break at midday. Darius became increasingly silent as the day progressed. It was normal for him not to speak aloud, but he didn't even communicate with me through our bond.

I watched as he got increasingly more irritated as he sharpened his blade. He quickly sheathed it and stood.

"I'm going to take a walk," he said before quickly making his way away from camp, not allowing anyone to even respond to him. Everyone gave me a look questioning what was wrong. I shrugged my shoulders in response. Their eyes stayed on me. I sighed and stood, following Darius into the forest. I hated it when he was in one of his moods, but I had to figure out what was wrong with him.

"Dar, wait for me!"

"Go back to camp," his voice was sharp. He didn't even turn to look at me as he spoke.

"No, it's dangerous to go alone!"

"I don't need you to protect me, doll," he snarled at that last word.

"What is wrong with you? Why are you being like this?" I finally caught up to him and grabbed his wrist. He turned towards me and grabbed me by my neck and slammed me into a tree. Pain vibrated down my body. His eyes were that blood-red hue I was too familiar with.

"What's wrong with me?" He chuckled. "*You're* what is wrong with me. I feel like I have to be fucking perfect when I am around you. I have tried to curb my hunger. I haven't fed off a human since the curse ended, because of you!" His grip around my neck grew tighter. He leaned in and breathed in deeply. "Your scent is still so intoxicating it drives me insane!" Darius' face was only an inch from mine, and our eyes locked.

My body shuddered. I had not felt like this since we had been locked in the dungeon together. I felt like that terrified human girl. I know I'm not that person anymore.

"Stop it. This isn't who you are," I whimpered to him.

"Is it not?" He dropped me, throwing his hands in the air. My back slid down the tree, causing my skin to burn as the bark scraped against me. I landed firmly on my ass. "I am a monster. I was before you met me. I am one now. That is how your people will see me!" Pain and rage filled his voice. He turned away from me, taking a few steps.

"That's not how I see you." My voice was soft as I looked up at him. I blinked, and he was now knelt in front of me. His face was still so close to mine, fangs visible. His entire body was predatorily still.

"How do you see me then?" His voice was low and quiet.

"As the man I love. The man I gave up everything to be with. The man who fights by my side. My people will come around. They will soon see you as the man who saved Serafina from the darkness."

"If they don't? What if they only see me as the one who let Serafina fall?"

"I am their Queen. They have no sway over who I choose to be with."

Darius said nothing in response for a moment as he stared into my eyes. I could feel the air charge around us.

"Even if I am a monster?" He gently raised his hand and stroked my cheek with the back of his fingers.

"Even if you are a monster."

"Good." A smirk grew across his face. He quickly grabbed me by my hair and yanked to expose my neck. His tongue ran up my neck. "Sorry, doll." His fangs sunk into my delicate skin. I didn't fight him. I knew if he didn't satisfy his hunger, things would only get worse between us.

While still feeding from me, his hand roughly grabbed my waist and pull down my pants. His fingers found their way inside me, and He continued to drink from me as he roughly played with my most intimate parts. I felt myself getting soaking wet for him. Soft moans escaped my lips, and I begged him for more.

He pulled away from my neck. Blood trickled down the side of his mouth. He wiped it away with his tongue.

"Look at you. What a little whore, begging to be fucked on the forest floor," his voice pulled me into him. I needed him. I needed all of him.

"Please..." Was the only word I could conjure.

"Please, what? I want to hear you beg for me."

"Please fuck me. I need you inside me. Please."

"Worship me, doll. Show me how much you need me," Darius chuckled as he stood, removing his cock from his pants.

My mouth watered as I got up on my knees and slowly licked him up and down. Darius shuddered as my tongue dragged across his cock. He placed his hand on top of my head to guide me. I licked my way down, taking his balls into my mouth, and sucked on them gently.

"Good little whore," Darius purred as I licked my way back up him. "Take me in your mouth." His voice was firm and demanding.

I obliged.

I opened my mouth and took his tip inside, circling my tongue around it. Darius pushed forward, forcing me to fall back against the tree. My body was pinned to it as he shoved more of him into my mouth. My eyes locked on his as he thrust in and out of my mouth slowly, his cock hitting the back of my throat.

Darius picked up his pace, causing me to gag on his cock. Keeping his hand atop my head to keep me in place, he used my mouth as his toy. Over and over, his cock pounded the back of my throat. My eyes watered as he showed me no mercy.

"This is what happens from now on when you run your bratty mouth. Do you understand, doll?" He groaned as he pushed in deep and held it there. I gagged hard and tried to pull away, but the tree and his hand kept me in place. "Nod if you understand."

I nodded.

This only caused him to destroy my throat. He went faster and harder than I imagined he could. My drool coated him and dripped down his balls. He pulled his cock out fully and sat it on my face, slapping it hard on my cheek. My eyes crossed as he sat it back in the center of my face, my mouth still open and my tongue out. Ready and waiting for more of him.

"Such a good little whore," Darius smirked as he smacked me again with his cock. He reached down and grabbed me, yanked me up, and pinned me against the tree. My legs wrapped around him, and he sheathed himself inside me.

"You feel perfect around me. Absolutely perfect," he groaned.

"Please don't stop," I pleaded.

"I love it when you beg." He leaned forward, pressing deeper inside me. My body quivered from the overwhelming pleasure. An explosion of stars filled my eyes.

His mouth crashed into mine. Hunger. All I felt was pure hunger as our tongues danced. His pace quickened.

He pulled his mouth away from mine. His tongue dragged across his upper lip. I dug my nails into his back as he slammed me down onto him. He roared as he came inside me, causing the trees around us to quake.

"Mine," he growled.

"Yours," I moaned in response.

Darius gently set me down and kissed me on top of my forehead. My legs felt numb under me, but Darius took my hand and helped me stay steady.

"Beautiful. Absolutely beautiful," he said softly as he helped me put my pants back on.

The purple mist was once again all around me. A feeling of hopelessness filled my core. I looked around frantically. I tried to call out to Darius, but when I opened my mouth, no words came out. I was alone.

I heard a familiar chuckle from behind me. Warm breath tickled my ear, causing a chill to run down my spine. I spun around, but no one was there. I tried again to call out for Darius. Silence. My mouth grew so dry.

"You did this," I heard that same male voice. "You allowed me to ruin Serafina." Again, my gaze went to where I heard the voice, but no one was there. From a new location, I heard the voice once again. "A blood whore doesn't deserve to be queen."

Those words stung deeper than anything I had felt before. My body grew numb as I felt the weight of my burdens overwhelm me. This mysterious voice was right. It was all my fault, and I was no closer to fixing the damage I had caused. I couldn't catch my breath, a high-pitched ringing filled my ears, And I felt a tremor beneath my feet right before a large boom sounded off in my head.

I crouched down, knees to my chest and hands on top of my head.

"Stop it!" I begged as tears streamed from my eyes.

I heard the boom once again. I swear it almost sounded like my name.

"Go away!" I commanded.

"Sabrina!" I heard Darius' voice call to me, pulling me out of the hell I had found myself in.

I shot awake. Darius was on top of me, hands on my shoulders, worry and concern all over his face. I couldn't seem to catch my breath as our eyes stared deep into each other.

"You were screaming for me," he said softly, "are you alright?"

"I have been having these dreams," I whimpered as tears still fell from my eyes. The feelings of hopelessness lingered in my waking world. "I am lost in the purple mist. A figure—a man — keeps taunting me, telling me that Serafina belongs to him. That he will destroy me and all that I love."

Darius pulled me into his chest. He held me in a tight embrace and gently played with my hair. "We will end him. We will reclaim Serafina and restore it to its glory. Look at what you did for the earth fae village. What you did for the lake. Change is coming, and you are the harbinger."

"You really think I am worthy? That I am strong enough?"

"I know you are. Sabrina, you are the most resilient person I know." He gently kissed the top of my head.

"I love you."

"I love you, too." Darius gently laid us down and held me tight in his arms. "Sleep, my love. I will protect you."

I looked over and saw the others were fast asleep. I wondered for a moment what they were dreaming about.

Finally calmer, I nestled into his chest, closed my eyes, and drifted back asleep.

Ten

The section of the forest we were in was the most confusing yet. It was incredibly dense, and there was not any evidence that a trail had ever been there. We had traveled for hours, and no matter which direction we went, we always came back to the same tiny burrow. It was the only hint that any animals still resided in this part of the forest.

"This isn't working," Daphne said from behind me. "Xander, you are just getting us more lost. Let someone else take the lead."

"No, I will find the way. I am very familiar with this village. I know where I am going."

"Clearly not," Ron responded. "Go this way. See those purple mushrooms? Follow them." He pointed down to the ground where mushrooms were scattered about. They seemed to lead off into the distance. Xander huffed as we all turned our horses to follow them.

The mushrooms led us through a clear and direct path through the forest. Ron was a genius. I wondered how he knew the mushrooms would guide our way. I also wondered what connections Xander had to the dark fae village we were headed towards.

Long before the curse, he was always a secretive one. He would leave the castle and be gone for weeks at a time, never telling me where he went or what he was up to.

If I knew then what I know now, I would have kept a closer eye on his affairs.

Hours after we started following the mushrooms, the village finally came into sight. It was surrounded by a wall of thorns. It was about ten feet tall. The thorns were so tightly woven there was not a spot for light to pass through. The colors of muted greens, blues, and purples mixed. My heart sank into my stomach as I recognized them. They matched the thorns that had overtaken my castle.

Carved out of the thorns was a single entrance into the village. Two dark fae men wearing deep purple armor, wielding halberds, stood guard at the entrance.

"They look friendly," Isa said under her breath. Daphne shot her a glare.

"You could try to be positive," Daphne retorted.

"That was me being positive." Isa rolled her eyes.

"I think you two should go talk to them," Andrei said to Ron and Xander. "You are both dark fae. They most likely will be accepting of you. Test the waters for us."

"You have a good point," Xander nodded. "Ready to meet more of us?" He turned to Ron, who glowed with excitement.

The two of them marched forward toward the village. The rest of us all stayed hidden a good bit away. I gently tapped my fingers against my thigh as I watched them with anticipation.

"Will you stop fidgeting?" Darius whispered in my ear, a bit of annoyance in his voice. "It's distracting. I am trying to listen to them."

"Sorry," I whispered back to him. "I'm nervous."

Darius gently grabbed my hand, squeezed it, and a wave of calm washed over me. Ron and Xander approached the guards and began to speak with them. They were too far away for me to hear anything being said. I prayed to the gods that everything was going well.

"The guards are cautious of them," Darius said. I craned my neck to look up at him. His eyes were glued to Ron and Xander. "They are surprised to see outsiders who are dark fae."

A cloud of purple smoke appeared in front of Ron, and every muscle in my body tensed. When it dispersed, a gorgeous woman was standing there. She had dark olive skin and sleek dark hair that fell to the waist. She wore an extremely sheer dress with a low-cut V in the front.

I looked over to Daphne, who gave me a worried glance in response. I had met many dark fae while I ruled Serafina, but she was not someone I recognized. Based on the look Daphne gave, she did not either. When I looked back towards the village, the woman was gone.

"It is a bit rude to spy," a seductive voice came from behind us. We all whirled around. The woman now stood behind us, a sultry look in her eyes. "Don't be shy. Come introduce yourself." She paused, then looked at me and gave a slight bow. "Some of you don't need introductions. Welcome home, Your Majesty."

An exact clone of her appeared by her side. Darius' eyes went wide with a confused look on his face. He reached out and tried to touch the clone, but his hand went right through it. Daphne and I were used to this kind of magic, but it seemed the others were shocked by it. Out of all the things in Serafina we have seen, I was surprised that they were shocked by anything at this point.

"I will take your horses to the stable for you," the clone said as she gathered the reins.

Darius quickly moved so that he stood between the mysterious woman and me. The woman chuckled and gave him a judgmental glance.

"Ah, such a big strong vampire you are. It's ok. I understand that the only person allowed to kill our Queen is you," she hissed. I heard Darius release a low growl in response. "Come along now. Let's get you all into the village, shall we?"

The woman floated past us and waved for us to follow her. Andrei and Darius gave each other a knowing glance, as I watched Andrei ready his dagger, just in case. We all followed her to the gate. Ron and Xander looked shocked as we approached.

"No one hiding in the trees?" One of the guards snarled at them.

"You are in the presence of the Queen of Serafina and her," she paused and gave Darius another judgmental glare, "partner, the King of Titus. Stand down and show some respect," she commanded them.

They stood tall and withdrew. "Our apologies. Welcome to Ombryth." They bowed toward us.

"Come along friends. Let me take you to our Elder." She took Andrei and Isa by the hand and guided them first.

Daphne came by my side, gently tugging me back to keep a bit of distance between us and them. "I do not trust her. Be on your guard."

I nodded, and we followed the group into the village. My eyes were focused on Xander as I watched him scan the scene around us. He was trying to hide the worry on his face, but I could see right past his facade.

This village was nothing like the earth fae village we had visited. The buildings here were constructed of dark stone and were all nestled close together. Cobblestone paths snaked their way through the village, with black metal lantern posts stationed throughout the streets that gave off a dim purple light. It appears the darkness that corrupted Serafina had not touched this village. The trees were healthy, full of lush purple leaves. I could hear the songs of birds for the first time since returning to Serafina. Many dark fae filled the streets. They all parted and bowed as we approached them.

I like it here. Seems like we get the respect we deserve. Darius spoke to me, mind to mind.

Something seems off, though. Isn't it odd how she immediately gravitated toward Andrei and Isa?

Are you jealous, doll? I mean, if you want a threesome, say the word.

Pervert. I rolled my eyes at his response and shut him out of my mind.

The woman guided us to one of the most beautiful churches I had ever seen. The dark stone seemed to shimmer as the purple fae light glowed against it. Each of the windows had stained glass artwork of one of our gods and goddesses.

I swore I saw Hinaki wink at me as we passed her window, and Tempuno and Stelini gaze proudly as we passed theirs. My eyes were stuck on the moon, the rain, and the stars featured in each window. We approached a beautiful mahogany door with ornate flowers and filigree carved into the wood. On each side of it were more stained glass windows; Astrid, goddess of day, was to the right, and Astor, god of night, to the left.

Both had an uncanny resemblance to Daphne and Xander. Astrid had a beautiful sunglow behind her, and Astor was shrouded by shadows. It reminded me so much of the day I reunited with Xander in his prison.

When we stepped through the door and entered the church, it was completely silent. Several people in tan hooded robes kneeled before an altar in the center of the room. On the altar was a shimmering gold sun and a matte black moon. The pews all faced toward the center and formed a circle. A few people sat in the pews. Some were praying, and some were reading. No one glanced up at us as we passed them and went to a staircase in the back of the church.

The stairs led us to a small office where an older dark fae sat at a desk, a quill in hand as he scribbled into a book in front of him. His hair was pale gray, peppered with evidence of what once was dark locks. His dark skin contrasted with his hair and his robes were different from the others. His were as black as the void, with golden accents on the edges.

He looked up and his black eyes met mine and he gave a warm smile and looked towards the woman who brought us here.

"Priestess Morgana," he acknowledged her presence. He then turned to Xander and his dark features lit up. "Xander! My old friend, it has been too long. I am glad to see you are doing well." He stood from his chair and approached Xander wrapping him in a hug, who to my surprise, hugged him back.

"It is good to see you too, Orlok. I am surprised you are still here," Xander responded. To be honest, I was also surprised. Orlok had been the Elder of the dark fae even when I reigned. I had met him several times, and he was always very clear on where he stood concerning the relationship I had with Darius. I was a bit nervous to see how he would respond to our return.

"You know the darkness keeps us young." Orlok's eyes then fell on Ron and then back to Xander. I saw a look of terror cross Xander's face as Orlok spoke. "A son! I cannot believe you have a son! I can sense his powers are identical to yours! You must be so proud."

Everyone froze and waited for Xander's response. No way was that true. He had been locked away for centuries. How could he have fathered a son? How could he not say a word of it to anyone?

"Yes," Xander swallowed hard. "I am very proud of him." I saw the look of betrayal cross Ron's face. His mouth pressed into a firm line.

"You are my father?" His voice shook as he spoke.

"I am," Xander said matter-of-factly. Orlok's face changed into a look of shock as if he was the one embarrassed by this reveal. Maybe he was? Maybe he was embarrassed to call it out.

My mind flashed back to that encounter on the porch. The way he looked at Ron and Cora. The way Cora looked at him. How, even in the times of the curse, Ron could control the shadows around him. The evidence was here all along. I was too wrapped up in my drama to notice.

Ron didn't say another word. He gave Xander a look of anger and disappointment before heading back down the steps. Xander did not stop him.

"I..." Orlok began. Xander quickly cut him off.

"Don't. The truth would have always come out. He was bound to find out, eventually."

"How? You were imprisoned. Why did you not tell anyone? Why did you not tell me?" Daphne began to fire off one question after another.

"Cora used to bring me my weekly supplies. At first, she would drop them off and run. Over time, she would stay and talk. We grew close. We fell in love and became intimate. She told me she was with child, I was over the moon. The week after, Silas started making the deliveries. I never saw her again and had no idea what happened to our child, until that day on the porch," his voice trailed off.

Orlok put his hand on Xander's shoulder. "I know what it is like to have a son you are not close with," he said somberly. "I have not spoken to mine since the Queen's death."

"I am sorry to hear that. I have always wondered how you two have been after all these years."

"Neither here nor there," Orlok said as he went back to his desk. "So, what brings you here?"

"We are investigating the Darkness that has taken over Serafina. We heard rumors that you may have some information," I spoke and came forward.

"How should we know what is causing it? Just because we are dark fae, you think we are involved?" Orlok's eyes narrowed. His face twisted with disdain.

"Orlok, she did not mean it that way," Xander spoke up on my behalf.

"You allowed them to come all this way to judge us? Shame. I always thought better of you," venom dripped on his words.

Morgana, who had been draping herself around Isa and Andrei, left their side and came to stand by Orlok. Her face filled with the same disdain.

"I meant no disrespect," I said softly, hoping to calm the situation. "Clearly, the rumors we heard were false."

"Disrespect taken. Please, all of you, leave," Morgana said forcefully.

"Orlok. This is a bit ridiculous. Is it not?" Xander asked. He took a step toward the desk. "Let us just start again."

"No. Out. Leave my village. All of you," Orlok said, looking back at his papers.

"Are you fucking serious?" Darius exploded. "Your Queen is here asking for help to restore Serafina, and *this* is how you treat her?" He pushed past us all to get to the front of the desk. His eyes were red and filled with rage. "Treat her with respect."

Orlok did not even look up from his papers as he responded. "The Darkness is your fault. You are nothing to us, Darius Dragomier. You do not deserve our respect. You never have."

I blinked, and Andrei was now in front of Darius. His hands were on his shoulders. "Come on, it's time we leave," Andrei said in a whisper to Darius. Darius snarled in response, and my body tingled with emotions as if they were my own. I stepped behind him, gently taking his hand in mine. He snapped towards me, then froze as he looked into my eyes.

"Let's go," I said softly. The tingling dimmed as he nodded. We all headed down the steps. Xander stayed behind.

"Serafina deserves better than the way you acted today." I could have sworn I heard Xander say through the sound of echoed footsteps.

Ron was standing outside the church, waiting for us. He was leaning against the cold stone, staring up into the sky. Next to him was Astor's window. I was sure that the face had changed to a more somber look. Ron asked what was wrong as we quickly stormed out of the village.

"The fae here have sticks up their asses," Darius responded as we finally cleared the gate. Four guards now guarded the entrance, making it very clear we were not welcome back. Once we stepped outside of the walls they blocked our path back in, their weapons ready. Darius gave them a vulgar gesture. Ron stood on the far side of the group, away from Xander.

We made our way to the stables where Morgana had taken our horses in silence. The revelation of Ron's lineage caused tension between us. Why would Xander hide this from me, his sister or his son?

Andrei walked by Darius' side trying to talk him out of slaughtering the whole village. This was not the first time Orlok had disrespected Darius, but Darius wanted so badly to make it his last.

Xander stopped in his tracks as we approached the stables. "Ron, I am sorry. That is not how I wanted you to find out. I did not know what Cora had told you, and I wanted to speak with her first before saying anything. I did not get a chance before we left the village," he said somberly.

We all stopped and faced him. Ron was the last to look toward Xander.

"So, my mother's feelings about this are more important than mine?" He said with anger.

"No. Not at all," Xander huffed. "I just... I don't know how to be a dad. I worried about you every day for fifteen years. I wondered who you were, what were you like, and if you were alright? When I finally realized you were fine, I did not want to ruin that." Xander stepped towards Ron. "In case you haven't noticed. I ruin everything. I don't want to ruin you, too."

A cool breeze hit our backs. Everyone stayed silent for some time as the two stared at each other. Before either of them could say anything else, a man in a tan robe came towards us. He was one of the men we saw at the church. I watched as Darius gripped the hilt of his sword and Andrei readied his daggers.

"I mean no harm," the man heaved as he came to a stop. He slowly extended his arm forward, a book in hand. "Take it."

I stepped forward to take the book. As soon as it was in my hand, the man ran off. He didn't say another word to us. I opened the book and flipped through it. It was a journal documenting the events after my first death. My heart dropped as I read the pages, and I could feel the world vibrate around me . Xander came before me and gently guided my hands to shut the book.

"Not here. Too many watching eyes," he said in a whisper. His eyes darted around. I tucked the book in my bag with a nod.

We entered the stables and readied our horses. We only had a few hours until nightfall. We needed to find a safe place to camp before then. Everyone had mounted their horses, except Ron.

"Daphne, can I ride with you?" Ron's voice was almost too quiet to hear. Xander glared in their direction and rode his horse out of the stable.

"Of course," she said. Ron got on the horse and took the reins.

"Come on!" Xander called from outside. "We are losing daylight." A sharpness stung his voice as he spoke.

We all made our way out of the stable and followed Xander into the forest. Without looking back at the rest of us, he spoke. "I know a cave near here that will be perfect for us to set up camp."

We followed Xander as he guided us through the forest. I leaned back into Darius and took in the sights around us. There was a stillness in this section that had been different from the rest. An overwhelming calm washed over me. I looked up at Darius, who had a twinkle in his eye and a smirk on his face.

The trees gave way to a rock face with a large cave carved into the side of it. The rock twinkled and had sharp, jagged pieces jetting out of it. This wasn't just normal rock, no, this was pure obsidian. We dismounted our horses and tied them to some trees right outside the cave. I had been here long ago. Just before the curse came to be. There was something odd happening here. I was never able to figure out what it was before I died.

I could hear a soft hum as we entered. It was coming from the crystal itself. The cold stone called to me, luring me to this place. As I approached the center, I fell to my knees as the hum filled my ears. I felt a magical force weighing me down.

"Sabrina?" I heard Darius call out to me. I didn't respond.

I couldn't.

I took the book out of my bag and sat it on the ground before me. The hum intensified. I heard a raspy voice deep in my mind and it told me I was safe. No watchful eyes. I heard the entire group now calling to me. Their voices were like tiny flies buzzing in my ears. Images flooded my head. I felt my power surge within me.

The book flew open. The pages flipped through so quickly before me. Images flashed through my mind, displaying the book's contents. The wind picked up around me, and I could feel my hair being tossed about. The images became so intense that I was fully submerged in them.

Eleven

*I*s the Queen truly dead?

Killed by her lover?

What is this wall?

Where have the Ancient Ones gone?

Is there no one to guide us through this?

A council will be formed to govern Serafina during these unprecedented times. One of each type of fae will join the council. Come to the castle, posthaste.

They did.

Fire, water, and air came first. They waited three days for light and earth to arrive. Dark was the last to arrive. A week after the rest.

For a time, they governed with unity. They put everything to a vote. They were able to rule together for ten years, but as they awaited the next Queen to be born, they grew impatient. It had never taken a queen this long to be reborn. Without the Ancient Ones' guidance, would they even find her?

More time passed, and they all grew hungry for control. Serafina fell into disarray as they argued. They only wanted what was best for themselves.

News spread of some sort of accident at the castle, but the details were shrouded in mystery. Half of the castle was destroyed in the blast. Only the dark fae council member survived.

A new council was formed shortly after the accident, but those new members were never seen again.

Three days after they entered, the purple mist began to leak from the castle.

The dark fae sat on the throne.

"This is the beginning of the end," he said to himself. His voice was like cold velvet.

Twelve

I gasped for air as the book slammed shut and the winds around me immediately died. My mouth was dry, my body felt weak, and I collapsed onto the cold ground. It was near impossible to keep my eyes open. When I opened them back up, the entire group was before me, with Darius knelt in front of me.

"I knew we shouldn't have trusted whatever that book was," I heard Xander say. I watched Daphne go to pick it up, but Xander grabbed her wrist, stopping her. "Do not touch it. Nobody touch it."

"Sabrina," Darius' voice was full of concern. "Sabrina, can you hear me?"

"Draven," was the only word that I could get out.

Everyone's eyes snapped back to me.

"What?" They all asked at once.

"Draven. His name is Draven. The one who caused the Darkness. Our enemy." I sat up. I tried to shake the feeling of hopelessness that overwhelmed me, similar to the feeling I had felt during my recent nightmares.

"I know him," Xander said in a way that sent a chill down my spine.

"What do you mean, you know him?" Ron shot a look at Xander. I watched as the shadows grew around him. "If you betrayed our Queen again, I will end you right here, right now!" His voice boomed off the cavern walls.

Xander put his hands up in surrender and took a step back, almost as if he was afraid of Ron. I wonder if he knew of what Ron had done to the men at the full moon celebration who disrespected me.

"Woah, take it easy. I told you I would never betray her again."

"Then explain. You have two seconds."

"Oh, you think you can go toe to toe with me?" Xander let out a low chuckle. "There is much you need to learn, boy," every shadow that Ron had quickly moved towards Xander. They shrouded around him, ready to strike on Xander's behalf. "You cannot out shadow the shadow master."

"Enough!" Daphne yelled to them. "You can have your dick-measuring contest after Xander explains how he knows Draven. Explain fast." Her words were sharp as she stared at both men, and the shadows faded back to their corners of the cave.

"He was my apprentice. He helped me create the curse." Xander looked away. He seemed ashamed of his words. "He was very powerful back then. I can only imagine the power he holds now."

"I never knew you had an apprentice," Daphne said in response.

"You do not know a lot of things about me, dear sister. Back then, you did not wish to know." The pain was deeply rooted in his voice. "The cottage he lived in is not too far from here. We should travel there in the morning, see if it brings us anywhere closer to our goal."

"Agreed," Darius chimed in. "We shall leave in the morning. I think it is best that we all get some rest." He finally stood and turned towards the others. "I am going hunting. Andrei, want to come with?"

"You know I do," Andrei readied his daggers, and the two of them were gone in a flash. Isa huffed at their departure, clearly annoyed by the fact she wasn't invited. My stomach rumbled. The last time I had eaten was early this morning, and that wasn't much.

Ron, Xander, and Daphne got to work setting up camp. They told me not to move an inch. I was glad to hear they were concerned about me, but I ignored their orders and went about building a small fire. I dug a hole into the ground, put in some wood and kindling that I gathered from just outside the cave, and used my magic to light it. Quickly, the cave was filled with warmth and a soft glow. When I looked up from the fire, Isa was gone. I looked toward others who gave me a shrug.

Ron picked up the book and started flipping through the pages. "Xander," he called out. "Want to look through this with me to see if there is anything else we can learn?"

Xander's face lit up. "I would love to."

I awoke to the sound of arguing. The sun gently kissed the crystals, causing them to look almost translucent. The morning light chased away the darkness. Too many times in my lives, I found darkness to be my best protection. I wished that I could hide within it now to escape the sounds coming from outside the cave.

I got up and walked outside to find Darius, Isa, and Andrei. All of which were very passionate about the conversation.

"Isabella," Andrei said firmly. His voice had more affliction to it than I had ever heard. "That is enough."

Darius looked over and sighed. "So much for not getting everyone involved," he said, rolling his eyes.

"What is going on?" I questioned as I joined their circle.

"I am done," Isa shouted at me. "I am over this wild goose chase you brought us on. I am over sleeping on the ground, I am over being attacked by wyrms, and I am certainly over everyone's bullshit."

"It was only one wyrm," Darius said under his breath.

"That's not the point!" She snarled, taking a step back.

"If you want to leave," Daphne said from behind me, "leave. You haven't helped us at all. Last night was a great example. When we set up camp, where did you go?"

"Where I went is none of your business."

"Isa, calm down. We are all going to get through this together." Andrei took her hand. She quickly snatched it away.

"Fuck you, Daphne, You think you are so much better than everyone."

"Hey! That's enough," Darius' voice boomed, causing my core to vibrate. "Isa, go home. Andrei, please go with her. Make sure Titus isn't falling apart." He grabbed Isa by her arm, pulling her to him. "Next time you disrespect anyone in this group, I will kill you. Do not say a word. Nod if you understand." His eyes were blood red, his voice like razors, and the fear in Isa's eyes grew as he tightened his grip. She nodded, and he released her. His eyes then went to Andrei. "Go, before I change my mind."

Isa rushed to Andrei. He whispered something into her ear, so quietly that I could not hear. She did not look up from the ground as she walked to their horse.

"Darius," Andrei said in a low growl.

"Save it," Darius cut Andrei off. "I am not sorry. I will not let her disrespect my wife, or her court. If Isa continues to be a problem, she will be removed." He took a step toward Andrei. "Do we have a problem?"

Andrei stood his ground. He took a deep breath before he said anything. "No, Sir. No problem." His gray eyes darkened as he spoke. Darius raised a single eyebrow and then glanced toward Andrei's horse. Without another word, Andrei turned and met up with Isa. As Andrei and Isa mounted and turned to leave, Darius called out to them.

"Andrei," he said firmly. Andrei stopped the horse and turned towards us. Darius shifted his bottom jaw. "Thank you for going back and checking on Titus. We will be home soon." His voice was now a bit calmer.

"It is my honor and my duty," Andrei responded before they rode away and disappeared into the trees. We stood there, watching the treeline for some time. The trees rustled as the wind danced around us.

Once they were out of sight, I turned back toward the cave. Ron and Xander were standing at the entrance, looks of concern plastered on their faces.

"Well, let's get camp packed," Darius declared. "We have wasted too much time already." He laced his fingers and stretched his arms outward as he walked back to the encampment. I followed behind him. As we passed Ron, I could have sworn he was whispering something to Xander about how Isa was not to be trusted.

Thirteen

T he forest transformed into a swamp as we traveled. The mud was thick and squelched as our horses traveled. The air was suffocating with the scent of rot as we passed through, making it a bit difficult to breathe. Purple and blue moss scaled the trees, and a rainbow of various sizes of beetles and giant scarlet millipedes climbed throughout it all.

Stacks of stones guided the way through the swamp, and veering off the trail a tiny bit caused our horses to get stuck in the muck.

The croaks of frogs echoed through the air. Every so often we would hear one of them leap into the water, causing a splash. This made all of us turn our heads toward the sound, no matter how many times we had heard it.

Roots wove in and out of the sludge, making the path a constant obstacle course. Mosquitos buzzed in our ears as we traveled. Darius continuously slapped them, and missed nearly every time.

"Stop fighting the air. It makes you look crazier than you already are," Daphne teased from behind him.

"I am not crazy," he snarled back at her.

I chuckled under my breath.

"What is so funny?" He looked down at me.

"Oh nothing," I broke out into a full laugh. He was crazier than I thought if he believed he was not crazy.

It wasn't long before we made our way to a small hill in the middle of the swamp. The grass was extremely tall and overgrown. I watched as a massive, bright green snake slithered out of the grass and into the water. This was the most lively part of Serafina we had been to so far, and the occupants made my skin crawl. There was nothing I despised more than snakes and bugs.

Atop the hill was a small wooden cottage. The wood was falling apart, the door lay flat on the ground, and moss nearly covered it. I did not want to think about what critters had taken residence under the door. We all dismounted our horses and stood near the entrance. All eyes fell on Xander. He huffed and accepted his fate, then turned towards the door.

We all watched him with bated breath as he entered and relaxed when he walked farther in. We followed Xander into the cottage. The place was a disaster. Lichen grew on the windowsills and some of the old wooden furniture. Broken glass was scattered about. We all spread out, examining different places in the cottage. We had no idea what we were looking for, just anything that would send us in the next direction.

I walked over to a desk and saw a busted picture frame. The glass was broken, and the photo was faded, but it was clear that this was a photo of Xander and Draven together. Draven towered over Xander. He was probably the tallest fae I had ever seen. His facial features were now faded from the age of the photo.

The photo was taken over with darkness, and the entire image was now flat black.

Ron came to my side and took the frame from my hand. His eyes were angry. "No need to reminisce about the past," he said in a whisper. It wasn't anger that filled his voice. No, it was pain.

"You're correct," I said just as softly. "We are all moving forward."

"Come take a look at this," I heard Darius call out from another room. "It's more writing in that ancient language."

We all made our way to him. Darius stood in what looked like might have been a study. It was hard to tell now with how destroyed everything was. Bookshelves with ruined books, fallen shelves, and a desk overwhelmed with paperwork. Darius stood examining some papers that were scribbled on the front and back.

Xander was the last to walk in. He chuckled as he made his way over to Darius. "It's upside down again. Could Dimitri not afford a proper tutor? Wasn't there a prestigious academy back in Titus?" Xander said as he took the paper.

"My father put more value on how quickly I could kill than on me being a scholar," Darius hissed in response. "What does it say?"

"Welcome back." Xander's brows furrowed as he flipped the paper over. "You were not missed."

On that final word, the paper exploded into a cloud of purple smoke. It expanded until it filled the room. It burned my lungs and throat as I breathed it in. By the sound of everyone's coughing, it had a similar effect on the others. I tried to use my air magic to clear the room, but nothing happened. The smoke was so thick that I could not see Darius, even as he grabbed me and threw me over his shoulder. He didn't say a word as I felt him race us out of the cottage. He was considerably slower than he had ever been, near human speed.

One by one, the coughing fits ended as I heard thuds on the floor. The smoke had filled the entire cottage. My lungs were a flame as I tried expel the smoke from them. My head felt light, and I couldn't keep my eyes open any longer.

"I…" Darius coughed as he forced out the words, "will… get you… out."

I surrendered to the smoke, no longer able to fight it, as everything around me went black and my body hit the floor.

Fourteen

Once again, I was lost in the purple haze. My throat still burned and my mouth was like cotton. A high pitch screech filled my head, causing me to clutch my head in agony and scream. No sound could be heard as I tried to force out my scream. My brain felt as if it was being stabbed a million times over.

The screeching faded, but the pain stayed, and I heard Darius frantically calling out for me.

"Sabrina!" he wailed through the mist. My vision spun in circles as I tried to put myself back together. The ground trembled beneath me as I heard him call out once again. "Sabrina! Where are you?" His voice was now coming from a different direction than before.

I spun in that direction and pushed myself forward. I wanted to find him more than anything. My bones ached for him. I tried to feel him through our bond, but felt as if our lines had been ripped apart.

It was then Daphne's voice that I heard from behind, then Xander's, Ron's, Isa's, and Andrei's. Their voices bounced around me coming from all over, booming in my head. They all called my name.

"I am here!" I was finally able to call out. "Please find me!"

Their voices became more distant as I tried to find them. No matter which direction I ran. The purple haze was never-ending. The farther I ran, the denser it became.

Their words turned into screams of agony as if they were being torn apart. I felt my heart being torn into pieces as, one by one, their screams extinguished. I fell to my knees as the sharp pain returned to my head. I let out a wail so powerful that the mist nearly cleared around me.

"That is how it will end." That cold velvet voice brushed against my ear. "All of you will die."

"Fuck you," I snarled. "You are the only one who will die!"

I felt a hand grip my hair tightly and pull hard, forcing my neck to crane. Standing behind me was a dark figure. He was tall and shrouded by similar shadows that clung to Xander and Ron. His features were blurred, and I was unable to get a good look at his face.

"Look how pathetic you are," he growled, "knelt before me." His voice sent a chill down my spine. The last time I had a similar feeling was when Darius and I had been locked together in the dungeon. I felt so small and helpless back then, and I promised myself I would never feel that way again.

I tried to yank away from his grasp. He gripped harder, pulling me back with so much force I fell onto my back. He released my hair, put a foot on my chest, and slowly applied more pressure, pinning me to the ground.

"See how easy it is for me to control you? Sabrina, I have you right where I want you," he knelt, digging his foot into me, causing me to groan in pain. He lifted his left hand and picked at his short, sharp nails. I watched a long, black tongue slither out of his mouth and drag across his top lip. "I am the game master. You think you are one step ahead of me? Wrong." He pushed his foot down harder and my rib cracked. I screamed, but I would not give him the satisfaction of hearing me beg for mercy. "I am ten steps ahead. Serafina is mine," he snarled the last word. "This is your only warning to leave." The man dug in deeper, causing more of my ribs to crack under him.

I coughed hard, blood pooled in my mouth, ejecting out with every cough.

Images formed within my mind that caused me to shudder.

First of Daphne. Beheaded. Ron was next. His body torched. Isa and Andrei were both impaled by a long sword in Andrei's attempt to save her. Xander was flayed, with crows picking at his flesh. Darius hung from the wall by silver chains that burned and burrowed into his skin. Small cuts covered his body from head to toe, and his clothes were torn to shreds. Blood dripped from every cut, and his throat was slit open.

As the images played out Draven's voice filled my head once again. "This is what I will do to them. You don't want to see what has been planned for you, little mouse. I am going to eat you alive, slowly." That final word was a purr that made my spine shiver in fear. "You know..." he paused, "I could just kill that vampire king now. Keep you all to myself. I would love to have you as my pretty little pet."

I quickly forced those images out of my mind. I would not let the people I love fall, and would not allow them to suffer. Not only could I not allow my family to suffer, but I couldn't allow the people of Serafina to continue to suffer. A blinding flash of light filled the space between Draven and me. I watched as the blast sent him back. I took a deep breath and felt my own body restore itself from the wounds Draven had inflicted.

"That may happen here, in this fucked up dream world you have crafted, but let me tell you how this is going to end for you, Draven." I stood and watched as the light pushed away the purple haze. Plush green grass and cherry blossom trees were revealed as I stepped toward Draven, who was now leaned against a tree. I clenched my fist, and roots shot from the ground and wrapped around him, pinning him there. "First, Daphne will blind you with her light. Xander and Ron's shadows will overtake yours and drown you. Isa and Andrei will tear you to bits. Darius will delight in peeling your flesh off your bones. As for me? I will eviscerate you." The roots dug in tighter to his dark skin. "Serafina is *my* land, and nothing will bring me more pleasure than ridding this world of you and restoring my home and my people." Shimmerthorne appeared in my hand, arrow ready, and I aimed directly at his blurred-out face.

"I like how feisty you are. I can't wait to break you, little mouse," he mused.

Rage contorted my face, and I released the arrow. Just before it connected, he vanished, and I watched as the arrow struck the tree and tore it in two.

219

Fifteen

The scent of almond and warm vanilla filled my nose as I jolted up. Furs gathered at my waist. My eyes darted around the small room. It had a round, tinted window above the bed frame, and I could barely see what was beyond it. The walls were a light wood that contrasted with the dark flooring. I twisted my body to allow my feet to hit the floor, and the maroon rug on the floor was soft against my bare skin. My body ached as I moved. A bookshelf and desk sat on the far wall. Books were neatly arranged by color and the desk was clear.

I stood and walked over to the door, and my heart pounded as anxiety filled me at the thought of being locked away again. I reached for the knob and twisted, releasing the breath I was holding as the door opened. The hall was filled with some of the most beautiful artwork I had ever seen. I focused on the painting directly across from the door I stood in. A cherry tree in full bloom with petals floating on the wind. The full moon illuminated the scene. The dark frame was in contrast with the light wood of the wall that made the painting stand out even more. I stepped out of my room onto the plush white runner and looked both ways. One way was a dead end, the other led down to a staircase. Three other doors lined the hall. As I took my first step down the stairs, a calm washed over me, like the moment after a rainstorm when the sky was hazy and the wind calmed. With each step I took, I became calmer. The scent of pine and cinnamon filled my nose as I got closer to the bottom.

When I reached the bottom stairs, I was led to a small sitting room. Daphne and Darius sat on the red velvet couch, with a roaring fireplace across from them. A stag mounted above it with rainbow antlers. They were one of my favorite creatures in Serafina. I used to wake with the first light to watch them graze in one of the fields beyond the castle.

My heart stopped as my eyes fell on an unknown face. A young man sat across from Darius. He was lean, freckles were sprinkled across his alabaster skin, and his amber eyes glowed from the dancing fire. The short bright red hair matched the fire in his eyes. He wore a burnt orange tunic with tan pants. I was so much in my head, overwhelmed by how we got here and what was this new place, that I didn't hear much of the conversation, but it seemed they all were getting along.

"Sabrina!" Daphne's voice was a sweet melody that pulled me back to reality.

Darius sprang up and was before me in an instant. He wrapped his arms around me so tightly that I felt his body tremble. "I..." his voice was soft and quivered lightly, "I am so sorry I couldn't save you." I looked up and saw the tears well in his eyes. "I am so glad you are ok."

Pulling away from his embrace, Darius pulled me in closer and held me tighter. I wondered if he had a similar experience as I did; I could only imagine the horror Draven would show him.

I am here. It is okay. I am okay.

He didn't respond, but slowly released me and turned away from the others, and brought his hand to his face.

Daphne and the man stood and walked to our side. "I am so glad you are awake," she said with a warm smile.

"Me, too. How long was I asleep?"

"Just a day longer than everyone else. Two days total here. But who knows how long you were asleep when our scouts found you in that cottage," the red-haired mystery man began. "My name is Archer. It is my honor to meet you, Your Majesty," he said with a bow.

"The pleasure is mine," I responded. "Where are we, exactly?"

Archer stood with an inviting grin. "Welcome to Tasumanza, the city of the resistance against Draven and the darkness he created."

"You know of Draven?!" I exclaimed, raising an eyebrow.

"Yes, my father founded this safe haven centuries ago. Unfortunately, we have not been able to defeat Draven yet, but we will."

"Where is your father?" Darius turned back to us. "I would love to speak with him and come up with a plan on how to kill Draven," hatred coated his name.

"He should return in a few days. He is currently out on a scouting mission to the castle."

I looked around. I had not yet heard a peep from Ron or Xander. "Where are the others?"

"They went to explore the village. They wanted to make sure it was safe for you once you awoke," Daphne answered.

"Would you like a tour, my Queen?" Archer asked. Darius reached his arm around my shoulder, pulling me to him.

"We would love a tour," Darius answered for me. I heard Daphne chuckle under her breath.

Archer motioned for us to follow him and guided us out the front door. We stepped out into the street and my heart fluttered. This was the Serafina I remembered. Shops and homes were carved into the large trees of the enchanted forest. Ropewalks connected the upper levels. The streets were made of light cobblestone. Rays of sunshine came down from the small openings in the canopy. Fae lights glittered in the air. All types of fae walked the streets with purpose. Children played without a care. The village was massive.

"How is this all possible?" Daphne questioned as we walked through the village. "The rest of Serafina is in total ruins."

"My family set up wards many years ago that have protected this section of the forest and the village. We are all grateful that Draven has yet to discover us."

My eyes met with an albatross that sat in a tree across from the house. Its eyes and beak were as black as the void, and there was a gouge across its beak. Shadows clung and danced around its wings. A feeling of dread washed over me. After a moment of us staring at each other, the bird flew off, and the feeling vanished.

As we walked through, people bowed. They welcomed me home. My heart was filled with joy as one by one, the villagers greeted me. I was glad to know there were fae here who fought the darkness and welcomed my return.

A young boy rushed up to us and grabbed my hand, and his eyes filled with wonder as he looked up at me. "You are so beautiful," he gasped.

His mother came rushing through the crowd, her orange hair rushing in the wind. "Ollie!" Her voice was filled with worry. As her gaze fell on me and she stopped abruptly, bowing before me. "My Queen! I apologize for my son!"

I looked up at her with a warm smile. "No apologies needed. He is a kind young boy." I guided him back to his mother.

"Thank you, my Queen," she took Ollie's hand.

"What is your name? It is a pleasure to meet you and sweet Ollie."

"Jessandra. The pleasure is mine." She bowed once again and motioned for her son to do so as well. "May the gods walk with you," she said as she scurried off down the street. My eyes followed them as they disappeared into the crowd.

"She seems kind," Daphne said.

"She is," Archer started. "She is the owner of a local tavern. She came here a few years ago when her son was just a babe. Jessandra had lost her husband in the fight against the Darkness. Though warded against Draven and his Darkness, if close enough it is easy for the lost to find this safe haven."

My heart ached as I learned of another who was affected by my absence. Darius squeezed my hand tightly, and I looked up to see he had an equally somber look on his face. He tried to act like things like that didn't bother him, as if he had no empathy, but he had more than most of us.

"Queen Sabrina!" I heard Ron's voice. It yanked me out of my own head. I looked up and saw him and Xander approaching. Xander had several boxes and bags in hand. Ron picked up his pace to meet us. "You should have waited until we returned with news of safety."

"Sabrina is capable of handling herself. No need to worry. As you can see, the people here love her," Xander said as he joined us and presented what was in his hand. "All of these are gifts for you from various shop owners in the village."

"Oh, I could not accept those. Please take them back."

"My arm was twisted to take these. I informed them that they were too kind, but they would not take them back."

"Too kind indeed," I responded.

"The villagers are very happy with your arrival. Tomorrow they have planned to have a festival in your honor," Archer said with a smile.

"A festival?" Daphne questioned. I heard the concern in her voice. I think we were both still haunted by the memories of the full moon festival in Titus.

Something in the magic-filled air told me that this festival would be different. I couldn't wait to truly mingle with the villagers.

"Shall we go back to my house, open these gifts, and have dinner?" Archer questioned.

"I think that sounds great. My arms are tired," Xander chuckled.

I sat on the bed, cross-legged, with the bags and boxes sitting at the foot of it. Darius leaned against the wall with his arms crossed.

"Go on. Open them," he said. "You can't just stare at them forever."

"I feel bad. I don't need these gifts." I looked down and fiddled with my thumbs. The truth was I did not deserve them. I did not deserve the kindness of the people in this village. It was my fault they were in this situation.

Darius pushed off the wall and strode to the bed and sat by my side. He picked up one of the small bags and put it on my lap. "Open it," he said firmly.

I looked up at him, met his gaze, looked back at the bag, and took out the soft white tissue paper. Inside, I found a note on crisp cream paper. I unfolded the paper and heat rose to my cheeks as I read the words. "This one is for you," I said as I handed him the bag.

"For me?" His eyebrows raised.

"The note said to let you open it."

Darius reached into the bag and pulled out a red chiffon nightgown. A predatory smirk grew on his face as he looked at me. "Well, I don't think this is my size, but they are correct. For my eyes to fall upon you while wearing this would be the greatest gift of all."

I took it out of his hand and giggled. "Oh, will it be?"

"Absolutely."

I took off my top slowly, exposing my breasts. Darius' body stiffened, and his eyes filled with anger.

"What is wrong?" I questioned him. I blinked, and he was in front of me, grabbing my arm and lifting it.

"What happened?" He snarled.

I looked down and my skin was black and blue, exactly where Draven had dug his foot into my ribs. I swallowed hard and looked up at Darius.

"What the fuck happened?" he demanded again, more firmly.

"When I was unconscious, Draven appeared to me," I whimpered. Saying his name sent a shiver down my spine. I told Darius of the encounter and the images he had shown me.

His jaw tightened. "He showed me things, too. I will make sure his wishes never come true. I will kill him. I will tear him limb from limb," he snarled.

"We will destroy him together."

His hand traveled down my body and gently brushed against my bruised skin. I flinched as he touched the darkest spot.

His face softened as he lifted me gently and carried me into the adjoining bathroom, sat me on the counter, and began to run water for a bath. "Wait here. I am going to see if there is anything in those gifts I can add to the water," he said as he exited the room.

I got off the counter and looked at myself in the full-length mirror that was across from me. I glided my fingers across my bruised ribs, flinching at my touch. I would never let Draven get the better of me again. What was even scarier was that even in the dream realm, he still had a real-world effect on me.

How far could he take it?

Once again, I touched my damaged skin. This time focusing healing energies through my fingertips. The bruise vanished where my fingers grazed. So much damage had been done to my skin that it would take more than magic to heal me. It would take time. It was sensitive to the touch, but I didn't feel any internal damage.

Darius came back in with his arms full of different herbs, salts, and soaps. He looked at me and sighed as he added them to the water.

"You don't know how to stay put, do you?" He said with a sly grin on his face.

"Absolutely not."

"You are such a brat," he said as he strode towards me. He gently cupped my cheek in his hand. "I found some healing tea in those packages. I'm going to make you some. Let me help you in the bath, and I will go make it for you."

"I don't need help, Dar."

"Please," his voice was soft, and a bit shaken. I rolled my eyes and nodded. He knelt before me, gently kissing my bruised ribs, making my heart flutter. I did not feel the need to flinch away. His kisses caused me no pain. He kissed his way down as he rolled my leggings off my body. When they were on the floor, he looked up at me with his bright green eyes. "I don't tell you enough how amazing and beautiful you are."

Heat rose to my cheeks, and I laced my fingers into his hair and ran them through without a word. He took my hand from his head and kissed the back of it. He rose to his feet. My hand was still in his as he guided me to the tub, and he held me steady as I stepped in and lowered my body into the warm, soapy water.

The scent of rosemary and eucalyptus filled my nose. My body shuddered in delight as the warm waters welcomed me in.

"I will be back shortly. Rest, doll. You deserve some peace." With that, he let go of my hand and left me alone. I heard the soft creak of the bedroom door as he left the room.

I closed my eyes and tried to put myself in a place of relaxation. To be honest, I could not tell you what that felt like. I could not think of a single time I felt completely relaxed, and I took a deep breath.

In.

Out.

In.

Out.

I tried to push out thoughts of the impending battle ahead. How my people were suffering. How we had barely made it out of the battle with Dimitri. How Draven was a far worse opponent than we realized. How Isa had no longer believed in me. How somewhere along the way I had lost her friendship. How Liam had died for this cause. How Ron put everything he had on the line for this—for me.

I dunked my head under the water as I continued to fight these thoughts, attempting to expel them as if I could free myself of them.

I couldn't get the image of Daphne's head rolling out of my mind. Xander's body torn apart by crows. I let out a sob. Water filled my mouth as I saw the image of Darius, once again hung in chains, blood drained, and throat slit.

That won't happen. Sabrina, you have to know we will not let that happen. You will not let that happen. There is a reason you are Queen. A reason my father feared you. Don't let the darkness eat you alive. Take my hand and come up for air. My eyes flashed open. A small window was above me where the bubbles had cleared. I saw a blurry image of a hand above the water. It ebbed and flowed with the motion of the liquid.

Take my hand.

I reached up and grabbed Darius' hand. He gripped me tight and helped me pull my head above water, where I gasped for air as I leaned against the side of the tub. A gray mug sat on the small wooden table nearby. His brow furrowed as he looked over at the mirror. I followed his gaze and stared at his reflection, getting lost in those emerald-green eyes.

Before I had met Darius, mirrors had been made of silver, making it so vampires had no reflection. When Darius visited Serafina and learned of mirrors and his predicament, he hired several artificers to solve his problem. It wasn't long before they created enchanted polished brass mirrors and they took over the industry and became the norm.

"Are you trying to drown yourself again?" He teased.

"I wasn't trying to that time, or this time."

"Good. I would miss you," he looked away. "Do you want me to go?"

"I need you to stay."

"May I join you?" A joyous grin filled his face.

"Of course."

That was all the invitation he needed before he ripped off his clothes and joined me in the tub, his large member already at attention. I blushed hard when the considerable length was eye level to me. Darius slipped into the tub behind me and put his legs on either side of my body.

"Such a dirty girl," he whispered in my ear, "blushing at the sight of my cock." He wrapped his arms around me and pulled me against his chest. His hard cock pressed into my lower back.

He reached over and grabbed the tea from the side table and put the mug to my lips, gently tipping it back. I opened my mouth and swallowed the warm liquid. Licorice and honey melted away any pain I felt as the last drop traveled down my throat.

"Good girl," Darius purred as he put the empty mug on the table. Even though my body fully relaxed against him, it ached for him. I needed him inside me. I needed that release. His hands traveled up my body and found their way to my shoulders. He kneaded his thumbs into them, massaging the tension away, and I let out a moan as he worked his way down in between my shoulder blades.

"You are very tense, doll. You need to loosen up a bit more."

As his hands left my shoulder, I looked up at him with pleading eyes.

He put a dollop of shampoo into the palm of his hand. Slowly, he rubbed his two hands together, into my hair, and slowly massaged the shampoo into my scalp. The scent of strawberries and cream filled my nose. His fingers laced through my hair and down the length.

"Your hair is so soft, Sabrina," he pulled his hands from my hair and bent down to kiss me. His lips were so soft against mine. He pulled away, and the air electrified. "I love you."

"I love you, too." My words were like sweet syrup on my lips.

He grabbed a basin and filled it with clean water. He laced his fingers through my hair and gently pulled my head back. Pouring the water through my hair, rinsing away the soap. "All clean, my love."

"There is one spot left untouched," I whimpered.

"There is?" One eyebrow raised.

I answered with a simple nod.

"Beg," he demanded.

"Please fuck me. I need you. I need all of you," my voice trembled.

"Is that all you got?" He teased.

"Darius, please fuck me. I need to feel your cock deep inside my pussy. Fuck me now. Fuck me hard. Show me no mercy." I felt my whole body tighten as I pleaded for him.

"Good girl," he growled. "Prove to me how bad you need it. Reach behind you and show me how badly you need me."

I reached around and gripped his girth, slowly stroking him from base to tip. A groan escaped and his cock twitched in my hand. He thrusted up into my hand. I could feel that he needed me just as badly as I needed him.

Darius's hands traveled in between my legs and brushed softly against my inner thigh. They made their way up until they coaxed at my entrance, his fingertips toying with me, teasing me. My most intimate parts tingled at his touch. He caressed me slowly, up and down, and circled his fingers around my clit, applying pressure to my most sensitive parts. I let out a moan as his fingers abruptly forced their way inside me.

"You are so wet for me, doll," he said as he thrust his fingers deep. My body quivered with pleasure as he played with me harder. I needed more of him. His fingers could not satisfy my hunger.

"Darius," I moaned. "Please." They were the only words I could get to escape my lips. His fingers melted away any logical thought I had left.

"Such a needy little whore," he groaned into my ear. He pulled his fingers nearly all the way out of me. They gently probed my entrance before slamming back into me. "Tell me what you need."

"I need your cock deep inside me. I need it now," I demanded.

Darius pulled his fingers out of me and roughly grabbed my hips. He stood, picked me up, and held me close as He stepped out of the tub. When he lowered us down to the floor, he laid me on my stomach and gripped my hair tightly, pinning me in place. My chest was flat on the floor and my hips were slightly raised. With his free hand, he lifted my hips and thrust inside me.

I moaned as his full length entered me and pressed back to get as much of him inside me as I could. He showed me no mercy as he fucked me into the floor. I felt my wetness grow for him the harder he went.

He pounded into my cervix, and I moaned louder with each thrust. Darius leaned down, his chest against my back. The hand that held my head in place moved to my mouth and pressed firmly.

"Shh. You don't want the whole village to hear what a little whore you are for your vampire, do you?" He snarled into my ear.

My vampire. Darius was mine. I was his. That thought was all I needed to send me over the edge. I felt myself start quivering around him as I was nearing my pleasure, squealing into his hand, and my eyes rolling back.

"Good girl, cum for me." He continued the relentless thrusting as I gave into him. My vision filled with stars as I felt overcome with pleasure, and his primal groans filled the bathroom as he muffled my screams. I couldn't tell if the puddle we laid in was from the bath water or my own arousal.

Darius pulled out of me, and in a blink I was sitting on the counter, and he was between my legs, ramming back into me. I arched my back as his mouth found my breast. His fangs grazed against my skin, sending a shiver down my spine. His tongue danced around my nipple as he took it into his mouth. He took the other breast in his hand and greedily groped it as he fucked me harder. I craned my head back and screamed as I exploded once again. Darius kissed his way back up my body and his mouth found my neck, wasting no time sinking his fangs into my delicate skin. A wave of ecstasy washed over me. My vision blurred as I entered true paradise. He pressed deep inside me and held it there. I felt his cock twitch and release deep inside me. I felt him groan into my neck as he found his pleasure.

He pulled away and our eyes met. Blood dripped from his lips, and he wiped it away with his thumb, slowly licking the crimson liquid off with his tongue. He did not pull his cock from me.

"Shall we continue our bath?" he teased as he leaned in and gently kissed my lips.

"We shall," I said softly, kissing him back. I looked in the mirror and noticed my bruises were gone.

Sixteen

By the next night, the village had transformed into a magical festival wonderland. The fae lights that hung in the trees and typically had a yellow glow were now a rainbow of colors to represent the different kinds of fae magic. Each shop and tavern had a booth set up with different food, beverage, artisan goods, and a wide array of crafts. Several bands and musicians were stationed about. Each had its own musical style. Somehow, each sound was distinct.

The population of the village was more than I had imagined. So many fae, of all kinds, filled the streets. They all seemed to be in harmony with one another. They all mingled with one another. Typically you would see each type of fae only interact with their kind, here it was like a huge melting pot.

The fae wine flowed. Several people walked around with carafes full of it and kept everyone's glasses full. Daphne and I once again refrained from drinking any. To be honest, after what happened the last time we enjoyed it, I am not sure if either of us would partake ever again.

We all were gifted clothing from a local clothier that had been dropped off early this morning. Daphne wore a beautiful golden cap-sleeve dress. The sweeping train cape made of silk gave her an ethereal look. Xander and Ron both wore matching dark blue, long-sleeve shirts and pants, each embellished with purple embroidery.

My heart skipped a beat when I saw Darius in his dark red tailcoat with matching golden embroidery on his vest. He smiled when he finally saw me. His eyes went straight to the deep V neckline that exposed much of my chest. I loved my dress. It was made with dark green tulle, and little golden flowers were embroidered on transparent, long puff sleeves.

Darius stepped before me and gently lifted my chin. "Beautiful," he said as he gently kissed my lips.

"We must stop by the clothier and thank them. They truly did an amazing job. This is some of the best craftsmanship I had ever seen. It reminds me of my clothier that made all my dresses before," I paused, "Everything."

"I wasn't talking about the clothes," Darius chuckled. I heard Xander cough under his breath. Both Darius' and my attention turned to Xander.

"Ron and I are going to explore the festival. We met some dark fae yesterday, and we're going to see if we can find them," Xander said, his eyes darting around a bit. I watched as he nervously pulled at the hem of his sleeves. It has been a long time since he has been around this many people.

"Don't get into too much trouble," Daphne said with a smile. "Sabrina, you have to come check out some of the food offerings! The things I have tried have been utterly delectable!" Daphne grabbed my hand and pulled me to follow her. I turned to Darius and motioned for him to come with us. He followed close behind us with his shoulders back and his eyes slowly scanning.

There was a full street where the tavern owners had set up their food offerings. It was clear that everything here was in abundance. There were different stews, bread, meats, and treats available.

"My Queen!" One of the vendors called out to me and waved me over. She was a water fae. She had beautiful navy skin, and her beautiful seafoam green hair was in a side braid. As we approached her booth, she did a small dance in delight and clapped her hands. "Oh yay! I am so happy you stopped at my booth! It is a pleasure!" She squealed.

"Well, thank you," I smiled and looked over the table that had tiny little bowls filled with yellow rice and perfectly seared scallops. "This looks delicious!"

"Please! Try some!" Her eyes looked up to Darius, who stood with his arms crossed. "Well, there is garlic in it, so you may not want to," she said meekly as she looked back at me. She reached down and offered a bowl to Daphne, then to me.

"Luckily for him, that is just a myth. This looks too delicious to pass up." I took the bowl from her hand and offered a warm smile. "What is your name? It is lovely to meet you!"

"Branwyn!" Her face lit up, and I took a bite. My taste buds danced in delight at the sweet, succulent scallop. I smiled and nodded to her as I swallowed. "I am so glad you like it! My tavern is called Buck's Tavern, for when you crave more!"

"This is delicious!" Daphne said with a smile. "Thank you for this! We will definitely be visiting your tavern while we are here!"

I then heard a familiar voice through the crowd. I turned my head and Ollie ran towards us. A huge joyous grin was on his face as he skipped through the crowd, calling for me.

"Queen Sabrina!"

I gave my attention back to Branwyn and gave thanks before running to Ollie.

He rushed faster towards me, taking my hand as he reached me. I looked down at the young boy. He had to be no older than six. Glancing around, there were many children his age ran free in the streets of the festival. The village must be very safe if this many children could play freely.

"Come with me! My mommy has something amazing! She's got the best food in the whole village!" He pulled me, forcing me to follow him.

As we raced through the crowd, I turned to see if Darius and Daphne were following behind me. The two of them walked side by side. Daphne's face was full of laughter, but Darius' lips were tight, his jaw tight, as if he was on edge.

I looked forward and continued to follow Ollie until we got to the end of the block and arrived at a tree with dark burgundy bark and scarlet leaves. Fae lights hung in the tree that mimicked fire. A door had been carved in the base of the tree and was wide open, and above it hung a sign: *Bear's End Tavern*. We walked inside and I was hit by the scent of warm spices that were foreign to me.

It was a small tavern. A bar was located on the back wall and there were a few booths on the sides. Though the place was small, it was packed. Every table was full, and a few people sat at the bar.

"Mommy! I brought the Queen," Ollie called out to his mother, who was behind the bar pouring a pint of ale for one of the patrons. She looked up at me and her golden eyes met mine. The tavern fell to silence as all eyes turned toward me. Darius and Daphne finally entered the tavern close behind me. I noticed some of the people avoided Darius' gaze as he walked past them and stood at my side.

He cleared his throat. "Nothing to look at. Mind your manners and get back to your meals," he announced firmly, and they did. We approached the bar, and we were greeted by Jessandra.

"Hello again, my Queen. Welcome to my tavern!" Her gaze fell to Ollie. "What did I tell you about bothering the Queen while she was here?"

"Oh, he was no bother at all! He is quite sweet!" I said as we sat at the bar. "This is your tavern? It is lovely!"

"Yes, I just opened this year. It was my dream to own my own tavern! When Bearyalis went to sell last year, I knew it was my chance!"

Darius reached across the bar, grabbed the pitcher of ale, and poured himself a glass. I shot him an angry look.

"Darius! Are you serious?" Daphne snapped at him as she took the glass from his hand. "I am so sorry, I didn't realize we brought a caveman with us instead of a king," she said, giving the glass to Jessandra. Darius huffed and leaned back into the chair.

"All is well. That ale had gone bad. That is why I allowed him to take it. Typically men who reach across my bar do not leave with hands," Jessandra said with a smile. She poured Darius a fresh glass and sat it in front of him. He sat up and brought it to his lips, taking a sip.

"Thank you. This ale has an interesting flavor."

"Lime! I add it to go with the food I make here. It is different from anything you have ever seen! Would you like to try it?"

"We would love to," I said with a smile. Jessandra went through a door behind the bar.

"You did not have to embarrass me, Daphne," Darius said under his breath.

"Then do not embarrass the Queen. You are her guest. Do not make her look bad," Daphne whispered back.

Jessandra came back with two plates. Each had a tiny blue piece of circle flatbread piled with poultry, a mixture of corn, tomatoes, peppers, herbs, and cheese.

"You fold it in half and then eat," she said with a smile.

Darius took my plate and held it to his face, examining it closely. "Is this safe? What is this?"

"It is totally safe! I call it a taco! I heard vampires don't eat, otherwise, I would have offered you one."

"Vampires do eat, but not the same foods as mortals. We prefer a more liquid-based diet." Darius sat the plate back down and slid it to me. I watched Daphne pick up her taco and take a bite and then followed to do the same. The spices from the meat warmed my mouth and then were cooled by the sweetness from the corn and the creaminess of the cheese.

"This is amazing!" I exclaimed as I took another bite.

"Thank you! I have seven different varieties, but this is the best seller! I am so glad you like it! I need to tend to the rest of the tavern, but please let me know if you need anything else. It's on the house," she said as she slipped down the bar to assist other customers.

Daphne and I finished our tacos. I was so elated to have tried this new dish. It was unlike anything I had ever had before. The three of us sat at the bar for some time, and a few people approached, asking us about our journey so far. I noticed even Darius dropped his guard after some time.

After another round of the lime ale, Darius dug into the pocket of his vest. He pulled out a coin purse and called over Jessandra. He took her hand and set it into her palm. "This is for you. An apology for my behavior earlier, and for the tacos that made my wife and her friend happy. Thank you."

My jaw dropped as the words came out of his mouth. I watched as Jessandra felt the weight of the coin purse in her hand.

"I...I can't accept this."

"You can. You deserve it," he said as he got up and walked out of the tavern without another word. I looked back to Jessandra and thanked her once again for the lovely meal. I motioned for Daphne to follow me as I also made my way out of the tavern.

Darius now stood in the center of the street with Xander, Ron, and Archer. Daphne and I joined them, and Archer greeted me with a warm smile.

"Ah! There you are!" Archer said. "Please come with me! I would love for you to come to speak to the village!" He took my hand, but before he could take a single step forward, Darius had a hold of his wrist.

"Do not touch the Queen," he said firmly. Archer released me.

"My apologies. I meant no offense or harm."

"No harm done. She doesn't like to be touched by strangers. Please guide us to where we need to be," Darius' tone was cold as he spoke.

We followed Archer to the center of the village in front of their community building. We stood on the front porch and Archer called for everyone's attention.

"Attention one and all," his voice extended through the streets. All attention was on us. Hundreds of eyes. "Our Queen has returned. She has brought to us the Ancient Ones and the Vampire King!" The crowd erupted in cheers. "This is what we needed to turn the tide. To finally restore peace to Serafina." Archer looked to me to speak.

I stepped forward, waved to the crowd, and took a deep breath as I met the faces of everyone before me. I saw the pain, the joy, and the hardships that Draven had caused.

"I won't sugarcoat this," I began, "this will be a long and difficult journey. There is still much to learn about Draven and the dark powers he harnesses. Together we will do all we can to gather information and destroy him. We will bring Serafina back to the light."

The crowd erupted once again in cheers. Darius took a step forward and took my hand. As he did, I heard a hollow whooshing from above and the sound was getting louder. We all looked up and saw the sky lit with shooting stars. One was coming directly at us.

Everyone else ran back. Darius and I did not falter. We had had this happen once before. Heat began to flood my body. Darius gripped my hand tighter as the star collided with us and burst like snow, washing us in stardust. A cool and calming feeling washed over me. I looked up at Darius, who now was covered in glittering stardust, with a smile. I knew that this was a blessing from the powers that be once again, as it was all those years ago.

The crowd was silent as I looked back at them. All eyes were on us in awe. The fae knew things like this did not happen unless the gods will it to be. One by one, they all fell to their knees.

"All hail Queen Sabrina."

<h1 style="text-align:center">Seventeen</h1>

A few days had passed since the festival. Ron and Xander had spent a lot of their time with the dark fae they had met. Xander had also begun training Ron to truly understand the extent of his power. The two of them seemed to be growing closer after the night in the obsidian cave.

It had been way too long since any of us had done any training. Now that we settled in the village, it may be a good idea for us to get a routine in place. Everything had been so chaotic since the curse broke. I know we all missed the sense of some sort of structure in our lives, especially Darius. He was the king of 'keep on schedule. If you're on time, you are late.'

I spent most of my time going through the journals that Archer provided me about the past missions the village had conducted, with Daphne's assistance. They contained details from every mission they had ever taken against Draven. Unfortunately, they had not gathered as much intel as I had hoped. All they had confirmed was that the castle was the center of the Darkness. Any time they traveled too close to the castle, someone would get hurt, many times it was beyond healing. I prayed that Archer's father would have more information for me.

To my surprise, Darius had spent most of his free time out in the village. What he had been up to, I was not exactly sure. When I asked him about it when he came back to the house, he would always say, "Oh, just here and there," or "You know, putting out the feelers." Whatever the hell that meant.

This morning Archer had taken us out to Bear's End for breakfast. Over the past few days, I had found myself coming here at least once a day for tacos. They were extremely delicious. To my delight, they also had crepes, my favorite. We ate in silence for some time before Archer finally spoke.

"Darius, I have heard about what you have been up to since the festival," he said as he took a bite of his eggs.

"I do not know what you are talking about," Darius grumbled as he leaned back into his seat.

"I have heard from thirteen struggling business owners in town that they received a generous donation to help keep their businesses afloat." Everyone's jaw dropped, and we all looked toward Darius, who was now looking up at the ceiling.

"Hm, sounds like that was someone else. That is not something I would do."

"Nope, definitely not the Darius we know," I said as I went back to eating breakfast.

Before anyone could say another word, the sound of a buisine horn filled the tavern, and the whole village for that matter. Archer's face lit up, and he jumped out of his seat.

"Jess, I will pay you later. We have to go. A team has returned! Hopefully, it is my father."

"You always pay your debts. Go on," Jessandra replied from across the bar.

"Aw, I was not done eating my breakfast," Ron said as we all got up from the table. The look of disappointment was all over his face as he gazed down at his half-eaten omelet with sausage and peppers.

"I will box it up for you, sugar bean, and have it sent to the house," Jessandra said as she approached the table. Ron thanked her as we all left the tavern.

Archer took us to the community center. He informed us that this is the first place that people returning from missions went so that they can debrief. The land in front of the building was packed with all kinds of fae who were excited to see their family members return home. From the talk of the crowd, they had been gone for several weeks.

We entered the building and saw a group of six fae, men and women of all types. The fire fae was the largest of them. His back was to us, but he stood well above the others and his muscles were well-defined. He turned to face us as Archer greeted the group of warriors. A chill ran down my spine as his amber eyes met mine and I saw the large scar across his nose. Something about him felt so familiar, but I could not place it.

"Father, welcome back," Archer said as the large fire fae man stepped closer. "Queen Sabrina, this is my father, Leon."

Leon stepped towards me and took my hand in his as he knelt before me. I heard Darius snarl under his breath.

"Welcome Queen Sabrina. The resistance has been awaiting your arrival," he said as he looked up at me through his brow. Darius stepped in front of me, forcing Leon to release his grasp. Leon stood and cleared his throat as he took a step back.

"Do not touch her again. How did you know Sabrina was still alive?" Darius said as he took a step forward, creating more space between Leon and me. The two stood nearly eye to eye. Leon had to be the tallest fae I had ever seen.

"There were rumors of a curse that kept our Queen away. I knew she would return to us one day. When the wall fell, I knew the rumor to be true."

"We are glad to be here," Daphne and Xander chimed in unanimously.

"We need to know everything you know about Draven," Darius demanded. Leon turned back to the warriors, telling them to go home, get some rest, and that they would debrief in the evening. When he turned back to Darius, I swear I saw fire and darkness in his eyes.

"There is much to fill you all in on," Leon began. "I would love it if the two of you come on the next scouting mission to the castle. That way, you can get a better idea of the area around the castle and the magics at play."

"Has anyone ever been inside?" Ron asked.

"Not any who have come out alive," Leon said matter-of-factly.

"How is it that you know so much?" Darius questioned. "We have traveled all across Serafina. So many have no idea what the Darkness is. Yet, you seem to have all the answers. Why not use this knowledge to protect all of Serafina?"

"I have spent centuries trying to fight Draven. I have done my best with the resources we have. Our magic can only go so far." Anger, that he was trying to hide, filled his voice. "Draven cannot learn that we know of him and are currently working against him."

"If it has been centuries, shouldn't you have more information? Shouldn't you have the knowledge and power to stop him?" Darius continued to push him. The others fell silent as we watched the two of them go back and forth.

"Well, *someone* had killed the most powerful fae in existence. Hard to win a war without our biggest player."

Darius let out a growl.

I could feel his anger building and that he was about to snap. Hoping to de-escalate the situation, I took his hand and squeezed. "Darius," I said softly. "It's alright."

He snatched his hand away from mine. He twisted to face me. His eyes were red, and his fangs bared.

I won't let him make a fool of me.

"Leon, I am sure you have done your best. The village is wonderful," Daphne chimed in.

"We would love it if you showed us the castle. Anything we can learn is vital," Xander said.

I stood there, eyes locked with Darius, and my heart pounded in my chest. I knew we did not have long until Darius exploded with rage.

Something isn't right with him.

Dar, you're just being overprotective. It is ok. We can trust Leon. He has been trying to defeat Draven long before our return. He is on our side.

Are you taking his side?

No, I am telling you that everything is under control. Not everyone is our enemy.

"I have been keeping journals containing everything I have learned about Draven in my private library. I would love to show them to you." Leon looked up at Archer. "Son, can you take the Ancient Ones to my home? I will meet you there shortly."

Archer nodded. Ron declared he was going with them.

Daphne came to me, pulling me into a tight hug. "Gods help you with that one," she said quietly in my ear.

I watched the four of them leave. The remaining warriors left behind them. My eyes fell back to Darius, who still stood there rigid with anger.

"I am not your enemy," Leon said in a calm voice as he strode to be in front of Darius, who let out a growl. He did not stand down.

"I am not so sure about that," Darius didn't even blink as he spoke.

"Darius," I said softly, turning back to him and taking his hand in mine. His head snapped to face me. As his eyes met mine, he squeezed my hand and his face softened.

Those blood-red eyes returned to the green gems I loved so much. He cleared his throat and looked back to Leon.

"I..." Darius said as his eyes lowered, "there has been a lot going on. I am on edge. It's nice to meet you, Leon. I look forward to working with you to destroy Draven."

The next day, Leon invited all of us to train. Just north of the village was a training arena with sparring, targets, and every weapon you could think of for practice. The morning air was nipping at my face as we walked into the grounds.

Ron and Xander immediately went towards the group of dark fae that they had met when we first got to the village. The three of them were begging Xander to show them anything he was willing to teach.

Daphne was greeted by twin light fae girls. They were very young, even younger than Ron. Archer had told me about the twins. They were the only light fae in the village. The duo had walked into the village alone a few years back, with no memory of their lives before them entering the village's wards. The two silently argued over which one should speak first. Eventually, the one with the green streak in her hair spoke.

"Excuse me," she said shyly as she looked to the ground and twiddled her fingers, "are you really Daphne? The ancient light fae?"

Daphne giggled and knelt to be at eye level with them as she confirmed who she was.

"Will you please show us how you use your magic? We have no idea how to use ours," the other twin said.

"I would be happy to show you," she said as she stood and took both of their hands. The three of them glowed as they connected, and Daphne took them to an empty section of the training grounds.

Darius seemed to have cooled off a lot since last night. We didn't talk about what had happened when we met Leon. I tried to bring it up once we had gotten into bed, but Darius quickly changed the subject when he dove in between my legs. My core still melted at the thought of his tongue sliding along my skin. A shiver went down my spine as I pushed the feeling of his fangs grazing my inner thigh out of my mind.

"Hey, vampire!" I heard someone call out from the sparring ring. Our heads turned in the direction of the voice. An earth fae stood in the center of the ring, shirtless, sweat dripping from his muscles. "I heard you think you're tough. Are you going to prove it?" A smirk grew across his face.

"Is that a challenge?" Darius' face lit up.

"Absolutely, unless you're a chicken."

Darius rushed to the ring., and I chuckled under my breath as I watched them shake hands and set the terms. No weapons, no magic, just bare hands. I stood there for some time, along with everyone else in the area. All eyes were on them.

Darius quickly had the fae pinned on his back. They went again, with the same results. The earth fae stood and wiped the dirt off him.

"Well, it seems that the rumors are true," the fae said.

"Indeed, they are. Want to go again?" Darius smirked.

"Absolutely. This time I won't lose."

Back at it they went, and again the earth fae lost. Other fae joined them, and they all took turns to see if they could defeat the vampire King.

I turned and made my way to the targets. Taking my bow off my back, I loaded the arrow. Finding my target, I aimed and my heart stopped. The albatross sat on the target, at which I took aim. Dark magic radiated from it. I felt a lump form in my throat. The bird stared directly into my eyes. It looked deep into my soul, making me feel more exposed than I ever had. It squawked in my direction, and the sound pierced my ears and my vision blurred.

I released the arrow and heat washed over me as the bowstring stung my inner arm. I had never once had that happen in my years of using Shimmerthorne. I glanced toward my arm and saw the bruise begin to form. My vision snapped into focus as the arrow hit the target and I watched it go up in flames.

The albatross was gone.

Commotion erupted behind me as I stood paralyzed, watching the fire quickly spread to other targets. I tried to move, tried to help, but I was unable to move. Three water fae rushed in front of me, using their magic to put out the flames.

One of them being Branwyn. All I could do was watch as she commanded the other two to use their magic in unison. It was clear she was the most powerful of the three. The waves she summoned nearly flooded the area. Just as the water hit the ground, the water magically disappeared.

I heard Darius' voice call out for me from behind, but I couldn't turn around to look as I felt a firm hand take my bow from me and hold my hand.

"Sabrina, you are burning up," like cold velvet in my ears. My head snapped in the direction of the voice. Leon stood there, looking down at me with concern.

Darius stepped into my vision and ripped Leon away from me. "I told you not to fucking touch her!" He raged towards Leon. I watched something shift in Leon's eyes. He looked to the sky and then back to Darius.

"I apologize. I meant no harm, just wanted to make sure she's fine."

"That's not your job. If you touch her again, I will fucking kill you." Darius took a step toward Leon, making sure to keep himself between me and Leon.

Archer and two other fae, one of them being the earth fae Darius had just sparred with, also placed themselves in between Darius and Leon, as if they could do anything to stop him. I raced towards Darius, wrapping my arms around him from behind.

"Stop," I whispered. I felt my own body trembling around him. I knew what he planned to do. I had seen it flash through my mind's eye. Leon's throat ripped out. Darius' mouth was covered in blood. Archer's neck snapped after he tried to stop Darius. "Please, please stop," I begged him.

Darius froze. He didn't speak or move a muscle for what felt like an eternity. After some time, he released the breath he was holding, stepped out of my grasp, and turned to me.

I am sorry.

Those three words flashed into my mind. I blinked and Darius was gone. I looked around and he had completely left the training grounds.

The crowd was silent. All eyes were on me. I felt as if I was about to explode.

"What are you all looking at? You aren't going to get any stronger staring at our Queen. Back to work!" Leon announced as he walked over to me. Everyone listened. Only Leon now looked my way.

"I don't know what got into him. I am so sorry." Leon cut me off with a wave of his hand before I could say another word. "No need to apologize. I understand where he is coming from. With everything going on, he has the right to be cautious."

"That gives him no excuse to act that way,"

"We do crazy things for the ones we love. I was about to head back to my house and go over some paperwork for the scouting missions that happened while I was away. Care to join me? We can stop at Buck's Tavern on the way?"

"Thank you for the offer, but I should really go try to find Darius," I said quietly, taking my bow from his hand. I saw that same shift, from flames to darkness, in his eyes as he looked down, then back at me.

"So be it," he said as he turned to Archer. "Come, son, we have much to discuss."

I looked all over the village for Darius. I couldn't find him anywhere. I went into every shop, and every tavern, and no one had seen him. It was nine PM before I gave up. I had hoped he would be in bed waiting for me, but when I got to the bedroom, it was empty.

A wave of exhaustion washed over me as soon as I passed through the threshold. I barely made it into my night clothes and bed before I passed out for the night.

I awoke to the sounds of screaming from outside. Heavy footsteps could be heard rushing down the stairs and the door flew open. I jumped from my bed and threw on a robe to cover myself. My heart pounded as I raced down the stairs in my bare feet and found everyone outside.

Everyone except Darius.

The streets were full of people rushing around. Everyone was in a panic.

"What's going on?" I questioned as I joined Daphne and Archer. Archer wore an angry expression. When Daphne's eyes met mine, I saw her face fill with worry.

"Darius went crazy. He slaughtered twenty-two fae overnight and into this morning. He was in a frenzy. No one could stop him," Archer snapped in my direction.

Leon joined our group, but I did not see where he came from. "Do not take your anger out on the Queen. She is not responsible for the monster's actions," Leon said to his son.

"He is not a monster!" I cried out. My stomach was in knots. There was no way this was happening. Darius wouldn't do this. I tried to reach out to him through the bond but felt nothingness in return. I couldn't reach him. "He wouldn't do that! That is not who he is!" Tears threatened to fall from my eyes, and I desperately tried to hold them in.

"My Queen, several people witnessed it, and we have the bodies in the hall of the dead to prove it. Their throats were ripped out, Sabrina," Leon said softly as he put his hand on my shoulder.

I jerked away from him. I could not stand his touch as it sent a freezing shock down my body.

"Where are Ron and Xander?" I stepped back, looking around, my breath quickening.

Daphne stepped in front of me and took my hands in hers. "Breathe. It's going to be ok," she said in a whisper. My eyes met hers and I saw hopelessness for the first time in them. I couldn't hold it in any longer, and my body fell into hers as I sobbed. She wrapped her arms around me. "Come on, let's get you inside."

Everything that we had worked for was destroyed. How could he do this to me? How could I defend him to my people when he had mercilessly killed so many of them?

Daphne guided me into the house and shut the door. I fell to my knees, tilted my head back, and wailed. Daphne put a hand on my shoulder and then knelt in front of me, our knees pressed together.

"Breath," she said calmly.

I couldn't.

The walls closed in around me. My chest tightened. My sight was blinded by tears. My body went ice cold, and then everything went black.

Eighteen

My lungs burned. My vision was blurry when I first opened my eyes, and when it came into focus, I was on my knees alone in the purple haze. The air was ice cold, and the silence was near deafening. When I stood, I felt a familiar tug from deep inside me and ran in the direction of the tug.

"Darius?" I called out into the haze. Frantically, I called out to him again and again as the tug got stronger. I slammed into a brick wall and the tugging vanished.

The silence filled with that dark laughter. The one that made my skin crawl. A rough hand gripped my shoulder and spun me around.

There he was, towering over me. Draven slammed me into the wall. He ran the back of his fingertips against my cheek, and I trembled at his touch. His presence was overwhelming. Draven's magic radiated off of him, it was incredibly powerful. The scent of moss and leather filled my nose. I was frozen as I looked up at him. I could feel the tears flowing down my face.

"See how easily the vampire King can be sent into a frenzy? He is no longer in the way. Serafina is mine. You're mine, little mouse."

Nineteen

I sat up quickly, gasping for breath while my heart was pounding wildly in my chest. My body was drenched in a cold sweat. Daphne, Ron, and Xander all sat in my room. Daphne was by my side, Ron at the end of the bed, and Xander sat in the armchair in the corner. Before they could say anything, the words flew out of my mouth.

"It was Draven. I don't know how, but Draven caused him to go into a frenzy. Darius would never do anything like that!" I tried to reach out through the bond again. Nothingness. I felt pure nothingness as I tried to feel his presence. My heart broke once again.

Daphne's hand found my knee.

"Darius is not a good person," Ron said before anyone else. "Your love for him doesn't diminish the monster that he is."

The room fell silent. A lump formed in my throat.

"Ron, that was harsh," Daphne snapped at him.

"No, he's right. That aside, I am telling you that Darius was not responsible for what happened."

"That's impossible. This village has been here for centuries with no sign of Draven," Xander said from his corner.

"Draven has been communicating with me," I confessed.

"What?" They all said in unison.

"Through my dreams. He was communicating with Darius as well. After I blacked out, Draven came to me and said he caused Darius to go into a frenzy."

"How is that possible?" Daphne questioned.

"I don't know. What I do know is that I need to go back to Titus." I pushed the blankets away from me and got out of bed.

"You can't give up and go back to Titus. We are so close. Staying in Tasumanza is the best thing for you right now. Continue to work with the resistance and learn more," Daphne said.

"I need to talk to Andrei and Isabella. If Darius is out in the forest in a frenzy, Andrei is the only one who can help."

"I will go," Xander stood from the chair and stepped out of the corner. His shadows clinging to him.

"No, you will stay. You know the most about Draven. Your job while I am gone is to get as much information as you can. You too, Ron."

Ron nodded in agreement. Xander said nothing for a moment, then agreed.

"Sabrina, please be careful. Ron and I will collect all the information that we can while you are away. Do you know how to even get to Titus from here?"

"In the scouting journals that I have been studying, there have been countless maps. They have scouted the wall so many times. I know exactly where to go. The journey will be a long one. It will take four days each way. Now that we have a map, we know exactly where we are going."

"You can't go alone," Daphne said.

"Never planned to. Pack your things. We leave in an hour."

We told no one other than Ron and Xander we were leaving. We made our way to the stables and found our horses. I had hoped that the stable would be empty. Unfortunately, that was not the case.

"Queen Sabrina!" an earth fae woman said as she brushed her horse's mane. "We weren't expecting you. Are you needing an escort?"

"Daphne is my escort." I looked toward her and got our horses out of the stalls.

"Will you be gone long?"

"We are just taking a ride to clear our heads,"

"With those bags?"

Daphne stepped forward and took the earth fae's hand. A soft glow formed around them.

"You never saw us here today." Daphne's voice was soft and melodic.

"I never saw you," the earth fae said in a trance-like state.

"I haven't seen you do that in forever," I said to Daphne as we mounted our horses.

"Haven't needed to. I do not like doing that. It feels dirty," she said with a shiver.

We quickly made our way into the forest. As we passed through the wards to exit the village borders, a sense of dread washed over me. Thoughts flooded my brain that I was abandoning my people. They needed me here more than Darius needed me to save him.

I pushed those thoughts away, and my head cleared more the farther away from the village we got. I needed to get away from Serafina — from Draven. I prayed that his influence wouldn't reach me in Titus.

I tried again to reach out to Darius through the bond. My attempts went into nothing as if we had no bond in place at all. That was what worried me the most. Even with the curse, I had always felt the tug that led me to him. To feel nothing left me feeling empty.

Daphne and I had gotten lucky so far with our travels. The forest had been desolate. We had not seen any more monsters, nor did we have to hack our way through thick vines. With the map I had taken from the journals, it had been easy navigation. After we set up camp for the third night, the two of us huddled in front of the fire, my head resting on Daphne's shoulder.

I never knew the woman who gave birth to me. I was taken from her at birth, As was every queen before me. It's not as if that person was my mother. When a queen died, another fae woman became pregnant with no male involvement. There was a point in my life I wished to know the woman who had birthed me, but that feeling left me long ago. In many ways, Daphne was my mother, and Xander my semi-absent father. The two of them raised me, taught me my magic, and taught me about life.

"We should arrive in Titus tomorrow if all goes as planned. Are you ready to be back? To see Andrei—and Isabella?" Daphne said softly, the crackles of the fire almost overtaking her voice.

"I would rather do anything else at this time than speak to Isa. I am still mad at her."

"Why?"

I sat up straight and looked at her with a raised eyebrow. Daphne knew damn well why I was mad at her. I was mad that she tried to turn her back on my people. I was mad about how she spoke to Daphne. I was mad that our friendship changed when we were both no longer human. Before I could, Daphne spoke once again.

"That anger does not serve you. It will give you premature wrinkles. Release it."

"You don't even like her. Where is this coming from?"

"She was a good friend to you. This anger will not serve us. It will not serve our kingdom, or when the two unite."

I had not even thought about what would happen once I reclaimed and restored Serafina. Would we unite our kingdoms? Would we finally wed as we had planned so long ago?

I hated to admit it, but Daphne was right. I needed to let go of any negative feelings I had for Isabella. She was my best friend. On top of that, she and Andrei are thick as thieves. Maybe once all of this is over, the two of them would marry. I was surprised that the two of them had not yet. Andrei was Darius' second in command. I wondered how Darius felt about their union. Darius had never hidden his negative feelings for Isa.

"Go get some sleep. We need to get up early in the morning to make sure we get to Titus before noon," Daphne smiled. I stood and made my way to my bed roll. "Oh, Sabrina. We will get him back."

I was so happy to be back in the city. I missed the luxury of cars. We were able to get one at one of the camps that lined the wall. They were still working on clearing the debris. That would be one of the first modern things I would bring to Serafina. We raced our way to the Golden Circle and the palace. We were stopped at the gate by one of the guards who looked like he saw a ghost when our eyes met.

"Lady Sabrina! Lady Daphne! You two were not expected. Where is the King?"

"This is urgent. I need to speak with Andrei. Where is he?" I responded frantically.

"Yes, Lord Andrei and Lady Isabella are here. I will ring them to let them know you have arrived," he said as he opened the gate. I pressed on the gas and made my way up the drive, parking directly in front of the front entrance, jumping out of the car, and rushing into the palace. Daphne followed closely behind me.

"Lady Sabrina!" One of the servants said as she bowed. "I was told to let you know the Lord and Lady are in Darius' office."

"Thank you," I said to her as I ran up the grand staircase and found my way to his office. The door was already open as I approached. Andrei sat behind the desk and Isa sat on top of it on the left side. As soon as I stepped over the threshold, Isa rushed to me and had me wrapped in a hug in an instant.

"I missed you," she whispered in my ear. "I am so sorry. For everything."

I embraced her back. "I am sorry, too."

Isa took a step back but still held my shoulders. "You smell terrible," she chuckled.

"I traveled four days through the forest on horseback to get here. Not everyone has the luxury of living in a castle," I teased.

"Where is Darius?" Andrei interrupted.

I informed them of Tasumanza and the resistance. I told them of the dreams Darius and I had been experiencing. Of the rage he felt when he met Leon, and when Leon touched me. How Darius had been missing that entire day, and how the next morning we were told he had killed so many innocents. A look of terror crossed their faces, Isa's more so than Andrei's.

Andrei stood from his chair and was at Isa's side in an instant. He had wrapped his arm around her tightly.

"When we returned to Titus, Isa had a similar experience."

"I killed six people," her voice trembled. "I will never forgive myself for what happened."

"No! What happened?" Daphne and I said in unison. Isa had always refused to drink human blood.

"I don't know. In Serafina, I felt so angry. I kept telling myself that I didn't need to be and that I was acting crazy, but I couldn't control it. As soon as we got into Titus, it was like a light switch."

"How did you get yourself out of it?" Daphne questioned.

"I heard Andrei calling to me, from inside me. It helped pull me back to where I needed to be. Please let me go with you. To Serafina. To find Darius."

"I cannot go. I am still needed here. It appears it was not the smartest to take both Darius and me away at the same time. Isa should be a great help. She will be able to sense his vampiric energies," Andrei added.

"The problem is, I can't feel Darius through our bond anymore," I whimpered.

"I couldn't feel Isa either while she was in her frenzy. Though our bond is different, our bond is a sire bond." The sire bond was a bond that happened between a vampire and anyone that they had turned. They had a vague sense of their location, could sense emotions, and in rare cases even speak telepathically and feel each other's pain. "It is nowhere near as strong as your bond that was gifted from the gods. I had to search deeply to find her. I was looking for the best in her. I had to shift my thoughts to look for the worst. All the good in her had vanished during the frenzy."

I had never thought of that. I had reached out to the kind, thoughtful, passionate Darius I loved, not the cruel, demanding, and selfish one who lurked deep within him. The monster he tried to hide from me. The monster we pretended he wasn't.

"Rest from your travels. Eat, bathe, and sleep. I will have everything ready for you three in the morning," Andrei said with a smile.

We were not as lucky on the way back. Somehow, the forest was darker and denser. The air stung as I breathed in. The purple haze was dense and made it nearly impossible to see in front of us. On the journey to Titus, the purple haze hung in the canopy. It had now fully taken over the air. Daphne had summoned orbs of light to help guide our way. They helped, but only enough to see the next step we were going to take. The worst part was the stench. The forest smelled like pure rot as if we were walking with the dead of Serafina decomposing around us. It was unnerving and put all of us on edge.

We had caught Isa up on everything that she missed while she was away. I was thankful that she and Daphne had been civil with one another. I could tell they were just trying to get along for me. We didn't need any more internal conflict. I worried that the history between them would make this journey incredibly awkward for me. The three of us chatted like we had been best friends for centuries.

I had not yet tried to reach Darius through our bond. I was too afraid of what I would find if I reached out to the worst parts of him. I thought back to before Darius and I had met, to the man he was back then. To the man whose blood lust could not be satisfied. To all the people he had murdered for fun. To all the times he had murdered me during the curse.

I was not ready to see that man again.

We had traveled for two days, praying to the gods that we were traveling in the right direction. Our horses stopped abruptly. They refused to move a single muscle. We all tried to get our horses to move forward, but they would not budge.

The silence of the forest was broken by a deep growl followed by cold velvet laughter that made my whole body tense. A sharp pain flashed in my ribs, a reminder of what was. The laughter faded, and the growl turned into a roar, then two, then three.

Daphne and Isa jumped off their horses. Isa readied her twinblade, and Daphne's hands filled with glowing magic. I stayed on top of my horse and took the bow off my back and prepared an arrow. Three dark beast silhouettes appeared in the haze.

I aimed and released the arrow I'd imbued with fire. It struck one of the beasts. Upon impact, it stood on its hind legs and wailed into the sky. The two others lunged at us. The beasts were now in full view, and we finally grasped what we were up against. Their form was similar to that of a wolf, but five times the size. They had fur as dark as the void, their eyes glowed purple, and shadows clung to them, similar to how they clung to Xander and Ron.

One lunged at Isa, trying to swipe at her with their long, sharp claws. Isa twirled her blade and lunged toward the beast. Watching Isa in battle was like watching the most elegant dancer I had ever seen. Each step was calculated. Each move of her blade was precise. She struck its extended arm, slicing through cleanly. That did not stop the beast from advancing toward her. She spun around the blade once again and jabbed forward with the other end.

Flashes of light filled our battlefield from Daphne's hands as she unleashed her magic toward the beast before her. Each white blast landed its mark, striking the beast in its chest and exploding on impact. The beast's shadows completely dissipated from Daphne's light. She relentlessly sent blow after blow to the beast, completely overwhelming it. The haze around us cleared from the battlefield from the light and commotion.

The smell of burnt flesh filled the air mixed with the scent of rot, and it was enough to make me gag. I pushed all these thoughts out of my head as I readied the next arrow and took aim at the beast I had previously hit. This time, swirls of red, blue, green, yellow, and black swirled around the arrow. I put everything I had into this arrow. I shot it and this time it landed directly in its eye. The arrow did not stop. It traveled through its head and burst out the other side of its head. The beast fell limp as the arrow struck a tree that was behind it.

I looked towards the others and saw they had both slain the beasts they were up against. Isa huffed a deep breath.

"We make a good team. Easy peasy," she said as she strapped her twinblade to her back.

"Indeed, we do. We are forces that should not be disturbed," Daphne responded.

The purple haze had completely cleared from the area. The forest was now fully in view once again. Even with the previous obstacles, we were exactly where we needed to be. A chill ran down my spine. A dark presence could be felt from behind me. I spun around and saw the albatross perched on a tree limb. My heart pounded as it opened its beak and screamed in my direction.

Suddenly, a bolt of light struck the bird directly in its chest. The albatross flailed its wings for a moment then went limp as I watched it fall from the tree, landing on the ground with a hard thud.

"Stupid bird," I heard Daphne say from behind me. "I am tired of that wretched thing following us and squawking outside my window before dawn."

"You had seen it before?" I questioned.

"Indeed. I could feel the dark power coming from it, but every time I went to strike it, it would vanish." Daphne said as she walked over to the dead bird and peered down on it. "I am glad it will no longer watch us with beady eyes."

Twenty

As soon as we returned to the village, we were bombarded with questions from Leon and Archer. Xander and Ron had not told anyone where we had gone, or for how long we would be gone. They had only told them that we would return soon.

I was a bit nervous about bringing Isa to the village. With Darius' attack, I was unsure of how they would respond to Isa's presence. I was pleased that everyone greeted her with open arms. They had been as kind to her as they had been to all of us.

The first two days of our return had been very busy, and we did not get much time to ourselves. We had found ourselves in several meetings with returning scout parties that were giving us information on how the darkness had worsened across the forest. Previous areas that were untouched now were added to the Circle of Death. Another scouting party had returned, and they had informed us that three of their members had been lured into the castle. The group said that they tried to stop them, but nothing they did would pull them from their trance-like state. They claimed they had even tied them up, but each time they would somehow get free. Somehow, the three got away before anyone could stop them.

I spent a lot of time with the families that were affected by Darius' attack. I made sure to visit each one and provide my condolences and gift baskets. I knew my words would mean nothing, but it was the least that I could do. Each was filled with things that I had purchased from the many shops around town. They all were appreciative of my visit, but I am sure many of them left words unsaid.

At the house, there was not much time where it was just Daphne, Isa, Xander, Ron, and myself. It seemed every time I entered, Leon and Archer were having a meeting with some of the warriors about their next move.

On the second night back, I found myself lying in bed, wide awake. The bed felt incredibly empty. My heart and body ached for the man that should be here by my side. I tossed and turned all night, begging for sleep and peaceful dreams. Neither came.

I took a deep breath and closed my eyes. My entire body trembled, yearning for me to try reaching out through the bond again.

My thoughts spiraled around me as I reminded myself of what Andrei said. I had to think the worst. Darius was a monster. He killed for fun. He tortured people. He had no regard for any life other than his own. He was controlling, jealous, and angry. He was a miserable son of a bitch. All I was to him was a toy and a food source.

Suddenly, I heard him roar in the back of my mind. My whole body heated as his roar grew louder. I opened my eyes and found myself in a bedroom. The walls were a dark red, the black double doors were shut, and a fire roared in the fireplace on the right side of the room. A black bedspread covered my body, and when I sat up, there was a tug against my neck. I reached up and felt cold metal. Looking behind me, I found that not only was I collared, but I was also chained to the headboard.

I tried to summon my magic to try to break the collar, but nothing came. My magic was gone. I pulled on the chain. I yanked and yanked, but it did not yield. My chest tightened and my body trembled more as I gave up on trying to pull free.

Trapped. I was trapped.

I screamed for help and pleaded to be let free. My cries were answered by silence. I was alone for hours in that room. Panic continued to build within me. This world wasn't real. This was in my mind. This was a dream. All I had to do was wake up and I would be free.

The double doors swung open, and a breeze flew in that sent a chill down my spine. I looked up to the door and watched as Darius strode in. He smirked at me, baring his fangs. His mouth was covered in blood, and his eyes were red and glazed over.

"Are you done crying?" He snarled at me. "You are so fucking annoying when you cry." He stopped at the foot of the bed, an expression of anger on his face.

"Unchain me," I demanded.

"Now where is the fun in that, doll?" The moonlight shone through the large window and illuminated his skin. His bare chest was on display.

"Dar—" he cut me off before I could even speak his name. He had lunged onto the bed and pressed his palm into my mouth.

"Shut the fuck up." Rage filled his voice. "When will you learn you belong to me and will do as I say?"

My body shook uncontrollably. I scooted away from him until my back found the headboard. Darius crawled closer to me. Running his hand across the silk of the red nightgown I wore, he slid his hand up gently. His eyes locked on mine, and that predatory grin crossed his face as he hooked his fingers under the strap. He yanked hard and snapped the strap. Darius continued to rip the silk off of my body to expose my most intimate parts. His tongue ran across his top lip.

"Much better," he purred.

"Darius, stop it. This is not the time for this. Where are you?"

"I will tell you what it is time for." He grabbed my hips and pulled me closer to him. His fingertips dug into my skin as my back hit the mattress. His breathing slowed, and I watched his chest rise and fall.

"Darius, I need to find you."

Before I could say another word, he took the ripped silk in one hand and grabbed me by my hair with the other. He wrapped the silk around my head, making sure it was tied tightly around my mouth.

"There we go. No more words out of that pretty little mouth of yours." His voice was dark and seductive, and despite the fear I felt, wetness grew in between my thighs. "I am so tired of worrying about anything that's not my cock and fangs buried inside you. If that piece of shit faerie thinks he can take you from me, he's wrong."

He quickly removed his dark-colored pants, and his cock sprang free, already fully erect.

He reached down, grabbed my thighs, and pulled my legs apart. His head lowered and ran his tongue against the delicate skin of my inner thigh and groaned. Darius wasted no time before he bit into my upper thigh. My body fully relaxed as pleasure ran through my veins. Darius gripped my legs tightly as he continued to feed on me. I began to feel lightheaded as he took more and more.

He finally pulled away from me and snarled as our eyes locked. I watched him rise. He bent himself forward so his face was just an inch from mine, and we shared the same electrified air. I felt as if my heart was about to jump out of my chest.

Darius lined himself up with my soaked opening and thrust in, holding himself deep inside me as I quivered against him. He slowly pumped himself in and out of me from base to tip. His hands found my knees, and he forced them open wider, pinning my legs to the bed. His pace quickened.

"You feel so good on my cock. You were made for me," he groaned. He pulled fully out. "Look at how you glisten against me, doll."

Once again, he plunged himself deep. I never felt such pleasure as I erupted around him. I moaned into the silk as my eyes rolled back. Darius let out a dark chuckle under his breath as he pounded into me harder, showing me no mercy. I arched my back, needing him deeper.

He hit my deepest inner wall over and over. I reached up, gripping his wrists. The look in his eyes was all I needed to find my pleasure once again. I felt myself drench his cock. My juices coated me and dripped down my legs. He drove himself as deep as he could and roared with his release. So hot and deep that I could barely stand it.

As he slowly pulled out, his seed leaked from me. He reached down with one hand and with two fingers and caught some of what had poured out. With his free hand, he pulled the silk from my mouth. Before I could say anything, he pushed his fingers past my lips.

"Suck our juices off my fingers, doll. Taste how delicious we are together."

I obeyed and looked up at him as I sucked his fingers clean, heat rising to my cheeks.

"Good girl," he purred. "You are so cute when you're my obedient little whore." He dragged his fingers out of my mouth, slowly brushing over my bottom lip. I watched a shift in his eyes. He looked down at me, quickly grabbed my legs, and folded them over my upper body.

"You know, doll," his voice became rough, "there is one part of you I have never claimed. How can you be fully mine if there are parts of you I have not touched?"

"Don't you dare," I growled at him. He reached forward, putting the silk back into my mouth, making it tighter than it was before.

"You do not tell me no. You are my toy to do with as I please."

He lined himself up with my untouched hole. Our juices coated us both and allowed him to ease in the tip. My eyes went wide, and I screamed into the silk as he stretched me.

He groaned to the sky as I felt myself clench around him. He looked back down at me. He released one of my legs and moved his hand to grip my jaw tightly. His index finger and thumb pressed into my cheeks. "Look me in the eyes as I take what's left of you, doll."

He slowly leaned his body forward, making me take another inch of him. He pulled out to the tip, then pushed in again, a bit deeper. Inch by inch, he stretched my tiny hole. My body writhed under him as he pushed in and out, over and over, until his full length was inside me. The feeling was completely overwhelming. I could not tell if it hurt or was the best thing I ever experienced. He made me watch him as he slowly pulled to the tip and then slammed deep inside me. Pleasure coursed through my body as he pounded into me. I gripped the sheets tightly and arched my back.

He released my face and grabbed the chain above me, gripping it tight and using it to support himself as Darius used me as hard and fast as he could with reckless abandon.

I found release like I had never experienced before, and through the pain, I had the best climax I had ever had. He continued to fuck me through my orgasm, and it threw me over an edge I did not know existed once again. He pulled on the chain so hard that it ripped from the headboard, giving him full control of my leash. With his other hand, he ripped the silk away from my mouth, and I let out a loud moan, grateful my mouth was finally free.

He yanked the chain hard towards him, forcing me to be closer. He held it tight as he lowered himself and his mouth crashed into mine. Our tongues danced as he ruined my last hole. The taste of blood filled my mouth as he bit my lower lip and pulled away from the kiss. His cock twitched as he shot inside me once again. This load was much more than the last. He held it there, not allowing my body any reprieve.

"Such a good little whore. Letting this vampire fuck your ass after what I did. You just can't help yourself, can you?" He snarled and began to slowly pull out, but halfway pushed back in. "You crave me, don't you, doll?"

I said nothing. He was right. I did crave him. I needed every inch of him inside every hole. If it was possible, I would allow him to fill all three at once.

He chuckled as if he knew my every thought. He most likely did. He fully removed himself from me. I felt so empty as he removed himself from me and both holes leaked his cum.

"Such a pretty little whore." He smirked as he got up from the bed and put his pants back on. I couldn't say a word until I watched him turn and head to the door.

"Darius, where are you? I need to find you so we can find Draven."

"Don't bother finding me. You are a distraction. I need to be free. I need to be me. I do not need you to kill that faerie. I will find him on my own, and I will kill him on my own. He thought sending me into a frenzy was going to take me out of the game. No, it fueled my drive to end him."

That's when it hit me. All twenty-two fae he had killed were dark fae. We were lucky that Xander and Ron were not included in that body count.

"He wants to own what is mine, fuck what is mine, destroy what is mine." Venom dripped from every word. "I do not like when people touch my things."

He strode out of the room just as he had entered it, taking that cold wind with him that had sent a shiver down my spine. The fireplace roared as I snapped back into my head and found myself staring at the ceiling of the house in the village, feeling empty and defeated.

259

Twenty-One

After that, no matter how hard I tried, I was unable to feel Darius through our bond. He had completely shut me out of his mind. I told the others to leave me be, instructing them to not interrupt me while I continued to reach out to him.

I was alone in my room for three days before I gave up. When the sun finally came through the window and warmed my skin, I got up from bed and walked downstairs. I did not bother changing out of my nightclothes, and my long hair draped around my shoulders in a loose mess.

I grabbed a pastry from the kitchen and joined Ron, Xander, Isa, and Daphne at the dining room table. They all stared at me in silence as I took a bite. I looked up at them through my lashes.

"What?" I snapped. I was utterly exhausted, and I was sick of them all looking at me like some fragile doll.

"Just surprised to see you up," Xander said from across the table. His arm rested on the table as he taped his fingers.

"Did you find him?" Isa asked quietly. I raised my gaze to match hers and shook my head before leaning back in my seat and taking another bite.

"What do you guys have for me? Anything on Draven?"

"Unfortunately, we do," Ron said. I raised an eyebrow in response.

"He is like you," Daphne said quietly.

"Like me?" I leaned forward and put my elbows on the table.

"He is no longer just a dark fae. He has access to all magics. Some we believe to be beyond this realm, unknown to you," Xander responded.

"Possibly unknown to us," Daphne added.

"On top of that, no one has seen him. We assume he is in the castle," Ron said.

"Ok, so we go to the castle," I said as I stood.

"No," Daphne and Xander said in unison. Daphne then added, "it is not safe. We do not strike until we get more information."

"I will continue to work to try to find Darius. I have not felt any vampiric energy in the area. I will widen my search," Isa declared.

"Are you still going to try to reach him through the bond?" Ron asked.

"No. If he wants to shut me out, I don't need him."

Later that afternoon, I made my way to the training grounds. I didn't know what, or who, I was feeling the most anger towards, but I needed to blow off some steam. Arrow after arrow, shot after shot, I hit the target's dead center. Each arrow splitting the previous one down the center as I hit my mark.

I tried to release my anger with each shot. I was mad that Draven had gotten the better of me one too many times. Angry that he had somehow sent Darius into a frenzy and that Darius refused to come out of it. Enraged that my people continued to suffer as I scrambled for some kind of solution.

I continued to fire until my quiver was empty. I walked back to the arsenal to restock it with more arrows than I had before. The fire that burned inside me would not extinguish.

"I hope you don't plan on setting anything ablaze with those arrows," Leon's voice teased from behind me. I spun to meet him. He grabbed a long bow off the wall along with a quiver.

"I did not know you did archery," I said with a raised brow.

"It's the only weapon I use. Something about pulling back the string and releasing your arrow is very cathartic."

"I agree."

"I had heard so many rumors of Shimmerthorne before your return. What is it like to have a magic weapon?"

"Shimmerthorne and I are one. She speaks to me as I speak to her. The feeling and connection we have cannot be described."

"Similar to your bond with the vampire King?"

"Similar, yet different. Also in ways I cannot describe, only feel. Why the interest in magic weapons?" I said as I turned to make my way back to the targets.

Leon followed me. "I just find the concept fascinating. How that bow appeared to you on your sixteenth birthday. Many say it was a gift from the gods."

No one knew of Shimmerthorne's origin. It was true that it appeared to me on my sixteenth birthday. Daphne said she had found it wrapped in a box on the castle steps that morning. There was no note with the box. As soon as I laid my hands on it, something clicked between us when I felt its magic rush into me and mine rush into it. We merged and became one that day. To this day, we all wonder how it arrived with no one noticing.

We made our way back to the targets. Leon sat on the bench to the left.

"Before I get started, I would love to watch you in action. If you don't mind."

"Not at all," I smiled and drew my bow, loaded the arrow, and pulled back the string. Melodic whispers filled my head as the bow gently controlled my motions as we aimed. I released, and the arrow flew through the air. Streaks of color surrounded it as it whirled toward the target. The arrow found its mark and struck. It did not stop. It ripped through and landed on a tree behind. The colors still dancing around the arrow, as if to show off.

"Magnificent. We could really use someone with such skill on our scouting teams," Leon said as he stood and walked toward my side. "I know you are wanting to scout the castle grounds. I am free to start the journey in the morning if you wish."

I needed to go. I had to see my home close up. Was Draven truly at the castle? Was my home truly beyond repair?

"Yes, let's go. Don't tell anyone. The others would think it foolish and dangerous." The others could not find out that I was going. They would never allow it. However, I am the Queen, and I decide what I need to do for my people.

"Understood. This shall stay between us, my Queen," Leon smirked as he raised a bow and readied an arrow of his own. "Meet me at the stables just as the sun kisses the sky." He released his arrow, but no lights danced as it struck the target, slightly off center.

Twenty-Two

I snuck out of the house before dawn with a pack ready and my hair braided back. Luckily for me, everyone was still snoozing in their beds. The village was just as quiet. No one had yet left their homes and greeted the day. I traveled through the shadows and made my way to the stables.

Leon was there and waiting with a single, readied horse. I looked around. Other than the two of us and the one horse, the stable was empty. He finished tightening the cinch strap and turned towards me with a grin.

"Good morning, my Queen. Ready to ride?" He reached forward and grabbed my bag for me and attached it to the saddle. "It will be about a three-day journey to the castle."

"Only one horse?" I raised an eyebrow. "Where are the others?"

"Another scout group went out last night," he said as he got on the horse and extended a hand to me. "Ambrosia is the last one. Good thing she's a sturdy horse."

I took his hand, and he assisted me up onto Ambrosia. I felt him adjust and press against my back. His arms wrapped around me as he grabbed the reins, steered us out of the stable, and headed into the forest.

It was high noon when we took our first break of the day. Leon said that after about another hour of travel, we would enter the Circle of Death. We dismounted Ambrosia and Leon tied her reins around a tree limb to keep her in place.

I reached up to the sky, stretching my aching body. Riding for long hours still made me extremely sore. I don't think I would ever get used to it. I watched Leon as he grabbed something from the saddle and made his way to a small patch of dirt. He knelt and scooped a small amount of the dirt into a tiny glass bottle. He corked it and then added some grass into another.

"What are you doing?" I walked over to his side as he rose.

"Every time I go out, I like to collect samples. When I return to the village, I test them to see how affected by the Darkness this section of the forest is."

"Test it? How?"

"Draven is a dark fae. Most of his powers are dark magic, including the curse on Serafina. I pass the samples to the dark fae of the village and they can tell how much dark magic is in the samples," he explained as he walked over to a tree and collected some bark.

"Fascinating." I found it slightly odd that out of all the written reports we had gone through, I had not read anything of these tests. Xander and Ron had gotten close to the dark fae of Tasumanza, but they had not mentioned any of these tests back to me.

The Circle of Death sent every one of my senses on edge. For a place so silent, I didn't understand how it was so loud. Death screamed all around me. The section we traveled was razed, a barren wasteland with nothing remaining. The sun was high but was lightly fogged by the purple haze.

Leon was tense behind me. He claimed there wasn't a single time he had been in the Circle where he had not been attacked by some terrible beast, and in some of the battles, he had been lucky to come out triumphant.

Nothingness surrounded us. I tried to assure him that we would see anything coming our way long before it got to us.

"Don't be so sure. Nothing is ever as it seems in the circle," he said matter-of-factly.

We traveled for many more miles before setting up camp. Several hours prior, the purple haze had gotten so thick that it had obscured all of the sun's light and its warmth, causing the night to be completely frigid. Leon made us a small fire as I set out my bedroll. I sat on top of it and crossed my legs, allowing the flame to warm my body.

Warmth quickly overtook me as I stared into the blaze. I watched the flames dance and flicker. My breath slowed, and I found myself unable to pull my gaze away. In the flames, I saw my kingdom rise and fall, then rebuild anew. A better and brighter Serafina.

"Queen Sabrina!" Leon's call pulled me from my vision. He had stood with a bow in hand and an arrow at the ready. Loud screeching filled my ears, and the sound was quickly drawing closer. I followed Leon's gaze and saw a hoard of giant bats heading our way.

I jumped up from the bedroll, grabbing my bow on the way up. Looking around for the quiver, I realized I had left it hung in the tree next to the horse. I was so tired of carrying it, as soon as I got off Ambrosia, I had thrown it off my back.

I rushed towards the tree as the bats were upon us. They swooped down in a mob. I used my magic to add force to the air and push them away. I continued to clear the path in front of me, trying to get to my arrows.

Heat rose and fell on my back as Leon's fire magic erupted behind me. I got just within arm's reach of the tree when one of the bats dove down, grabbed onto the strap of the quiver, and flung it up into the sky. The arrows flew through the air and out of my reach. I froze for just a moment, but that moment was all they needed.

Another bat took that opportunity to fly down and attack. Its razor-sharp teeth dug into my upper arm, and a piercing, sharp pain coursed through my body as it tore into my flesh. I grabbed it by the back and threw it as hard as I could. I raised my blood-drenched arm to the sky, squeezed my fist together, and slammed it downward. As if gravity intensified, the bats around me slammed into the ground.

I turned to Leon and watched him set the ones around him ablaze. Each of his motions was forceful and direct. He punched forward, and flames burst out, enveloping the bats directly in his path.

I released my fist and raised my hand once again in an open palm. Roots came shooting out from the ground and wrapped around the bats, tightly constricting the ones who were unlucky enough to be caught. I heard their bones snap as the vines squeezed harder.

Leon fought through the swarm until he was by my side. Our magics intertwined and worked together to bring down the last of the bats. As the final one was eliminated, I fell to the ground, overwhelmed and exhausted. The pain in my arm was minimal during the battle, but now that it had ended and the adrenaline began to fade, it was nearly unbearable.

I looked at the bite and was met with a horrifying sight of torn flesh and an incredible amount of blood, covering my arm and the ground around us. Leon said nothing as he walked over to the saddlebags, pulled out a small kit, and returned to my side. He knelt beside me and opened the kit to reveal medical supplies.

"I will warn you, this won't be pleasant. However, it is better than letting this fester," he whispered as he gently took my arm in his, beginning to clean the wound.

It stung like hell. I winced and pulled back my arm. "Fuck, that hurts!"

"That means it's working. Those bats have so many nasty bacteria in their mouths. We need to kill them before you get infected." He grabbed my arm and held it tighter and continued to clean it. I clenched both my fist and jaw as he began to close the wound with a needle and medical string. Once he was done, he held his hand over it gently and my entire body was overwhelmed by heat and pain. I wailed into the sky.

"All done," he said as he lowered his hand. I looked at the wound. It had been stitched together and cauterized. For the first time since the battle's end, I finally got a good look at Leon. He did not have a single injury from the attack. I, however, was going to be left with a terrible scar and was covered in my own blood. I stood and thanked him for patching me up. He rose as well and nodded.

I looked up to the sky and heavy rain began to fall and washed away the evidence of battle from our bodies. Leon's magical fire still danced several feet from us.

"Leon, turn around. I need to shower and change from my battle-worn attire."

"Yes, my Queen," he said as he turned away and looked up into the sky.

After three long days of travel, we finally made it to the castle. A feeling of despair washed over me as soon as we stepped onto the grounds. We entered through the orchard where every tree was still standing but was completely devoid of life. The bark that had once been many shades of brown, white, and green was now drained of all color.

I dismounted Ambrosia and walked into the center of the orchard.

"Be careful! We do not know what traps lay hidden," Leon called out from behind me. I did not care. I could see my castle in the distance. We were so close, yet it seems a million miles away. To see how my home was destroyed up close was more than I could handle. I fell to my knees and sobbed. I heard Leon dismount and approach me from behind. Each step he took amplified in my mind. They got louder and was the only thing I could focus on. I felt my power explode out of my control. The air rushed and the dried leaves whirled around me. My magic wrapped me in a cocoon, not allowing him any closer.

Images flashed through my mind of how things used to be. The prolific orchard. The gardens were lush and beautiful. My home that I once loved and cherished. It had cherished me in return. That castle had taken care of me in ways that no one would understand. In ways that I did not fully understand myself. There was magic that flowed through the stone that had taken care of me, and every Queen before me.

Suddenly, I felt something tug inside me that made me dig deeper into my mind. The images of my home transformed into something new—something bigger. The cosmos flashed in my mind's eye. I saw worlds being destroyed and renewed. I felt a new power grow inside me and beg for release.

As the air slowed, my tears vanished, I stood and took two steps forward. I could hear Leon say something to me from behind, but I could not make out the words through the noise in my head. No, my head was filled with voices, too many voices to count, but they all screamed the same thing. They demanded I released them. I lifted my gaze and my hand. A golden ball of light appeared before me. It shined and glimmered like nothing I had seen before. This was life itself. The warm energy exploded and the area around us came back to life.

I watched in awe as the grass grew, and the trees regained their colors and blossomed before my eyes. Fae lights appeared and danced in between the tree limbs as if to welcome them back to life.

I felt a tight grip on my shoulder as Leon quickly spun me around, rage contorted his face.

"We need to go," he growled.

"No! Look what I can do! I can restore all of the castle grounds like this!" I pulled away from him, but he advanced towards me once again.

"My Queen," he took a deep breath to regain his composure, "something, or someone, is coming. We must go. Now."

He took my hand and held it tightly as he pulled me towards Ambrosia. He picked me up, forcing me to get into the saddle. Something was not right about his reaction. I sensed no others around. Was Leon upset about my newfound power?

He forced me to mount Ambrosia and rushed away from the orchard. "It was too risky to bring you here."

Twenty-Three

The ride back to the village was extremely awkward. Leon barely said a single word to me the entire time..

Xander and Daphne rushed us the moment we entered the village's wards. As soon as the horse came to a stop, Xander grabbed me by my arm and pulled me down off the horse.

"What were you thinking? Where have you been?" He demanded.

"Do you know how worried we have been? Do you know how dangerous it is to go alone?" Daphne's tone was harsher than I had ever heard her.

"She was not alone. I was there," Leon said angrily from behind us. Xander's gaze snapped to him.

"What happened to her arm? Are you ok?" He snarled. "I swear to the gods Leon—"

"We went to the castle. We were attacked by bats on the way. Leon patched the bite up. I am fine." I interrupted him before he could speak further.

Isa, Ron, and Archer joined us.

Isa rushed to my side and wrapped me in a hug, squeezing tightly. "I was so worried about you," she whispered. She stepped back but still held my shoulders. "Don't do that again."

Leon dismounted the horse and walked over to his son. "Well, how was the village in my absence?"

"Fine. Everything has been running smoothly."

"Has that scouting group come back yet?" I questioned. "I would love to hear their reports."

"What scouting group? You two were the only ones who were gone." Archer raised an eyebrow. My heart dropped. If we were the only two gone, why were all the horses missing from the stable that morning? Why would Leon say another group had left? Isa's voice pulled me from my inner downward spiral.

"Unfortunately, I do not have any updates on Darius. I can't pick up on his scent anywhere."

"You should not worry about that. Darius is long gone," Leon said nonchalantly. Everyone's attention snapped to him.

"Why would you say that?" Ron asked in a lower pitch than normal. There was a tone in his voice that made me think he had theories of his own about the situation. Leon shifted his body and crossed his arms in front of him.

"After his frenzy, he ran into the woods alone, he probably got lost and was eaten by one of many monsters that lurk out there." His tone was defensive. I saw a shift in his eyes, just like the one I saw in the training area when Darius had exploded on him.

"I know that's not true. I connected with him. I know he is out here."

Leon's face fell as shock took over. "You connected with him? Through the bond?"

"Yes. He would not tell me where he is, but I know he is out there."

Leon cleared his throat. He stepped back to Ambrosia and remounted her. He looked down at us and took a deep breath. "We just got back from a long journey. Take today to rest and tomorrow at first light we will go out to look for him. I will gather a search party if it is that important to you."

Before anyone could respond, he rode away, heading towards the stable. Archer bowed toward me and rushed to catch up to his father.

I raised a single finger, signaling for them not to say a word. Once Leon and Archer were out of sight, I lowered it. The words rushed out of my mouth as I told them all of what had happened during the journey. How I summoned an orb of life to resurrect the orchard, and how Leon had rushed us away directly afterward.

"I think he made up the fact something was coming to get us to leave. I felt nothing other than our energies. I don't know why he would do that."

Ron approached to stand directly in front of me. "My Queen, if I may," his tone hushed, "I see more than people think. I have noticed things about our good 'friend' Leon that make me want to proceed with caution. Things that want me to suffocate his flames with my shadows." With those final words, his shadows grew and raged around him. Xander stepped to his side and placed a hand on his shoulder. I watched as Ron's shadows simmered and merged with his father's.

"Whatever you want to do," Xander spoke, "we are with you."

"We are always with you," Daphne added, "Just tell us what you need."

"Please don't run away again," Isa said, her voice cracking.

I saw all my friends for what they truly were: family. No matter how much we fought, how far I would take them, they would always be here for me.

"We go without Leon. We leave the village as soon as possible and go to find Darius on our own."

"Let's return to the house and pack immediately for the journey," Xander said. "What is the plan after we leave the wards?"

"I suggest we go to where it all began," Daphne said. "To where the bond was created. See if there is still magic left behind from the star that could reconnect you to Darius."

"Brilliant. Let us not waste any more time," I smiled as I began to run towards the house.

We all packed and rushed to the stables to get our horses. When we got to the stables, we found Leon, the stable keeper, and two tall earth fae outside. Xander extended his hand forward, not allowing us to advance closer. Leon now had an injury on his left arm that mirrored mine.

"It is true. The Queen has gone mad since Darius left. I am sure he has some sort of spell on her. Do not allow any of them to leave the village and do not let any more vampires in. They cannot be trusted. "

"I cannot believe she bit you like that. It sounds horrid," the stable keeper said. It was the same woman who Daphne had used her magic against to convince her that we were never there.

"She was like a rabid animal. It was like nothing I have ever seen," Leon added. I felt a fire grow inside of me. How dare he slander my name? How dare he create some story to villainize me?

"Are you sending guards to watch the house? She should not be allowed to wander the village freely!" one of the earth fae spoke, fear rattling his voice.

"Yes, they should be arriving now. I am going to go check on them. Care to join?"

The two earth fae agreed to go, and we watched as they headed back into the village. I felt Ron and Xander's shadows surround us, to keep us hidden from sight. My heart pounded into my chest as I watched them until they disappeared.

When I focused back on the group, Daphne had already approached the stable keeper. I could vaguely hear Daphne's honeyed words, but I knew they hit their mark. The rest of us met up with Daphne just as she had finished her conversation and the stable keeper turned and made her way into the stables.

"She's going to gather our horses. There will be no issues with her." Daphne's voice was cold as she spoke. So cold that a chill set around me. Just a moment later, she came back out with five horses, one for each of us.

"Thank you for your visit, my Queen," she bowed before me.

We wasted no time as we mounted the horses and sped into the forest.

We arrived at the orchard three days later, grateful that nothing slowed our travel. The moon hung in the sky. Its soft glow illuminated the land. It was now booming with life. Cherries, peaches, apples, and citrus hung all around us as we traveled through the trees. A serene calm washed over us. The magic seemed to stop at the edge of the orchard and returned to the decay we had grown too accustomed to.

We exited the orchard and back into the Circle of Death, where everything lay barren. My eyes were on my castle the whole time. Up close I could finally see the destruction in full detail. Stone crumbled into dust. Thick thorny vines weaved in and out of any window and hole in the wall. The towers had fallen and left wreckage on the ground. Only one tower remained standing. The vines coiled around it but left the top window free.

After a few minutes of riding, a small hill came into view. That hill was where it all began. A perfect circle where Draven's Darkness had not touched. The grass was lush, and wildflowers flourished. Atop the hill was a cherry tree in full bloom. A small breeze passed that caused a few blossoms to come free and float to the ground.

I dismounted my horse and rushed up the hill, not saying a word to anyone as that familiar inner tug pull me in. I lay in the grass under the tree and stared up into the sky. My breathing slowed, and I stared up into the night sky, waiting for something. I was not sure what I was doing or what to expect.

"Is it working?" I heard Isa question. "Can you feel him?"

"Why don't we give her a minute before we ask her," Xander responded.

"How will we know if it's working?" Ron chimed in.

Their chattering was not helping the cause. I sat up and looked down at them. The four of them stood together at the bottom of the hill. Their voices rang in my head as they all went back and forth.

"Silence," my voice boomed, "I need to concentrate."

They all apologized, taking a step away from the hill. I took in a deep breath once again and laid back down in the grass, gazing at the stars, waiting.

I could feel the magic that still lay in this ground. It was a steady hum underneath me like it too was also waiting. I tried to think of Darius and our bond. How I needed to find him. How we needed each other to get through this.

I laid there staring into the void for what seemed like an eternity. I watched the stars above dance. The full moon traveled overhead, and it was the only thing that helped me keep time.

A star raced across the sky. Then another, and another. The sky eventually was flooded by shooting stars that glittered in the sky. I felt the magic under me vibrate harder. I closed my eyes, squeezing them tight, and reached deep within myself to find the thread that connected us.

Images began running through my head of every moment Darius and I had spent together. At the end of my vision, I was left in the void with a red string held taut hovering in the air. It was not dye that caused it to be red.

No, it was dripping in blood.

I reached forward to grab it. As soon as I did, everything snapped into place.

Twenty-Four

Darius

R age. All I felt was pure rage.

I wanted to kill everything I came in contact with.

I would kill my way to the castle. I was going to find Draven and tear him limb from limb, and I would savor every moment. He didn't deserve to live after all he had done. He did not deserve a peaceful death.

He had destroyed Sabrina's home. He had shown me how he was going to destroy her body and mind. I would never allow him to touch her. I had felt like such a miserable failure when I saw that bruise on her rib. How could I protect her from the unseen?

My blood boiled as those images crept back into my mind. I had been fighting off those nightmares ever since they first entered my mind.

I had been lost in this forest for weeks now. No matter which direction I traveled in, I always ended up at this fucking golden tree. This was the fifth time today I had passed it, and I felt madness creep in a little more every time.

My throat went dry as a delicious scent passed my nose. My head snapped in the direction of the smell. There was a rainbow stag standing barely fifty feet from me, making my mouth water.

I pounced, and my fangs tore into its flesh. Its blood coated my mouth and dripped down, covering my front.

I roared into the sky as I devoured my meal.

Twenty-Five

Sabrina

I sprang to my feet and rushed toward my group. Tears flooded my eyes as I got to the bottom of the hill.

"Sabrina! What is wrong?" Xander questioned, worry all over his face.

I quickly mounted my horse. I had no time to waste. I had to get to Darius.

"I know where he is! Hurry!" I exclaimed as I raced through the castle grounds.

That golden tree had been the ticket to finding him. I had felt it pull him in, leading him to it every time he attempted to stray during the time I was in his mind. That tree was one of our mystical wonders. Very few people were able to locate it. The tree decided who was allowed under its golden canopy. It had healing powers that not even our greatest scholars understood.

There were many legends of how the tree came to be. Many claimed that it was because of the goddess of the harvest, Kori, and the goddess of life, Mortess. As a token of their forever bond, they had planted a tree that would be forever in bloom and forever healing.

After we wed, we had planned to go to that tree and ask for it to cure Darius of his bloodlust — of his vampirism.

Unfortunately, we never made it. I wondered if, after all this, was that something he still considered?

The others mounted their horses and followed me back into the forest. It would take us four days to get to our destination.

I hoped that the tree would hold him there until we arrived.

The golden tree hummed as we approached. This section of the forest was untouched by the darkness. The forest had slowly transitioned from the dead trees and twisted vines to a tropical forest full of life and the song of birds. The golden tree sat in the center of a clearing. The grass was lush, and wildflowers grew all around. Fae lights danced between the branches of the tree, giving it a soft, golden glow.

The area was silent and empty except for the rainbow stag that lay at the edge of the clearing. Its flesh was torn from its body. It was several days old now. The stench of rot hung in the air but vanished as we approached the tree. The smell of sweet apple blossoms filled my nose.

"He's not here," Xander announced as I dismounted my horse.

"He will be. I know it," I responded as I looked around frantically. I needed to see him before he saw me. My heart pounded in my chest. I could feel him. He was just here. I stepped closer to the tree and sat at its base. I closed my eyes and reached out for him.

Come to me. Please. Come back to me.

I pleaded in my mind, hoping my message would reach him.

"My Queen, as beautiful as this place is, I do not think this is a good time for meditation," Ron said. His voice pulled me back to this place. My right eye opened, and I shot him a glare. Isa giggled under her breath.

"Please, no more interruptions. I'm trying to connect with him."

"You look like you are trying to contact the beyond," Xander added. "He is not here. Let us keep moving."

Be careful what you wish for, doll.

He snarled in my mind. In a blur, Darius appeared from nowhere, tackling me and pinning me to the ground. His eyes were blood red, and his fangs were on display. He was just about to rip into my throat when shadows filled his mouth. Darius jumped back, and more shadows rushed him, pinning him to the golden tree.

I looked over and saw Ron off his horse and quickly approaching. The shadows around him erupted forward toward Darius, and Ron's eyes were solid black as he stepped directly in front of him.

"I will not allow you to hurt her," Ron growled as he removed the shadows from Darius' mouth.

"You fucking faerie bastard! Release me!" Darius spat. He fought against the shadows but was no match for them as they kept him pinned to the tree.

Xander grumbled from behind me as I stood and walked toward Darius. I tried to steady my breathing and keep calm as chaos erupted around me. Darius' gaze snapped back to me as I approached.

I saw that familiar hunger in his eyes. The same one I had seen so many times before he had ripped out my throat and drained me dry. My vision tunneled and all I could see was him. His screaming turned into a loud ringing in my ears, and the words from the others faded away.

I gently guided Ron out of the way to step in front of Darius. "Stop it," I breathed, "this is not who you are."

"You're a fucking faerie whore. You don't know who I am!"

His words stung.

"Darius Dragomeir. I know exactly who you are, and this is not it."

He tried to lunge at me, but the shadows kept him in place. I tilted my head upwards, looked up into the golden canopy, and I prayed that the goddess who planted this tree would help me reclaim my mate. That somehow they would be able to return him to his normal state.

I felt a sharp pain in my chest. What if this was his normal state? At the beginning of this journey, he had told me he was a monster. When I had made contact through the bond, I had thought of the monster that he was.

My eye gazed back down at Darius. The monster. My heart thumped deep in my chest, and everything clicked into place.

"Darius," I said calmly as I looked him directly in his eyes. "You are a monster and a terrible person. The absolute worst."

"Yet, you still hunt me down and wish me mortal."

"No. I wish for you to be who you are. If this is who you want to be, so be it." I felt tears threaten to fall, but I would not allow them. I turned my back to him and began to walk toward my horse.

"Don't turn your back on me!" He snarled.

I did not respond. The others stayed silent around us, waiting and watching.

Please, don't turn your back on me. You're all I have left.

I paused. There was that voice I craved to hear. The voice that showed any emotion other than anger.

"Release him," I demanded.

"What? Are you nuts?" Xander questioned.

"Ron. Release him. That's an order from your Queen." I spun to look at Ron. He nodded and, without a single word, his shadows whirled away. They did not fully disarm; no, they were ready to strike on command.

Darius fell to his knees and sat there with his head down. I took a single step forward.

"Well?" I growled at him. He lifted his gaze and looked at me through his eyebrows. His eyes were emerald green, and dark circles shadowed his under eyes as if he had not gotten any sleep in weeks.

"Tell the others to go away and wait," he said under his breath.

"No. You don't call the shots anymore since you want to be an ass."

"It's embarrassing," his gaze shifted away. I took a few steps closer.

"Good. Maybe you will learn something."

I knew I was being harsh. But that is the only way he would respond to me.

Monster versus monster.

"I'm sorry. I don't know what got a hold of me. I didn't want to say those things to you," he finally raised his gaze and looked at Ron, "or to you. I am sorry."

"Look, it seems an old dog can learn new tricks," Isa said, a snicker under her breath. Darius' gaze shot to her. He looked as if he was ready to strike, then his gaze softened.

"Yes, I suppose they can. Sometimes," he said in response.

"What happened? How were you thrown into a frenzy?" Xander finally asked the burning question we all wanted to be answered.

There was a moment of silence before Darius' face shifted as if he was trying to recall the memories. "To be honest, I do not remember. After what happened in the training area, I left the village, but only to clear my head. When I came back that evening, Leon met me at the wards to talk about what had happened. After that, almost every memory is gone."

"Almost everything?" Daphne questioned. Darius cleared his throat and then looked at me, his face flushed.

"Yes, almost everything. You guys really do not want the details of what I do remember."

My eyes went wide. Was the only thing he remembered when I was finally able to contact him through the bond? How he had me chained and at his mercy?

"I think we should hear everything you remember. It may help us piece everything together," Ron added.

Darius tightened his jaw. Before he could say anything, I spoke.

"I was able to reach Darius once through the bond. I believe that is the only thing he remembers. Trust me, you do not want those details."

"Yes, *that* is very clear in my mind." He stepped closer to me and took my hand in his.

"Do you two do anything but fuck?" Xander asked in a rough tone, and I felt heat rise to my face.

"Xander!" Daphne and I said in unison.

"What? I mean it is true," he replied.

"Yes, but I really don't want those images in my head. I think the rest of us agree," Daphne laughed.

"Right, let's move on," Ron said in a quickened tone. His face was just as red as mine.

We caught Darius up on everything that occurred in his absence. How Daphne and I had retrieved Isa. How Leon and I had gone to the castle. How I revived the orchard. How Leon had been so upset that I had done it. How upon returning to the village, he had told people I had gone mad and attacked him, and how we were not allowed to leave the village.

I saw that familiar rage return to Darius' eyes.

"I knew there was something off with him," he said between his teeth.

"I think at this point, we only have one option," Xander said as he walked back to his horse. We all watched him in silence as he mounted.

"What is that?" I questioned.

"We go to the castle and see for ourselves what is going on."

Twenty-Six

We arrived back at the castle with no issues. To our surprise, the Circle had been completely devoid of any beasts waiting to claim us. Darius had requested that we stop in the orchard before making the advancement to the castle. He wanted a place to stretch his legs and relax before we continued forward. We all agreed for that to be our final rest. For what was head would be our most difficult challenge yet.

The sun was to come up in just a few hours as we entered the orchard.

We dismounted our horses and tied their reins to a tree. I sat under a peach tree and leaned my back against its bark. My head rested against the tree, and I closed my eyes for a moment taking a deep breath. The journey had finally caught up to me and I was totally exhausted. Finally opening my eyes, I looked out and saw my castle in ruins, leaking that purple haze. My eyes followed the purple haze as it crawled into the forest of petrified wood.

Daphne and Isa came and sat on either side of me. With Daphne to my right and Isa to my left. Daphne had picked two peaches and handed one to me.

"I wish I could have seen it in its glory," Isa said. She had spent her whole life in Titus. A barren waste of a place. Dimitri destroyed everything he touched. His own country was no exception.

"It was beautiful," Daphne smiled. "I dream of it every night. The marble, the florals, the people. Oh, the people," she sighed.

My court was made of some of the kindest and most loving people there were. Every single member was an essential part of Serafina. My eyes shot to Xander, a few feet away, sitting with Ron. I could barely hear his words, but it sounded as if he was telling some history of Serafina.

He was the reason my court fell. When they came to retrieve me, he was the reason they were massacred. He had done well so far to prove himself worthy of forgiveness, but I was not sure if I ever truly would forgive those lives lost.

"I cannot wait until I can rebuild and put all this turmoil behind us," I sighed and looked up to the sky.

"Oh, the battle ahead is just the beginning," Daphne said. "The real work is after that."

"We will be with you every step of the way," Isa said as she leaned against my shoulder.

Darius approached us with his hands in his pockets. His eyes were aimed toward the sky. "Mind if we take a walk?" He said as his gaze fell on me, his voice shaking a bit as he spoke.

"Don't wander too far. Who knows what is waiting for us," Daphne called out as I stood.

"We will be safe," I responded as I took a step toward Darius, glancing back toward Daphne and Isa.

"I will keep her safe," Darius said as he wrapped his arm around my shoulder.

With that, he and I walked through the orchard and away from the others, not speaking for some time. Darius was the first to break the silence.

"Thank you."

"For?" I looked up at him with a raised brow.

"Saving me. You pulled me from that dark place. I do not want to be there ever again."

"Trying to turn a new leaf?"

"I want to be a man worthy of being at the side of the great fae Queen." Darius pulled me close and turned me to face him. My heart pounded in my chest as I felt heat rise to my cheeks. His hand gently cupped my chin and lifted it, and our lips met with a tenderness I had not felt from him. My core melted from his soft touch.

He pulled away and looked in the direction we came from. The others were not out of view. Darius smirked as he looked back at me.

He picked me up and laid us down in the grass with him on top. His mouth found mine once again. His tongue entered my mouth and danced with mine.

I arched my back and pressed my body into his, wrapping my arms around him and running my fingers through his hair. He hardened against me, pressed his lower body into me, and ground against me softly.

His hands found their way to the waistband of my pants. I lifted my hips to make it easier for him. My whole body shivered with anticipation. After he pulled my pants down, he unfastened his own to free his cock. Darius' mouth traveled down to my neck. He slowly ran his tongue over my skin.

Moaning his name, my body flooded with heat as I felt him line himself up with my slick entrance. His tip slipped inside me and paused before he slid deeper, pumping his cock into me gently.

Pleasure overwhelmed me as he twitched deep inside me. My body exploded from pleasure. My arms wrapped around him and I dug my nails into his back. Darius continued to pleasure me through my climax by thrusting harder into me.

"Go on, doll. Cum like a good girl," he purred. He pushed himself deep inside me and held it there as his eyes locked with mine. "Such a beautiful little doll."

I found my pleasure again as he praised me and continued to fuck me. I begged for more, for him to use me harder. I had never known Darius to be a tender lover, but at this moment, he was embracing it.

"Beg, and maybe I will fuck you like the little whore you are."

"Please. Please, Darius. I need it." I wiggled my hips to tease him.

"All you ever want to do is cum on my cock. To be fucked by me. Isn't that right?"

A breath of laughter escaped my lips as I continued to grind against him.

He snarled at my response and flipped me onto my stomach, placing one hand on my back to hold me in place. His other hand grabbed my hair tightly and pulled it to keep my head looking forward.

Darius began to plow into me roughly, his cock pounding against my cervix. I pushed back against him. I needed as much of him inside me as I could get. It was not enough; it was never enough.

Darius pushed his hand harder into my back to keep me in place, and I let out a soft scream as he again pulled on my hair. I felt him throb with his release.

"Such a good girl, Sabrina," he teased as he released my hair and pulled out of me. He rolled me to my back and leaned down and pressed a kiss to my lips. As he pulled away a smile crossed his face.

Darius found my waistband once again and pulled my pants back up. He stood and assisted me up. I brushed the dirt and grass off me.

"We will have a lot to explain when we get back. Xander was right," I smiled up at him.

"I mean, the man has only been wrong once," he responded as he fixed his pants, "when he sided with Dimitri."

We walked back into the view of the others. All eyes were on us. Xander opened his mouth to speak, but I interrupted him before he could get a single word out.

"Save it," I teased.

Xander responded with a smirk.

The sun finally rose, and we made our approach to the castle. Everything around us was completely silent. We had left our horses in the orchard, thinking it may be easier to approach on foot. Each step I took felt as if I was walking through dense mud. My mind and body did not want to deal with what was to come.

My muscles were tense. My vision blurred and funneled toward the castle. I stopped in my tracks when my brain screamed for me not to take another step. To leave and not look back.

To run.

The others continued moving forward and were a few feet in front of me when Darius stopped. He was before me in an instant, forcing my attention on him. He took my hands in his and squeezed. The world around us vanished into expanding black, and we stood together in the void. I felt as if the weight of the world had been lifted off my shoulders, and a soft piano melody began to play, filling the air around us.

"Sabrina," he said calmly.

"Yes?" I craned my head up to look at his face. He looked so kind at this moment, kinder than any expression I had ever seen on his face.

"Do not give up. I will not allow it."

"What if this all is for nothing? What if we fail?"

"We won't fail. We never have."

"We failed Liam."

The music stopped abruptly, and Darius stepped back as he looked at the ground. After a moment of silence, he took in a deep breath, then exhaled. "We won't fail again. I can promise you that."

"How? How can you make that promise?" My volume rose as I took a step towards him and closed the distance.

"I will not allow any more of our friends to fall. We will all make it through. The only ones who will fall are any who stand in our way. That includes Leon and Draven."

"I hope you're making a promise you plan to keep."

"I am." Darius winked and the world came back into view around us.

I watched as the others were finally turning toward us as they realized we were behind them, now a good bit away.

"Everything ok?" Daphne and Xander called out in unison. Darius turned to them, and we both nodded. Hand in hand, we caught up with the group.

We made it to the steps of the castle. My stomach was in knots as I looked up. Everyone was dead silent as I took a step ahead of them. I could feel their gazes burning a hole in the back of my head. Though the marble pillars were crumbled, the steps somehow were still intact. Before any of us could take that first step, we heard three horses approaching us in a full gallop. They had seemingly come out of nowhere.

We spun to see Archer and two other fire fae I did not recognize. They were all armed. They halted their horses directly in front of us and dismounted.

"We cannot let you go any further," Archer said.

"Oh, you cannot let the Queen return to her castle?" Xander snarled.

"Sabrina betrayed all of Serafina when she chose the vampires over us. We all know the plan is to allow the vampires to take control," one of the other fire fae, the one with the golden eyes, said.

My jaw dropped. Is that what Leon had been telling people? That I was going to let someone else take over? To plunge Serafina into more chaos?

"That is not true. I want to bring Serafina back to its glory and restore the forest. I would never do harm to my land, or my people."

"My father says otherwise." Archer stepped forward. Ron, Xander, and Darius also took a step forward, as if to create a wall between me and the fire fae.

"Your father is wrong. I think he is the one betraying Serafina," I told Archer of the odd behaviors Leon had been exhibiting. How he was so angry and pulled me away after restoring the orchard.

"You lie!" Archer spat. The two other fire fae readied their weapons. One a short sword, the other a mace. Archer's brows furrowed. "Stand down," he commanded them. "We are not to attack."

"We have different orders," one said.

"Orders to leave no survivors," the other said as he raised his mace and swung it towards Darius.

In a blur, Darius dodged his attack, grabbed onto his wrist, and twisted it so hard that the fae's arm snapped and dislocated. He let out a scream as he released his weapon.

The second fae man did not have the chance to attack. Xander and Ron's shadows merged and pounced on him in an instant, completely overpowering him until he was coated in darkness. We saw his sword hit the ground and not a single sound from him.

I did hear a low chuckle come from Xander's lips.

Archer stood there in total shock. He did not move a single muscle as he watched in terror.

Darius did not release the fire fae's arm. He continued to twist and pull until the arm was ripped from his torso. After throwing down the arm, Darius picked up the mace that the fae had dropped and bashed the mace into the fae's head repeatedly. He did not stop as the body fell but continued slamming the mace into the fae until his head was not recognizable.

The shadows recoiled and returned to the father and son duo. My eyes went wide as I saw what hit the ground. An emaciated shell of a man lay on the ground. His skin was gray, and his jaw was slack as if he was screaming, or had his mouth ripped open and had something shoved down it.

The men looked up to Archer. We all stayed silent and still, waiting for what he would do. Archer looked down at the two dead fae that lay before him, lifted his head, revealing his extremely pale face, and took a step back. He stammered to find his words as he raised his hands in surrender. His voice shook as he spoke.

"This was unexpected. I did not know of the orders they spoke of. I was only told to speak with you and bring you back to Tasumanza," his eyes darted between us as he took another step back. "I need to get back to the village to figure out what is going on. Something is not right."

"Go," Darius said. I looked at him in shock. Darius was not the second-chance type of man.

Or was he?

Archer mounted his horse and raced away, and we all stood there watching him for some time.

"Was that smart of us to let him go?" Ron questioned.

"It is not too late for our shadows to drag him back," Xander responded.

"Let him go. Something tells me he is our ally. He will be valuable to us another day," Darius turned and faced Isa. "Isabella!" He called out. She turned to face him. "Follow him. Make sure my suspicions are correct that he is indeed an ally. If not, kill him."

She nodded in response, and a blur continued after him.

Darius turned to face the castle and walked forward. "Let us not waste any more time."

Twenty-Seven

As we walked deeper into the castle, the purple haze was so thick it was impossible to see through. I reached deep inside myself and was able to channel the same magic that helped me revive the orchard. A flash of gold surrounded us and immediately cleared the mist.

My heart broke when I finally saw the true state of the castle. Everything was in total ruin. Many of the halls and corridors were blocked by fallen debris, although the path to the throne room was clear. Marble archways were fully collapsed. Paintings that once hung on the walls were now on the ground, ripped, blacked out, and the frames were broken and scattered across the floor. Dead flowers littered the halls.

As we walked in, I realized the throne room was much different from anything in Titus. While the throne room in Titus was cold and empty, except for the throne, well, two now that Darius became king. He had a second one installed for me to sit by his side during his court meetings. The walls were dark, there was no art. The people who worked in the castle were mostly unfriendly.

My throne room was open and warm. The people of my court were kind. There was no ceiling, allowing the sun and moonlight to fill the space. It had magical runes and enchantments to protect the room from the weather.

There was one entrance at the south of the room. The east and west walls had two archways each that led to gardens. The east garden bloomed at night. The west bloomed during the day. Ivy and wisteria climbed the columns of the arches. It was now all shriveled and decayed.

In the center of the floor were blue opal moon phases in a circle embedded into the marble flooring. The full moon pointed north and the new moon south. In the center of the moons was a citrine and carnelian sun.

At the north end of the room sat a single throne on a dais, with two columns on either side. The west had a carnelian sun, and the east had a blue opal moon, which was where Daphne and Xander used to stand by my side in front of the pillars.

The north wall behind the throne was once full of ivy and hid one of the many secret passages and emergency exits I had in case of emergencies. That wall was now just dried vines and cold stone.

Not only was this a throne room, but it was also a ballroom. Every ball I ever hosted was held in this room.

The room was now in ruins. The gardens were wilted, the columns were crumpled onto the floor, and the archways had all collapsed. The crystal inlays in the floor and pillars were dull and cracked.

Ron was the first to walk deeper into the throne room. The rest of us were still too shocked to move. Darius squeezed my hand tight and stepped forward. I followed every step he took.

I looked up at the dais, and while columns around it were completely destroyed and in piles of rubble on the ground, the throne itself was untouched. The rose gold finish was untarnished and scratch-free, the latticed back was still covered in flowers that were somehow in full bloom, and even the soft pink velvet cushion on the seat itself was dust free.

Darius guided me across the throne room, stopping at the foot of the dais and releasing my hand.

I will be right here. Go and reclaim what is yours.

His voice was so calming. I could feel his gentle fingertips brushing the back of my mind.

I stepped onto the dais and sat on my throne. Looking out at my throne room, I locked eyes with my friends who were staring back at me, waiting for my next move.

Xander and Daphne stepped up and stood on their respective sides.

"Together," they said in unison. We had finally made it home. Sitting on my throne with these two by my side, everything once again felt whole.

"Together," I breathed. I closed my eyes and reached for that golden energy once again. As my eyes opened, the room was filled with near-blinding golden light. Warmth overtook my body. The light quickly faded to reveal the room being restored inch by inch.

First, the pillars by my side rose, rebuilding and repairing their crystal inlays. I looked behind me and the wall of ivy behind me came back to life, and flowers of pinks, reds, and purples filled the wall.

All of the purple haze that lingered in the throne room and the garden completely vanished. The air felt light and fresh, with the scent of sweet peaches and cherries filling the space.

I took a deep breath and shut my eyes, reveling in the perfect moment. I could feel that golden power grow within me. It filled me with warmth and comfort.

I felt a sudden, sharp, and burning pain in my shoulder. The golden light completely vanished, and I could no longer feel the magic. My eyes opened wide to find an arrow in my shoulder. From across the throne room, Leon stood at the entrance with a bow in hand.

"Now, now. I can't have you doing that," he teased, his voice like cold velvet.

Darius rushed forward, putting himself between me and Leon. I pulled the arrow from my arm and roared in pain. The tip dripped a mix of a purple liquid and my blood, and the scent was a clear indicator of what it was.

Morning glory. The only true poison to the fae. The same poison Dimitri had used against me during the full moon festival to weaken my magic and keep me weak.

"Why are you doing this? You are the leader of the resistance! Shouldn't you want the restoration to happen?" Daphne questioned.

Leon stepped fully out of the shadows of the throne room's entrance. As the sun hit his olive skin, I watched him transform. The color of his skin darkened, his red hair turned black, and his facial features contorted. Leon was not Leon at all.

He was Draven.

"None of you were supposed to come back. Serafina is *mine*," he snarled.

Darius knelt before me, examining my wound.

Are you ok?

Not at all. It burns. I can't feel my magic.

We will handle this. Try not to move so the poison doesn't spread.

Darius stood and faced Draven as he drew his sword. Daphne and Xander stepped off the dais in unison.

"Draven," Xander spoke first, "you don't have to do this. Let the Queen reclaim her throne. Let her restore Serafina."

"Fuck you," Draven spat, "You have no room to say anything. Your betrayal of Serafina allowed all of this to fall in the first place."

"I was wrong back then." Xander took another step forward. "I was so wrong. About everything."

"Destroying Serafina cannot be what you want," Daphne spoke, looking at Draven. "You created a safe haven for people who wanted to escape the destruction. You would not have made them a sanctuary if the destruction of Serafina was what you truly wished."

"I started the resistance so that I could keep a close eye on my enemies. Anyone who got too close to the truth was eliminated. I also wanted a safe place for my son to live."

"I know all about wanting a safe place for your son," Xander said as his head turned toward Ron.

I finally summoned enough strength to stand. Darius glared back at me as I took a step forward. "I can give your son a safe place to live. Please. Let me restore the forest," my voice cracked as the burning sensation spread through my body.

"You will never reclaim your throne. Serafina will not be restored. You allowed this to happen when you brought a vampire into your bed and became nothing more than a blood whore."

Shadows erupted from Ron and flew through the air. Draven raised his hand and dissipated them without a glance.

"I was raised in your father's shadow, boy. You cannot harm me with them."

"You're wrong," Darius' voice boomed. "It is our love that will rid this world of you and free the people of Serafina."

"Oh, don't act like some hero. We all know your plan was to kill Sabrina so that your father could rule these lands. Your father was right about you. You are worthless."

I could feel the sting of Draven's words in Darius' chest and the rage that was building within him through our bond.

Darius lunged toward Draven, who once again raised his hand without care, and sent Darius flying into the garden of night. Purple vines erupted out of the ground and constricted around him, covering him completely.

I screamed his name and took another step forward, but collapsed before I made it off the dais. The burning pain was overwhelming and was spreading rapidly. I felt so weak as I once again tried to rise and failed. Daphne and Xander both ran to my side, kneeling and trying to help me stand.

Draven let out a cold laugh as he took another step forward. The ground cracked beneath his feet and the purple haze surrounded him. "I suggest you all leave, return to Titus, and reconstruct the wall. You are not welcome here."

Xander looked down at me, at Draven, then back to me.

"I promised you I would make this right," he said in the most hushed tone before glancing up. "Sister, are you ready?"

Daphne stood and stepped to Xander's side. "Oh yes, brother. I am ready," she replied with a smirk.

"Ron," Xander said in a disgruntled voice, "stay with the Queen. Keep her safe at all costs."

Ron did as he was told and rushed to my side.

A flash of darkness and light exploded around Daphne and Xander. When they came back into view, they looked different than I had ever seen them.

Daphne was now tall, wearing pearlescent armor, and had large white feathered wings tucked behind her. Her hair and skin gave off a soft white glow.

Xander was just as tall as Daphne. His armor was black as onyx. His wings were black, feathered, and just a little larger. The shadows that normally clung to his skin had darkened and tripled in size.

I could feel immense power from them. It was greater than any power I had felt from them, or anyone. The two of them were even more like those stained-glass windows from the church. They were almost exact clones of the god and goddess, now with the power to match.

They began the onslaught against Draven with their dark and light magic. Bright flashes exploded around the room while dark shadows snaked across the ground toward Draven and wrapped around him.

Draven had magic of his own that he threw our way and used every type of fae magic to his advantage. He had become a master of the elements. I watched as he perfectly executed each type of fae magic. This power was supposed to be mine, and mine alone.

I felt helpless as I watched the three of them dodge each other's magic. Their magical energies clashed against each other, causing explosions all over the room.

I tried once again to stand, but still couldn't find the strength. Tears threatened to fall from my eyes as I tried to push through the pain. I reached through the bond to see if I could feel Darius, but it failed. My heart broke when I couldn't.

The battle continued to wage before me. The poison made it seem like time had slowed. It seemed as if they were evenly matched. None of them had been hit. They all danced and dodged each other's assaults.

I blinked and Draven had vanished. Xander and Daphne froze for only a second. Once realizing what had happened they searched around for him in a panicked state. I heard that cold velvet laugh from behind me. Ron spun to meet the sound. Glancing back, I saw Draven standing on the seat of the throne, a lightning bolt in his hand.

Draven's gaze wandered to Ron, and a dark grin crossed his face. He then looked up at Xander and winked as he hurled the lightning bolt toward Ron. In an instant, Xander pushed Ron out of the way, just in time for the lightning to strike Xander square in his chest causing his onyx armor to shatter.

"You always told me love makes you weak," Draven cackled, "it appears you were right."

I looked up at Xander as the darkness faded from his eyes. A hole was burned through his chest. The scent of burnt flesh filled the air. He fell to his knees. His wings went slack.

"No!" Ron cried out as he rushed to his father's side.

"Do not cry for me," Xander coughed up blood. "I will always be with you. In the shadows." With those final words, Xander's body fell limp to the floor.

Daphne ran towards him, kneeling by his side, cradling his head in her lap. Golden tears flowed down her face. "No. No. No, no, no," she sobbed.

The world flew into darkness, and I looked up to see the sun in a total eclipse.

Dark clouds filled the sky and thunder rolled. The ground shook as something slammed into the ground in the center of the throne room.

No, not something. Someone.

Two people now stood in the center of the throne room, dust covering their features. As it fell, it became clear who stood before us. A lump formed in my throat as I gazed up at Astor and Astrid, the god of night and goddess of day. They were two of the most beautiful creatures I had ever seen and looked almost identical to Daphne and Xander in their true forms.

Astrid stepped forward, a look of rage all over her face. Each step she took covered the ground in fire. "Daphne, my child. What happened?" her voice echoed, sounding as if she was both here and far beyond at the same time. She looked down at Daphne and Xander, and there was a fire in her eyes that warmed my soul.

Daphne looked up to Astrid, and not a single word escaped her lips. Astor did not move, did not speak. The rage that filled his eyes was cold and devoid of life. It snuffed out the warmth that Astrid provided.

Both of their gazes rose to Draven, who still stood atop the throne. He did not falter as he raised his hand and formed another lightning bolt in his hand. As he grasped it, a beam shot down from the eclipse. It was dark with gold dust twinkling throughout, and struck Draven, causing him to release his bolt of lightning.

"You think yourself to be a god," Astrid and Astor spoke in unison, "You are nothing more than a mouse. To rule Serafina you must be chosen by the gods. Today you chose to kill the god's kin. Because of this action, the gods have decided for you to end, for we are the albatross that claims you as prey."

The beam vanished, leaving nothing but dust flying through the air in its wake. Just like that, Draven was gone, completely vanished from the world. From the night garden, I heard Darius roar, and when I turned towards the sound, I saw those purple vines wither and his body breaking free.

"Light and dark must stay in the balance," Astrid said.

"For it is our grandson that will continue forth as the darkness," Astor followed up. He lifted his hand, slowly dragging it through the air with his palm up, With shadows dripping from his long and sharp black nails.

Everything began to feel fuzzy around me, and The pain from the morning glory was so intense I could no longer resist it.

The last thing I saw before I passed out was Ron being consumed by darkness.

Twenty Eight

T he scent of sweet strawberries and cream filled my nose. I had awoken in the most comfortable bed I had ever been in in a long time. I took a deep breath and sat up, looking around in shock.

This was my bed chamber. Everything was exactly where I had left it in perfect condition. Vines with pink blooms draped from the bed canopy. The window to the left of me was open and a warm sweet breeze swept in. The bookshelf to the right was perfectly organized with my romance novels, journals, pressed flowers, framed butterflies, and crystals. The silk sheets felt divine, and for a moment I had forgotten everything that we had gone through.

I jumped out of bed and rushed into the hallway, calling out for the others. Where were they? How was the castle back in pristine shape? My chest tightened as panic set in. A piercing pain went through my head and my body ached as I moved.

As I rounded a corner, my body slammed into something. I fell onto my ass and looked up and saw Daphne standing in front of me, Back in her everyday form, with her dark hair in perfect ringlets.

"It's alright," she said softly, "it's over." She extended her hand to me. I took it and she assisted me up.

"Where is everyone? What happened? How long have I been asleep?" The words flew out of my mouth.

"Two weeks. I was beginning to worry you wouldn't wake up. Everyone is downstairs waiting for you. Let's get you changed. I am sure you do not want to address the court in your nightgown," Daphne said with a giggle. I followed her back to my room. "After you passed out and my parents vanished, the castle rebuilt itself. It is exactly the way we left it."

We entered my room and went straight into the attached walk-in closet. The smell of strawberries and cream, my signature scent, filled my nose. It was just as big as my bedroom and full of dresses and accessories.

"Is Xander..." I whimpered as I watched Daphne look through my dresses. Her head fell, and she gave a small nod.

"He was buried three days ago." Her voice was soft and broken.

"And Ron?" I was almost too afraid to ask.

"He is adjusting to his new powers. It's been hard on him. Xander and Ron had just started to get close, and I fear he will always be left with a feeling that he missed what could have been between the two of them."

Alive. Alive and well. That was all I needed to hear. Daphne pulled a dress from the rack.

"This one is perfect," she said with a smile.

I walked into the throne room with my head held high. Daphne had chosen for me a dark green dress with a square neckline and long balloon sleeves. The crown atop my head was embellished with the most breathtaking rubies.

The throne room was filled with people. The crowd parted as Daphne and I walked toward the throne. Silas and Cora had made the journey from Titus. Tamir and a few of his warriors bowed as I passed them. Carlow's skin had darkened to a beautiful cerulean shade. Even Morgana and Orlok were here. Both avoided eye contact with me. Branwyn, Jessandra, and Ollie all lit up at the sight of me. Archer stayed behind them, also avoiding my gaze. At the foot of the dais stood Ron, Andrei, Isa, and Darius.

My heart fluttered at the sight of him, and as soon as he smiled, I felt everything around us melt away. He extended his arm to me.

Glad to see you finally awake. You look absolutely beautiful.

I blushed hard as I took his hand, and he guided me up the dais and to the throne. I turned and sat down, looking at the crowd, and Darius sat on the arm of the throne. Once we settled, Daphne and Ron both stepped up onto the dais and stood at their pillars.

Butterflies filled my stomach as I looked over the people. The darkness was gone and we could now begin fixing everything that had been done.

"I can't believe it," words finally escaped my mouth. "I cannot believe that I am finally here, looking at all of you. This has been an extremely tough journey. The Darkness may have been cast out of Serafina, but the true work has just begun. We must all unite and work together to rebuild Serafina into something even better than it once was."

The crowd cheered as I paused. Darius sat his hand on my shoulder, and I looked up at him and gave him a warm smile. I gazed back at the crowd.

"I would not be here without every single one of you. Today we will rest, we will celebrate. Tomorrow the real work begins."

After my speech, we took the rest of the night to celebrate. Music played, the court members danced and feasted, and the fae wine flowed. For the first time since being in Serafina, I let myself partake. I even saw Daphne having a few glasses.

Jessandra and Branwyn had made a wide variety of different foods. Jessandra brought three kinds of tacos. My favorite of them was the one with shredded beef and corn. She put a creamy and tangy sauce on top that was to die for. Everything I tasted was absolutely delicious. The lemon bars that Brandwyn made were to die for. They were perfectly tart and sweet.

"I am glad to see you alive and well, Lady Sabrina," Andrei said as he and Isa approached me. Isa wrapped me in a hug so tight it stole my breath. After she released me, Andrei wrapped me in a hug just as tight. "I don't know what we would do without you," he whispered in my ear.

"Andrei, let the Queen breathe," Darius said, putting a hand on Andrei's shoulder. Andrei released me.

"How does it feel to be home?" he questioned.

"It feels unreal. I never thought I would see my castle like this ever again. I am excited for the road ahead."

Archer approached our circle. He cleared his throat and clenched his bottom jaw as the group turned to look at him.

"My Queen, may we speak?" He said in a nervous tone.

"We may," I responded.

"In private?"

"Anything you have to say to me can be said in front of the Titus royals."

Archer cleared his throat again and straightened his jacket. "I want to apologize for everything. I had no idea that my father was Draven if that was even my father. I want you to know that all of his allies have been removed, and I will do whatever you require for me to gain back your trust."

"Thank you, Archer. That means a lot. We can discuss your service to the crown tomorrow. For tonight please enjoy the party." I glanced toward Isa and Andrei. "You two as well. Please go have fun. We will discuss business another day."

Archer bowed and returned to the party. Isa and Andrei looked toward Darius, who gave them a nod before they turned and joined the crowd.

"You can follow your own advice. I can hear your thoughts swirling," Darius purred as he pulled me close and began to dance with me.

"You know I can't calm my mind."

Darius gently lifted my head by my chin so our gazes met.

"Let me help," Darius' voice was a melody that wiped away everything around us.

We were now in a clearing in the center of a sunflower field. Darius guided our movements as we danced. A calm feeling washed over my body, and my mind was silenced. Nothing else mattered as the smell of summer rain filled my nose.

"I love you, Sabrina," Darius said in that same melodic tone as he held me closer.

"I love you, too." I rested my head against his chest. Darius' hand gently petted the back of my head as we danced. A smile appeared on my face when I realized we could still hear the music from the party.

We had danced for what seemed like an eternity when reality snapped back into place. Ron had gently tapped Darius' shoulder.

"Mind if I cut in?" he said in a low and quiet voice.

Darius released me and took a step back. "Go ahead. I need a drink anyway." He smirked as he walked off into the crowd.

"Can we head to the garden? There are too many people in here," he said.

"Of course."

Ron and I walked into the night garden, and he sat on a black iron bench.

"How are you?" I questioned.

"I am managing," he said in a somber tone. "Just as I finally started to connect with my father, he was taken away. The new powers I was given are very overwhelming." The shadows that surrounded Ron were larger and darker than they had been before.

"Is there anything I can do?"

"Daphne has been a great help. She has explained to me my new role. Being the god of shadows is a lot to take in."

"I am sorry, what did you just say?" My breath caught on his last words.

"I am the god of shadows. Astor and Astrid gave me Xander's powers at the end of the battle."

"I did not know Xander was a god."

"He and Daphne both are. Daphne is the goddess of light."

My heart skipped a beat. Daphne and Xander had always been in my life. I had worshipped the gods my whole life. Not only did I not know that there was a goddess of light and god of shadows. I had no idea that Daphne and Xander were gods.

"Excuse me, Ron. I need to go speak to Daphne."

I rushed out of the night garden and searched the throne room for my dearest friend. I found her sitting in the garden of the day.

"Why didn't you tell me?" I demanded.

"It was not my place to. Ron should not have told you, either. We need to stay hidden. If it is known what we are, the world will fall into chaos to take advantage of us."

"I would never take advantage of you."

"I know, but there are many others that would. Please do not take it personally. It was decided long before you were born that it would be kept secret. Please, keep our secret. Do not tell a soul, not even your mate," Daphne stood and looked me dead in the eyes. Her tone was more serious than I had ever heard.

"What secret?" I smiled. "Shall we head back to the party? I need more of those lemon bars."

Daphne smiled back and hooked her arm into mine. "Yes, I agree they are delicious. Let's hide the rest before anyone can get them."

We walked back to the table of desserts and filled a plate with our favorites. Everything looked so amazing it was hard to pick between them. It was Daphne who decided. Why bother picking when we could have them all?

Morgana and Orlok approached us, and it was Orlok who spoke first. "Your Majesty," he paused, "I need to apologize for how I responded. I had a suspicion that it was Draven who was the cause of the Darkness, but I did not want to accept it."

"So, you had information that could have helped us, but you knowingly refused to share it?" Daphne said with anger in her voice.

"I am sorry. Draven was my only son. I had hoped that when he went missing that that was not the case. I would have done nearly anything to protect him. Daphne, I am sure you understand wanting to protect your child."

"I do," she responded the anger in her voice retreating.

"We had made a mistake in not providing that information. Please allow us the opportunity to make up for it," Morgana bowed, and Orlok followed her motions.

"Please stand," I said to them. "We can discuss this more once we are done celebrating."

The two of them stood and thanked me. Orlok began to select treats from the table. Morgana made her way through the crowd and found Isa and Andrei, joining them in conversation.

We celebrated throughout the night. The full moon was high in the sky by the time I finally snuck away to return to my room. Darius had vanished from the party about an hour before, I assumed to feed.

When I entered my bed I found a note on my bed in Darius' handwriting.

S.

Meet me at our spot.

D.

I made my way to the hill where the stars had fallen. Atop the hill, Darius leaned against the tree. A picnic was set up at his feet.

"What is all this?" I questioned as I made my way up the hill.

"I thought we could chat and look up at the stars," Darius said as he sat down on the blanket he had laid out. I sat by his side, and he opened up the basket and pulled out some fruit, wine, and cheese. "Peaches, brie, and moscato. Those are still your favorite, right?"

"Yes, it is. I am surprised you remember that."

"I also remember that these crackers and honey are your favorite too," he said as he brought more out of the basket. His voice shook a bit. Darius had a nervous look in his eye that I had only seen once before.

"Is everything ok?" I raised my eyebrow at him.

Darius cleared his throat and adjusted a little as he looked at me. "Now that everything is over," he began, "I was wondering if you would please let me court you again. So much time has passed. It would be nice to have a fresh start." He reached over and took my hand in his.

"Darius, I thought you would never ask. Besides, you still owe me that date you promised."

"Oh, you will get your date, doll. It will be the best date you have ever been on," Darius chuckled in response.

I leaned in and gently kissed him on the lips. As I pulled away and looked up to the sky, a million stars glittered above us. A few shot down onto us, covering us in stardust. Darius let out a laugh that could be heard throughout Serafina.

I could not wait for what was to come.

Blood Origins

Willow Asteria

The Lovers

One

Sabrina

The Masquerade of the Vernal Equinox was one of the most important celebrations in all of Serafina. Nobles from near and far traveled to partake in the festivities. Not only was this the day the fae of Serafina greeted life and light into our lands, but it was also the queen's — my birthday.

I sat on my throne with my elbow rested on its arm, my fist supporting my face. Looking out, I took in the sight of the crowded ballroom.

There was one exit to the south of the room that led into the main section of the castle. On the east and west walls were archways that led into the gardens, each currently adorned with bright green vines and flowers of pinks and purples. I took a deep breath and leaned back into my throne.

"They are all here for you. At least pretend you are enjoying yourself," Xander said from my left.

"The ball is almost over. You can fake it for a little while longer," Daphne said from my right.

The Ancient Ones stood in front of the pillars on either side of my throne. Each of the columns represented them. Daphne's pillar had a carnelian sun embedded into the marble. Xander had a blue opal moon in his. Both imbeds mimicked their magic.

Daphne was life and light.

Xander was death and shadows.

Straightening in my seat, I put on a fake smile. I hated my birthday, and I hated large crowds. By the time everyone had come and granted me birthday blessings, my social battery was fully drained.

I focused on the string quartet that played in the center of the room. They sat, in white pearlescent chairs, atop an inlay of carnelian and citrine formed into a sun. Circling the sun were the phases of the moon in blue opal. The crowd danced around the band, and for a moment I let the music take me away from this place and fill my soul. My eyes followed the golden fae lights that floated through the air.

As the song came to a close, my eyes locked on a man that I did not recognize. His long white hair flowed as he danced with a noble from a fae land from across the sea.

"Who is that?" I questioned.

"An emissary from Titus," Daphne and Xander said in unison.

"Where are the Titus Royals?"

"They have never attended. We do send them an invitation every year," they responded.

I pressed my lips into a firm line and signaled one of the servants to come over. Stepping up onto the dais, she bowed. I gave her a soft smile as I examined her simple muted blue knee-length dress with a large bow in the back.

"Yes, my queen?"

"Fern, can you please inform that gentleman over there," I pointed my perfectly manicured finger towards him, "that I am requesting his audience?"

Fern nodded, rushed over to the man, and gently tapped him on the shoulder. After whispering to him, he looked in my direction, nodded, and walked toward me. His amber eyes, through his black mask, locked on mine. He stopped at the foot of the dais and bowed.

"Happy birthday, Your Majesty. My name is Vlad," he said as he straightened his back. "I am an emissary sent by King Dimitri of Titus, who sends his well wishes." He smiled, his elongated fangs on display.

I clenched my jaw and gave him an up-and-down look of disapproval. After glancing at Daphne and Xander, I maintained a straight face and gave him my response. "You may leave. Please inform your King that if he cannot bother to come, not to bother sending anyone at all."

The vampires and the fae never had the best relationship. Many wars have been fought between our people in the past. My entire reign I have worked to mend our relationship and was met with cold indifference by their king. It was time I put the ball in their court. I will no longer be entertaining this one-way relationship or lack thereof.

I snapped my fingers and two guards appeared seemingly out of nowhere, grabbed Vlad by his arms, and dragged him out of the ballroom.

The party continued as if nothing had occurred. Every year, we had at least one fool dragged out and thrown out on their ass.

Two

Darius

I squeezed tighter around the human's throat as I plowed my dick into her. She was a decent fuck. I had experienced better, but she certainly got the job done. She writhed under me as I gave her the best experience of her life. Moans escaped her lips as I forced my way deeper inside of her.

I didn't plan on bedding a human today, but when I went to the dining hall to pick my meal, she threw herself at me. Instead of draining her right then and there, I decided to take her back to my room for some fun. Could anyone blame her for wanting to take a ride on the vampire prince?

My cock twitched as I found myself close to release. My spine stiffened as I heard the door open behind me. The human tried to get up, but I held her down by her throat to keep her in place. Her annoying voice filled my ears, but I paid her no mind.

"This better be important," I grated out.

"The King requests your presence immediately," Andrei said.

I turned my head to face him. If looks could kill, Andrei, my right hand, would be on the floor and I could continue with my toy.

"Can't you see I am busy?" My gaze returned to the human as I squeezed her throat harder and fucked her as if my best friend wasn't watching.

"Well, he said I can't come back without you, and if I don't bring you back, it will be my head," Andrei said as he sat on the edge of the bed and gently stroked the human's cheek. "Cute human, though. Save her for me when we are done dealing with your father? You know I love blondes."

A snarl escaped my lips as I pulled myself out of the human. I reached for the rope that was attached to the headboard and tied her by her wrists.

"Wait here, pet." I winked as I found my clothes and put them back on.

I looked over and saw Andrei grazing his fangs over the human's nipples. She let out a soft moan as he teased her

I rolled my eyes as I opened the door. "Come. We wouldn't want to keep father waiting, and besides, you know the rules. I get the first bite."

Andrei and I walked into the throne room. The room had entrances on the south, east, and west walls. You could tell maroon and black were my father's favorite colors, as the windowless walls were painted that dark red. Gold sconces lined the wall, the fires gave off a warm dim light. A dead body laid on the black cold stone at the foot of the dais. My father sat on his throne with two guards by his side, and his favorite servant, Barnabas, behind him.

We stopped just before the corpse and looked down at him. Blood pooled on the floor out of the man's neck. Gazing at his blank stare, I realized that this was the emissary my father had sent to Serafina. I slowly looked up at my father's stoic face.

"He failed. That faerie bitch sent him back saying we are not welcome to her stupid ball. We are cutting all contact with Serafina as of today."

Three

Sabrina

Almost a year had passed since I had heard from Titus. I suppose the King did not like the message I passed on through his emissary. Though, not hearing from him hurt Serafina none. I hoped their people did not suffer due to Dimitri closing trade and communication with us. We had several trade routes established with them, but they were mostly out of pity. Titus had very little that we didn't. I was keenly aware of the lack of farmland in the kingdom to the north.

I sent out the invitations to the Masquerade a few weeks ago. Daphne, Xander, and I sat in my study, going through the responses. I noted one was not received from Titus. Though the Ancient Ones advised against it, I sent out one final invitation to extend an olive branch. If they did not show up, it would be my last.

"Do you think Titus will show up?" Xander questioned as he neatly stacked the pile of responses.

"It has been over a year since we have had communications with them. I doubt they will," I said as I opened the response from Nouavara. King Tristan and his sister Ursula would be attending.

"If they do, we shall be ready," Daphne said softly. "For whatever happens."

Four

Darius

I stood at the foot of the dais, dissociating while my father rambled on about politics. I hated when he got into one of these moods. He would lecture me about the state of the kingdom, and how to stay strong we must be feared.

Everyone feared me. My name sent a shudder through the spines of those who heard it. For the ladies, it was for more than one reason. Not only was I known for my bloodlust and strength, but also known to have my way with the fairer sex. You bed one, or two, courtiers and quickly the tales of your skills travel. My attention snapped toward one of the guards as he broke up Dimitri's monologue.

"What are your plans for the Masquerade in Serafina this year?"

Dimitri shot the guard a look that could kill. "We will not respond to the invitation, nor will we attend. I am thinking of building a wall to fully separate us from them."

"My King, if I may," he did not pause to wait for permission before continuing, "This year has been hard on Titus since the embargo on Serafina. Many of the villages in the Wastes relied on those crops from Serafina. So many people have moved into the city, we are now needing to ration supplies. Maybe it would be wise to reopen communications with the fae? I have heard that Sabrina is a kind and fair queen, maybe she will be open to the idea as well?"

My father shot me a look and slowly tapped a singular finger on the arm of his throne. Before his nail could touch the dark stone, I was already snapping the guard's neck and throwing him to the floor.

My father gave me a look of approval that was almost a smile. "Titus does not need Serafina to prosper," Dimitri snarled.

I returned to my royal suite and found Andrei lounging in the sitting room, his legs up on the red velvet chaise.

"I had hoped you had a human up here. Everything in the dining hall displeased me," he said with a smirk.

"Well, pack a bag. We will find you a snack on the way."

"On the way to where?" Andrei sat up and raised an eyebrow.

"We are going to see who has gotten under my father's skin so badly."

"I like the sound of that." Andrei stood, prepared to head to his chamber.

"She's just a little girl, who turned of age last year. She should be easy to conquer and win my father's favor." A wicked grin grew across my face.

I had heard few things about the fae queen. Every year I would hear how the emissaries we sent spoke of her. I gathered she was small and absolutely delicious looking. I couldn't wait to have her scream my name and submit to me.

Five
Sabrina

Another year, another Masquerade. I sat on my throne as one by one my guests approached me and granted me birthday wishes. Xander and Daphne, as usual, stood on their respective sides of the throne. I could feel my energy being drained more and more as new people continued to approach the dais.

I focused on the grand pianist in the center of the ballroom. We never had the same musician attend the ball twice, but she played so well that I was considering hiring her to be the court musician full-time.

King Tristan of Nouavara approached the dais and bowed. I gave him a faint smile in response.

"Queen Sabrina, may I say, you look more and more beautiful every year. Green truly is your color," he purred.

This year Daphne had chosen for me to wear a dark green velvet gown that shimmered like the night sky. The circlet atop my head was adorned with emeralds to match. She said it made my normally bright blue eyes look like the sea.

"Thank you, Tristan. You need not to be so kind."

"I would love it if you would grant me a dance," he said as he extended his hand. His muted blue suit matched him perfectly. Tristan was a water fae and a powerful one at that. He was known as the storm-bringer throughout the lands. He could command the rain and lighting at will.

"I appreciate the offer, but I will have to decline. I am not much of a dancer."

As his bright blue eyes shifted to navy, Tristan, the king of Nouavara, took in a deep breath. "Understood. Happy birthday, your Highness." Turning on his heel, he quickly disappeared into the crowd.

Xander chuckled as he looked over at me. "You won't win a husband that way."

"She does not need to win a husband," Daphne snapped at her twin.

"No male has ever caught my attention. If I am to allow anyone by my side, it will be for the best of Serafina."

The room went silent. I turned back towards the crowd and jolted up from my throne, looking around to see what had happened.

Two men stood at the entrance of the throne room. One had blonde, slicked-back hair and wore a simple tux and a black mask. My focus was pulled to the man by his side. His green eyes pierced me all the way across the room through his golden mask. His green tie matched my dress perfectly. No one wore green to the Masquerade but me. Everyone knew that green was my color. It had been since birth.

"Well, hello. Don't stop the party on my behalf," his voice was like music to my ears. His smirk exposed his fangs. My heart skipped a beat as we locked eyes, and he walked in my direction.

"Who is that?" I said as I sat back on my throne.

"The Prince of Titus," Daphne and Xander said in unison.

I watched as the Prince strode in my direction. I couldn't look away. Everything about him was alluring, from the confidence in his walk and the glimmer in his emerald eyes. I tried to push those thoughts out of my mind as he stopped at the foot of the dais with his blonde companion by his side. With a twirl of his wrist, he bowed deeply, and when he lifted his head, his long dark hair dangled in his face.

"Happy birthday, Queen Sabrina. It is an honor to meet you. I am Darius Edward Alexander Dragomeir, Prince of Titus." He stood up with his last word.

"Your initials spell DEAD?" I raised my eyebrow at him, hoping that wasn't an omen of what was to come.

"Oh, darling, I am death personified," He smirked, and my heart skipped another beat. The Prince snapped his fingers, and the blonde man gave him a small black velvet box from his pocket.

"Thank you, Andrei," he said, as he stepped up onto the dais.

When my guards moved for him, I raised my palm, signaling for them to stand down. My gaze followed him downward as he kneeled before me and presented me with the small black box.

"A gift, to show my good intentions," his voice was smooth and dark. A sinister smirk grew on his face as he looked up at me through his brows.

Noticing the ball was still silent, I gazed back up at the crowd and saw all eyes on us. Looking back down at Darius, I took the box from his hand, my skin gently grazed against his for just a moment. Darius licked his lips in response, and heat rose to my cheeks.

I opened the box and pulled out a thin black chain adorned with tear-shaped rubies.

"What a beautiful necklace," I said with a smile. Darius stood and winked at me.

"That is a collar disguised as a necklace," Xander snapped as his shadows extended toward me and took the necklace from my hands.

"I don't keep fae as pets. Though your queen is so pretty, she would make a good doll."

"How dare you speak to our queen in such a manner," Daphne shot at him.

"Now, now," I cut Daphne off before she could continue. "It is no issue, for vampire males make good toys," I smirked up at him as he towered over me.

Darius licked his lips and chuckled in response. He stepped off the dais and returned to Andrei.

"I shall leave you be, Your Majesty. I must see what is so great about the Masquerade that not everyone can get in."

Six
Darius

I snaked my way through the crowd. None of the masked faces compared to anything of the beauty I saw within the queen. I found myself constantly looking back at her. Her velvet dress hugged her curves just right, making me want to do anything to kneel in front of her throne, slide between the slits of her dress, and feast between her thighs.

Gods help me. I could sense her magic radiating from her. She was the most powerful creature I had ever met. I had heard many stories of the Ancient Ones that she kept close, but they did not hold a candle to her.

Andrei and I made our way to the bar in the southeast corner of the ballroom. I leaned against the dark wood and ordered two shots of liquor.

"She may not be as easy to conquer as I expected," I sighed as I tapped my short, pointed nails on the bar top. My signet ring reflected the moonlight. When I entered the room, I was shocked to see that it had no ceiling. I looked up and gazed at the night sky that was glimmering with stars. I had never seen a throne room like this. Not only was it full of life, but the open concept made it feel free. The two gardens on either side of the throne room were filled with beautiful botanicals. Even the throne room itself was filled with ivy wrapped columns and the wall behind the throne was filled with flowers.

For the first time, I felt as if I could truly breathe.

"What are you going to do?" Andrei questioned as the bartender sat the two shots in front of me.

"Enjoy the party," I chuckled as I quickly took the two shots back-to-back. Andrei gave me a disappointed look.

"Damn, I thought one of those was for me."

"Get your own."

Andrei ordered his drink, and I made my way into one of the gardens while he waited. Everyone rushed out as I entered. Seems my reputation preceded me. I turned my head and saw a group of women huddled under the archway, all of them had their eyes on me. Their whispers and giggles were not as quiet as I assumed they hoped. I gave them a wink and turned away before I could see their reactions.

The garden was like nothing I had seen before. The foliage was extremely diverse and ranged in hues of greens, purples, and reds. I walked over to a very large white flower and examined it. The stem and leaves were black, and the stoma of the flower was bright red. A sweet scent filled my nose as I leaned down to take in the aroma. My ears perked up as

I heard soft footsteps approaching me from behind. I took a deep breath as the scent of strawberries and cream filled the air.

It was intoxicating.

"After not hearing from Titus for a year, I am surprised you came. I was even more surprised you gave me such a beautiful gift."

Sabrina's voice was so soft and sweet, and I immediately wondered if her voice matched the touch of her lips. I turned to face her. "To be honest, my father was very offended by what you told our emissary." I took a step closer to her and sucked in a deep breath. The scent of strawberries and cream filled my nose, causing me to crave her even more.

"Are you not?" She teased.

"I am not so easily offended, especially by beautiful women." I stepped closer. One more step and my body would be on hers. My mouth watered at the thought.

"I am not so easily fooled by handsome men. I could feel the enchantment on the necklace," her tone now had a bit of bite to it. She was a fighter.

Good, I liked that.

"Can you blame me for wishing to make you mine? To have you wear a pretty little collar for me?" I grabbed her wrist and pulled her toward me. Gods, her skin was so soft. I smirked down at her as she tried to pull away, and I gripped tighter.

"Let me go," she demanded.

"If I refuse?"

Before I could react, I watched as she used her free hand to grab a dagger from her thigh and she stabbed it into my chest. I released her and staggered back. Blinking down at her, I grabbed the dagger and pulled it out. My injury immediately healed.

A smirk grew on my face and turned into wild laughter.

"Oh, I like you." I examined the dagger. "Oh, doll, this is too small to affect me. Next, I will show you something bigger that could finish the job." I licked my lips.

"Guards! Remove the Prince of Titus immediately!" She called out for them. A group of guards charged into the garden, with Andrei close behind them.

"Come, Andrei. It is time for us to leave." Before the guards could reach me, I rushed out of the garden and the castle completely. The fae may have magic, but they will never beat my vampiric speed.

"What the hell happened?" Andrei growled as he caught up to me.

"I think I have started to hunt the most elusive of prey."

$Seven$

$Sabrina$

Three days later, Daphne and I strolled through the royal orchards. They were one of my favorite parts of the castle grounds. Serafina was known for its good harvests, and the royal orchards were the most prolific of the land. The fruit was like nothing you could get anywhere else. They were sweeter, juicier, and had a more complex flavor.

Daphne and I had so far been discussing upcoming events of the kingdom and appearances that I would need to make. Daphne stopped at one of the pear trees and picked a low-hanging fruit.

"The Masquerade went well," she chuckled as she took a bite of the pear. I rolled my eyes and chuckled as well.

"It was certainly... something. I don't think anyone will forget."

"I don't think the vampire Prince you stabbed will forget either," Daphne pushed her curly dark locks out of her face. I looked up at the fae lights that danced between the leaves. A cool breeze passed through, causing them to rustle and the sweet scent of cherries and peaches filled my nose.

The thought of Darius made my spine tingle. I could still feel his hand wrapped around my wrist. How my heart pounded in my chest as he pulled me close to him. Gods, I hated the fact I could not get his scent from my nose, how I now craved the scent of pine and cinnamon. For the first time, I found myself intrigued by a man and the larger weapon he had promised to show me. Heat rose to my cheeks, and I forced those thoughts away.

"I am sure we have not seen the last of the Prince of Titus." I couldn't help but smile.

Eight

Darius

"How dare you disobey me!" My father screamed at me from his throne. His face contorted in anger as he spat with every word, and the vein on his forehead bulged. My normally cool and collected father had completely unraveled in his rage.

The throne room had been cleared upon Andrei's and my return. Only my father, a few guards, and Barnabas remained. My father was the type of man to demand total submission to his whim in every aspect of his life.

Unfortunately for him, so did I.

"I went for the good of the Kingdom. I went to get information so that we may use it against them," I spat back at him. Didn't he understand that we both wanted Titus to be the powerhouse of the continent?

My father released a low chuckle from his lips before his eyes snapped back to me.

"You think you know what is best for this kingdom? You know nothing. You are a weapon. You are not to think. You are to follow orders!" My father shifted his gaze to Andrei, who stood by my side. "This is what happens when you think." My father snapped his fingers and two guards grabbed Andrei and forced him down to his knees.

I watched as Andrei said nothing as he kept his gaze on the King and clenched his jaw. A third guard had come up behind him with a cat-o'-nine-tails. My body tensed as I heard the crack of the whip and Andrei grunt.

Andrei had been through this before and was very good at not giving in to the pain. I refused to look at him as my body tensed at the sound once more. The whites of my knuckles showed from how hard I clenched my fists in an effort to maintain my composure. I released the breath I was holding, then relaxed as my eyes met my father's.

"Andrei is my pet. What do I care if you whip him? I whip him often." I walked over to the guard with the whip and took it from him. I cracked the whip against Andrei's back, holding my father's gaze as I did. I went to lift the whip again, and my father raised his palm.

I lowered the whip. Never pulling my attention from my father's. The two of us were in a game to see who would crack first, and it would not be me.

"Enough. Tell me what you learned in Serafina," he demanded.

The guards dropped Andrei, and he collapsed to the floor. I would not look at him. I would not allow Dimitri to see that I cared. Anytime I showed any emotion other than hate and anger, I was punished for it, and I was nearly at my breaking point.

It was hard to tell when I snapped if I would burn this entire kingdom to the ground, or if I would give my free will over to the King who saw me only as a weapon.

"Sabrina is extremely powerful. She is not the weak little girl I thought her to be. She also has the Ancient Ones by her side for protection. Their power, however, isn't even close to hers."

I watched as my father's face returned to that lethal calmness I was more familiar with. A low growl escaped his lips. "She must be destroyed. Write to her, and request to see her again. You will find out all you can, return to me, and then I will destroy her."

"Yes, my king," I said as I bowed before him, accepting my role as a spy.

However, in the back of my mind, something ached about the thought of something so beautiful being destroyed.

Nine

Sabrina

Every full moon, we held a festival on the palace grounds. The festival was to give back to the magic of Serafina. A huge bonfire had been set up in the center of the field behind the castle., and fae of all kinds flooded the field and danced around it.

Music filled the air and multi-colored fae lights floated and danced through the sky to the beat of the music. Many food offerings were available and were provided by castle chefs as well as chefs from throughout Serafina. The fae wine flowed as if it were water. Several people walked around with carafes to keep everyone's glass full.

Daphne and I sat in a gazebo. Ivy and flowers climbed the columns and decorated the entry into it. Two swings sat inside facing each other. This was one of my favorite spots in the kingdom.

As queen, it was my duty to replenish the magic of Serafina. The ritual had left me feeling totally drained. Every time I completed it, I felt as if the forest took more and more from me. I was not worried about it. I knew in the morning my magic well would be filled. The lands of Serafina will flourish for another lunar cycle.

"Do you need to retire for the night?" Daphne questioned.

"No, I am enjoying the spring breeze. Besides, before I leave, I need to have another serving of the meatballs that the earth fae chef made."

"Ooo! The ones with the cherry-soy glaze?" Daphne's face lit up.

"Oh, yes. They were delicious." I smiled, gazed out toward the night sky, and took a deep breath. "I just want to enjoy this moment for a little while longer."

"You do have quite the packed schedule for tomorrow."

"Dear gods, yes. Have you seen all the letters I need to respond to?" There were several stacks of letters on my desk that I needed to get back to, but I had been putting them off for weeks. I honestly thought that if I did not respond the senders would stop sending them. Some were updates from the Elemental Elders, personal letters from friends from across the kingdom and beyond, invitations to all sorts of events and celebrations, and messages from my spies about what was happening at the border, and from inside other kingdoms.

"It seems you have many from the King of Nouavara," Daphne chuckled.

"Indeed," I signed. "He has sent me four letters requesting to visit. I did respond to the one he sent after the ball, telling him I was too busy to have visitors. That has not deterred him from trying to find a time that works."

"Interesting. What about the stack of twenty letters with the Royal Seal of Titus?"

"They are all from Darius, also requesting to visit."

"Look at you. Two men vying for your affection at once. Such a harlot you are," Daphne teased with a laugh.

"Stop it," I giggled in response. "I have no interest in the King of Nouavara. It is not my fault he can't take a hint."

"You have interest in the vampire prince?"

"I did not say that."

"You do not need to. I cannot tell you what to do, but I recommend staying away from him. He said it himself. He is death."

The next morning, I sat at my desk and was organizing some of the loose paperwork I had lying about. There were to-do lists, budgets, schedules, and a few letters that still needed to be responded to. Daphne and Xander always said my desk was too messy, but I disagreed. It was organized chaos.

I picked up the crimson envelope with the black dragon wax seal, and my heart fluttered as I thought of the man who sent it. The scent of pine and cinnamon filled my nose, and my skin turned to gooseflesh. Using my rose gold letter opener to free the letter that was inside. I unfolded the cream paper, and a smile appeared on my face. Internally, I fought with myself. Darius was a royal jerk. Why was I excited to read his words?

My Dearest Sabrina,

I write to request to visit your magnificent Kingdom. I was fully enthralled by the fae lands and a certain inhabitant, and would love to see more of the natural wonders Serafina has to offer.

Eternally Yours,

Darius Edward Alexander Dragomeir

Prince of Titus

I chuckled as I sat down his letter and picked up a piece of my signature pale pink parchment. With a quill in hand, I wrote my response and then sealed it in a pink envelope with a gold wax seal of a cherry tree in full bloom.

The cherry trees were always in full bloom here in Serafina. Trees from this region transported to another never lost their blooms, even in the coldest of winters.

"Fern," I called out. The earth fae ran in and bowed as soon as she crossed the threshold. Her silvery green braid fell in front of her shoulder.

"Yes, my queen?" She asked meekly.

"Can you please send this letter out post haste?"

"Yes, of course!" She stood and rushed over to me, taking the letter. She left my study as quickly as she entered. I leaned back in my seat and smirked.

Ten

Darius

I sat on the foot of my bed and held a pink envelope with both hands. The scent of sweet strawberries radiated from it. Everything about Sabrina was good. She was beautiful. She was powerful. She was pure. I needed to destroy her like I destroyed everything else in my life. But something deep within me told me that by destroying her, I would destroy myself in the process.

The King's orders had to be followed.

My gaze lifted as I heard the door opening. Andrei leaned against the door frame in his night pants, his golden hair slicked back.

"You have had that letter for a week. You really should open it before Dimitri hears you are hiding correspondence from Serafina."

"What if it's bad news?" My heart sank at the thought. I needed to see Sabrina again.

"Worried it will bruise your ego?" Andrei chuckled.

"Nothing can bruise my ego. You know how my father feels about people who fail him," I said softly, looking back down to the envelope. The room fell silent for a moment before I looked back to Andrei. "About what happened with my father…"

"Don't. I understand the game we must play." Andrei sighed and came to sit by my side.

"One day he will pay for all the pain he has caused you," I growled.

My jaw clenched as I thought about all the times my father had harmed Andrei to punish me. Everything was always a lesson about discipline when it came to my father, even when I was young.

I used to be a wild child when my mother was still alive. I would sneak out of the castle to explore. Andrei was one of the first people I met that would talk to me during my time in the city. He wasn't afraid of who my father was.

He should have been.

When my father learned that I had been sneaking out of the castle to hang out with a human, he forced me to kill Andrei's family. I am still haunted by their screams as I ripped out their throats one by one. When I was done, I was to turn Andrei into a vampire. He was the first and only person I had ever turned.

The two of us have never once spoken about that night. Something inside of us broke at that moment, but something else ignited in our cores.

"We have a lifetime to deal with that. For now, focus on that letter," Andrei said with a calm and steady voice. Somehow, he was always the calm one. No matter what we faced, he had a level head.

I opened the envelope by cracking the golden wax and pulled out the pink parchment. A smirk grew on my face as I read the letter, and I looked over to Andrei.

"Pack your things. We are going on a trip!"

Eleven

Sabrina

I paced back and forth in my room. My thoughts raced as every possible outcome of Darius' visit played through my mind. This was either going to go extremely well, or he was going to leave with my kingdom up in flames behind him.

Daphne stood in front of my bookshelf, examining a new piece in my collection. I had gathered many framed butterflies and moths from Serafina. My newest had been a bright green moth with tiny golden moons on the bottom tips of its wings. It was like nothing I had ever seen, so when the oddities merchant came to the castle a week ago, I knew I had to have it. Daphne glanced over at me and sighed.

"Calm down. What is with you today? I have never seen you so nervous."

I paused and faced her. "What if you were right? What if this was a bad idea?"

"Based on how things ended last time, I am probably right. I hope that I am not, but if I am, you have very powerful magic to protect you."

She was right. I was extremely powerful in my own right. The garden encounter did not exactly go as planned. He had bested me physically. I could have taken control of the situation if I used my magic, why didn't I? This time, I was better prepared. I walked over to my jewelry armoire and opened one of the drawers to reveal its green, velvet-lined interior. Pulling out a few jewelry boxes, I showed them off to Daphne.

"What is that?" Daphne asked.

"Oh, I had my jeweler make me a few pieces I thought would be useful during his visit." I opened one of the boxes and showed off the pure silver jewelry. I had heard that the touch of silver harmed vampires, so I prayed that it was truth. Other than the emissaries that Titus sent to the Masquerades, I did not have much experience with vampires.

She took the box from me and examined it. Looking up at me with a smile she said, "Seems like you are all set. You should rest. Tomorrow will be a busy day for you once he arrives."

That night I tossed and turned, getting very little sleep. My inner monologue ran one hundred miles a minute playing out every possible scenario. Without my morning latte, I don't think I would have gotten out of bed. I chose a pink silk gown with long bell sleeves and shoulder cut-outs. The thought lingered in the back of my mind what Darius would think of this dress.

I sat on my throne. My body was stiff as I took in a deep slow breath. I looked up at Xander and Daphne, who stood in front of their pillars. Daphne gave me a small nod. I faced forward, and motioned toward one of my servants across the room. She bowed and rushed out of the throne room. A few seconds later, returned with Darius and Andrei.

My heart skipped a beat as our eyes locked, and I watched as he swaggered in my direction, smiling at me. The rest of the throne room faded to black as I focused solely on him. The vampire prince was devastatingly handsome. Without the mask, I took in his full beauty. Gods, this man is going to be my ruin.

My focus was broken when Andrei spoke, and I gazed toward him and saw him bow.

"Thank you for your invitation. We appreciate you giving us another chance, especially after our first meeting," Andrei said. Darius' emerald eyes glared in his direction.

"You are welcome. I am excited about starting over. Do the two of you always travel together?"

Andrei's back straightened as I asked the question. "Someone needs to keep the Prince in line," he chuckled nervously.

"Do a better job this time. There will be no more chances," Daphne and Xander said in unison.

"No more chances will be needed," Darius smiled, his fangs on display.

I stood from the throne and stepped down from the dais, stopping right in front of Darius. I looked up toward him, and my throat bobbed at how he towered over me. The man had to be at least two feet taller than me.

"Please allow me to give you a tour of my castle," I said to Darius trying to hide the nervousness in my voice.

Twelve

Darius

I tried to pay attention to the layout of the castle, but my focus was fully on the beauty providing the tour. Everything about her was intoxicating. Her pink silk dress hugged her body just right. Her body was absolutely perfect, curvy in all the right places. Unlike other royals I had met she wasn't thin as a rail. Her face was soft and delicate, and her blue eyes tore into my soul. It took all the self control I had to keep my composure.

If Andrei wasn't along for the tour, I would have had her against the wall and moaning my name while I claimed the fae queen as my own. Though at the beginning of the tour, Sabrina shooed away the Ancient Ones, I could still feel their presence. What a site that would be to watch their queen submit to me.

When I wasn't fantasizing about shoving my cock through her pouty little lips, I was in awe of how beautiful the castle was. The halls here were lined with windows that allowed light to shine in. In Titus, I avoided the sun as if my life depended on it. Though the sun doesn't cause me direct harm, it always made me feel uneasy. However, in these halls, I craved the warm comfort the sun provided.

Sabrina had first shown us the garden that was the twin to the one we had our first entanglement in. This one was full of flowers that bloomed during the day. Sabrina informed us that the two gardens were enchanted. One was eternal night, and the other was eternal day. The night garden was filled with dark colored flowers and the day garden was filled with a rainbow of vibrant and pastel pinks, reds, and oranges. Both had a pond filled with koi. The day had black ones and the night had white.

Everytime she looked up at me with those bright blue eyes I wanted to pull her close to me. I needed to know how her lips felt against mine. Were they as soft as they looked? Sabrina turned around to continue the tour. Andrei nudged me in my rib and my gaze snapped to him.

"What?" I tried to keep my voice quiet to not allow her to hear, but she looked back at me just as I snarled to Andrei. To my surprise, she turned back around and acted as if she never saw or heard anything.

"You are looking at her like she is prey. Can you cool it for a minute?" Andrei whispered back to me with judgment in his eyes.

I did declare she was prey when I left the castle. Here she was, allowing the lion into her den. I was so close to getting the approval from my father for the first time in my life. Looking at her small frame in front of me, I did not know if I could destroy such a beautiful creature. Sabrina's soft voice pulled me from my mind.

"He can look at me anyway he pleases. I don't mind the attention." She stopped and turned to face us. "As long as he knows that the queen is the most powerful piece on the board. This time everything we do will be on my terms." Her lips quirked into a smirk.

"There hasn't been a game that I haven't won." I took a step forward to close the gap between us.

She quickly spun away, causing her long black hair to toss back and hit me. "There is a first time for everything," she gave a soft giggle. Appearing at my side, Andrei gave me another nudge.

"If you don't marry her. I will," he teased

Sabrina took us into the Royal Library, and I was shocked at how large it was. This was at least three times the size of the Royal Library in Titus. There was a second-story balcony that wrapped around the library. Both the second and first stories had bookshelves full. There were rolling ladders attached to the shelves. A large stained glass window was on the far wall with an image of a cherry blossom tree in full bloom and the full moon high in the night sky. To my right, there was a roaring fireplace in the center of the wall. Back home that fire would be used to set books ablaze.

"I have never seen so many books in my entire life," I breathed. Serafina was more remarkable than I ever expected to be. I wondered if this knowledge was shared with the people, or was it kept locked away in the castle?

"Oh? Do you enjoy reading? What is your favorite genre?" I watched as her face lit up at the prospect of me enjoying literature. I took a deep breath and glanced over at Andrei. Anxiety filled me as I knew I was about to ruin my image in front of the fae queen. Andrei gave me a knowing glance. Sabrina raised an eyebrow.

"Darius has many strengths. Reading is not one of them," Andrei answered for me.

"My father thought it was a waste of time," I sighed, trying not to remember the beatings I'd received any time my father had caught me with a book in my hands that my mother had given me.

"You can't read at all?" She questioned. Studying her facial expression, I did not detect any judgment or disdain. Instead, I found concern. I am not sure why, but I knew that I could trust her with this.

"I can. Sometimes it takes me longer than others." I paused to steady my voice. "I would appreciate you not telling anyone about this."

"I will not tell a soul. Maybe if we have downtime while you are here, I can read some of my favorites to you." Her cheeks turned rosy. The stone and ice around my heart cracked as she reached out to take my hand in hers. Her skin was so soft. Smiling down at her, I gave her hand a small squeeze before I released. The thought of us curled up to the fire as she read to me filled my heart with an unfamiliar feeling of joy.

It had been too long since I felt a comforting touch. Violence controlled everything back home. For the first time, I found myself dreaming about how things could be.

I looked away from her gaze and stepped back. All of these feelings were too much for me to handle, and I shoved them into the box in the back of my mind where all of my emotions go to die. A large piece of glass hung on the wall. I walked over and looked up at it in confusion. I reached my hand up and ran my fingertips along the gold frame with engraved flowers. For all the things I had seen in this castle, this seemed very strange to me. Never had I seen anything like this. It showed an image of the library within the glass, that moved when I moved.

"What interesting decor," I said, trying to be polite. Sabrina walked over to me, and I was shocked when I saw her reflection in the glass and not my own. A look of confusion crossed my face as I stared at her image.

"This is a mirror. They are made using silver. That is probably why you cannot see your own reflection," she explained.

I turned to Andrei and snapped my fingers. "Andrei, take notes. I need one of these that will work for our kind." The thought of being able to see my reflection excited me. It wasn't fair that the world was able to gaze upon my face, but yet I could not.

"I will get right on that. Speaking of which, I would love to spend more time in the library and learn what it has to offer. Would you allow me to stay here while you finish the tour?" Andrei asked.

"Of course. I will have one of the servants check in with you when you are ready to be shown to your room," Sabrina said in her sweet voice.

Finally, I would get a moment alone with her. Well, as alone as I could be. I still felt the presence of the Ancient Ones lingering.

Andrei bowed, thanking her for allowing him to stay behind. He went over to one of the shelves and examined the literature.

Thirteen

Sabrina

Darius and I stood in the center of my orchard. I watched as Darius' head was on a swivel, looking at all of the varieties of fruit. A warm breeze hit our backs, and leaves and flower petals floated down to the ground.

"These are my pride and joy. We are known to have the best fruit in the land."

"I wish I could test that," Darius chuckled.

"We do have some ripe peaches ahead. You are welcome to have one."

"Vampires do not eat mortal food. Even if I tried it, it would taste like nothing. The only thing a vampire can taste is blood," he explained.

I spun toward him and smirked. "What a shame. How unfortunate for you." A soft giggle escaped my lips.

"Oh, not so unfortunate. Some blood has the best taste imaginable. Fae blood is particularly sweet," he closed the gap between us, and my heart fluttered. "I bet yours would be the sweetest." Darius licked his lips as he stared at my neck. My skin grew hot as I imagined his fangs grazing over my skin.

"Over my dead body, would I ever let you taste it," I lied. Every part of me screamed to let him do as he pleased with my body.

"A vampire can dream," he teased.

I quickly spun away from him and continued to walk through the orchard. I needed to put some distance between us before I gave in to my deepest desire to press my lips to his.

"You should be careful. You wouldn't want a repeat of our last encounter," I toyed, quickening my pace.

In a blink, Darius was in front of me, and I halted. He reached up into the tree and plucked a perfectly ripe peach. I watched as his fangs bit into the peach and the juices dripped down his chin. I couldn't help but think of what it would feel like if he had bit into my delicate flesh, and if it was my juices that dripped out of his mouth. Darius pulled the fruit away from his lips.

"I am imagining that this sweet nectar is your own, doll." He licked his lips. "I would love to find all the ways to make you gush all over my face."

My core melted as Darius slowly dragged his thumb against his lower lip to wipe away the excess juice. He then gently lifted my chin and locked our gazes. My whole body trembled, and my heart ached for him to close the gap.

"Would you like that, doll? For me to lick your juices?" Darius grabbed my wrist. As quickly as he took it, he jerked it away with a hiss. I lifted my arm to allow my long silk sleeve to fall and reveal the silver bracelet.

"Oh, I warned you. If you touch me, it will be on my terms," I smirked as I walked around him. "We should head back to the castle. It is getting late. I wouldn't want the twins to worry about me." I turned my head back to see Darius facing me with a smirk of his own.

"I agree. Let us return. You shouldn't be out alone so late with a predator." Darius and I walked back to the castle through the grassy field. We walked in silence for a moment, tension filled the air. I did not want to hurt him, but I needed the silver for my protection. He didn't seem mad, I hoped he wasn't hiding his true feelings.

"Why is that one cherry tree in the center of this field and away from the orchard?" He questioned, pointing to the lone tree on a small hill.

I informed Darius of the history of that tree. "It was the first cherry tree in all of Serafina. Many of us believe the gods planted it and that it is the source of the magic in Serafina. Many cherry trees popped up throughout the forest as the years went on."

Fourteen

Darius

Later that night after we retired to our room, I had provided one of the servants with a letter to deliver to Sabrina. I believe her name was Fern. She had come to check on how Andrei and I were doing after dinner. Sabrina had hosted a grand feast to celebrate our arrival. My only regret was that we could not enjoy the delicious looking food. The only thing I wanted was to sink my fangs into the queen's neck and have a feast of my own. When I handed Fern the letter, I informed her that it was an urgent matter. Based on the fact Sabrina had not yet met me under the cherry tree, Fern obviously did not take 'urgent' very seriously. It had been hours and she still did not arrive.

That had to be it, right? Sabrina wouldn't have received the letter and ignored my request. Would she? She had to feel the same attraction I did. It had taken everything to control myself earlier in the orchard. Even when I started to lose control, that silver bracelet snapped me back. It had been wrapped around a rose gold one as if it was barbed wire.

Nothing kills an erection faster than the burn caused by silver. It felt as if my entire body was aflame.

My mind calmed as I heard those familiar delicate footsteps from behind me. I turned and caught her gaze. The moonlight shone on her pale skin and illuminated her dark hair.

"You know, I don't think it's very smart meeting the vampire Prince in the middle of the night." She smirked as she walked up the hill and paused on the other side of the tree.

I walked to the side of the tree and leaned against it. A large grin spread across my face that bared my fangs.

"That's quite brave of you, doll." My eyes were glued to the queen. She wore a beautiful pale green silk dress with the thinnest of straps. If I hooked my claws under it, I could easily cause it to snap. My eyes were glued to her face as she walked closer to me and stopped just at arm's length. The moonlight reflected in her eyes almost caused my knees to buckle.

Why was I feeling so weak for this small fae woman? She should be my prey, I should not be vulnerable to her. There was something about her that made me want to fall to my knees and worship her. Again, I took those emotions and stuffed them away.

"So, what did you need to see me for that was so urgent?" Sabrina raised an eyebrow as she asked.

"I wanted to show you my good intentions, so I asked around and found out your favorite snacks." I smiled and motioned to the ground behind me. Under the tree, I had set up a full picnic, complete with a dark green and gold linen blanket laid on the ground. A wide selection of cheeses, fruits, nuts, pickled cucumbers, and a bottle of her favorite fae wine were laid out for her.

I hadn't known much about fae wine before traveling to Serafina. There were many different kinds based on the grapes and how long it was aged. Each style provided a different effect. Before my father placed the embargo on Serafina, I was very familiar with the one kind that got me extremely intoxicated. I had no idea what it tasted like, but I craved the feeling it gave. The fae wine that was given to me by the kitchen, I was not familiar with.

Sabrina's face lit up as she made her way to the picnic. Her bright blue eyes took in the food I had laid out for her.

"That is very kind of you."

"I can be kind when I want to be." I strode to her side, and she spun to face me. I watched as heat rose to her cheeks.

"You want to be kind to the girl who stabbed you?" She questioned.

"I want to be kind to someone as amazing as you. I need someone in my life who won't take my shit," I breathed nervously as I cupped her chin, my thumb gently brushed against her bottom lip. I lifted her chin so our gaze locked. Sabrina just stared up at me with those eyes that were as endless as the sea. The air electrified as a warm breeze blew through us.

I leaned down and crashed my lips into hers. They were softer and sweeter than I could ever imagine. She pressed her body into mine as she melted into my kiss, surrounding me completely with her intoxicating scent. Gods, I would kill to be frozen in this moment. My hunger for her grew the longer our kiss went on. Images flashed through my mind of my fangs piercing her delicate flesh. She let out a soft squeak as I held her tighter. My eyes went wide, and I quickly jumped away from her.

"I apologize. I did not mean to hold you so tightly," I said, embarrassed, and a wave of anger grew within me.

How could I be so reckless? How could I hurt her?

"No need to apologize," she teased, closing the gap between us once again. "It was just unexpected."

"You better eat before this all goes bad," I motioned down to the picnic. Sabrina smiled and sat on the blanket on her knees.

Fuck, seeing her on her knees was a sight to behold. It took every ounce of control I had not to grab the back of her head and thrust my cock down her throat.

Taking a deep breath, I sat by her side, watching as she grabbed a plate and filled it with a variety of offerings. Good lord, she liked mini-pickled cucumbers. She had eaten three of them, then put four more on her plate. I found myself wondering what they tasted like. I was born a vampire, so I never got the chance to eat anything like this.

"May I ask you something?" She questioned as she took a bite of the pickle. I couldn't help but to think about her lips wrapped around something else.

"Anything."

"Why did you go against your father and attend the ball? Why come here now if you know he would be unhappy?"

"He may be king," I looked up toward the sky and took a deep breath, "but I want to be my own man."

On my last word, I watched stars race across the sky. I had never seen anything so magnificent in my entire life. In Titus, the night sky was as black as the void. Sabrina scooted closer to me and leaned her body into mine while we watched the meteor shower. Unable to resist touching her again, I wrapped my arm around her and pulled her close. I was completely content in this moment. A serene calm washed over my body that I had never felt. It was a strange emotion, but I knew it was something that I would welcome into my life.

Unfortunately, I knew this moment was fleeting. I would soon need to return to my father and find a way to convince him to leave Sabrina alone. That type of disobedience would not be tolerated. If defending her was the hill I died on, so be it.

My eyes went wide as one of the shooting stars raced in our direction. My body was paralyzed. I wanted to throw Sabrina out of the way, but every muscle was frozen. Sabrina did not move, and I wondered if she was as immobilized as I was.

The star collided with us and burst into a glittery snow-like coating. A warmth washed over me, and I felt a tug within myself to look over to Sabrina. The stardust clung to her hair, and I swear it looked like she was glowing. Her gaze was still up at the stars in confusion.

"*What the hell was that?*" I heard her voice inside my mind. I could feel her heartbeat and was hyper-aware of every word she said.

"*That, I believe, was the craziest thing to ever happen to me.*" I sent my thoughts to her mind. I don't know how I did it. It was now something that was a part of me. Sabrina's head snapped to me, and her eyes went wide.

"How did you do that?" She demanded out loud.

"The same way you did, I suppose." I shrugged. Indeed, this was odd, but something inside me said this was how it was supposed to be. Again, I felt complete.

"Dar," she whimpered. Her voice was so soft.

"Yes, doll?" I breathed in response.

She looked up at me so nervous. Another wave of emotions washed over me, and I didn't know how much longer I could hold down my urges. They intensified the longer I stared into her eyes.

A single word did not escape her lips. Within my mind, I heard us both say in unison.

"*You are mine. You can't get rid of me now. We are bonded.*"

I could no longer resist the amazing woman in my arms as her sweet scent filled my nose and permeated me entirely. I pounced on her, causing her to lie back on the grass. My mouth quickly found its way to hers, and she wrapped her arms around my neck and kissed me back. I could not get enough of her taste. I kissed my way down to her neck and gently sucked on the flesh before grazing my fangs against her.

"No," she breathed, and I pulled my lips away from her neck. "No... I meant no fangs. Don't stop kissing me."

"Is there anything else you don't want me to do?" I asked, not wanting to make a wrong move. For once in my life, I did not care about my own desires.

"I... I'm not sure... I will tell you as you go," she whimpered oh so softly and it had me stiffening again. I hooked my fingers around those dainty little straps and gently peeled them down off her shoulder. I pulled her dress down until her breasts were free. Gods, they were the most glorious things I had ever seen.

"Will you be a good girl for me, doll?" I questioned. She nodded, and I quickly freed myself . I mounted her and laid my cock on her sternum. "Squeeze your beautiful tits around me," I growled.

She obliged. As she pushed them together, I thrust myself between her full breasts.

Her supple flesh was absolutely euphoric. She arched her back and moaned for me as I stroked my cock against her.

"Open your mouth," I demanded. Again, she did as I told her.

I loved how obedient she was for me. After all the fight she put up since I first met her, she now obeyed my every whim. I thrust the tip of my cock into her mouth. Her lips wrapped around the head as she sucked gently, and my eyes rolled back, and I groaned as she swirled her delicate tongue around the tip.

"Such a good girl," I moaned as I lifted myself and pushed deeper into her warm mouth.

"Don't stop. Please don't stop." Her voice sang in the back of my mind.

I restrained myself from fully fucking her skull into the ground. Slowly, I pumped myself deeper until I hit the back of her throat. Her eyes were crossed as she looked up at me. Gods. What I would do to bring her back to Titus with me and have her constantly kneeling before me? My cock twitched, and I released another groan of pleasure as I came into her mouth.

"Don't swallow it," I commanded. I slowly pulled out of her mouth and stood, slowly fisting my erection. "On your knees." She moved quickly. Gods, I loved having the fae queen follow my orders. Did she know that I would follow hers as well? "Open your mouth. Show me what you made me do to you."

She opened her mouth and showed me the cum that was pooled on her tongue. I brushed my hand through her hair and smiled down at her.

"Good girl. Swallow for me." As she did, my cock shot out another rope and it landed on her face. "Thank me."

"Thank you," she moaned.

I kneeled in front of her and licked my lips. Sabrina looked so beautiful with her tits out and my cum on her face. She was mine. I needed to continue to mark her as such.

"Do you enjoy pleasing me, doll?" I questioned.

"Yes," she breathed, her face flush.

"Do you want to continue to pleasure me?" I teased, as I brushed a stray strand of hair out of her face.

"More than anything."

"Such a good girl. Have you ever had a man please you before?" She shook her head in response. "So precious. I will be gentle, doll." I gently leaned her back into the grass and hiked up her dress, revealing her soaked panties. Slowly, I pulled them down and revealed her glistening sex.

I lined myself up with her and slowly pushed in the tip, releasing a groan as her pussy squeezed me. It was as if she was made for me.

"Tell me if I hurt you," I mused as I slowly pushed deeper into her. She arched her back and moaned as she accepted more of me. I pulled back to the tip and pumped myself back into her deliciously tight pussy.

"Please more," she pleaded.

I obliged and thrust into her faster. Sabrina writhed under me. Her pussy clenched against me as she grew closer to her climax. I reached down and teased her clit with my fingertips. She let out a loud moan of pleasure that shook the tree we fucked under.

My cock twitched. There was nothing more that I wanted than to pump her full of my seed as I drank her blood. Just the thought of her taste caused me to find my pleasure once again. My release flooded her, and I thrusted to force it deeper inside her.

"Oh gods," she moaned.

"No gods, dear. Just me. Your vampire." I leaned down and kissed her lips gently. As I pulled away, she reached up and grabbed my shirt and pulled me back down to her, kissing me harder.

I forced my tongue into her mouth, and I pressed my body into hers. I couldn't get enough of her. After what felt like a blissful eternity, I pulled away and she allowed it.

"Do you want me to walk you to your chamber?"

"I would love you too, and to stay with me."

"It would be my pleasure."

Fifteen
Sabrina

The morning sunlight hitting my face caused me to wake from the greatest sleep I had ever experienced. My heart fluttered as I thought about the night we had. Darius was an amazing lover. I had found my pleasure several times before finally passing out from sated exhaustion.

When we returned to my room, we continued to make love. He was gentle, just as he promised. The way he commanded me made me want him even more. I had never been known to be submissive in my life, but for him, I would obey his every command. Heat rose to my cheeks as I craved his touch once again.

I still could not get over what had happened between us. The star that had fallen somehow gave us a deeper level of connection. I had heard rumors of the gods bonding people together to serve a greater purpose. It had not been recorded however in hundreds of years, or with anyone outside of the fae. For me to be bonded with a vampire, the gods must have something up their sleeves.

It was not for me to question the gods. Never in my life had I, but for the first time I found myself wanting to know exactly what they had planned.

I rolled over to face the man I had allowed to sleep in my bed. He was gone. Only the lingering scent of pine and cinnamon remained. I sat up, my blanket fell to my waist, and revealed my bare chest. My bedroom door was closed, and I looked around and my heartbeat quickened. I twisted at the waist, so my bare feet hung off the side of the bed.

"Darius?" I called out and was met with silence. I stood, completely bare, and walked over to the frosted glass door of the adjoining bathroom. I gently knocked on the door, and again was answered by silence. Grabbing the golden handle, I twisted it and opened the door. An empty bathroom was all that I found. Steam fogged the mirrors, and I relaxed a little. He was just here. Maybe he had gone to get something to eat.

Walking into the closet, I looked at all my dresses that were hung up and organized by color. A red dress with a black bow tied in the back was what I chose to wear today, hoping that my vampire enjoyed the color choice.

I made my way down to the dining hall, and my heart sank as I walked in. Neither Darius nor Andrei were here. I walked over to the head table where Xander and Daphne sat eating their breakfast. Xander had a plate with an extremely fluffy waffle, topped with more chocolate than I could ever eat in one sitting, and a mountain of whipped cream. Daphne was giving his plate a side eye; she had a bowl of fruit and a poached egg on toast.

"Have either of you seen our guests?" I questioned them. Xander shoved a large piece of waffle into his mouth as he looked up at me, confused.

"They left this morning," he said with his mouth full.

"What do you mean, they left?" My voice raised in pitch as I spoke. Daphne swallowed her piece of toast. Her gaze burned my skin as I watched her eyes narrow.

"They left about two hours ago. Darius said there was an emergency back in Titus he had to handle," she said calmly before taking another bite.

"Well, I hope everything is ok," I sighed. In my soul, I could sense it was not true. There was no emergency. He lied so he could leave. Everything he said was a lie.

Daphne was right. Darius would bring nothing but pain into my life. I turned away and took a step.

"Aren't you going to stay and eat breakfast?" The twins said in unison.

"No, I am going to my study. I have lots of work to do."

Sixteen

Darius

There was no way I was bonded to a fae, especially not the fae queen. She was my enemy. It was my job to destroy her. I could not allow myself to fall for her. I could not, would not love her.

Taking in a deep breath, I looked out the window of the carriage and watched as the trees went by. It took everything I had to force out the thoughts of the beautiful fae queen, *my* fae queen.

In the deep recess of my mind, I could hear her cries, and her pain flooded my body. For once in my life, I did not enjoy the misery that I had caused.

I had claimed her fully under the moonlight, and several times once we returned to her room. Her scent still filled my nose, making me crave her even more. I never knew anyone to be so sweet. She was perfect, and she was mine.

But I could never be hers. I belonged to Titus- to Dimitri. I had to follow his orders. I had gotten too close to her, and it would ruin me.

Andrei's voice snapped me back into focus.

"Are you going to tell me why we had to leave so quickly? What is this emergency you spoke of?"

"I don't want to discuss it," I snarled.

"If there is an emergency in Titus, shouldn't I-"

I cut him off before he could finish. "There is no emergency in Titus," I said plainly.

Andrei gave me an up-and-down look before he sighed. His eyes met mine, and I saw nothing but sadness behind his stormy blue eyes.

"Do you want to talk about why the fae queen's scent clings to you as if you bathed in her perfume?" He continued to question me.

My anger boiled inside of me, and I banged on the carriage wall behind me. "Stop at the next village," I demanded. "I need to blow off some steam."

It wasn't long before we found a village and stopped. We found a small inn, if there was not a sign out front we would have thought it was a house. Andrei and I walked into the inn, and everyone's eyes were on us. The pub area was filled with fae, there were very few open tables. This part of the forest did not seem well-traveled. The road we traveled was bare of travelers, and some parts were overgrown. I assumed this was the first time that these fae had ever laid eyes on a vampire. Some of the patrons looked confused by our presence, others angry, and I noticed a few women making bedroom-eyes toward me. I informed Andrei before we exited in the carriage not to get in my way.

I locked eyes on a fae woman with long, dark hair, amber eyes, and dark olive skin. She was one of those aforementioned women. Her being all alone was the cherry on top.

She would do.

The woman smiled at me as I made my way over to her and slid into the booth next to her.

"Well, hello there, stranger," she teased.

"Hello to you too, darling," I purred.

She bit her bottom lip and set her hand on my thigh. As she leaned in closer, the scent of sweet peaches filled my nose. The scent brought up the memory of Sabrina and me in her orchard. When I had bit into that peach, I was fully going in for the joke but was pleasantly surprised when I could actually taste it. Was my mind playing tricks on me, or was the fruit of Serafina was so good that even a vampire could enjoy them?

I pushed those feelings deep into the back of my mind to a section where I locked away all feelings other than hate. That was the only emotion I could allow myself to have, especially for the fae queen I needed to destroy.

"I have never seen your kind around here before," she mused.

"I am just traveling through while returning home."

"What a shame. I would have loved to have you stay here at the inn for a while." The fae grazed her hand up my thigh and stopped just below my groin.

"I can spend all the time here I need to, darling." I leaned in and roughly kissed her lips. I didn't care that the whole bar still had their eyes on me. Let all of Serafina know that the vampire Prince preyed on the fae.

She bit my lower lip and grazed her teeth against it as she pulled away, making me groan as she did. "Come, I have a room upstairs. That way, we have more privacy," she cooed.

"What? You don't want me to bend you over this table and fuck you with the whole bar watching? I will. All you need to do is say please."

Heat rose to her cheeks, and she slid out of the other end of the booth, motioning for me to follow her. She led me to a small room upstairs with a single bed, chest, and a writing desk.

The fae woman wasted no time. As soon as the door closed, she got on her knees and freed my erect cock. She slowly dragged her tongue up and down my length, and a groan escaped my lips as I tilted my head back. The fae swirled her tongue against my tip just before she took me into her mouth. I ran my fingers through her hair before I roughly grabbed it and fucked her throat the way I wanted to fuck Sabrina. The tiny fae woman gagged as I hit the back of her throat over and over. Her hands gripped my thighs. They pushed against me, as if she was trying to pull away.

Yes, little fae, fight harder.

I closed my eyes and pretended it was my fae queen. Gods, I would kill to see her bright blue eyes looking up at me as I skull fucked her. No matter how much I pretended the whore was her, it was no use. This mouth did not feel nearly as good as Sabrina's.

I pulled the fae off me after a while, a string of drool connecting my cock to her lips. I held her in place as she licked the tip.

"I have never seen anyone so big," she moaned.

"You never will again." I threw her down to the ground.

"Bend over the bed and show me your pathetic cunt," I demanded. Obeying, she got up quickly and bent over the bed, pulling up her skirt. The whore wasn't wearing any panties.

Quickly, I lined myself up with her aching cunt and plunged myself into it. Clenching my jaw, I was reminded I craved the feeling of Sabrina's tight pussy, but this was nothing like it. This fae woman did not feel half as good. I reached forward, gripped her hair, and pulled as I thrust into her over and over. She screamed and moaned for more. What a disgusting whore for throwing herself at an unknown vampire. I am sure if it wasn't me, it would have been any man who sat in that booth.

My balls tightened as I released inside of her. My cock twitched as I came. Though, it was unsatisfying, as if my body had done so just to get this over with. I pulled out of her and quickly flipped her to her back.

"Give me your neck," I commanded. She tilted her head, and moved her hair away from her skin. Leaning down, I bit into her skin, but as soon as her blood flooded my mouth, I spit it out. I jerked away from her, looking down at the now blood-covered whore.

"Repulsive," I growled as I fastened my pants. I turned and quickly left the room, not listening to the obscenities she now spat at me.

I went downstairs and found Andrei sitting at the bar speaking to two fae males. Their conversation stopped as I approached them.

"Come," I demanded. "It is time for us to return to Titus."

As soon as we got back to Titus, some of my father's guards escorted us to the throne room. The castle was dark, and devoid of life, and I could feel my soul withering away with every step I took. If Serafina was the embodiment of life, Titus was the exact opposite.

How much longer would I allow it to drain me?

Dimitri sat on his throne. His face contorted in anger. I swore it was the only face he had. He did not even wait for us to approach the dais before he jumped from his seat and rushed toward me. His hand gripped my throat and squeezed. I did not flinch.

"Where have you been?" Dimitri spat.

"I went to Serafina, as you commanded. To be a spy, I need to leave Titus every so often," I growled.

Dimitri released me and in a blink, he was back on his throne with his ankle over his knee. He leaned back and waved his hand at me. "Go on," he said as he rolled his eyes. "Tell me what you learned."

I told him about the library in the castle and how much more knowledge it stored compared to ours. I also informed him of the mirrors that I discovered, and how they showed the reflections of all who weren't vampires, as they were made with silver.

"That's it?" He questioned in an annoyed tone.

"Yes, for now. I am still earning the queen's trust. Her advisors are making it difficult for me to get in." I lied. She was so open with me, and I barely saw her advisors while there. I could never let Dimitri know that Sabrina and I were bonded, he couldn't know that I took her to bed, that I craved her.

Dimitri looked me up and down slowly, not saying a word. He leaned forward and released a single breath. "Remember what happened to the last woman you were stupid enough to love," he snarled. "Having feelings makes you weak."

Images flashed through my mind of the last time I saw my mother. It was right here in the throne room. I remembered the sight of her head rolling on the floor. Cut off by my father's sword. He had his guards hold her in place as he lectured her about how my attachment to her was making me weak.

I had one purpose, and that was to be a weapon. His weapon. There was no room for kindness in my life.

My mother would be ashamed of the man I have become. I gritted my teeth and locked eyes with my father. "The only feelings I have are hatred and anger."

<h1 style="text-align:center">Seventeen</h1>

<h2 style="text-align:center">Sabrina</h2>

I had called Xander and Daphne into my study three days after Darius had left. My room had become my sanctuary during this time, no one was allowed in or out. Alone time was what I needed. I was hurt by Darius leaving, but I was even more hurt that I allowed myself to give him a part of me that was so sacred.

Disappointment filled me. I always wanted to save my first time to be with someone that I loved and fully trusted. After we were bonded, I was flooded with desire, and I could not resist the pull I felt toward him.

That pull called to me long before the bond was in place. It was dull, but I could not deny how I felt a connection with him as soon as he walked into the ballroom on my birthday. It was like I had waited for that moment my entire life.

Xander and Daphne were in shock when I told them about what had happened the night before Darius left. About how once the star fell upon us, we had an instant connection into each other's mind. How I had felt an intense desire to be with him.

"You and the vampire Prince are bonded?" Daphne questioned.

"It is impossible. There is no way you are bonded to him. Bonds of this nature are extremely rare, and there is no way the gods would choose for a vampire and fae to be bonded together," Xander added.

"Unfortunately for me, we are," I sighed. "Trust me, I am just as thrilled as you two are about it."

The two looked at me, stupefied. Daphne broke the silence after a moment. "The two of you seemed to be getting along when you gave him a tour of the orchard."

"No! The two of you being bonded would be terrible. This would mean the end of Serafina. There is no way the gods would do this," Xander raised his voice.

I stood from my chair and raised my palm to him. A silent command for him to silence himself. He did.

"They did, and I plan to make the most of it. There has to be a good reason the gods have bonded us." I picked up a letter from my desk and called for Fern to come into my study. "I want to improve relations with Titus. I plan to send them a peace offering."

Even though my heart was broken by him disappearing, I knew that this was all in the gods' plans. I was chosen by them to be queen. I would not want to disappoint them. I did not know what they had in store for Darius or I, but I will prove to them that I am worthy.

When Fern entered my study, she bowed. "Yes, my queen?"

Walking over to her, I permitted her to rise, and she did. She reached out her hand to take the letter I offered her and the instructions on what to do with it. One of our cherry trees would make a fine offering to Titus. The royal arborists dug up one of the trees and prepared it for travel. Fern nodded and rushed out of the room as quickly as she had entered.

"You are making a mistake," Xander said from behind me.

"Enough. I am queen," I said, without turning to face him. "What I say is final. I do not want to hear another word." I left the study before he could respond.

Eighteen

Darius

My blood boiled beneath my skin as my anger raged inside me. I stood in the center of my private training room, punching my target. My wrappings had begun to fray as I worked out my anger. Losing all sense of time, I wasn't sure if I had been here for only a few minutes, or a few hours.

I still could not get the smell of her or the taste of her away from me. Sabrina had consumed every thought I had. I needed to be with her. I needed her to be mine. I needed to be hers. It had been nearly two weeks since I had left Serafina, and I regretted it every day. Somehow, I could feel her heartache, or was it my own? I had been so numb to my own emotions for so long, would I even be able to feel them if I had them?

Beyond frustrated, I punched the target so hard that it finally exploded upon collision, sending sand spraying all over the ground. The tips of my claws dug into my skin as I clenched my fists. I wasn't done. The aggression in me was building and I needed to release it. Footsteps approach me from behind. Perfect, just what I needed, another target. I spun, whirling my fist at whoever was behind me.

My eyes went wide as I stopped my fist just an inch from a very familiar face.

"Well, hello to you too, brother," Andrei let out a chuckle as I lowered my fist.

"What do you want?" I snarled at him.

"I haven't seen you in a few days. I wanted to come and check on you." Worry filled his voice, and it did nothing but fill me with more anger.

"I don't need you to check on me," I said angrily, pushing past him.

Andrei followed me as I stomped up the stairs and into a large sitting room in a part of the castle that was not used often. When we found the secret passageway to the large square room below, I knew it was going to be my perfect hiding place. Across the castle there were many secret passages that led to tunnels or secret areas. I knew about some of them, but not all. Andrei and I found this one by mistake many years ago when I had pushed him up against the wall. His head smacked into the stone that opened up the hidden entry.

"Darius, stop running from me," he said with some force in his voice. I heard the secret passage slide shut behind me as Andrei finally entered the sitting room. I continued to ignore him and walked out of the room. I heard Andrei's steps quicken behind me. I needed him to stop caring about me.

I was a monster. Didn't he know that?

Everyone else did.

I stormed through the castle, trying to rid myself of this pest that I had created. His voice was like a fly buzzing in my ear. His words went in one ear and out the other. I did not know where I was even going, I just needed to get away from him, from anyone who could care about me.

Red filled my vision as I continued to move through the castle halls.

Clarity snapped back into focus as my body ran into something hard. I looked down at the small earth fae male who was now sitting on the ground. I realized that I had walked all the way to the castle entrance and was just about to exit through the gates. I looked back at the fae male and extended my arm out to him to assist him.

"I apologize." Fuck, who was I becoming? Had I ever apologized for running into someone? Was it not always their fault for being in the vampire prince's way? "I should watch where I am going." The words spilled out of my mouth before I could stop them. Andrei had come to my side and gave me a sideways glance.

The fae man took my hand, stood, and brushed the dirt off of him. That is when I noticed the cart behind him. Had he been pulling the cart all by himself? I knew earth fae were strong, but I was shocked seeing it in person. On the cart was a beautiful cherry tree in full bloom. The roots were wrapped in a muslin cloth.

"Thank you for your assistance," the fae spoke. "My name is Aspen. I am looking for the King of Titus. I have a delivery from the Queen of Serafina."

"Welcome Aspen. I am the prince. The king is currently not in," I lied.

I could not let my father see the gift from Serafina. Thoughts raced through my mind of what would happen if he did. Knowing him, he would burn the tree and destroy its beauty. I could not allow Sabrina's gift to be destroyed.

"I will accept this gift on his behalf," I said with a smile.

Aspen handed me a letter in the queen's signature pink envelope. Her scent filled my nose, and I struggled to hold in a groan of pleasure as I took it in. After opening the envelope and removing its contents, I stared at the page for a moment, taking a deep breath. I knew the fae stared at me. I prayed he thought it was just a long letter.

To the Kingdom of Titus,

Please accept this gift of an ever-blooming cherry tree. These are sacred to my people, and I hope that this can be symbolic of the relationship between our two kingdoms.

Sabrina Alexandra Saison, Queen of Serafina

How could she still want a relationship with this kingdom after what I had done? Could this mean she still wanted a relationship with me? I did not deserve such a forgiving woman.

"Thank you, Aspen, for bringing this to us. I will pay you double what she paid you for you to deliver this to my castle in the western mountains," I said to him as I put the letter in my pocket.

The castle in the west was my sanctuary from this hell. My father had built it many years ago as a gift for my mother. Though, he only did that so he could send her away so that she would not be aware of what he was up to. When she died, she left the castle to me.

"Double?" Aspen raised his eyebrow.

"Double. Make sure that this also stays between us."

"Agreed," he said as he told us the total. Sabrina truly spared no expense.

I looked over and nodded at Andrei. In a blink, he was gone. While he was gone, I had Aspen take out his map, and I provided him with directions on how to arrive at the castle in the mountains. Just as I finished providing him with the instructions, Andrei reappeared with a coin purse in hand. He gave it to Aspen as well as a nod in thanks.

"I must be on my way." He grabbed the bars of the cart and lifted it. Andrei and I stood in silence as we watched him run off.

Even once he was no longer in view, we still stood there for some time. It was Andrei finally who broke the silence. "Well, are you ready to talk about it now?"

"Not here. Come with me to my chambers."

Andrei sat on the edge of my bed as I paced in front of him. The words fell out of my mouth about how I was so drawn to the fae queen, how I thought she was the most beautiful woman I had ever seen, and how I wanted to care for her, even when Dimitri wanted me to destroy her.

I told him of what had happened under the cherry tree, how the stars had fallen on us and bonded Sabrina and me together. Andrei was silent as I informed him that Sabrina and I could now communicate telepathically, and even so far away, I could still sense her. I explained to him the tug I felt on my heart that begged for me to return to her.

I finally paused, faced him, and finally took in a deep breath after my long-winded monologue. He looked up at me, his elbows on his knees and arms hanging down.

"Okay," was all he said.

"Okay?" I questioned. He nodded. "I just dropped that all on you, and all you have to say is okay?" My anger rose once again.

"Well, you told me the events. You have yet to tell me how you feel about it," he added. I paused and looked down at my feet.

"I am angry about it."

"Why?"

"Because I love her, and I am not allowed to. I have never felt anything like this in my entire life. I am making a fool of myself. No matter which path I take, it will end in misery. If I do what my father asks, I will kill another thing I love. It is my fault my mother is dead, my fault your family is dead, and my fault you are a vampire. I do not know if I can handle killing another I care about. If I choose Sabrina, my father will destroy us." For the first time in a long time, I felt tears threaten my eyes. "I don't know what to do."

Andrei stood up from the bed and took a step, so he stood in front of me. He grabbed me by my shoulders and pulled me close, wrapping his arms around me. My eyes widened and my body stiffened as he hugged me. There was always an unspoken promise between us never to show emotion or affection. He patted my back then released me and took a step back.

"Brother," he breathed, "it is good to love. Your father is wrong. Love is not weakness. Love is strength."

"What do you know of love?" I snapped, bitterly.

"I've loved. I never told you about her. Her name was Isadora."

"Was?"

Andrei nodded sadly. "Dimitri found out, and we all know what he does to the things and people we love," he said softly.

I saw the pain in his eyes, and the tears that threatened, but never dared to fall. "We keep ruining your life. Why do you stay?"

"No, not we," he corrected. "*He* ruins my life. *You* are my best friend. I will not leave you alone with that monster."

"Thank you," I said as I took a deep breath. "I would be lost without you."

"And I without you." He walked over to my desk, grabbing a pen and a piece of parchment. When he turned back and extended them toward me, I raised my eyebrow. "Well, don't you want to show her where you put the tree?"

"I think that is a wonderful idea," I smirked and took the paper and pen from his hand. I walked over to the desk and wrote out a formal invitation for Sabrina to join me in my castle in the mountains.

Nineteen

Sabrina

I was in my study with the twins when Fern delivered the letter from Titus. My heart fluttered as I accepted, wondering what they had to say about my gift. I hoped Dimitri was receptive to my attempts at trying to repair the relationship between our Kingdoms. I was shocked when I opened the letter to find it was from Darius.

My dearest Sabrina,

Please accept my invitation to join me at my castle nestled within the western mountains of Titus. I'd love to see the place of honor I've given your generous gift. I too hope that your gift will be a symbol of our relationship.

Eternally yours,

Darius Edward Alexander Dragomeir, Prince of Titus.

The twins were too eager to see what the letter said. Xander snatched the paper from my hands and I watched as his olive skin turned pale as he read. His gaze met mine.

"My queen," he sighed, "I implore you not to accept this invitation. Please heed my warning. A relationship between the two of you will ruin Serafina."

"Serafina and Titus improving relations can only be good for the whole of Serafina. I will not want to hear any more of this. I *will* be going, and Daphne will be joining me as my escort. Xander, you will be staying here and keeping an eye on things."

I watched as the wheels turned in Xander's head. I could see his thoughts zooming through his eyes. He clenched his jaw and swallowed hard as if to swallow down the words he wanted to say.

"Yes, my queen," he finally said as he stood and exited the study.

I had never been outside of Serafina's borders. I was a bit anxious as we made our way through the forest, across the border, and into the Wastes of Titus. I had never been anywhere so devoid of life. For miles were long stretches of desert. There was nothing but sand and a few settlements along the path to the mountains. It seemed impossible for life to exist here, and I found myself wondering how these settlements fared. Passing through

351

the Wastes left me with an uneasy feeling. I was glad that I had my carriage to keep me separated from the outside world.

I was thankful when we could finally see the mountains in the distance after hours of traveling. The jagged mountain range was full of life. For the first time since entering Titus, I saw lush green trees. The Kikaro mountains had a dense forest enveloping them. The only break from the trees were the roads that traveled up the mountain side. Fog clung to the road as we traveled up the mountain range.

We finally arrived at the castle that was nestled in the mountains. I gazed up at it in awe. Ivy clung to the dark stone and climbed the towers. I was most interested in the tower in the back of the castle that had a large glass dome atop it. My thoughts immediately wondered what was inside the dome.

As I stepped out of the carriage, Darius rushed forward, stopping just a few feet in front of me. My stomach twisted as I looked up at him. I should be angry with him, but something within me would not allow it.

He stood in front of me, and I noticed the feeling of the tug of my heart had stopped. Darius bowed and tilted his head to look up at me. A few loose strands had fallen out of his pulled-back hair and dangled in his face.

"Welcome to my castle," he smirked. I caught the subtle emphasis on 'my'.

"Thank you for having us," Daphne said as she came to my side. It was then I noticed that Andrei stood a few feet behind Darius with a smile on his face.

"Hello, Andrei," I gave him a wave.

"Hello, Queen Sabrina," he waved back.

"Sabrina is fine," I said to him.

"Oh no. That is far too casual for someone like yourself." He raised his palms in protest.

"Andrei, please. I insist."

"Lady Sabrina is what I can offer you," he chuckled.

"Lady Sabrina it is," I giggled, and focused my attention back on the handsome prince that stood before me. Before I could speak, Darius did.

"I would love to give you a full tour. However, before I do, please allow me to take you to my gardens. I have a surprise for you." His smile warmed my soul.

"That would be wonderful," Daphne and I said in unison.

Darius and Andrei guided us through his castle. I stayed a few steps away from Darius. He would not regain my trust so easily. The two of us exchanged longing glances, but never spoke of the elephant in the room. It was nothing like the architecture of Serafina. While my castle was filled with open spaces, sunlight and foliage, Darius' castle was dark, suffocating, with not a single ounce of life other than the four of us that roamed the halls. How could anyone live like this?

Darius abruptly stopped and turned to face me. "I need you to close your eyes," he said with an urgent tone.

"I'm sorry, what?" Daphne and I questioned.

"Do you trust me?" Darius asked.

"No. Not even a little bit," Daphne chuckled.

Andrei laughed as well. "She's got you there, Darius. You haven't really given them a reason to trust you," Andrei said.

"Please," Darius said softly. "Close your eyes."

"If it is that important, Sabrina can. Mine will remain open to keep her safe," Daphne snapped at Darius.

"That is agreeable," Darius said.

"Let's not talk about me like I am not here. Darius, I'm not sure why, but I do trust you. Do not make me regret it." I closed my eyes and felt him gently grab my hand. A shiver went down my body as our skin connected, and I had not realized how badly I needed his touch. Darius guided me a bit further, and then I heard Daphne gasp.

"What is it?" I questioned. "Is everything ok?'

"Open your eyes and find out," Darius said softly.

I opened my eyes and my jaw dropped. The cherry tree I had sent sat in the center of the courtyard garden. Opal moons laid in the ground and circled the tree. Many tropical flowers and plants were planted in the garden beds.

What left me in awe the most was the butterflies that filled the garden. There were so many different varieties, many of which I had never seen. It was absolutely amazing.

"Darius," I breathed as I took a step into the garden, "this is beautiful." Tears of joy threatened to fall.

"I am glad you liked it. I was inspired by your gardens, and I took plants from your day garden and mixed it with the decor from your night garden," Darius said as he stepped in front of me. A golden butterfly flew around his head and landed on his nose. He crossed his eyes to look at it, and I chuckled. With a scrunch of his nose, the butterfly flew off. "I had the butterflies imported from all over the world. I knew they were your favorite. I wanted a place you could easily go to see kinds you typically would not be able to."

"Color me impressed, Darius. It seems that even *you* can go beyond expectation," Daphne said. I looked over at her and saw she was inspecting some of the flowers in one of the beds. I recognized them as the vitella flower, a very rare plant with healing properties. Each color bloom had its own effect. I had never seen them in person, only in botanical encyclopedias. They were native to a continent across the sea called Elswynth. We had not had contact with them for centuries, for their human king was not fond of any of us magic folk that shared this world.

"He worked very hard to get this all put together before your arrival," Andrei said from behind me. I turned to look at him and he was leaning in the archway. "It was quite entertaining to see him work so diligently."

I turned back to Darius, whose face had turned bright red. "I love it," As I smiled. Darius took a step forward, and I heard his voice in the back of my mind.

I am glad. I would give anything to see you smile like this.

Darius broke our stare and looked over to Andrei. "Will you show them to their guest chamber? I need to finish something up before dinner," Darius then looked back at me. "Please join me in an hour in my private dining room for dinner. I had hired chefs from the city to travel here to make you the best meal you have ever had."

"I am excited to see if that is the case. I have two amazing chefs in Serafina. It will be hard to beat anything that Brandilyn and Genevieve can make."

The private dining room Darius had set up was absolutely beautiful. A fireplace was on the back wall, with red and black tapestries hanging on either side, with a large stag head mounted just above the mantle. Above the table hung a grand chandelier, the black metal was twisted into a beautiful design. The long table had a red velvet runner with a gold trim running down the center . Down the runner were candelabras, flowers in clear vases, and crystals of varying colors and shapes.

Darius was standing at the entrance of the dining room when we walked in. He guided Daphne and me to the table where two place settings were set. My eyes went wide as I saw that the plates were gold, and the cutlery matched. Andrei appeared seemingly out of nowhere and greeted us. Darius had pulled out the seat to the left of the head of the table for me. I took my seat. Daphne sat across from me. Darius took his seat at the head of the table, the fireplace to his back. Andrei sat across from him.

"Thank you for coming to Titus," Darius said as she snapped his fingers. As he did, four servants entered the room. Two of them had golden chalices, and they were delivered to Darius and Andrei. The other two presented Daphne and I with stemless glasses filled with white wine. "I had some of your favorite wine imported before your arrival."

"Thank you," I smiled. "We are certainly happy to be here."

Daphne took a sip of her wine and nodded in approval. Darius lifted his chalice and gently swirled the liquid inside it. He took a sip and looked down the table towards Andrei.

"If you do not eat," Daphne started, "What do you plan to do during this dinner?"

"I plan to enjoy your company," Darius said as he took another deep sip.

"We are hoping that we can reform and strengthen our alliance," Andrei said.

"Without the King?" Daphne raised an eyebrow. With another snap of Darius' fingers, two of the servants came back out and placed salads in front of Daphne and me. One of the servants, who was very tall and pale with dark hair and glasses, informed us that it was a bed of romaine lettuce with dried cranberries, cinnamon pecans, and an apple balsamic vinaigrette.

"Thank you, Kiam. You are dismissed," Andrei said. Kiam and the other servant quickly exited the room.

Silence built for a moment as we all stared at Darius. He took another sip and then sat it on the table in front of him.

"My father can never know of this meeting," Darius finally spoke.

"Why is that?" Daphne and I spoke in unison.

I watched his shoulders drop, as he gave Andrei a pleading look.

"Dimitri will never understand," he leaned back in his seat and looked me in the eye. "All I want is to be free of him."

"Let us change the subject to something more pleasant," Andrei said. I looked toward him and he, too, leaned back in his seat, sipping from his chalice. "Tell us, how are the salads?"

I finally took a bite and the flavors burst on my tongue. Everything tasted extremely fresh. The sweetness from the dressing went perfectly with the spice from the pecans and the crisp taste of the lettuce. I looked back over to Andrei, letting him know that it was absolutely delicious. Darius did not speak for some time, and it wasn't until we had finished our salads that I turned to him.

Before I could say anything, he snapped his fingers, and Kiam and three other servants came out with him. Two came and took our plates and filled up their chalices. Once the salad plates were removed, our main course was sat in front of us. Kiam informed us that it was a pepper and rosemary-crusted lamb chop with butter and garlic couscous and roasted asparagus. We thanked him, and the servants exited the room.

"Darius, this is truly amazing," I said, looking over to him. "It smells divine."

"Thank you. I was hoping you would like it. Please enjoy."

I took a bite, and the meat melted in my mouth. "I will say, you were right. This does give anything I've had from Brandilyn and Genevieve a run for its money."

"I am glad to hear it." A smirk grew over Darius' face. "Please, tell me how the journey here was. Do not spare a single detail."

The rest of the dinner was amazing. For dessert, we were served a vanilla-orange souffle with a brulee topping. After we discussed our journey from Serafina, the conversation moved to Darius' day-to-day life here in Titus. Apparently, He spent most of his time within the castle, awaiting Dimitri's orders. This year, he had only left Titus's borders to visit me in Serafina.

After dinner, Darius asked if I would join him for a stroll through the castle. I agreed. Daphne said she was going to retire for the night. After the trip we took, she was exhausted. She wanted to take a bath and do some light reading. Andrei said he also had work to do.

Darius and I walked side by side as we left the dining room. I still made sure to keep some distance in between us.

"I have something I want to show you," he said softly.

"Something else?"

"You will see. It is a bit of a walk to get there."

"Good that means we can talk," I said to him with a sting in my voice.

Darius cleared his throat. "I am sorry," he said so quietly that I could barely hear him.

"What was that?" I questioned. I heard him, but I wasn't letting him off the hook that easily. I stopped walking. If he was going to apologize, he was going to do it until it met my standards. Darius took three steps before he realized I had stopped. He spun to face me. He took a deep breath and stared down at the floor, avoiding my gaze. I took a step forward.

"Feeling your heartbreak down the bond nearly killed me. I am so sorry, doll," he said as he finally looked up at me.

"Why? Tell me, why did you leave? Why invite me here?"

He let out a deep sigh. "I am not a nice person. I was born and raised in hatred. My father despises you and wants you destroyed. I could not imagine a world where I was bonded to someone, let alone the fae queen that is my kingdom's enemy. When I awoke that morning, I panicked. I did not know what to do, so I ran." Darius closed the gap between us. "Every moment away from you has been torture. I could not escape the smell of you-the taste of you. I need you in my life, Sabrina." We stood there for a moment as the air electrified around us, and gooseflesh ran down my spine as he leaned down and gently kissed my lips. "Please forgive me."

"I will consider it," I breathed.

He straightened his back and smirked down at me. "Good, now come along. We have a ways to go before we get to what I want to show you." He quickly turned on his heels and made his way down the hall. I followed closely behind him.

After a fifteen-minute walk through the castle, we passed through an archway, and a spiral stone staircase came into view, and we climbed it. Once at the top, I realized we were in the large glass dome I saw when I had first arrived.

There was a fire pit in the center of the large circular room, and a large couch sat near it. There was a wicker swing sitting facing out toward the amazing view of the mountains.

"This is the most beautiful view I have ever seen," I breathed.

Darius came over to me and stopped just behind me. I felt his breath on my ear, causing a shiver to run down my spine.

"I could think of something more beautiful," he purred. Heat rose to my cheeks. "Want to come sit with me on the swing and enjoy the view?"

"Absolutely."

Darius wrapped his arm around me, and we walked over to the swing. He sat on it and I took my place next to him, leaning against his shoulder. Almost immediately, Darius's arm looped around my body pulling me in tight.

"This is perfect," he said softly, and I nodded in response. Exhaustion from the day began to take over my body, and I gave a little yawn. "Rest, little doll. I will keep you safe."

I laid my head on Darius' lap. He gently pet my hair as I closed my eyes and let sleep take me.

When I awoke, the moon hung high above us.

"Good morning, sleepyhead," he chuckled.

I sat up, stretched my arms above my head, and yawned. The sound of an owl in the distance filled my ears.

"How long have I been asleep?" I questioned.

"Just a few hours," Darius mused. "I just enjoyed the view while you slept. It was quite peaceful, actually."

I stood and smiled. "I am glad you had a moment of peace."

"It is probably the last I will get for a while," he said, and his gaze went out of focus as he stared out over the mountains. His focus snapped back to me and he gave a sad smile. "It is late. I am surprised Daphne hasn't torn down the castle looking for you. Shall I walk you to your room?"

"Daphne is very protective of me, and I am grateful for it." Daphne had always been there for me. She would go to the end of the world for me. Not that Xander wouldn't. He would just fight me every step of the way. "I would love for you to walk me to my room. I worry I will get lost."

Darius stood and came to my side, wrapping his arm around my shoulder. "Well, I wouldn't want that happening. Follow me."

With his arm around my waist, Darius guided me back down the spiral staircase and through the castle halls. I was very glad he had walked me here, it felt like a much longer walk than I remembered, with so many turns I would have gotten lost. Darius stopped directly in front of the door of the suite, turned to face me, and took a deep breath.

"Good night, Sabrina. I look forward to seeing you in the morning," he said softly.

"Good night, Darius," I giggled. Heat rose to my cheeks as he gently cupped my chin, his thumb just beneath my bottom lip.

"May I kiss you?" He pleaded.

"Please," I breathed.

Darius leaned down and gently brushed his lips to mine. As he pulled away, my thoughts screamed for him to not stop, for him to never stop. I would never get tired of his lips on mine.

Darius chuckled. "You do not need to think so loud," he planted another kiss upon my lips. "All you need to do is ask. Anything you wish, I will deliver." Again, he gave me another soft kiss. "Good night, Bri," he whispered.

"Good night, Dar," I said as I stole another kiss before turning away and entering the suite.

Daphne sat in the velvet armchair, the fireplace roaring in front of her. Her amber eyes met mine and a mischievous grin crossed her face.

"It's so late," she teased. "Did you have a good time?"

I rolled my eyes in response. I laid on the couch next to her armchair, rested my head on the arm, and looked up to Daphne.

"Darius was just showing me around the castle," I said.

"Oh, I am sure that was all that he was doing," she teased. "I have never seen such a predatory look in one man's eyes."

I rolled my eyes. "You are insufferable."

"That I may be, but you love me."

"That I do." I gave another yawn.

"Good, because you and I need to have a hard conversation."

I sat up and raised my eyebrow to her. "Oh?"

"Yes," she breathed. "Though he has been a very generous host, I do not trust him. I have heard many stories about the vampire prince. I find it very hard to believe he would go against his king."

"I believe him. I can feel it through our bond. I hear his thoughts, sense his emotions."

"You are sure that they aren't just what he wants you to feel? I can't help but worry you are falling into a trap that you won't be able to get out of."

"I know this is not a trap. The vampire prince's words are genuine. I trust him." I stood and walked over to my bedroom door.

"If you trust him, then so shall I. Are you going to bed?"

I nodded in response. Daphne stood and walked over to me, wrapping me in a tight hug before retiring to her room. I slipped into my room and barely made it into my nightclothes before falling into bed and letting sleep take me once more.

The next morning, Darius had sent a servant to our suite to inform us that breakfast would be served to us in the private dining room again once we were ready.

I put on a green tea-length dress with golden embroidery and waited for Daphne to be ready. The servant guided both of us to the dining room where Darius sat waiting for us, drinking from his golden chalice.

"Where is Andrei this morning?" I questioned as Daphne and I took our seats.

"He is currently in his study. He said he had a bit more to research about those... What did you call them? Mirrors! He is almost done figuring out how we can make them work for vampires. When he gets into something, he cannot stop until it is complete."

"I can respect that," Daphne said as two servants appeared and sat a cup of coffee in front of Daphne and me. The warm scent of the roasted beans and vanilla filled my nose. A wide grin crossed my face as I took the warm mug in my hand and brought it to my lips. This was absolutely delightful.

"I am disappointed that you will be leaving us today," Darius said sadly. "I have quite enjoyed your company."

"Oh, have you?" Daphne chuckled, looking up at me through her mug. I gently kicked her leg under the table in response, and she shot me a pointed glare. Two more servants came out, setting a plate down in front of Daphne and me. Daphne's plate had two pieces of bacon, toast, and two sunny-side-up eggs. My plate made me salivate just by looking at it.

There was french toast topped with bananas foster and powdered sugar.

"This looks amazing!" I was delighted as I cut into it. Daphne glanced over at my plate and let out a joyous laugh.

"You eat like Xander. You know that is not healthy for you," Daphne said as she dipped her toast into the egg yolk.

"It is healthy for my soul." I took a bite and smiled at her while I chewed. My response even caused Darius to laugh.

"Yes, I will miss this indeed," he said, taking another sip from his cup. "When can I see you again?"

"Soon," I promised.

Twenty

Darius

I dreaded every second as we traveled back to the city. I wished that Sabrina and I never had to be apart, and that the two of us could stay in the castle in the mountains and hide from the rest of the world. Anxiety filled my chest as the main castle came into view, and the closer we got, the more I wanted to peel off my own skin.

It did not help that as soon as I exited the carriage, one of the servants informed us that Dimitri requested our immediate presence.

Could he not allow me a moment of reprieve?

Andrei and I entered the throne room, and Dimitri sat on his throne. The gods themselves did not understand how badly I wished to set the throne on fire with him on it.

Barnabas stood behind him. I hated that little rat of a man. He was always lurking in the halls, gathering any information he could to report to Dimitri.

"Where have you been?" Dimitri growled.

"Must we do this again, father?" I responded with a pinched expression.

Dimitri gripped the end of the armrest so tight that I swore I heard wood crack as the white of his knuckles showed. He released a deep breath and then let go.

"Yes, now do not make me ask again," he snarled vehemently.

"I went to Serafina to visit a village near the border to get some information. Those faeries are incredibly annoying," I lied. I could never tell Dimitri where I truly was.

"Did you learn anything *this* time?" He leaned forward. My heart pounded in my chest. I had not thought that far ahead.

"No, not yet."

Dimitri leaned back into his throne and rolled his eyes, sitting silently for a moment as he clenched his jaw. I looked over to Andrei, who stood by my side, fully unphased by everything. I wondered if he was with us here, or if he had disassociated. I heard the king's claws tap on the armrest. I looked back to him and my heart stopped when my eyes locked on Dimitri's.

"Leave the City," he demanded. "Do not return until called upon. Go find useful information."

Without a word to Dimitri, I turned and walked out. I stood in the doorway, and without looking back, I finally spoke. "Andrei, come."

Twenty-One

Sabrina

I was so happy to be home. The scent of flowers filled my nose as I walked through the halls of my castle. Daphne and I made our way to the southwest tower, which was not open to anyone in the castle other than Daphne, Xander, and myself. We used it when we needed to speak to Xander about urgent matters. His bedchamber was atop the tower and his study was just below. He was most comfortable in his study. The bookshelves were filled with some of the oldest tomes of Serafina that depicted our history.

When we got to his study, we were surprised to find him not at his desk. Xander spent most of his free time locked away up here. Daphne walked over to his desk and looked down at it.

"Looks like my dear brother left us a note," Daphne said as she picked up a piece of parchment off his desk. It was folded in half. The top of it had Daphne's name written on it in Xander's handwriting. I watched as she read the paper and rolled her eyes. "Well, he will be gone for some time."

"Some time?" I questioned.

"He did not say how long he would be gone."

"Of course, he didn't." I rolled my eyes and let out a groan.

"You know how he is. Do not let that get you worked up. I am sure he will be back before the tithe."

"He better be," I growled.

The summer heat had finally set in. I was very lucky that my castle had been magically enchanted to keep us protected from the overwhelming warmth.

During the tithe, held during the middle of each season, each of the Elemental Elders visited the castle to pay taxes and voice any concerns they had concerning the kingdom. Normally, we did not have many issues. The people thought I ruled Serafina fairly, and we had had centuries of peace between the elemental groups.

I had always welcomed the six elders into my home. I considered them to be great council. Almost every decision during my rule had been discussed with the Elders. They were my direct connection to the people, and as queen, it was my job to make sure my people's needs were met.

Orlok, the Dark Elder, was the first to arrive. He always believed that being on time meant you were late, had arrived five days before the tithe, and was disappointed that his close friend, Xander, was not here. With Xander being what many believed to be the first dark fae, the two of them were very close.

This also went for Daphne, who people believed was the first light fae, and Nelda. Daphne and Nelda seemed to be more like sisters than close friends. While Xander and Orlok often debated about everything and anything, Daphne and Nelda often just enjoyed each other's company when Nelda was visiting the castle. The two of them often were in the library exchanging books, recipes, and gossip from all across Serafina. Nelda was the second to arrive, just a day after Orlok.

Three days later Petra, the Earth Elder, and Vulcan, the Fire Elder, arrived. The two of them always arrived and departed together. They even requested that their suites be close to one another. Daphne had told me once that the two were in a secret relationship, that wasn't so secret. She also said once she found Petra sneaking out of Vulcan's suite in the early hours of the day. Their relationship was always funny to me. Petra was kind, calm, and thoughtful, which was in stark contrast to Vulcan's fiery temper. He did not think before he acted, and seemed to act upon every impulse.

Like a cool spring breeze and a gentle flow of a stream, Ayla, the Air Elder, and Hale, the Water Elder, came to the castle the day before the tithe.

Ayla was the embodiment of a free spirit. She quite literally went wherever the wind took her. I was just grateful the wind brought her here on time. There had been many times where Ayla arrived late, or much too early. There was one year in the fall when she had missed the tithe entirely and arrived a month later.

Hale always went with the flow. They were always where they were meant to be at that moment. Hale always arrived just before they were needed and left right after business was concluded.

I sat on my throne on the day of the tithe with Daphne in position. The fact Xander was not here made my blood boil. Xander had never missed a tithe, and he better have a damn good reason for doing so once he returned. I worried his absence would make me look weak. Without the unified front of the Ancient Ones, would Serafina take me seriously as queen?

As queen, I was chosen by the gods, and it was the Ancient One's duty to guide the Queen in her role. Without Xander here, would it look like I had lost the gods' favor?

The Elders were brought in one by one by Fern. Hale was the first to meet with me. They informed me that all was well within the tides of Serafina. Lake Kikami and the marshes of the east were well. The people were healthy and peaceful. The water fae were content and had no concerns at this time.

Ayla floated in before Fern could bring her to me. She had requested my blessing. The air fae had been spread out throughout the kingdom, and she had hoped to build a fae village in the north to bring her people back together. So far she had a small village together, and they had been working very hard to find more air fae to move there and allow the village to grow. I wished her well in her quest. Out of all the fae, the air was the rarest. They traveled often, never staying in one place for long. To try to have them settle in one city would be a mighty task indeed.

Vulcan came in like a bat out of the underworld. Fire was on his heels as he rushed in front of me. He informed me that there were no issues, paid his taxes,bowed, and left as quickly as he entered.

"Well, that was fast," Daphne chuckled.

"Vulcan is a man of few words when he isn't worked up about something," I turned toward Daphne and smiled.

"That is very true."

I called for Fern to bring in Petra, and she too had nothing bad to report. However, she did mention how each time she had seen me this year, I appeared more glowing than the last. When I questioned her about it, she said she couldn't explain beyond that. Something about my aura being brighter than it had ever been, as if my inner light had finally kindled.

Nelda made similar comments. She said that she had never seen me so happy. When I heard Daphne giggling under her breath, I shot a glare at her. "What did you tell her?" I said through my teeth.

"Oh, nothing," she teased.

"Just that you have a potential suitor," Nelda cooed.

Heat flooded my cheeks. "You could say that," I looked back at Nelda.

"Daphne wouldn't give me any details. She claims it is too new. However, she claims she sees into the future and sees the two of you entangled for centuries to come."

Shock took over my face. "Daphne, is this true? Have you had visions of us?"

"Indeed, I have. However, they are very blurry. The only thing I can tell is that he will be around for centuries. Seems your lives are intertwined."

My heart raced at the idea of Darius and I being together for centuries. I could not help but imagine what that future would look like.

"I am excited to see what is to come of that," I mused.

"As am I," Nelda added. "When do I get to learn more about this mystery man? Do I know him? Is he from Serafina?"

"He is not from Serafina, and I will not provide anything more at this time. Not until we are more established," I responded.

"Awe, you are no fun," she chuckled.

Orlok was the last of the Elders that I needed to meet with for the tithe. I was grateful that so far everything had gone smoothly, even with Nelda's teasing. I had not yet thought about how the Elders would respond to my relationship with the vampire Prince.

I wondered if they would be as apprehensive as Xander, or be accepting as Daphne has been.

After Orlok entered the throne room, his gaze was fixed on the pillar that Xander should have been standing by. He stopped at the foot of the dais and bowed.

"My queen," he said as he straightened. "I see Xander has not yet returned?" His eyes narrowed as he spoke.

"He is away on business," Daphne quickly responded on my behalf. I was grateful for her to do so.

"Well, hopefully, he will not be gone for long. We have an issue that needs to be addressed."

"An issue?" I leaned forward on my throne.

"Yes," he took a deep breath as he looked at me with worry in his eyes. "There is a disturbance near the dark fae village. The obsidian cave just west of the village has a strange power coming from it."

"What do you mean?" Daphne and I questioned in unison.

"A purple mist has filled the cave, and no one has been able to walk through it. The cave is a sacred place for our clergy. They used to hold daily rituals within it. They believe the mist is a sign from our gods, and whatever is happening is a punishment."

"Is that what you believe?" I believe whatever it is, is suspicious and has a malevolent presence."

"We will make sure to handle this as soon as possible," I leaned back into my throne. "Please advise your people to avoid going near it at all costs. I do not want any of them getting hurt. Is there anything else we should know? How long has it been like this?"

"It started about two weeks ago. Thank you for looking into this so promptly. I know you will find a solution." Orlok bowed his head.

"I will do my best," I said to him. I was very interested in learning more about whatever was happening. Nothing like this had been heard of. What was the source of this magical mist? I wondered if there would be anything in the library that could provide more information before I traveled south to investigate.

I knew what I would be doing for the next several days.

Twenty-Two

Darius

Andrei and I had returned to the castle in the mountains after Dimitri had demanded I leave the city. I was thankful that he did. I hated being in that place. I would never return if my duties allowed it. I had been here for about two weeks already. I tried to keep busy, but I found myself either in the garden or in the observatory. Thoughts filled my head of the queen that I could not have.

I paced circles around the cherry tree in the garden. Andrei sat in the grass, looking up at the butterflies that fluttered around him. We had been here for what seemed like hours, passing the time in silence. I had tried to sort all of my swirling thoughts, but they continued to rage in my mind. It was Andrei who finally broke the silence.

"We haven't talked about your plan to get your father to accept your relationship with the fae queen. Have you given it any thought?" He asked as his gaze shifted to me.

I stopped my pacing. Out of everything that I had in my mind, that was the last thing I wanted to think about. "No, not even in the slightest," I sighed. "I know in my soul that I belong with Sabrina in Serafina, but I feel obligated to stay here in Titus by my father's side as his soldier. It's all I have ever known."

Andrei stood, sadness welling in his eyes. He took a few steps and stopped before me. "Even if being his soldier is destroying you?" His voice cracked as he spoke.

I broke his gaze as I turned to face the tree and looked up into its branches. Pain filled my chest, a pain that I was unfamiliar with.

Could this be my soul tearing in two? One half to follow my heart, and one to follow my duty. I felt my own eyes begin to well with tears. I sat with it for a moment before stuffing those feelings down, deep within me.

I heard the sound of racing footsteps from beyond the garden coming this way. I turned toward the entrance as one of my servants appeared.

"My Prince," he said as he caught his breath. "An urgent letter arrived for you from the castle." He extended his arm with an envelope in hand. I waltzed over to him and took the envelope from him. I examined it and saw my name written in Dimitri's handwriting.

It took every ounce of control I had to not crumple the paper in rage.

Twenty-Three

Sabrina

Three days later, I was standing at the entrance of the obsidian cave, staring at the wall of purple mist. The mist was nearly hypnotizing as it danced and flowed, as if a breeze teased it. Daphne and I stood in front of the cave, and a dark presence washed over me as I took a step forward. Gooseflesh ran down my spine.

Daphne released a blast of light from her palm, and the mist wall cleared away. The dark feeling vanished with the wall. Something about the magic felt purely evil, and I was glad to no longer feel its presence.

"What a strange feeling that darkness had," I gave a soft whimper.

"Indeed. It felt familiar, yet off. Definitely strange magic at play," she said as she took a step into the cave.

I followed her. The purple mist drifted along the cave floor, the magical feeling it had now gone. It was now just normal mist with a strange purple glow. The jagged walls of the cave appeared to be normal until we reached the back of the cave. A large chunk of the stone looked as if it had been blasted out, leaving a crater in the stone wall. Shiny red shards covered the ground.

I knelt and picked up one of the red shards, and immediately dropped it as an overwhelming feeling of despair washed over my body. It was similar to the feeling at the cave entrance, but a thousand times worse. Death was coming for me, and soon. A vision flooded my mind, Xander was screaming asking someone what they had done. Ice took over my veins. I could not see who he was talking to, before I could the vision was gone. I leaned forward, and the contents of my stomach spilled onto the ground. With it, a part of me had exited my body. When I was done heaving, I felt like a shell of myself.

Daphne ran to my side and placed a hand on my back. A feeling of warmth and comfort overtook me, and I could breathe again. I stood as I wiped my mouth with the back of my wrist.

"I do not know what happened here, but whatever it is, it wasn't good," I finally said.

Daphne reached down and picked up one of the shards. My eyes went wide as I watched her inspect it. How was she not feeling its effects as I did?

"I will take this home with us and investigate more. Maybe once Xander returns, he can take a look at it and figure out what this is." Daphne pulled out a small piece of silk from her pocket, wrapped the shard, and placed it back into her pocket.

The two of us turned around to head back to the cave entrance. Orlok was waiting for us just outside. "I am glad to see the purple mist is gone. Did you find anything of interest?"

"Yes, I was able to clear the mist with my magic," Daphne said.

"We did find a large chunk of the obsidian missing, and red shards on the cave floor," I reported to him. "Please make sure the villagers stay away from this cave until we can figure out what is happening."

"Thank you, my queen. I truly appreciate you looking into this. I will make sure this area stays off-limits for now."

I had taken a few days to myself once we returned to the castle. The emotions I felt in the cave still overwhelmed me. Death was coming for me. As soon as I touched that stone, it confirmed it. It was a feeling deep within me that I could not release.

I laid in my bed and stared up at the ceiling and couldn't help but let my thoughts wander to Titus. I felt that tug on my heart that pulled me toward the Prince I was bonded to.

I wondered if from so far away, could he hear and feel my thoughts. I felt a distant presence, and while I knew he was far, there was no insight about his thoughts or feelings. Part of me hoped he was also lying awake and thinking of me.

There was a gentle knock on my bedroom door, and I sat up and called for whoever it was to enter. Fern entered the room and bowed her head. "Good evening, I am sorry to bother you, Your Majesty," she said softly.

"Fern, you are never a bother. Is everything okay?"

"Oh yes, it is. I just received this letter for you from Titus. I figured you would want it right away."

My eyes went wide as I scooted to the end of the bed. "Yes! Thank you, Fern!" I extended my hand to her, and she gave me the envelope.

I opened it and was shocked that it was not Darius' messy handwriting I was met with. I was not familiar with the beautiful script on the paper. I had never teased him for it, especially once I learned the Prince was barely taught to read. It all made sense. I wanted to offer to teach him, but I did not want to hurt his pride. It was very obvious it was a touchy subject. Shaking my head, I pulled my focus back to the letter.

Queen Sabrina,

I hope this letter finds you well. I would like to extend a formal invitation to our Blood Moon Festival. The castle of Titus welcomes your stay for the duration of the festival. The festival will begin when the moon is three-quarters full and last two nights.

Dimitri Viktor Dragomeir, King of Titus

I could not wait to attend! I knew very little about this festival, but I had hoped receiving an invitation from the King would mean that we could improve our relations. Butterflies filled my stomach at the thought of seeing Darius once again.

Twenty-Four
Xander

"I was expecting to meet somewhere more appropriate for someone of your stature," I said as I met the gaze of the King of Titus.

I was shocked when I arrived at the coordinates he had provided me in his letter. The wood had nearly rotted away, and lichen had taken over most of the outside of the building. I expected the door to fall off its hinges when I opened it. The inside was filled with dust, and had a few pieces of furniture. It was obvious that they were out of place as they were not as coated in filth as everything else and none of the metal on the chairs and tables were tarnished.

"I am sure you could understand why I would need to be discreet. Besides, no one would believe you if you told anyone that you met me here," he responded as he took another step into the room.

I did not break eye contact with him as he continued to walk closer. I knew the game he wanted to play, and I would not allow him to play it with me. I would not allow the king to break me, as he did so many others.

I could feel how nervous my apprentice was. This was the first time he had ever left his village, let alone Serafina. When I told him that we were crossing the border to meet with the vampire King, I thought his soul was going to leave his body. I glared over at Draven as I heard his teeth chatter and his foot tap against the floor. He immediately stilled as my eyes locked on his. I shook my head and then returned my attention to Dimitri. "You swear if I give this to you, you will keep your son out of Serafina?"

I had been plagued with visions of what would happen if Sabrina continued down the path she was on with Darius. I saw total chaos and destruction. Images filled my head of the forest dying, and the castle falling into ruins. What worried me most was I saw my own end.

A young man looked at me with horror in his eyes as I drew my last breath. He had my eyes; he had my shadows.

I couldn't help but wonder if I would still meet my son if I removed Sabrina from this path of destruction.

"I swear on my late wife's grave. I will keep him out of Serafina and away from your Queen." Dimitri pushed two fingers to his lip, then raised them to the sky as he mumbled something in the old vampiric tongue.

I looked over to Draven and nodded in his direction. He scurried out of the room. "He will be back with it shortly. After this, you and I are done," I spat at the King.

A devilish grin grew across his face, and he bared his fangs. "You will be done when I say you are," he dropped his tone as he spoke, "as long as you want me to keep your secret, God of Shadows." Venom dripped off his tongue on those last few words.

Daphne and I had spent our whole lives keeping our true identities a secret. I was not sure how Dimitri had learned the truth, but when he did, I begged him to keep Daphne out of it. He promised to keep our secret and keep my sister out of it as long as I supplied him with the magic of Serafina.

What he did not know is that in every piece of magic I provided, I had put in a fail-safe. In case he tried to use the magic to harm Serafina, he would meet his end.

Dimitri may have turned me into a puppet, but I was no fool.

Draven came back into the room with a small wooden box in hand. He gave the box to Dimitri and then ran to stand behind me. As the vampire king opened the box, his eyes went wide. The reflection of the red orb gave his green eyes a ruby appearance. I did not think that the vampire King could look any more terrifying until I saw him with red eyes.

"The obsidian has already been imbued with the required magic. All you need to do is complete the ritual," I said to him.

Dimitri snapped the box close and turned on his heels. "Thank you, Xander. It's been a pleasure." In a blink, the king of Titus was gone.

Twenty-Five

Sabrina

Anxiety filled my chest as we sat in our carriage and rode through the streets of Titus. The moon hung high in the sky and was bright red.

I was nervous about meeting with Dimitri. Would we be able to make amends and form an alliance? Could this be the first step toward Dimitri accepting a relationship between Darius and me?

The streets of Titus were filled with vampires and humans. We did not have many humans in Serafina, and I had maybe only met two in my lifetime. It was clear that anything went here in Titus. I wondered if it was just for this festival or if it was like this year-round.

Heat filled my cheeks as I watched a vampire male pin a woman to the brick wall and fuck her face. I could hear her gagging from the carriage. I turned away and looked out the other window, where I saw a vampire woman drinking from a man's neck as she rode his cock.

"This is absolutely barbaric." Daphne looked back down to her book. I focused my gaze on her.

"I did not realize that it was... *this* type of festival." My gaze shifted down to my twiddling thumbs, hoping that the Titus royals celebrated the festival in a more civilized manner.

To be honest, I knew nothing about the Blood Moon Festival or vampire culture in general. I wish that I had done some research before I arrived.

The rustic streets turned golden as we traveled deeper into the city. The dirt and cobblestone transitioned into what appeared to be pure gold streets. According to the map, this section of the city was referred to as the Golden Circle, and the castle was in the center of it all.

The palace came into view and our driver drove us up to the entrance. It was much larger than the castle Darius invited me to in the mountains. It was made of light colored stone. The first thing I noticed was the lack of windows. Six towers were erected around the perimeter, even those lacked windows. Daphne leaned forward and gently took my hand in hers. The carriage came to a stop and the door opened. I stepped out and Daphne followed behind me.

A tall man stood just outside the door. He had long dark hair that was loose and hung just under his shoulders and green eyes that matched Darius'. I tried not to shudder at the malevolent energy that radiated off of him. Daphne came to my side and gripped my hand so tight that it almost hurt. I wondered if she could also sense his dark energy. The man gave a grin and revealed his long fangs.

"Welcome, Queen Sabrina. I am glad the two of us could finally meet." His voice was deep and dark, like the ocean during a storm that threatened to swallow me whole.

It finally clicked in my head that the man before us was Dimitri. I straightened my shoulders, trying not to falter under his intimidating gaze.

"Thank you for inviting us to your home. I am excited to learn more about this festival and your culture," I gave a small smile.

"Oh yes, the vampiric culture is unique. There is much to learn and see." A deep chuckle escaped his lips. It reminded me so much of Darius, and I wondered if this was what he would look like in a few centuries. To be honest, I wouldn't mind it. Even though Dimitri was terrifying, he was very handsome. "Please, allow me to give you a tour of the castle."

"That would be lovely," Daphne said.

The king turned and walked into his castle. We followed him in, and once we were through the threshold, a chill ran down my spine. Something here was not right. My body screamed for me to run out the door and never look back, but I stuffed those feelings down. I did not want to offend Dimitri more than I already had. Since I sent away his emissary, I had been on thin ice with him. My breath got a bit shaky as my vision tunneled. The deeper into the castle we went, the more my blood ran cold.

I smiled and nodded as Dimitri spoke, trying to at least pretend I was not dissociating during his tour. Over the years, I had gotten pretty good at faking being present, even if my mind was elsewhere. Normally, it was only a few moments before I snapped back into focus. I was not sure how long I had been going through the motions before I felt the familiar tug on my heart that pulled me back to reality.

Dimitri opened a dark wooden door and guided us into a study. My ears were filled with a sound I would know anywhere. I froze in the doorway and my eyes went wide as I took in the scene that had unfolded before me.

My stomach twisted, and it took everything I had not to spill out its contents.

A human woman was nude and bent over. Her arms were pulled behind her back. Blood was dripping down them. Andrei and Darius were feeding from her wrists. To my horror, the two men were also nude. Andrei was positioned behind the woman, thrusting into her dripping sex. I was unsure if the liquid dripping from here was her own, or his. Darius' dick was deep down her throat. The room filled with the sound of her gagging to the rhythm of his thrusts.

Andrei was totally unaffected by our entrance. Darius locked eyes with me, and he froze for a moment then pushed away from the human. His cock dangling between his legs and her drool dripped from it.

"Bri? What are you doing here?" His voice was higher pitched than I had ever heard it.

"That is what you are going to say right now?" Tears welled in my eyes and I quickly turned away. I would not allow him to see them fall. No longer caring if my behavior was offensive, I rushed out of the room. A sharp ringing sound filled my head.

I needed to get out of here. I needed to go home. I needed to lock myself in my castle and never look back.

Hurried footsteps echoed behind me. I heard Darius' voice, but I did not understand the words that came out of his mouth. I hope he choked on them. His firm hand wrapped around my wrist, and he spun me to face him. His touch sent fire through me. The ringing in my ears vanished, and for the first time, I recognized that a monster stood before me.

"Stop!" His voice boomed. "It's not what it looks like!" I looked him in the eyes to see tears streaming down his face.

"Oh? Is it not?" I pulled away and took a step back from him. "Because it looked like you were just balls deep in someone who you aren't bonded to! I am not interested in anything you have to say." I threw up a wall of pure ice to separate us so I could escape him.

Twenty-Six

Darius

I stared at the wall of ice before me. If only she let me explain. Maybe she would not be so mad.

I turned around and saw Daphne leaving the study and walking the other way with one of our servants. She snapped her head toward me and I could feel the rage emanating off her. I swallowed hard, and for the first time in a long time felt fear. I did not want to feel the wrath of an Ancient One. My heart cracked inside my chest. I never meant to hurt Sabrina, and looking into her eyes and seeing the pain that was in them killed me.

Dimitri walked out of the study and looked at me with a mischievous grin. Rage boiled, and something within me snapped. I let out a roar as I rushed toward Dimitri and pounced on him. We fell to the floor, and I pounded my fist into his face.

"You son of a bitch!" I screamed. My vision was filled with red. "I will fucking kill you!" I released all of the rage that I had held in for years.

It was time for payback for my mother, for Andrei, for all the terrible things he had me do.

Someone hooked their arms under my shoulders and pulled me off Dimitri. I fought against them, but they held tighter. I heard Andrei's voice screaming in my ear for me to calm down. I watched as Dimitri stood and rage contorted his blood covered face.

"Get the fuck out!" He screamed as he wiped the blood from his mouth.

I continued to fight against Andrei. *I will kill Dimitri. Now is the time. It is now or never.* After I finally escaped from his grasp, I was able to take a singular step before Andrei's hands grabbed my head. He quickly twisted it, and a loud pop filled my ears before everything faded to black.

Twenty-Seven

Sabrina

I sobbed for the first several hours during the carriage ride home. Daphne sat across from me. I could see her out of the corner of my eye as I looked out the window. Daphne had her head down in her book and had avoided looking at me during the ride.

Neither of us wanted to talk about the events that occurred. I didn't want to relive my heart break, and Daphne didn't want to admit that she and Xander were right.

Gods, I did not want Xander to find out what had happened. Maybe I would tell him that Darius just bored me, so I no longer wanted to continue trying to make it work between us. Would Xander believe that? I truly hoped so, because I know he would never let me live down the fact he was right.

The city skyline faded as we headed into a desert. For miles, it was nothing but open road. Wiping the tears from my eyes, I finally turned my gaze toward Daphne. She lifted her head to me, shut her book, and placed it in her lap. We sat in silence, staring at each other for a moment before I finally broke it.

"You must think I am a fool," my voice cracked as more tears fell.

Daphne leaned forward, placed her hand on my knee, and looked at me with a down-turned expression. "A fool, no," she said with a heavy sigh. "A girl hopelessly in love, yes."

Shifting in my seat, I turned back toward the window. Focused on the dark clouds near the horizon and watched patches of the clouds illuminate from lightning, a calmness began to wash over me. I wiped my eyes and tried to hold in any more tears that threatened to fall. "I refuse to be in love with a monster such as him," I spat. "Never again will I fall for his charms."

Daphne removed her hand from my knee and leaned back in her seat. A forced chuckle escaped her lips, making me turn back to her with a raised eyebrow. "I see many things in your future, my queen. He shall return."

"He will regret the day he does."

When we arrived back at the castle, the sun was shining. Feeling the rays warm my skin as I stepped out of the carriage brought me joy. I had always believed that there was no problem that a little sunshine could not fix. I hope that to hold true for my broken heart.

As I walked through the halls, Fern caught up with me and filled me in on everything that had happened in the castle during my absence. Thankfully, Everything was business as usual.

Good, that was what I needed to hear. I don't think I could deal with another crisis at this time.

I needed to push away my personal issues and focus on the full moon festival that was coming up shortly.

"Fern, can you fetch Xander for me and ask him to meet me in my study? We need to prepare for the upcoming full moon," I said as we continued to walk down the halls.

"My queen, I regret to inform you that Xander has yet to return," she said meekly. I stopped in my tracks, cursing under my breath. Daphne and Fern took a few more steps ahead of me before they realized I had not continued with them. They turned to face me, both with a look of confusion.

"Fern, you are dismissed," I said through my teeth. She bowed and scurried off.

Daphne took a step toward me. I saw her mouth moving, but all I could hear was the pounding in my ears caused by my rage.

"If Xander doesn't want to be here, fine. I do not need him," I said over my shoulder.

The full moon festival was in full swing a few nights later. Again, the castle grounds were filled with fae from all over Serafina. Music flowed from several areas around the castle grounds, and all sorts of food. Fae danced around the bonfire as we began our preparations for the ritual.

I was extremely nervous that Xander was not in attendance. We had never completed the full moon ritual without all the Elders, both of the Ancient Ones, and the current reigning queen. Would we still receive blessings from the gods and distribute magic throughout the land?

I sat in a gazebo alone, eating a few crab balls I had swiped from one of the many chefs that had attended this festival. I took a bite of the fried ball, and the sweet and flakey crab meat filled my mouth. The water fae chef had informed me that this species of crab was found in one area in all of Serafina. The body of water was called Marpeake Bay, and this crab was known for its electric blue shell. As I popped the final one into my mouth, Daphne approached me.

"Everything is in place. Are you ready, my queen?" She said with a smile.

"Let us begin."

I stood and walked over to the bonfire, calling for everyone's attention. The Elders were already in position around the fire. The music died, and the voices hushed as all eyes turned to us. Daphne and I took our places in the circle.

"Thank you to all in attendance at tonight's full moon festival. We gather here to perform the ritual to ask the gods for their blessings and distribute magic through the forest," I announced to the crowd.

One by one I called out the names of the Elders, thanking them for their part in the ritual. I saw Orlok raise an eyebrow as I thanked the Ancient Ones for their guidance. I could tell he was getting suspicious about Xander's absence. The eight of us chanted in the ancient fae language. The fire rose and grew brighter. I could feel the magic within me ebb and flow, as if the land had taken it from me and the gods refilled my magical well. The fire flashed green, blue, red, purple, white, and yellow, and we chanted louder. Everyone stayed silent around us as the ritual took place.

My vision blurred and my ears filled with a high-pitched ringing as we continued. My stomach flipped and a sickening feeling washed over me.

What was happening? Never in all the rituals I had completed had it felt like this. Just as I was about to release the contents of my stomach, my vision snapped back into focus just as the bonfire went out three seconds too soon. The illness had vanished with the flames.

The ritual concluded, and when I looked around, it appeared no one else noticed the fire going out early. I wondered if they had also felt that sickening feeling, but everyone was acting normal. There was no indication that the ritual did not go as planned. I prayed that the missteps were just because Xander was not here, and not a bad omen.

Twenty-Eight

Darius

The rain pounded on the glass of the observatory as I paced back and forth, letting the rage build inside of me. Lightning cracked and illuminated the space around me, perfectly reflecting my volatile mood.

Andrei sat in one of the chairs in the center of the room near the fire pit. He had not said a single word to me since I had awoken and found myself here.

As soon as I gained consciousness, my head was flooded with memories of what had happened. It killed me that I had hurt Sabrina once again. I never expected her to attend the Blood Moon Festival. Dimitri knew exactly what he was doing when he had sent that letter requesting me to return home for the festivities.

"How dare he set me up," I raged. I couldn't tell if it was my voice or the thunder that caused the glass to shake. Andrei had opened his mouth to speak, but I cut him off. "How dare she not let me explain about the Blood Moon? It is one of our most sacred rituals!"

During the Blood Moon, we celebrated our god, Alarik. We drank blood and released all inhibitions. In exchange, Alarik granted us his blessings and power for the upcoming year.

Again, Andrei opened his mouth to speak, but I was not done.

"How dare you stop me from killing that miserable son of a bitch! Whose side are you truly on?" I spat at him.

Andrei shot up from his seat and, in a blink, was directly in front of me. "Darius, I could not let you kill your father!" He spat back. His pale features turned red. "You do not think of the consequences of your actions!"

I released a growl in response. How dare he step up to me? Gods, if he was not my only friend, I would snap his neck for his insolence.

"I *do* think of the consequences! If that asshole is dead, I will be king. I will make the rules. Sabrina and I can be together without persecution! Humans would no longer need to fear the vampire king. I would not force them to be slaves. I would not burn their homes for becoming friends with a vampire. I would not steal their children from their beds to create soldiers! I have thought about the consequences of his death in great detail!" My pitch raised with every sentence I spoke.

Everyone thought me to be a weapon with no thought behind the eyes of a killer. The truth was, I had too many thoughts, and often all at once.

Andrei staggered back, a look of shock on his face. He composed himself and took a deep breath. "The vampires would not accept her as your bride, as your queen. Dimitri has many loyalists. If you murdered him, they would never accept you as king. You will have a hard time getting them to accept you as king, even if Dimitri passed peacefully. The dreams you have for vampires, humans, and fae to leave in peace are just that — dreams. You will find that even harder of a task."

I clenched my jaw and spun around, walking over to the edge of the room. Looking out over the forest. I watched as the droplets ran down the side of the glass.

I hated to admit it, but Andrei was right. No one in Titus would accept the relationship between Sabrina and me. I did not belong in this hellscape of a kingdom.

"Andrei," I breathed. "You are right. I will go to Serafina and beg for forgiveness. I will abandon my crown and prove my loyalty to Sabrina." I turned back to face Andrei, who looked at me with wide eyes. The redness in his face now turned ghost white.

"That is not what I meant," he said in a shaky tone. I rushed toward him and wrapped him in a brisk hug before releasing him and making my way to the stairs.

"Thank you, Andrei! I don't know what I would do without you!" I called out to him. "Pack your things! We are leaving first thing in the morning."

Twenty-Nine

Dimitri

I leaned forward in my chair, looking over the papers that Xander had provided with the orb. It seemed like the ritual to keep my son in line would be more difficult than I believed it to be.

As soon as I returned home with the orb, I had fixed it onto a staff with a dragon wrapped around it. I could not let anyone know what my plan was. Unfortunately for me, my son was smarter than I wanted him to be. If he learned of my plan, he would surely stop it before I was able to finish.

Maybe it was not the best idea to have him turn that human all those years ago. I had hoped that the boy would hate Darius for killing his family and forcing him to walk the path of night, but it seemed like it just brought them closer.

Gods, I should have snapped that boy's neck when I had the chance. I would love to see the look on my son's face while I did it.

Tapping my claws on my desk, I read over the text. The ritual Xander provided was just the start of my plan. I would keep my promise to the God of Shadows by keeping my son out of Serafina. I needed something that would keep him obedient to me, and I needed a way to rid the world of the faerie queen.

After my son was born, an oracle came to the castle, telling me of many things that were to come. She told me that my dreams of conquering the continent would come true, and that my son would be my greatest weapon in that effort.

She also told me how my whore of a wife would conspire against me. When I caught her trying to sneak out of the castle with Darius, I knew everything the oracle told me to be true. I did not shed a single tear when I cut off her head. She was an obstacle just as that slut of a faerie queen is now.

The oracle told me that Darius would meet a fae queen and my entire empire would crumble. When I first received the invitation to her Masquerade, rage boiled within me. I knew I had to keep Darius out of Serafina. I kept him in the castle or northern territories. Everything I did was to keep the two of them from meeting. When she began to send us invitations to her ball, I knew we would never attend. Emissaries were sent in our place, hoping to keep her away. I planted spies in the castle in the mountains to make sure he was where he said he was. It took everything in me not to go to the mountain castle when I received word she was there.

Everything I worked so hard for was about to fall apart, and I could not allow it. I had one more player in the game that I was waiting for. Once he brought me what I needed, everything would fall into place just as I wanted.

Sabrina would be dead, and Darius would be mine.

I heard footsteps approaching my study and rolled my eyes as I looked up and saw Barnabas enter. I clenched my fist so hard that the quill I was holding snapped in my hand.

"I hope you have a good reason to disturb me," I snarled at him. He bowed toward me and took a step closer as he rose.

"Yes, Master. The shadow boy has returned and is requesting to see you right away," his voice shook.

Barnabas had been very loyal to me during my reign; however, he was still an extremely weak man. When he came to me all those years ago, begging for power, I knew he would be easy to corrupt into my compliant pet.

After I gave him the gift of vampirism, Barnabas learned too late that he would be mine until he took his last breath. I sometimes wondered what happened to his family that he sold his soul to protect. Then I remembered I sent in soldiers to burn down that small village in the Wastes. Barnabas had forgotten all about them, and so had the rest of Titus.

"Bring him," I said in a low tone as I sat back in my seat. Barnabas scurried out of the room, and I took a deep breath. My claws tapped on the arm of the chair as I waited for them to return. After a moment, he returned, bringing Draven with him.

He was no longer the cowering boy he was pretending to be with Xander. He stood tall, his breath even, and had a look in his eye that screamed he was up to no good. That didn't bother me, because neither was I.

"I assume this means you accepted my offer?" I questioned.

"If I provide this additional ritual, will Serafina be mine?" He questioned.

"If you provide what I seek, your queen and the Ancient Ones will vanish. Serafina will then be yours to do with as you please." I stood and walked to the front of my desk, leaning back against it as I met Draven's gaze.

"Perfect, so it's a bargain." A wicked smirk grew on his face.

"A bargain we have."

Draven reached into his pocket, pulled out a scroll, and handed it to me.

"I must go before they notice that I've been gone too long," Draven said just before he vanished into thin air leaving a puff of purple mist.

My eyes met with Barnabas' and I released a deep chuckle as I pushed off the desk and walked over to him.

"How loyal are you to your king?" I questioned, and watched in delight as his throat bobbed.

"Extremely, my king," he did not hesitate. He never did. He would follow me into the underworld if I asked him.

"Kneel," I demanded.

Barnabas quickly fell to his knees and looked up at me as I slowly circled him. Stopping behind him, I grabbed the back of his head and pushed him down to the ground.

He did not fight me. Barnabas stayed on his knees with his head on the floor.

"You must understand that you now know a secret that can never leave these four walls." I walked over to the front of him, placing my foot on his head, and pressed lightly.

"Yes, my king. It won't ever escape my lips," he whimpered. I heard his heart begin to race and could smell his fear.

Gods, it was absolutely delicious.

"No, it won't," I said in an even tone.

Just a second after, I applied more pressure and crushed Barnabas' skull beneath my boot.

Thirty

Darius

Andrei lectured me the entire way to Serafina. He did not think that it was the best idea to go to her unannounced. I did not agree with him on that. I knew deep in my soul she would appreciate my grand gesture of coming to her.

I felt that tug on my heart gain more force as we got closer to the castle. Once she saw me, I hoped our bond would not allow her to refuse me.Our carriage pulled up to the castle, and there were ten guards outside to greet us. Wonderful, she knew how important it was for me to be here, and I was glad she sent a welcoming committee. Andrei and I stepped out of the carriage and three of the guards stepped forward to block our path.

"Whatever you think you are doing here, you are not welcome," one of them said with his hand on the hilt of his sword.

I chuckled under my breath. Did they not know they would need an entire army to stop me? A few fae men were easy prey. For her, I would prove I am a patient man.

"Tell your queen I will not leave until she grants me an audience," I said firmly, looking down at the three fae I towered over.

The three guards let out a laugh. I clenched my fists so hard that I felt the tips of my claws dig into my flesh.

How dare they laugh at me? I was not funny. This was not a joke. Gods, I wanted to snap their necks.

"Good thing you are immortal," another one of them said. "As soon as you crossed her border, she made it clear you were not welcome here."

I looked back at the carriage driver, calling for him to park in the stables, and watched as he pulled away before turning back to the guards. I smirked at them as they all looked at me with a raised brow.

"You aren't welcome here. Why are you sending your ride to the stables? Do you plan to walk back to Titus?"

"No, I am not leaving until I speak with Sabrina," I said as I sat on the cobblestone. "I will wait until the world ends, if that's what it takes."

Andrei released a heavy sigh. I looked up at him and he rolled his eyes at me before he sat by my side. "You are insufferable at times. Did you know that?" He teased.

"Yes, and since I am your sire, you will put up with it."

"No, it is because you are my brother."

Thirty-One

Sabrina

I sat at the desk in my study, resting my chin on my hand. I was supposed to be going over budget reports for the month, however, I found myself staring out the window, watching the rain pound against the glass. Lightning cracked across the sky, causing the study to illuminate brighter compared to the light given by the sconces.

Daphne walked into the room with a pale pink mug in hand. She sat it down on the desk next to me, and the sweet scent of vanilla and espresso filled my nose. "I thought you could use a little pick me up," she said as she sat down in a green velvet armchair near the window.

"Thank you," I said softly as I took a sip of the latte, and it warmed me to my core.

"You know he is still waiting out there," she said as she looked out the window.

"It has been three days. You have to be kidding me," I sighed. "Is he really out there in this storm?"

"Yup," she chuckled. "Andrei is out there as well. He looks pissed. According to the guards, he is not happy with the vampire prince."

"They will be fine. If they don't like it in the rain, they should return to Titus."

I took another sip of the latte and returned my gaze to the reports.

I tossed and turned in bed that night. I could not get comfortable. The thunder continued to crash, and it jolted me awake each time I finally thought I would find sleep.

I could feel the tug on my heart pulling me to Darius. I tried to ignore the feeling as I turned onto my back and stared up at the ceiling. The sound of the rain finally began to lull me to sleep. Just as I found peace, a deep, familiar sound filled my mind, and this time it was not thunder. and it was not thunder.

"I will wait as long as you make me." Darius' voice echoed in my mind, and I picked up my pillow and held it to my face as I screamed into it. All I wanted was sleep, and the constant interruptions were making me very irritated.

It was becoming very clear that sleep would not find me tonight.

"Get out of my head." I demanded him. I still was furious about what happened during the Blood Moon. After leaving Titus, I made a promise to myself that I would not let him charm his way back in, and it was a promise I planned to keep.

"I wouldn't be in your mind if you didn't want me here."

"I do not want you here. Fuck off."

His deep chuckle filled my head and then went silent for a moment. I hoped that he followed my order. Letting out a frustrated breath, I rolled back to my side and held my eyes shut.

"You need to let me in if you want to fuck, doll. Unless you plan on coming out here. I wouldn't mind helping you find your pleasure under the tree once again. Maybe this time I will fuck you against it."

Something within me snapped, and I jumped out of bed, quickly ripped off my nightdress, and threw on one of my knee-length dresses before I stormed out of my room and down the halls. My blood boiled as fire built in me. I made my way to the front gates, and the guards looked at me in shock as I walked past them and went outside.

As soon as I took a single step outside, the rain stopped, and the clouds cleared to reveal a starry sky. I locked eyes with Darius, who was sopping wet, chuckling internally as I imagined how miserable he must have felt. Andrei and Darius stood, and Darius took a step forward toward me.

Heat flooded my body as I approached him. I stopped a few feet away from him and looked up at him, ignoring the pain in his eyes.

"Leave," I demanded.

"I will not," he said matter-of-factly. Andrei stepped behind him and grabbed his shoulder.

"Darius, it is time to go," Andrei said to him softly, but not weakly. When Darius pulled away from his grip and shot a glare back at him, Andrei took a step back and bowed his head.

I heard many footsteps from behind me. I turned my head to see more guards coming outside, with Daphne leading them. She had an amused expression on her face. I nodded to her and turned back toward Darius.

"You say for me to leave, but you have not said you don't want me," he snarled and closed the gap between us. "Tell me you don't want me."

"Leave," I said once again. My breath grew heavy, and my heart pounded in my chest. He gently brushed the back of his fingertips against my cheek.

"Tell me, doll," he breathed. "Tell me that you don't want me. Tell me you don't love me."

My heart pounded harder, and gooseflesh ran down my spine. "Darius," I whimpered. "Stop it." My eyes followed him down as he fell to one knee.

"Tell me that you love me, and I will submit to you. I will abandon my crown. You will be my queen."

I stared at him in shock as a lump formed in my throat. I really did not know what to say. Staggering back, I swallowed hard before I spoke.

"Swear there will be no one else. Swear you won't have relations with anyone else."

Darius explained to me about the Blood Moon Festival. He told me how it was the most important celebration of the vampires. Even though I hated it, I understood. We have many rituals with similar customs. I had never participated in those rituals, but I knew how important they were to our culture.

"I will never participate again. You are the only one I want to be with. I will defect from Titus and serve as your soldier," he said as he looked up at me with his emerald eyes.

"I don't need a soldier. I need a partner."

Darius stood and took my hands in his. I took a deep breath and the scent of pine and cinnamon filled my nose.

"Why can't I be both?" He smirked down at me, and bared his fangs.

Thirty-Two

Darius

Sabrina had two guards take Andrei and I to our guest suite. They stood just outside the closed door, and I heard them tell each other they would not let either of us out of their sight. It truly amused me that they thought they could stop me from doing anything.

If I wanted to take over this kingdom, I would with no issue.

As soon as we entered the suite, I went to my bedchamber, pulled off my soaking-wet shirt, and tossed it into the hamper. I shook out the excess water from my hair.

Of course, she had sent the storm that had made my time waiting outside miserable. I should keep in mind that she loves to torture just as much as I do. I turned and saw Andrei leaning against the door frame, his blonde strands still clinging to his skin from all the rain.

"Are you sure this is what you want?"

"I have never wanted anything more. For the first time in my life, I feel free to be my own man. Let Dimitri and Titus rot."

The next morning Andrei and I were summoned to Sabrina's study. I had changed my shirt three times before deciding on a dark green button up, and rolled the sleeves up, so they sat just below my elbow. Panic grew in my chest as I walked down the halls. Part of me worried she was calling me to her study just to have me removed from her life.

What would I do if she did? I was never going back to Titus. I refused to be Dimitri's puppet any longer.

As I walked into her study, the sweet scent of strawberries and cream slammed into my senses. Gods, she was intoxicating. My eyes fell on her. She sat at her desk, her long dark hair in a side braid, and a gold and emerald circlet sat upon her forehead, that matched her green and gold dress.

Yes, this was the Queen I was born to serve.

Upon hearing the clash of metal from behind me, I turned my head to see the two guards standing in the doorway with their swords crossed.

"What is this?" Andrei spat.

"Sit down. We need to talk," she demanded. Gods, the force in her voice had me at attention. I was so focused on Sabrina that I barely noticed Daphne standing behind her, leaning against the wall.

Complying, I sat down in the chair in front of her desk. Andrei stood behind me. I could taste his anger building.

Am I in trouble? I looked Sabrina in her eyes as I spoke into her mind.

She shook her head, and I relaxed my shoulders just a bit before looking over to Andrei. The look I gave him must've said it all because he sat in the seat next to me, releasing a low growl as he did.

"What do we need to talk about?" I questioned.

"Did Dimitri really send you to spy on me so he could destroy me?" Sabrina said with a raised brow.

"He did," I nodded in response. I saw the look of terror wash over her face and could taste the bitterness of her fear. "I have never told him anything that could be used against you. I would make things up or tell him that I was still trying to get information."

"How can we be sure what you are telling us is true?" Daphne asked from behind Sabrina.

I looked up at her and met her gaze. I swallowed hard and broke away from her intense stare. I took a second to compose myself and extended my hand to the queen. "Take my hand. I will show you."

Sabrina stood from her seat and walked to the front of her desk, stopping right in front of my seat. I looked up at her and stared into her bright blue eyes. She took my hand, and I gently held it. Through our bond, I showed her every interaction with Dimitri. I could have done this without the physical contact, but I didn't know how much longer I could go without feeling the sensation of her delicate flesh touching mine.

Sabrina's eyes went wide as they flashed with all the memories. I relived all of them with her, and sucked in a sharp breath, trying to keep my composure. She gently pulled her hand away as she turned toward Daphne and gave a small nod before sitting on top of her desk.

"We are glad you have kept our secrets," Daphne said.

Sabrina stared into her lap, her feet dangling above the ground.

"When you stabbed my heart when we first met, I know you meant to cause me harm. Instead, you set it free."

"You need to go back to Titus," she said, as her voice cracked. Andrei and I snapped our heads toward her.

"I made it clear that I will not be going back. You are stuck with me, doll," I said to her.

"You heard the queen," Daphne spoke up.

"No," Sabrina said as she raised her gaze to me. I could see the tears she was trying to hold back. "Not long term. I need you to go back, pretend everything is ok, find out all you can of Dimitri's plans, and report back to me."

I took a deep breath as I realized what she needed from me. She needed a man on the inside to make sure Dimitri stayed blind and dumb. She needed an alert just in case whatever he had planned was put into action.

I stood, walked over to her, and lifted her chin so our eyes met. Taking a moment to lean into the comfort of being this close to her, I fought back my own tears before I spoke.

"For you, I will endure living with that monster for a little while longer. I will do whatever is needed to keep you safe."

Thirty-Three

Sabrina

I laid in bed, tossing and turning as heat flashed over my body. I could not get comfortable to save my life. My mind ran with thoughts of what would happen after Darius left tomorrow. After the images he showed me of the monster Dimitri truly was, it killed me to send him back.

He could pretend all the things the king did and made him do didn't bother him, but I could feel every ounce of torment that went through his brain. I prayed that he wouldn't have to stay in Titus for long. I wanted to keep him here, with me.

That familiar tug on my heart had me jolting up, the thin sheet bundling in my lap.

"Unlock your door." His dark voice invaded my mind.

I twisted my body to get off my bed and walk over to the door, and unlocked it, just as he commanded. I had always been in charge of almost every aspect of my life and all the people around me. There was something comforting about giving up control to Darius.

Everyone around me told me not to trust him, but I knew in my gut that he was someone I should trust above all else.

After I took a step back, the door swung open, and Darius was before me in an instant. He tossed me onto the bed and pinned me to it. I couldn't help but to smile at him. His dark locks dangled in the space between, and a predatory grin crossed his face, baring his fangs.

"I cannot leave this place without making you mine once again," he growled.

I quivered under him as our eyes locked. "I am yours," I breathed. lifting my head to close the gap between us, my lips pressed to his. He pushed against me hard, causing my head to hit the pillow as he kissed me with passion. His tongue slipped into my mouth and danced with mine.

One of his hands released the wrist it was holding and slid down the length of my body. He played with the hem of my nightgown for just a moment before his hand went under and found his way to the wet spot on my panties.

A moan escaped my mouth as his lips pulled from mine and his fingers rubbed the spot to coax more wetness from me. Pulling my underwear to the side, he pushed his fingers against my slick folds. My body pulsed at his touch.

"You are so wet for me, doll," he said as he leaned down and kissed my neck. I arched my back and pressed my chest into him. Darius pushed two fingers into me, and I let out a soft moan. "Do you like it when I finger your needy little pussy?" He pushed them in and out of me faster.

"Yes, please don't stop," I pleaded. I hated how I craved being his toy. Hated how I loved being played with like a slut.

"Stop?" He released a dark chuckle. "You mean like this?" His fingers slowly pulled out of me until his tips were just prodding my entrance.

"Darius!" I cried out. "Please!"

"Please what? Tell me what you want, doll."

"Please don't stop playing with me," I whimpered.

Darius sat up on his knees and stared down at me with an evil grin. I began to sit up, but he pushed me back down. "I did not tell you that you could get up," he snarled at me. "Remove your panties before I rip them off."

I obliged, quickly removing my underwear to reveal my bare sex to him. He knelt in between my legs and looked up at me through his brow as he dragged his tongue up my aching slit. I shuddered at his touch.

"Fuck," he groaned, "you are delicious." His tongue moved upward and found my clit, and my eyes rolled back as he flicked his tongue over it. I reached down and grabbed his hair as he licked the most sensitive part of me.

"Don't stop," I begged.

He gazed up at me as he feasted, his dark green eyes full of lust. A whirlwind of pleasure ran through me as I met my climax. Darius' tongue found its way inside me and lapped up my juices.

"Sabrina," he groaned as he pulled away. "Please let me taste you." I knew what he meant. He wanted to sink his fangs into me and drink my life's essence. My eyes widened. "Please. I have never wanted anything more."

Terror and excitement coursed through my body. I had heard stories about how it was a very thrilling experience. I wondered if those were true, or just lies the vampires spread to provide willing victims.

"Sabrina," he breathed. "If you do not wish for me to, I will not. I can sense your heart pounding. If you do allow me, I promise it will not hurt, and if you ask me to stop at any point, I will."

I nodded. He checked with me once again to confirm that this was what I wanted. When I confirmed, he gently sank his fangs into my inner thigh.

When his tongue dragged against my delicate flesh, I released a moan as pleasure filled me once again. Stars flooded my vision. The rumors were not correct. This was better than I expected. I hated myself for not allowing him to feed from me sooner and cried out as I found my pleasure twice more while he drank from me.

Darius finally pulled away from me just as I felt dizzy from the blood loss. A small trail of blood leaked from the corner of his mouth. He used his thumb to wipe it before licking it away.

"Thank you, my love," a genuine smile flashed across his face. "I have never in my entire existence tasted something so sweet." He leaned forward and gently kissed my lips.

I bit my bottom lip as he pulled away. The feeling of pleasure still lingered within me. I felt fully satisfied, but there was something about him that left me wanting more. He got off the bed and faced the door.

"Darius?" I sat up and called out to him. He turned his head toward me, longingness in his eyes.

"Yes?"

"Don't go." My heart once again broke from the idea of him returning to Titus. Not just for the horrors he would have to deal with, but for the fact I would truly miss him. "Stay the night with me?"

He turned back toward the bed. I saw his eyes begin to mist. "It would be my honor."

Thirty-Four

Darius

Leaving Sabrina the next morning was one of the hardest things I ever had to do. My heart ached as I watched her castle get smaller and smaller until it finally disappeared over the horizon.

Rage boiled under my skin as I thought about what laid ahead for me. I could already hear Dimitri's voice badgering me about where I had been and what had happened after I had last seen him during the Blood Moon festival.

My gaze finally moved toward Andrei. I prayed to the gods that Dimitri would not punish him for what had happened. Was Dimitri even aware — grateful that Andrei had saved his life that day? I could still taste my rage, still hear those thoughts in my head from that moment.

Kill him. Kill him, and right his wrongs.

I made a promise to myself in that moment as I watched Andrei flip a page in his book that this would be the last time.

The last time we played Dimitri's game.

The last time he would hurt us.

The last time he owned us.

No one greeted us as we entered the main castle in Titus. The halls were bare, and there was not a single staff member walking about, which was odd for this time of the day.

Andrei and I waltzed right into the throne room, where Dimitri sat atop the dais, as he always did. Sometimes I wondered if he had been glued to that seat, or if it had some sort of enchantment that constantly drew him to it. Four guards stood at the foot of the dais. It was then I noticed who was missing.

Barnabas.

Before I could say anything, Dimitri spoke.

"Ah," he said with disdain. "If it isn't my sorry excuse for an heir, and his..." he paused, glancing at Andrei, then back to me, "even more useless companion."

I clenched my jaw, swallowing the words I wanted to say to him. I shoved down the thoughts of me rushing to the dais and ripping his head from his body. I needed to remember the part I was to play. I knelt on one knee, and Andrei did the same. I looked down to the floor and took a deep breath.

"I apologize," I breathed. Fuck, this was harder than I thought it would be. I continued to force out the words. "for my behavior during the Blood Moon. I was not feeling like myself."

I did not look up as I heard footsteps approach me. Dimitri's boots came into view after a moment.

"Rise." His voice was cold. I did as he said, looking my father in the eyes. He gave me an up-and-down glance. "You may not be as incompetent as I thought. Glad to hear you have come to your senses. Come." Dimitri turned to the left and walked out of the throne room. "Your pet is dismissed," he flung over his shoulder.

Andrei now stood, and I gave him a nod before I followed Dimitri. My right hand exited to the right and I assumed he was heading to his chambers to make preparations for what was to come. I turned my attention back to Dimitri as we walked down the hall in silence. Our footsteps echoed off the cold stone.

I stared into the back of his head. It would be so easy for me to attack him now and end his miserable existence. I needed to bide my time.

Justice would come soon.

"Where have you been?" Dimitri questioned without looking back at me.

"At the castle in the mountains," I lied.

A firm hum escaped his lips. We walked a few feet more before he spoke again. "Your mother loved that castle so much. I should have had it destroyed after I killed her, so you didn't have a place to hide."

I paused in my tracks. My throat dried and my pulse pounded in my ears. For the first time in a long time, my mind went silent.

How could he say that without care? To him, my mother's death was just another Tuesday. She deserved so much better. My mother was the kindest woman I had ever met. How she ended up with a monster like Dimitri confused me.

Soon, mother. Soon I would do much worse to him than he ever did to you.

I stifled those emotions and quickened my pace to catch up to my father, who was turning and heading into the library. He did not notice that I had fallen behind.

My eyes fell on the two strangers as we entered. They sat at a table across from one another, going over a few books. The man was about my father's age. He had fair skin and a long black beard, which had a few braids woven in, and his short hair was slicked back. His gray eyes met mine as he stood and smiled.

"Ah, your son arrived," the man said as he looked toward Dimitri.

"Just as I said he would," he released a dark chuckle. "Darius, this is Lord Godrick from Zentari." He motioned over to the young woman who now stood by Lord Godrick's side. Her eyes matched his, but a tint darker. They reminded me of an incoming summer storm. Her hair was in a braid that wrapped around the crown of her head. "This is Lady Evalyn, his daughter."

"It is a pleasure to meet you, your highness," she bowed, never breaking her eye contact with me.

"The pleasure is mine, Lady Evalyn," I responded.

"Please call me Eve," she said with a smile. She straightened her back and took a step closer to me. My skin crawled as she nearly closed the gap between us. The scent of sour cherry and musk filled my nose, and I nearly gagged from it.

"The two of them will be visiting us for some time," Dimitri said. "Tomorrow you will give Lady Evalyn a tour of the castle."

I nodded. " Yes, father. It will be my pleasure."

Eve's face lit up in delight as I agreed.

Thirty-Five

Sabrina

Daphne had awoken me with news that the Elders had all gathered to speak with me. My heart pounded in my chest as I raced to the throne room. I worried that something terrible had happened in Serafina.

Never in all my years as queen had the Elders gathered unannounced.

I entered the throne room in a simple green dress, with my hair loose around my shoulders. There had been no time to prepare for the day. The six Elders stood in the center of the throne room, all whispering to themselves.

"What has happened?" My voice boomed as I approached them. I could sense Daphne's presence behind me.

They all turned to look at me. My heart skipped a beat as I saw the worry on all their faces, and I couldn't help how my thoughts ran through every possible scenario.

"Nothing is wrong, my queen," Nelda said softly.

"Nothing?" The pitch of my voice rose. "Never once have you all gathered unannounced! This is clearly not 'nothing'!"

"We just have concerns," Petra and Vulcan said in unison.

"Concerns?" My eyebrows raised.

"You know I am never one to meddle, but we are worried about the vampire prince," Ayla responded.

"Yes, we are more than worried," Orlok said with anger in his voice. "Where is Xander? Is he missing because of Darius?"

"Darius is known to be cruel. We want to make sure he is not hurting you," Hale's soft voice arose from the crowd.

"Darius is on our side. He wants what is best for this kingdom," I responded to them.

"How can you be so sure?" Vulcan's fair skin turned red, and Petra placed her hand on his shoulder.

"What he means to say is that he is known to have a reputation to destroy. His father is even worse, and you know apples do not fall far from trees," Petra spoke up for him.

Rage boiled within me. How dare they judge him without knowing him? Sure, he had a reputation, but who didn't? I know in the other kingdoms I am perceived as a bitch, but this couldn't be further from the truth, and my people know it. Rumors. They were all rumors and my Court had fallen for the bait.

"He is kind and loving! Yes, he has had to do some terrible things that his father forced him to do! He is nothing like Dimitri." I raised my voice with each word. "This is my kingdom. If you do not like my decisions, you are welcome to sail to Nouavara!"

"No!" they all said together.

"That is not what we meant," Nelda said.

"We are just worried about you." Ayla's voice quivered.

"Our alliance is to you, my queen," Hale added.

I released the breath I was holding. My gaze went over each one of them, taking in their concerned expressions. I could not fault them for being worried about me.

"Come, you all must be famished from your journeys. Let's go eat breakfast," I smiled at them before turning on my heels and headed out of the throne room.

Thirty-Six

Darius

Eve and I walked through the castle halls side by side. We had started the tour in the throne room, and I had already shown her the west wing. I hated every moment I spent with her. Her voice was the most annoying thing I had ever heard. It was very high-pitched, and all she spoke about was herself. She wore an extremely low-cut purple dress that fell just below her knees, and was constantly pushing her breasts together to put them even more on display.

What a desperate whore.

Andrei walked with her guard, Nox, a few feet behind us. By the way Eve and Nox looked at each other, it was very clear that they hooked up nearly every chance they got. His scent was all over her and they constantly gave each other longing glances. It made me laugh, watching his face contort as she flirted with me. If only he knew how little I cared about her.

"This is The Hall of Kings," I said to her as I quickened my pace. All I wanted was to get this tour over with. On top of that, this hall always made me feel uneasy. The walls were lined with portraits of every king of Titus, and I could always feel their eyes on me. I had always imagined what it would be like to have my portrait hung here, but now I knew that will never be the case.

Eve matched my speed and caught up to me, looping her arm in mine. I pulled away and glared down at her. A low growl escaped my lips.

"You are such a bad boy, aren't you?" She gave a flirtatious giggle.

"I suppose." My eyes rolled in response.

"I mean, you have done a lot of bad things. You don't like to follow the rules."

"I don't bother myself with such things."

I heard Andrei chuckle from behind me. I glared back at him, and he put his hands up, palms facing me, in response. I gave him a smirk before I turned back and continued walking.

"I find it so very attractive that you like to rebel and cause trouble." She went to grab my arm again, but once again, I pulled away. If she tried again, I would rip her arm off. "Once we are married, you will need to lose the bad boy persona. All that nonsense will need to end, especially your relationship with the fae queen," she sneered.

I paused in my tracks, for the first time turning to look at her dead in her eyes. A scoff escaped my lips before I spoke.

"I am not marrying you."

"Yes, you are. That is why I am here. Our fathers are finalizing the marriage contract as we speak, and we all expect a formal proposal before my father and I return to Zentari. Our wedding is in the spring," she giggled as she twirled her hair. "You won't have any time to sneak away to that faerie whore's ball."

My anger released on those final words. I would not allow anyone to speak about my queen with such disrespect. In an instant, my hand was around her throat, and I slammed her into the wall. Her head smacked into the stone so hard I heard it crack. I was disappointed it wasn't her skull.

"How dare you speak of Sabrina in that manner!" I raged. "I should rip out your throat!"

She cowered under me. Good, she should be scared. She said it herself that I did not play by the rules. I was not above killing anyone, especially if they disrespected my queen. I saw a glimmer of light out of the corner of my eye. Nox was charging at me with a silver dagger in hand. Interesting that he would wield silver weapons. Being vampires themselves, they should understand how it harmed us. It was almost like he expected to fight — to kill me.

I dropped the girl and spun to face Nox, chuckling under my breath as I rushed behind him. He did not realize I had moved before it was too late. I quickly snapped his neck, and Eve's scream rang in my ear as I dropped his body to the floor.

"Darius!" Andrei called out.

"Stay out of this!" I commanded him.

My gaze fell back to Eve, who was now on her knees sobbing in front of Nox's corpse. I slowly walked to her. Stopping directly in front of her, I grabbed her by her hair and yanked her gaze up to meet mine.

"If you ever insult Sabrina again, you will be next," I said in a low tone. I released her hair and turned toward Andrei. "Come." I walked past Eve and exited the Hall of Kings.

Thirty-Seven

Sabrina

At breakfast, Hale told me a very interesting piece of information about one of the priestesses they worked with. The news had me rushing to get a carriage to visit Lake Kikami right away to see her. I had not been to the lake in years. Hale normally had everything under control. They never gave me any reason to worry about what was going on in the water villages.

Daphne and I arrived at the lake village just a day later. As soon as we exited the carriage, a woman greeted us. Her navy-blue hair was in loose waves around her shoulders, and two small braids framed her face. The simple seafoam green dress she wore stood out against her pale blue skin. My eyes fell to her very pregnant stomach, and I smiled up at her.

"Priestess Kila!" I went in to hug her, and we held each other in a tight embrace for a moment. Kila was one of the last descendants of the great Priestess Kikami, who the lake was named after. She led her people here centuries ago, and this lake granted them greatness. Lake Kikami was full of magical energies that not even Daphne and Xander understood fully. "Hale told us the joyous news! I had to come to offer you my blessings!"

"It is an honor for you to visit, my queen." She released herself from my embrace and looked over to Daphne. Her face lit up, and she skipped over to her, wrapping her arms around the Ancient One of Light. The two of them had been friends for centuries. My heart warmed as I watched them reunite.

"It is not often that us fae are blessed with children. We had to come as soon as we heard the news," Daphne chimed.

"Thank you. It means so much to me that you have come," Kila said as she released Daphne. "Follow me to the temple." She turned and guided us through the small village.

The houses were made of dry stone and were white with bright blue rounded rooftops. The streets were filled with water fae who were going about their day-to-day life. They all stopped and bowed as I passed them.

We arrived at the temple on the lake shore after a short walk. This building was much larger than the others in town, and the roof had a golden wave mounted on top of it. The round windows had no glass and allowed the warm lake breeze to blow in. She led us up the stairs of the temple to her bedroom suite. I was in awe of the view of the lake. The sunlight sparkled against its surface. I was always enamored with the aquamarine waters of Lake Kikami. It was the largest lake in Serafina, and many water fae called this lake their home.

"How far along are you?" Daphne questioned as she sat in a white and fluffy egg-shaped chair.

"A little over eight months," she said, sitting on the chaise across from the chair, putting her legs up. "I have been very lucky that the magic of the lake has kept me from falling ill during the pregnancy."

I had heard how terrible pregnancy was for many women. It was not something that I was truly excited about experiencing for myself. Maybe if it ever happened, I would build myself an estate here on the lake and use its water to keep me well.

"We are glad to hear you are doing well! Just another month and your little bundle of joy will be here!" I smiled at her as I sat in a teal armchair by the window.

"Oh! We brought you a gift!" Daphne chuckled as she snapped her fingers. A large box appeared on the floor in front of the chaise, and Kila sat up in surprise.

"You did not have to do that!" She squealed in delight and pulled on the bright blue ribbon to untie it. The Priestess lifted the lid of the white box and sat it in her lap, releasing a gasp as she peered into it. She reached in and pulled out a mobile. The top ring was gold and golden strings hung from it, holding a variety of shells, bubbles, and little fish in a rainbow of colors. Kila looked up at us, her bright blue eyes slightly misted.

"I am so glad you like it! When you hang it, it will spin on its own and play lullabies," I said to her.

"This is beautiful! I love it!"

"You haven't told us what you are having?" Daphne questioned. "Do you have any names picked out?"

"I am having a boy, and am naming him Carlow."

Thirty-Eight

Darius

The door to my room flung open, and I sat up from the bed. Dimitri rushed into my room, anger contorted his face.

"What have you done?" He raged.

I took a deep breath and rolled my eyes. "I did nothing that wasn't necessary," I said nonchalantly.

"You have no idea how badly you have ruined my plans!" He spat as he spoke. "Godrick was *this* close to assisting me into forcing all humans into farms! The Vampires could have total control of Titus *and* the north!"

I jumped up from the bed and rushed to stand directly in front of him. "I do not think that is how Titus should be ruled!" I spat back at him. "Yes, humans are worthless, but they should still have their freedom."

Dimitri's eyes widened, and his nostrils flared. "You are not the king. I. Am. King! You are nothing more than a useless worm! A dog for me to use as I please! You ruin everything you touch! Leave Titus, now!" He demanded.

"Gladly," I growled as I rushed out of my room.

After my fight with Dimitri, I quickly grabbed Andrei and left Titus. As soon as I crossed into Serafina, a huge weight lifted off my shoulders, and once the castle came into view, I felt at home. I felt safe.

As soon as we entered the castle grounds, we were greeted by Fern. She informed us that Sabrina and Daphne were both away on business and would return in a few days. My heart ached that she was not here. Fern guided us to the library, informing us that the Elders were all visiting and that she thought I should meet them.

After we walked into the library, the laughter and conversations died. My eyes fell to the round table where six fae sat. All of their eyes on me.

"Hello, Fern," the one with dark skin and white hair said with disdain in his voice. I hoped it was not toward the sweet little earth fae. Fern had shown me nothing but kindness, and I hoped that people here showed her that same kindness.

Fern introduced me and Andrei to the Elders. Orlok and Vulcan both seemed irritated by our presence. Nelda, Petra, and Ayla seemed a bit warmer in their greeting, but still a bit stand-offish. Hale gave a small wave, not saying a word.

When she was finished with the introductions, Fern quickly left. We all looked at each other in silence for a moment as tension hung in the air.

"Queen Sabrina is not here," Vulcan said.

"You may want to go somewhere else until her return," Orlok added.

"What do you mean?" Andrei said, raising his eyebrow.

"What I mean is," Orlok stood and stepped toward me. "We do not need the vampire prince and his companion in our business."

I chuckled under my breath. "Understood," I said. I pushed down the thoughts I had of ripping off his head. "We will be in our suite until Sabrina's return."

I turned and walked out of the library, Andrei's footsteps echoed behind me.

Thirty-Nine

Sabrina

When Daphne and I returned to the castle, I was informed that Darius had also returned a few days ago and was waiting for me in his suite. Apparently, he had not left it since his arrival after he met the Elders.

I prayed that they got along.

The Elders had made it clear they did not like him, and Darius was not the friendliest person I had ever met, but I hoped nothing had happened between them in my absence.

I made my way to his suite and knocked on the door. That familiar tug on my heart felt as if it was about to pull me through the solid cherry-wood door.

Darius' dark and calm voice sounded from behind the door, calling me to come in. I gripped the golden handle and turned the knob. The door glided open to reveal Darius sitting on a red velvet chair with a golden chalice in hand. His head spun to face me, and his emerald eyes lit up as they met mine. He jumped from the chair and rushed in front of me.

"Darius, I did not expect you back so soon! Where is Andrei?" I looked around the sitting room, noticing his absence.

"He is out hunting and will return soon." Darius furrowed his eyebrows as he looked down at me with a pained look in his eyes. "Are you not happy that I returned?" He swallowed hard.

"I am elated that you are back," I said as I wrapped him in a hug. He staggered back for a moment before wrapping his arms around me, holding me tight.

"I know that I should have stayed longer," he said softly as his fingertips played with my hair. "But I could not stand it any longer. I could not stand how they spoke about my queen."

"That's ok," I breathed, looking up at him. "You belong here, with me. Not with people who harm you."

Darius gave me a small smile and then bent down to gently kiss me. The fire roared behind us as our lips met. My core heated as I deepened the kiss, and my tongue slid into his mouth. I did not realize how badly I missed his touch in his absence. Darius released a low growl as he matched my hunger. I slowly pulled away, against my better judgment.

"Do you think Andrei will be back soon?" I blushed at the thought of Andrei walking in and finding Darius in between my legs.

Darius smirked as he picked me up and tossed me over his shoulder. "Well, let's go somewhere a little more private in case he returns," Darius said as he brought me into his bedroom. He kicked the door shut behind him as soon as we entered and tossed me onto the bed. I landed on my back and my eyes fell on him as he stood at the end. "Spread your legs and lift your dress, doll."

I obliged and pulled the pink silk up around my waist and allowed my legs to fall open, revealing my delicate underwear. In a blink, Darius was on the bed and in between my legs. He ripped off my underwear and smirked down at my bare sex. Kneeling down, he gently dragged his tongue across my glistening slit. His body shuttered from the taste.

"You have such a delicious pussy, doll," he growled as he lapped at me. His thumb found the sensitive bundle of nerves atop my slit and rubbed it in slow circles. I arched my back as blissful agony took over my body and reached forward to rake my hands through his hair. Darius' free hand found its way to my outer thigh and squeezed it.

I released a moan as his tongue slipped inside of me and pressed against my upper wall. His pace on my clit quickened as his tongue went harder. Just as I was about to climax, he pulled away.

"Not yet," he teased. "Now that I have you all wet for me, it is time to have more fun." He quickly got off the bed, stood at the end of it again, removed his pants, and his cock sprang free. Heat rose to my cheeks and my mouth watered at the sight of it. "Oh, do you want a taste before I plunge it into your sweet little pussy?"

I nodded in response. He raised his hand and motioned me closer with two fingers. I sat up and moved to the edge of the bed, getting onto my knees. He motioned with his fingers to look up at him. I did. My heart raced, and I swallowed hard as he slowly fisted himself in my face.

"Show me what a good little cock sucker you are. Go on," he instructed as he removed his hand.

I leaned forward and slowly dragged my tongue up the shaft. Darius let out a groan as my tongue reached the tip and circled it. He reached down and fisted my hair and held me in place. The head of his shaft was just a sliver away from my lips. "I thought I had patience. I do not. Open your mouth, doll."

My lips parted, and he thrust himself into my awaiting mouth. Half of it made it inside before it hit the back of my throat, causing me to gag. He slowly forced his shaft in and out of my mouth, causing my eyes to roll back into my skull. Drool coated his considerable length and dripped down his balls as he quickened his pace. Darius pushed himself as deep as it would go and held it there.

"Such a good little cocksucker," he purred. I felt him twitch in my throat, and he slowly pulled out. A line of drool connected my bottom lip to his tip. "Get on your hands and knees for me, doll."

I quickly spun over, put my head on the mattress and my ass in the air. He traced his fingertips down my spine, and I quivered. He tightly gripped my hip with one hand, and his tip teased my entrance.

"Darius," I breathed, "please."

"Please?" A chuckle escaped his lips. "Please what?" His tip prodded my entrance once again, and all I could think about was how badly I needed him deep inside of me.

"Please fuck me," I begged.

On that final word, he plunged himself inside of me full force. I let out a squeal as he reached the deepest part of me. Darius groaned as he unsheathed himself, then shoved back inside of me. I begged him not to stop as he fucked me, and gripped the sheets, trying to stay steady as he pounded into me full force.

He thrust so hard that I inched forward. Darius got up onto the bed, pushing me flat on my stomach. His hand pressed against my back in between my shoulder blades, keeping me in place. He fucked me harder. My body clenched as stars filled my eyes. A moan of immense pleasure escaped my lips as I climaxed.

"Such a good girl. Cum for me," He groaned as I felt his cock twitch inside me and he slowed his pace, dragging out my pleasure.

"Oh gods," I moaned.

Darius leaned down, pressing his body against mine. His bottom lip grazed against my ear. "Do not thank the gods for the pleasure I give you," he growled, pressing himself deeper inside of me. "Try again."

"Darius," my breath caught as I spoke. His pace quickened once again. I arched my back, pressing into him. My eyes rolled back as he slammed against my deepest wall. His hand pressed down firmly, keeping me in place. His release spilled into me, filling my core. He plunged himself deep into me and held it there.

"Fuck," he groaned. "You feel so perfect around my cock." It twitched again inside me before he slowly pulled out, and I felt his essence leak from me. I turned back to Darius and saw the look of pleasure plastered on his face. His eyes then went wide, and he released a chuckle. "Well, I am glad that we moved in here. I just heard Andrei return."

Heat rose to my cheeks as embarrassment set in. If Darius could hear Andrei, did that mean that Andrei could hear us? Darius leaned forward and planted a kiss on my forehead. As if he was reading my mind, he responded.

"Don't worry, doll. No one will know how much of a little slut you are for your vampire."

The next night I held a feast to introduce Darius and the Elders formally. The feast was held in my private dining room. A bright green silk runner ran down the center of the table with large flower arrangements of varying colors and glimmering white crystals arranged down it. Golden fae lights danced through the air, which gave the room a warm glow. I sat at the head of the table. My dress matched the color and material of the table runner, and I wore a golden circlet adorned with emeralds. Daphne sat to my left, Darius to my right, and Andrei next to him.

He was so handsome in his dark red button-up shirt and black tie. The light reflected off his golden cuff links. The Elders and their companions took their seats at the table. Each Elder had an aide that they typically brought along with them during their travels. Most of them stayed quiet in my presence. I knew very little about them.

In hopes of keeping the peace, I assigned everyone's seat. Nelda, Ayla, Hale, and their companions were closest to us. Vulcan and Orlok were seated at the far end. The two of them were most likely to cause issues.

Once everyone had settled into their place, the first course was served. Servants went around and provided everyone with drinks and a leafy green salad with shredded salty cheese, a creamy dressing, and garlic croutons.

The tension in the room could have been cut with a knife. Everyone ate in silence, many with their eyes glued to the plate, some with their eyes glued to Darius and Andrei as they sipped from their chalices.

I cleared my throat to gather everyone's attention. Once all eyes were on me, I spoke.

"Thank you all for coming to this feast. May the drinks continue to flow, and the food be extra delicious." I smiled at them before continuing. "I wanted to formally introduce you to a very special guest of the Kingdom." I motioned toward Darius, and he raised his glass. I heard a scoff from the end of the table. My eyes shot in that direction. "I hope you all treat Darius with the same kindness and respect that you treat me."

"May I speak?" Darius asked. I turned to him and nodded, and he looked toward the rest of the table. "I know I am not wanted here, but when I say that I want what is best for Serafina and Sabrina, I mean it. My past has not given you a reason to trust me. I understand that. Going forward, I will not be the man my reputation portrays me as. I look forward to gaining your trust."

"Darius, I think that is very sweet," Nelda said with a small smile.

"I do not trust you," Hale said with a sneer, "but I look forward to seeing what you do. Do not give me a reason to remove you from the Queen's presence. She will always come first, and I will not allow harm to come to her."

"Thank you, Hale," Darius responded. "I will not make you regret giving me a chance."

Vulcan and Orlok stayed silent and resumed eating their salads. I heard one of them mumble under their breath, but I could not make out the words.

"Is everything okay down there?" I questioned. "Is the salad not to your liking? The next course should be much better. It is a chicken breast served with a marsala and mushroom sauce served over a bed of angel hair pasta. The mushrooms were just foraged this morning. It is very fresh! I have been looking forward to it all day."

"Oh no," Vulcan said. "The food is fine."

"It is the company that is the problem." Orlok's gaze shot to Darius. "I don't understand why you would want to keep the companionship of such filth."

"Enough!" Darius' voice boomed, causing the room to shake. "Hate me all you want! Say whatever you want to me. Remember, though, she is your queen and you are to show her respect or I will show you the door!"

The room fell silent. All eyes were on Darius. My heart pounded against my chest.

"I believe the vampire to be correct," Petra spoke up. All eyes shifted to her. To my surprise, I had not heard her say a word all night until now. "We should all be mindful of how we speak to the queen and her guests. Queen Sabrina has never once done us wrong. I trust she is making good decisions for our kingdom."

"Very well put," Hale responded.

Vulcan let out a huff and sank into his seat. I watched as his eyes shied away from Petra.

"Are you kidding me?" Orlok's aide, Ronnan, exclaimed, jumping from his seat. "How can we watch this and allow this to happen?"

"Ronnan, sit down!" Orlok shot him a glare.

"I will not! Sabrina is a fool for bedding a vampire! He will destroy Serafina and turn our queen into a blood whore!"

In a blur, Darius was across the table and snapped Ronnan's neck. Everyone jumped from their seats in shock as gasps and screams filled the room.

"I warned all of you," Darius growled. "I will not allow anyone to mistreat Sabrina or speak to her or about in that manner." He shifted his attention around the room, looking each person in the eyes. "Who is next?"

The room fell silent. I could not believe what I had just witnessed and swallowed hard before I spoke.

"Enough of this!" I called out. "Guards! Please handle Ronnan's remains. Send them back to his family. The feast is over. You all are dismissed."

I stormed out of the dining room. I was not angry about how Vulcan and Orlok treated Darius. I was not angry that Ronnan had called me a blood whore. I was not angry that Darius had killed him. I wasn't angry that the entire night was ruined.

I was angry that I could not eat the chicken marsala that I had been so excited about since breakfast.

Forty

Darius

I could still feel the stag's blood running through my veins. It was the first time I had drank animal blood. The taste and feel were different than I had ever expected. It was gamey and rich and filled me with a sense of life that I had never experienced.

I promised Sabrina that I would never touch another, and I intended to keep that promise. I would do anything to keep her happy. She had not spoken to me since the feast yesterday. Worry filled my chest as I found a note on my bed requesting for me to meet her in the orchard.

I wasted no time and rushed to meet her. Sabrina sat under a gazebo. Each side had a wooden swing, and it's ropes had golden flowers braided through them. She softly swung on the left swing, her feet dangling above the ground. Variegated ivy wove its way around the lattice of the gazebo, providing the illusion of privacy. Golden fae lights danced around it, giving it a warm glow. My heart melted at the sight of my queen sitting in her soft pink dress, her hair in loose waves that framed her delicate face.

Nerves exploded in my chest as I walked toward her. She turned toward me and gave a warm smile.

"You summoned me?"

"I did. Please sit." She motioned to the swing across from her.

Stepping into the gazebo, I sat down on the swing she had ushered me to. I looked down at my lap and took a deep breath. Her tone gave me no clues to if she was mad or not. I wish she would just come out and say it. Instead, we sat there for a few moments in silence. Finally, I looked up and met her gaze.

"I will not apologize for defending you. Anyone who speaks out against you will meet the same end. I will defend you until my final breath."

My blood ran cold as she stood from the swing. She stepped forward and stopped when she was directly in front of me. I swore my chest was about to explode from how hard my heart was pounding. A wave of calm washed over me when she gave me a warm smile, reached out, and grabbed a piece of hair that had fallen from my bun, tucking it behind my ear.

"I expect nothing less from my soldier and partner." Her voice was like a soft melody. She sat in my lap and gently pressed a kiss to my lips. I wrapped my arms around her and smiled.

Forty-One

Sabrina

Daphne and I spent the entire morning planning the next Masquerade of the Vernal Equinox. I could not believe that almost a full year had come and gone since I had met Darius.

I never thought that this would be the turn of events after I had stabbed him in the chest, but I am glad it was.

"Are you excited?" Daphne questioned as she sat the stack of papers down on the desk.

"You know..." I breathed, "I feel like this year will be different. I was never excited before, but this year I cannot wait until the ball!"

"All the invitations have been sent out. I wonder if King Tristan will attend since you rejected him last year," she chuckled.

I had felt somewhat bad about ignoring his many letters, but he eventually got the hint and stopped sending them.

"I do not think he will. I heard he is to be wed on the Summer Solstice to an earth fae noble of his kingdom."

"Ah yes! I did hear about that!" She exclaimed. "Her name is Athena. Rumor is she is a very powerful earth fae and extremely beautiful."

I had also heard about her magic. It was very interesting how different the fae of Nouavara and Serafina were. While earth fae here are smaller with darker skin, the earth fae of Nouavara are taller, with paler skin. Each of the fae types had slight differences between the kingdoms.

The monarchy there was also by bloodline. They did not have a fae who could use all of the elemental magics. No one knew why our kingdoms had similar magics, but so many differences.

I looked up to Daphne as I felt a pit in my stomach grow. "Did you send an invite to...?"

"No," she answered before I could even finish my question. "I thought it best not to."

I leaned back in my seat and sighed in relief. Before I got too comfortable, gooseflesh took over my body seconds before the double doors to my study burst open and darkness flooded in. I jumped up and quickly grabbed Shimmerthorne, my gods-gifted bow, off the wall. I aimed and pulled back the string and a magic arrow formed. Daphne also stood and her hands gave off a bright white glow.

Xander appeared from the darkness, and I lowered my weapon. The energy around Daphne's hands vanished. Anger contorted his face.

"You let him come into our lands and spill fae blood?" He spat as he came closer and slammed his hands down onto the desk, looking me dead in my eyes. The usual amber hue was gone, and his irises were completely taken over by darkness. His shadows flared around him more than usual. "The vampire Prince is too dangerous to be allowed within Serafina's borders!"

"I did not let him do anything!" I shouted back at him. "Ronnan had it coming. I have heard that was not the first time that he has spoken out against me, just the first time he was brave enough to do it in my presence." My body grew hot the more I spoke. My magic was ready to explode and release. "Darius was protecting me and this court! Which is more than I can say about you! Where have *you* been?"

Xander staggered back. A wounded look crossed his face for just a moment before returning to anger. "I have dedicated my entire life to this court! Everything I have done is to protect you and our kingdom!"

"Answer the question!" I demanded. "Where were you? You missed an extremely important ritual! Orlok has been questioning my authority!"

"Where I was is none of your concern! I had personal matters outside of this castle that I needed to attend to!" His shadows grew around him and snuffed out all the light in the room.

I went to respond but was interrupted by a bright flash of white light and a serene calm wash over me. The shadows cleared away, and it was Daphne who spoke.

"Enough. What is important is that you have returned and you can assist with the ball. We can worry about all this drama afterward." Xander and I simply nodded in agreement. "Wonderful. Come along. The royal florist is awaiting us, so we can select the arrangements. Afterward, we have to meet with the chef to select the menu."

"That sounds wonderful," I responded through my teeth.

"Dear brother, If you could go meet with the Elders and try to calm any of their worries. That would be most helpful."

"Yes, sister," Xander let out a grumble.

Forty-Two

Darius

I paced back and forth by the fireplace. My eyes were glued to the shut door that led from the suite to the castle. One fist was clenched so tightly that my claws dug into my skin. With my other hand I was rapidly snapping my fingers.

What could be taking so long?

The door finally opened, and my heart stopped. Turning toward the door, I watched Andrei walk in. He looked too calm for how late he was, and I rushed over to him.

"Why are you late? It should not have taken that long! Did you get it?"

"Yes, I got it. Everything is in place. No need to worry." He shrugged and slid past me. Andrei threw himself on the green velvet chaise and put his arms behind his head.

"The ball is tomorrow!" I spat at him. How calm he was really annoyed me. "You almost ruined everything!"

"I ran into slight complications, but everything is in place for tomorrow."

I walked over to him and leaned down. My face was just a few inches from his and I bared my fangs. "You better hope for your sake it is."

Forty-Three

Sabrina

I sat on my throne, looking out into the ballroom. Like last year and the year before, the room was full of women in beautiful gowns and men in dapper suits enjoying the festivities. Xander and Daphne stood by my side. Xander and I had not spoken since his return. It was probably for the best based on the last interaction we'd had. I didn't want to fight with him, but he had no right to come back the way he did.

My eyes scanned over the crowd, searching for Darius. The ball had been going on for a few hours now, and my heart sank that he was not yet here. I wondered if he would come at all, or if he would avoid the ball to avoid any issues between him and the Elders.

Maybe it was for the best that he was not here.

My gaze fell to Tristan, who approached me with a woman hooked on his arm. He wore a navy suit, and she wore a glittery blue dress that reminded me of the sea. I gave them a warm smile as they bowed.

"Happy birthday, Queen Sabrina," Tristan said as he straightened his back.

"Thank you! I am glad you came! I wasn't sure if you would have made it with your wedding so close!"

"Thank you for having me. I would not miss this for anything. I wanted to introduce you to the future Queen of Nouavara," he waved his hand toward her, "Athena Greenbriar!"

"It is an honor to meet you," she said softly, but not weakly. Her sage green hair was braided into a coronet and had baby's-breath woven within it.

"It is my honor to meet another fae Queen."

"I did not wish to decline the invitation, but we will be leaving early. There has been some turmoil back home with the human kingdom to the north. I cannot be gone for long."

"When you return home, will you send us a report on the situation?" Daphne asked.

"We may be able to send aid," Xander added. The fae had not been to war in hundreds of years. Hearing that Nouavara was having issues with Selona made me a bit nervous.

If things continued, would Serafina be at war with Titus? Would Dimitri take it that far?

"Of course. We are hoping it won't get to that point. If it does, we are glad to have you as allies."

"Thank you for coming, Tristan and Athena. Please enjoy the ball, and safe travels."

With that, they bowed and returned to the party. After an hour, I saw them leave the ballroom. I had given up hope that Darius was going to attend. I tried to reach out through the bond to Darius, asking him where he was and what he was doing, but he had shut me out. I leaned back on my throne and tried to hold in my tears. All of a sudden the music stopped. I sat straight up and saw Andrei walk into the ballroom, alone.

"May I present to you, Darius Edward Alexander Dragomeir and his birthday gift to the beautiful Queen Sabrina! Please clear the floor," he called out, and I watched the crowd part.

They moved into the gardens and stood in the archways, and all eyes were on Andrei. He snapped his fingers and a new band walked in and began to play. The throne room filled with some of the most beautiful music I had ever heard.

The music then changed to an upbeat, energizing sound, and behind the band came in acrobats, who entered via back handsprings. They performed for a few moments. We all watched their flips and tricks. Once they were done, they stepped to the side and jugglers entered the room.

The music changed once again to a more dramatic sound. The room filled with gasps as the balls turned into pure flame as they juggled. A few of them got onto their hands and juggled with their feet. I had never seen anything like this.

I leaned forward more as my gaze intensified on the show. They then cleared the floor, and the music fell silent for a moment. I gripped the arm of my chair and waited for what was next. The music then picked up again in a robust tune.

Animals filed in pairs. First was the rainbow stag, one of the most beautiful creatures in all of Serafina. Followed by white tigers, male peacocks with their iridescent feathers on display, pale pink elephants from the western continent, shimmering gold giraffes, deep purple bears, and green-striped zebras.

They circled the room, and once they made three laps, they exploded into millions of butterflies, and the music shifted into a soft and enchanting melody. The entire performance was absolutely stunning. There were so many species in a rainbow of colors it was hard to pick which ones caught my eye the most. My gaze followed them as they flew around the ballroom, then up into the open sky.

The music changed again into a more fluid rhythm. Ribbon twirlers entered and had ribbons of dark green and red. I had gotten lost in the flow of the ribbons when Daphne's voice pulled me out of it.

"This is wonderful. I have never seen anything like this."

"He certainly has a passion for theatrics," Xander let out a deep sigh.

"I think it's sweet," I said softly as the floor cleared and a large group of people walked in.

They all wore white robes that hit the floor. One by one, they walked up and laid red roses at the base of the dais. Once hundreds of roses were at my feet, the music changed to a gentle piano tune. I felt that familiar tug on my heart, and I looked up to the entrance, which was now filled with fog.

When Darius walked through it, my heart skipped a beat. He smirked at me and adjusted the lapels of his jacket. He slowly walked to the center of the ballroom, eyes locked on me.

"From the moment I met you, I knew that I loved you," he said as he continued my way. "There was something so amazing and wonderful about the bright-eyed faerie queen who stabbed me. That dagger melted away the ice that had taken over my heart. When the gods bonded us together, it was truly a blessing. I knew this is where I belonged."

I stood from my throne and stepped off the dais. My hands shook as he continued toward me.

"I came from a world that saw love as a weakness. You taught me that love is a great strength. I would go to the ends of the world for you. I never deserved your kindness, but you are the type to show kindness to even the darkest of souls, if it meant pulling them back into the light." He stopped directly in front of me, got on one knee, and pulled out a small square box from his pocket. My heart pounded in my chest, and I looked down at him with wide eyes. "Sabrina Alexandra Saison, will you do me the honor of being my wife?" He opened the box and revealed a rose gold ring with a round pink stone in a halo setting.

All eyes were on me, and heat rose to my cheeks. "Are... are you sure?"

He chuckled. "Yes, doll. I am sure. Don't leave me waiting down here. The marble is hard on my knees, and everyone is staring."

"Yes! A million times, yes!" I squealed.

He took my hand and slid the ring onto my finger. It was a perfect fit. Darius stood, and I threw my arms around his neck and kissed him hard. He wrapped his arms around me and lifted me off the ground.

A blood-curdling scream filled the ballroom. Darius dropped me to my feet, and we all turned toward the sound.

Forty-Four

Darius

Screams erupted through the ballroom, and chaos ensued. The crowd flocked toward the exit. The ribbon dancers I hired had transformed into assassins. Blood sprayed across the ballroom as one of the guests had their head removed from their body.

"Congratulations on your engagement. The King of Titus sends his well wishes."

I heard a low voice say from behind us. I spun and saw a man coming at Sabrina with a dagger. I grabbed him by his wrist and twisted his arm behind his back, and took the knife from his hand. He let out a scream as I heard his arm pop out of joint. I let him suffer for a moment before I sliced his throat and threw his body to the ground.

I looked out to the crowd and saw Andrei as he ripped one of the assassins away from one of the patrons and snapped his neck. Xander and Daphne were also already in the fray. Their magic filled the air. I watched as Daphne shot her light through the assassins and Xander choked them out with his shadows. Seeing their magic in person was terrifying, and I reminded myself to stay on their good side.

My attention turned back to Sabrina. Her bow was in hand. Where had it even come from? I had heard many stories of Shimmerthorne, but this was the first time seeing it in person. She pulled back the string and a magic arrow formed. Releasing the string, she loosed the arrow, and I watched it pierce one of the assailants in the eye.

Panic welled in my chest. I knew she could hold her own, but I couldn't bear the thought of her getting hurt in the chaos. I grabbed her arm and pulled her toward me.

"I am getting you out of here!"

"I am not leaving!" She yanked away from my touch. "I will fight for my people."

"It is my job to keep you safe! You are getting out of here!" I grabbed her again and yanked her toward me. I looked her in her eyes and held her gaze. "Go to sleep. I will handle this." She collapsed into my arms, and I threw her over my shoulder. I called out for Andrei, and he was before me in an instant, covered in blood. "Take her somewhere safe! I will come to find you when I am done here."

"Yes, sir," he said as she took her from me, and in a blink, he was gone. He rushed through the crowd. I watched as Xander whipped his shadows to clear the attackers out of his path. Once he was out of sight, I tilted my neck to the left and right and heard a cracking sound in my ears. My eyes locked onto one of the assassins who had their fangs buried into a small woman.

My heart sank as I saw who it was. Blood dripped from her green hair. He threw her body to the floor, and Fern's eyes were devoid of life. I looked back at him, and he was wiping his mouth with his forearm. In an Instant, I was in front of him. Taking his arm, I pulled it so hard that a popping sound could be heard over the screaming. Blood splattered as I ripped his arm from his body, snapped his neck, and threw him to the floor.

I looked down at Fern and suppressed the tears that threatened to fall from my eyes. She was one of the sweetest girls I had ever met. She was very kind and never judged me for my reputation. I could not allow myself to grieve, not yet. Leaning down, I slid my fingers over her eyelids and shut them, then stood and looked out at the room. Most of the guests had fled, leaving the room filled with dead bodies, and the white marble stained with blood.

"Darius!" I heard Xander's voice from behind me. I spun and saw one of the attackers coming at me with a silver dagger. I smirked and dodged out of the way just before he made contact. In a flash, I was behind him, and before he knew it, I snapped his neck. "Who's next?"

Forty-Five

Sabrina

My whole body ached, and my head felt as if there was a fifty-pound weight sitting on my brain. My eyes gently fluttered open and my gaze locked on to Darius, who sat in an armchair that had been pulled up to my bedside. I sat up as the memories of what happened flooded my mind.

"Easy," he said in a soft voice. He leaned forward and placed a hand on my thigh. I pushed it away.

"What happened? How dare you compel me to sleep! I should have helped my people!" Images flooded my mind of the dead, and their screams still rang in my ear.

"I know you can handle yourself, but I needed to make sure you were safe. I do not know what I would have done if something happened to you. As your soldier, I took care of the threat."

"As my partner," I snarled, "you should have let me make that choice!"

Darius leaned in, his face just an inch from mine. "I won't apologize for keeping my queen safe. Daphne, Xander, and I handled it. I will not allow you to stay in harm's way."

I couldn't hold it in any longer. A wail escaped my lips and tears began to fall. I fell back onto the bed and laid on my back. Darius got out of the chair and crawled into bed by my side. He pulled me into him, and I buried my head into his chest, soaking his red cotton shirt with tears. The comforting scent of pine and cinnamon filled my nose.

His fingertips gently pet the back of my head. I don't know how much time had passed, but when I finally looked up at him, my eyes were sore and my throat was hoarse. He dragged his thumb under my eyes to wipe away the tears.

"The next time I return to Titus will be my last, and it will be to kill Dimitri for what he has done. I won't let him get away with this."

Nodding in response, I sat up. A vanilla latte magically appeared on my nightstand. I reached over and held the warm mug with both hands and took a sip. Looking over at Darius, I let out a sigh. "Thank you for staying with me, and for protecting me and my people."

"I will be by your side until I take my last breath." He sat up and locked eyes with me. "I will do everything I can to sever all ties with Titus."

I looked down at the mug I held just above my lap, not allowing it to touch my skin. "All ties?" I questioned, without looking up at him.

"Of course. I hate that I am associated with such a terrible place and king."

"I think I know of a way to do that."

"What do you mean?" He raised his eyebrows and leaned in.

"There may be a way to cure your vampirism," I said plainly. I held my breath, awaiting his reaction.

"I was born, not made. Would that make a difference?" He spoke in such a soft tone, I could hear the pain in his voice.

"I will ask Daphne to look into it. I have heard whispers, but she should be able to get more information."

"Do it tomorrow. For now, please rest." He pulled off his shirt and revealed his bare, chiseled chest. He took the mug from my hand and put it on the table beside him before he pulled me close and laid us down. My head rested on his chest as he leaned down and placed a kiss atop my head.

One by one, I watched as the families of the fallen added another log to the pile that sat in the center of the field behind the castle. This place where festivals were once held, now had a somberness that hung in the air. My heart broke more and more as I watched each family add to the stack.

I swore I heard an audible snap when Fern's family added a log for her. Her twin sister and her two young boys were all dressed in black. I could tell Juniper was trying to keep it together for her boys, but I could feel her pain. Maybe it was my own. Fern was not just someone who worked in my castle, she had become a close friend over the years.

I stood in between Daphne and Darius, holding both of their hands tight. Xander stood next to Daphne, and Andrei next to Darius. We said not a word to each other as we watched the pile get higher and higher. The final family set their log on the pile, and I gave Darius' and Daphne's hands one last squeeze before releasing them and approaching the pyre.

"Citizens of Serafina." I could already feel myself start to choke on my words as I looked at the sea of mourning souls. "Last week, we witnessed one of the greatest tragedies to happen on our soil. Too many mothers, fathers, sisters, brothers, and friends were lost during the Vernal Equinox. Let me announce to the world that justice will be done, but tonight, allow us to help guide the lost souls to the beyond and celebrate their lives."

The crowd was silent as I turned to face the pile of logs and raised my arms with upturned palms. My core heated, and then it spread through my arms and into my hands. Flame ignited in each palm and I shot the flames into the pyre, causing it to set ablaze.

We had no graves in Serafina. The caskets of the dead laid under the logs and we would allow them to burn until nothing but ash was left. We believed that the ash would float into the sky and each soul would become a star to watch over us.

I turned back to the crowd and felt the fire rise behind me. Tears streamed down my face as I locked eyes with Juniper. I mouthed to her 'I am so sorry' just before I fell to my knees and sobbed.

These deaths were all my fault. I should have known, sensed that something was off. I should have done more to protect my people. A firm hand gripped my shoulder. I looked up and saw Darius standing there. He took my hand and helped me stand.

"You are not alone. Don't hold the weight of this all on your shoulders. I promised I would be by your side for eternity, and I meant it," he said in the faintest of whispers before he turned to the crowd.

"To the families of those who were lost, I extend my deepest condolences. I take full responsibility for what occurred. Queen Sabrina is right. Justice will be done. I will bring down the man responsible. It will not make the ache in your chest lessen, but I hope it will help bring you some peace knowing that the one responsible will pay for this crime the way that the people of Serafina have paid, in blood."

I saw a fire ignite in the eyes of my people. They did not shout at him to go away. They did not blame him. I looked over to Daphne and Xander who now stood with the Elders, relieved to see all of them had a look of approval written on their faces.

Forty-Six
Darius

The sound of a slow and steady drip filled my ears as I walked through the halls of the dungeon. Andrei and Xander walked behind me. We did not speak a word to each other as we made our way to the cell at the end of the hall.

Xander used his shadows to keep us in darkness. They leaked into the cell as we gazed upon the man we had chained to the wall, with nails driven into his hands and feet to keep him pinned in place. His head hung down, and his golden hair was caked in blood. My gaze followed as a shadow slivered in and up his body. It gripped his head and jerked it upward, forcing the prisoner to look forward. The cell door swung open, and I smirked as his eyes filled with horror as the three of us entered the cell and stepped out of the shadows. I twirled my silver dagger in between my fingers as I approached him.

"Ready to play?" I mused.

"Fuck you," he spat at me. Another shadow rushed up and filled his mouth. I let out a deep laugh as I watched him struggle for air. As his skin gained a blue tint, I raised my hand and the shadow quickly vanished. The prisoner gasped for air.

"Let's try that again, shall we?" I used the tip of my blade to guide his chin upward, so he met my gaze. "Why?" I asked with a growl, baring my fangs.

"I won't tell you anything!" He bared his fangs right back.

Andrei appeared by my side. He grabbed the prisoner by his forehead and slammed his head into the cold, dark stone. He let out a groan, and the scent of fresh blood filled my nose before I watched it trickle down the wall.

"You may want to answer your prince's questions. You don't want this to get ugly," Andrei said as he leaned into the prisoner's ear.

"My Prince?" He scoffed. "He is a disgrace. He betrayed us for some faerie cunt!" He spat.

I chuckled and raised my dagger. The shadow held his head up and I watched fear flash in his eyes. I know he hoped for a quick death, but it would not come for him. I acted as if I was going to impale his heart, but at the last second, I took my blade and slowly dragged it from the nail in his palm down to his shoulder. He screamed, but the shadows returned and filled his mouth.

"I don't think anyone wants to hear him whine about a little cut," Xander said from behind me, in a voice so cold it even sent a shiver down my spine.

"Are you going to tell us what we want to know, or do I need to make the other arm match?"

Xander allowed him to struggle for a moment more before removing the shadows. He gasped for air once again.

"You better hurry," Andrei taunted, "our prince doesn't like waiting."

I lined my dagger up to his other palm and heard the sizzle of silver touching vampiric flesh.

"Wait! I'll tell you what you want to know," his voice was hoarse as he pleaded.

Andrei and I took a step back and looked down at him as we waited for him to continue. He told us how Dimitri had put this plan into motion the moment I left Titus after killing Nox, and nearly ruined his deal with Godrick. His plan was to ensure Sabrina was killed in the massacre. I had never been so glad to have removed her from the situation.

Originally, Dimitri had planned for the assassins to be disguised as guests, but when he heard of my proposal, he hatched a better plan. My blood boiled the more that he spoke.

"Dimitri is furious that you are in Serafina. He wants you all to himself. You are Titus's most dangerous weapon! He won't risk losing you."

I stepped back to the prisoner and locked eyes with him. "Now I am the most dangerous weapon in Serafina," I said with a deep chuckle as I plunged my silver blade into his heart. Blood spilled from his mouth, and I watched as the life left his eyes. When I was sure he was dead, I straightened my back, turned, and left the dungeon without a single word.

Forty-Seven

Sabrina

I threw myself into my work after the ceremony. I needed to keep myself busy, so I had no time to stop and think of the horrors that had occurred. I looked over the reports that Tristan had sent over from Nouavara, and my heart sank as I read of the trade caravans attacked, and villages near the borders burned. They definitely had a war brewing. I lifted my gaze when I heard the door open, and Daphne walked in.

"You know you can take days off. The kingdom will not fall apart if you relax for a single day," she said as she approached my desk, sitting down a mug with a vanilla latte. She and I thought there was nothing a caffeine boost couldn't solve. She was right. Whenever I had one, it always made me feel better. I took the mug and sipped from it.

"You know I have never been relaxed a day in my life."

Daphne chuckled and sat in the armchair across from my desk. "I know. You should really try it sometime. If you keep allowing yourself to be so stressed, you will wrinkle. Maybe go take a hot bubble bath!" I giggled in response. That did sound pretty nice right about now. "I was able to get more information on how to cure Darius' vampirism and the golden tree." She spoke in a more serious tone.

"Is it real?"

"Oh, it definitely is. It is very difficult to find, but I was able to get some information on how to get there and confirmation that it will cure Darius."

"How did you get this info?" I questioned. Daphne somehow was able to get information about everything. If she did not know something, she knew someone who did. She was also very tight-lipped about where she got her information.

She pressed her lips into a firm line and looked up in contemplation. Her gaze then met mine before she spoke. "Priestesses of Kori and Mortess had knowledge of the location of the tree and its power."

That evening I visited Darius. I gently knocked on the door and it swung open. He leaned against the door frame, shirtless, and heat rose to my cheeks as our eyes met. I swallowed hard as he smirked.

"My, my," he cooed, "such a naughty girl coming to a man's room so late at night."

"Oh, stop it! I am here to talk to you about something important."

"Oh, are you?" He raised an eyebrow. "Who comes to a man's room so late at night for 'important' things?" He leaned down so his face was just an inch from mine. "If you want to ride my cock, all you need to do is ask."

My eyes widened and my core heated. "Darius," I breathed.

"Say my name like that again, doll. I dare you."

"Daphne said she found a way to cure your vampirism," I said forcefully, trying to change the subject back to the initial reason I came to see him. Darius straightened his back.

"Really?" A look of shock overtook his face. I nodded and told him about the golden tree.

"We will go after the wedding. For now..." He wrapped his arm around my waist, lifted me off the ground, and threw me over his shoulder. "I don't think I can wait until our wedding night to have you again."

"Darius! Let me down! Where is Andrei?"

"I will put you down when I get you to a bed. Andrei is out. Be a good girl and stay quiet for me."

I blushed harder as Darius walked me into his room and shut his door with his foot. He reached behind him and locked the door just before tossing me onto the bed. The playful smile faded from his face.

In a serious tone, he spoke. "Strip." I obliged and took off the dress I was wearing. "Such a good girl." I blushed harder in response.

"Darius," I whimpered, and in a blink, he was on top of me. He grabbed my wrists and pinned me to the bed.

"I told you what would happen if you said my name like that again." He leaned down, pressed his lips to mine, and kissed me hungrily. I lifted my head and met his passion, but after a moment, he pulled his lips away. "Let me taste you," he breathed, and I nodded. He kissed his way to my neck and grazed his fangs against my skin.

A shiver shot down my spine, and a soft moan escaped my lips. Darius' fangs pierced my flesh and pleasure coursed through my body. One of his hands slipped down and under my panties. His fingers pressed against the most delicate part of me.

"Dar," I moaned as he pushed inside of me and coaxed my pleasure.

His lips finally pulled away from my neck. "You are so wet for me, doll." I arched my back, and he drove deeper inside me, and ecstasy built inside me. He slowly removed his fingers from me, and a trail of wetness connected his fingertips to my body. He brought his fingers to my lips and slipped them inside my mouth.

"Taste how sweet you are for me," he said as he brushed against my tongue. He pulled away from my mouth and quickly shoved them back inside my pussy. He thrust three times before he pulled them out and brought his fingers to his own lips and dragged his tongue up them. "So delicious," he groaned. "You didn't think I was going to let you keep your sweetness all to yourself, did you?"

"Darius, I need you," I pleaded.

"You need me?" He raised his eyebrow. "Use your words. Tell me how you need me."

"I need your touch. I need you deep inside me."

"I can't hear you," he purred.

"Darius, please!"

"Oh, alright. Since you said please like a good girl." He ripped my panties off of me, gripped my knees, and forced them apart. He pulled out his cock, lined himself up, and plunged himself deep inside me. I arched my back as he hit my most inner wall.

"Fuck yes!" I exclaimed as I gripped the sheets.

"Such a dirty mouth. Keep it up and I will have to fuck that next to punish you." He quickened his pace as he pressed his palm to my mouth. "The only things I want to hear are my name and your screams. Nod if you understand." I nodded in response. "Such a good girl."

He removed his hand and gripped the headboard as he continued to thrust inside me. My body quivered as I erupted from pleasure.

"Darius!" I screamed as my eyes rolled back into my head.

"Cum on my cock. Fuck, you feel so good," he groaned. The wood groaned as he gripped it tighter. As he continued to fuck me through my orgasm, his other hand reached down and squeezed my throat. "Mine. You are mine!"

"Yes! I am yours."

"And I am yours," he said as he slowed his pace. His cock twitched, and he spilled inside of me. He continued to push it deep, as he leaned down and kissed my forehead before releasing my throat. He pulled himself slowly out, and Darius fell to my side and pulled me to him.

"Darius," I breathed.

"Shh," he said as he pulled me close to him. "Enjoy tonight. We will worry about the weight of the world tomorrow."

Forty-Eight

Xander

My shadows clung to me as I paced through the abandoned cabin. I sent a letter directly after the ball, demanding that Dimitri meet with me. After three hours, that son of a bitch still had not shown up. If I had to storm Titus and give that asshole what he deserved, I would.

Finally, I heard the front door open, and I raced to it. Dimitri looked down at me with a pitched expression. "You wanted to see me?"

"What the fuck is wrong with you? Attacking Serafina was not a part of our deal!"

"I had to send a message," he chuckled under his breath. "I hope my son and your queen learned something."

"You fool! You brought them closer together!" I screamed at him. "You were supposed to make your son go mad and instead you attack my kingdom on one of the most important days of the year! You are lucky my queen shows mercy, or you would have a war on your hands."

"Oh?" He raised an eyebrow and took a step forward. "Is that a threat? What are you going to do, truly? I will tell the world your secret. I will tell your queen that you betrayed her. Who will have a war on their hands then?"

My shadows flared around me. "I don't know when or how, but you will pay for this."

He rolled his eyes in response. "Have your queen send a declaration of war." On his final word, he vanished.

Forty-Nine

Sabrina

Months passed, and the soft breeze of spring had transitioned to the scorching heat of summer, and the tithe was being held once again. I sat on my throne with Daphne in place and Darius sitting on the arm of my throne.

Xander had not been seen for a few months at this point. I had so much going on that I did not care where he was. I did not have the time to care.

The Elders joined us in the throne room. They had still not fully warmed up to Darius, as I had hoped. Vulcan gave Darius a sideways glance before whispering something to Petra. Orlok had his gaze glued to Darius, anger seeded in his eyes.

"Does he need to be here?" Vulcan finally spat.

"Yes. He is my soon-to-be husband, and this is the future of Serafina," I responded.

Vulcan opened his mouth to speak, but Darius spoke before he could. "I don't think that I should have to remind you about what happened last time someone disrespected our queen." He picked at his nails, not even lifting his gaze. The room fell silent, and I sat back in my throne, looked out at them, and waited.

"We should all show Queen Sabrina and her fiancée respect," Daphne said in a stern tone.

Daphne and I sat in my study later that evening. My desk was littered with fashion drawings and design mock-ups of dress options. On the floor sat fifteen different floral combinations. On the cart by the door sat a tray of twenty-seven cake flavors.

There was still so much to do and so little time to get everything together. My executive dysfunction had taken root. I could feel the frustration build as more decisions needed to be made.

"Sabrina, take a deep breath," Daphne said softly as she gathered the papers from my desk. "I will take care of everything. I will make your wedding perfect."

"Thank you. This is just too much for me to handle." I said as I leaned back into my seat. I looked up at her and sighed. "Have you heard from Xander?"

"Not recently. He said he was searching to see if there are any more spies hidden within Serafina."

I relaxed a bit. At least I knew he was doing something to better Serafina. There was always a dark thought that lingered in the back of my mind while he was away. "Good luck to him. He is good at finding what is hidden in the shadows."

Fifty

Darius

I sat at the table in the library, tapping my fingers against it as I. bounced my knee anxiously. My heart felt as if it was about to burst out of my chest. Andrei gave me a sideways glance.

"Will you relax?" He said to me in an annoyed tone.

"When have you ever known me to be relaxed?"

"Good point." He put his hands up in surrender.

Everything weighed on this moment. I was far more nervous about what was about to happen compared to when I asked Sabrina to be my wife. We were getting so close to the wedding.

I had written one final letter to my father and let all of my feelings bleed onto the page. How I hated him for how he killed my mother, turned me into a weapon, and treated everyone around him like they were nothing. How I hoped Titus would burn to the ground. How from this moment forward, I would be free of him. I would be a better husband, a better father, a better man than he ever would be.

I set the letter a flame and freed myself from the anger and resentment that I have harbored for all these years.

I was pulled from my thoughts as the door to the library opened and the Elders walked in. They looked around, confused.

"Where is the queen?" Hale asked as they brushed a loose strand of hair from their face.

"She is not here. I am the one who summoned you." I stood and walked over to them.

"You cannot summon us at your leisure! We have villages that need our attention!" Orlok exclaimed.

"We cannot lie about the castle with our dicks out," Vulcan added with venom on his tongue.

I took a deep breath and released it through my mouth. Gods help me through this. "I summoned you because I need to speak with you all. Soon, I will be married to your queen, or have you forgotten?"

"And? That won't make you king. You won't be in charge," Orlok spat.

"No, you misunderstand me." I clenched my fists so tight my claws dug into my skin. "I do not want to be king. This is Sabrina's kingdom and your homeland. I understand, but also you have to understand that I truly love her. I have given up my crown for her. I just want to be by her side and keep her happy. There is no alternative motive."

"Darius," Nelda said softly. "Please understand, we have heard so much about you."

"How do we know that this all isn't some pretty little compulsion lie?" Vulcan shouted over Nelda before she could finish speaking.

I turned to the table and motioned to Andrei. He stood and moved some of the boxes off the table, and I grabbed the others. The two of us gave a box to each of the Elders.

"If I lie, use this on me."

I watched as they opened the boxes and looked in shock at the silver stakes in each box. They all looked up at me. It was Vulcan who spoke.

"Hopefully, we never have to," he said with a warm smile.

<h1 style="text-align:center">Fifty-One</h1>
<h2 style="text-align:center">Sabrina</h2>

I had forgotten one of my journals in my study, and rushed back from my room to return to it. When I saw the door to my study was slightly ajar, I paused and lifted an eyebrow. The door was always shut after I left. Before yanking the door open, I conjured a small ball of fire in my hand. I released the breath I was holding when I found the study empty.

Walking over to my desk to retrieve the journal, I found a folded piece of parchment sitting in the center of it. I picked it up and the scent of pine and cinnamon filled my nose. A smile crossed my face as I unfolded the paper.

My love,
Do me the honor and meet me in the east wing for a surprise.
Eternally yours,
Darius

Not wasting a second, I quickly made my way across the castle to the east wing. Music filled the halls of a soft piano melody. I followed it into a large sitting room and found Darius playing the piano. The rain gently tapped against the glass of the large window behind him and added to the music.

I stood in the doorway, listening and watching as he played. His fingers stroked each key with such precision. Darius' hair was pulled up, but a few pieces hung in his face and swung with the music. His eyes were closed as he swayed to the music he created. My heart melted as the music filled the room. It was the most beautiful melody I had ever heard.

An ache filled my chest as the music ended. Truly, that piece would live within my soul for the rest of my days. Darius turned toward me and offered a smile. "Did you like it?"

"I loved it. I did not know that you could play." I walked over and sat next to him on the bench.

"My mother taught me before she passed away. She was a famous pianist in her youth before she was wed to Dimitri. I am glad you like it. I wrote it for you as an early wedding gift."

"It was absolutely beautiful."

"Just like you." He leaned in and gently kissed my lips. His tongue slipped into my mouth and danced with mine.

I scooted closer to him to close the gap between us, and he lifted me and had me straddle his lap as we continued to kiss. He thrust up and grinded against me. I could feel him through his pants, feel how ready he was for me. He picked me up and walked us over to the red velvet chaise in front of the fireplace.

He lifted my dress and pulled down my underwear. His lips parted from mine, and his warmth left me as he shifted onto his knees at the end of the chaise, grabbed my legs, and pulled me to the edge. Hunger filled his gaze as he looked up at me through his eyebrows.

"Please, my queen," a soft plea escaped his lips.

"Beg," I teased.

"Please let me taste you. I crave your sweetness. Allow me to drink from you and feast upon your soul."

My heart skipped a beat as he spoke. I nodded as words failed to escape my lips. He ran his tongue up my thigh and shuddered before sinking his fangs into my skin. Heat and pleasure flooded me as I arched my back and let him feed from me. Moans escaped my lips as he drank.

He pulled away from my thigh as my euphoria peaked and my head felt like it was in the clouds. He gently kissed the bite marks. Blood smeared on his bottom lip. "Your taste is so intoxicating," he groaned. "Now," he leaned in closer in between my thighs, "I get to eat this delicious little pussy of yours." He gripped my legs tighter to hold me in place before his tongue slowly dragged against my slit.

"Oh, gods," I moaned.

"Not gods. Me," he growled. "When you call for someone, you will scream my name." His tongue found my clit and quickly flicked against it, and two fingers slowly push inside me. My eyes rolled back into my head as his tongue and fingers met in rhythm. It was not long until I found my release.

Darius pulled his fingers from me. "Let's practice," he said as he freed his cock and lined himself up with me. "When I fuck your pretty little pussy, scream my name like the good girl you are." In one thrust, his full length entered me.

"Darius!"

"Good girl," he purred. "Again." He slowly pulled out to the tip before himself into me once again.

I screamed his name, and he fucked me harder and faster. Over and over, his name escaped my lips until my throat was coarse. My body quivered and my toes curled as I came undone. His pace slowed as he coaxed me through my orgasm. He leaned forward and pressed his lips to mine.

Pulling away, he also pulled his cock from me, leaving me feeling empty. Almost immediately, he grabbed my hips and flipped me over. My legs now hung off the chaise and my torso was pressed against the velvet cushion. He pushed my dress up once again and kept it bunched at my waist. Without warning, he plunged himself back into me, then gripped my hair and pulled it.

"Such a good girl. Take my cock," he demanded. He pulled my hair so hard that my neck craned. "Tell me how much you love being fucked by your vampire."

"I love being fucked by my vampire!" I repeated. "Please don't stop."

"Oh, I don't plan to until I break you, doll." He pressed himself deep inside me, and it twitched twice before he pounded into me once again.

I couldn't tell if the heat was from the fireplace roaring beside us, or from the passion between us. I found my pleasure three more times before he found his, and more heat flooded deep inside me.

"Darius," I panted. My body was overwhelmed by the pleasure.

He released my hair and leaned forward. His chest pressed against my back, and he gently kissed my ear. "Sabrina," he breathed. "You are my salvation."

Fifty-Two

Daphne

"No, No!" I exclaimed. "The flower wall is to be in front of the dais. Make sure the archway is centered on the Queen's throne."

The two men nodded and put it in place. Gods, I drew them an exact blueprint of how everything should be, but it was so hard to get good help these days. I turned to examine what was happening in the rest of the throne room. It was the night before Sabrina's wedding, and this would be the last time I could make sure everything was perfect for her special day.

I made sure there was enough seating for all the ceremony guests. The aisle runner was perfectly centered down the aisle under the large arched tunnel, the roof of which was variegated ivy. Workers frantically hung ivy and delicate white flowers on the pillars and archways that led into the gardens.

The room fell quiet as I locked eyes with my brother as he entered the room. Anger welled in my core. We had so much to do, and so little time. *Of course*, he would wait until the last moment to return. I could guarantee the look of worry plastered on his face was because he did not want to receive the tongue-lashing I was about to give him.

I marched over to him and furrowed my brow. "There you are! It is about time you showed up. Rein in your shadows, you are letting them spread and are making something so beautiful, very dark and gloomy!"

"Daphne," his voice trembled, "I need to speak with you. Now. I fucked up." His amber eyes met mine, and I saw the worry seeded deep within them.

"No! Not today you didn't!" I corrected him. "There is too much to do, and I will not allow you to ruin Sabrina's wedding. It's bad enough that you hate the groom. You can tell me all about your issues after the wedding!"

He took a deep breath and his shadows snapped back to him as he straightened his posture. Gods, mother would be so disappointed by how badly the God of Shadows slouched. I saw pain flicker in his eyes.

"You are right, dear sister. Tell me where I can help."

Fifty-Three

Darius

I jolted out of bed. My head ached and my mouth watered as the delicious scent of strawberries and cream filled my nose. Everything around me was in a haze.

I needed her now. I needed her blood.

Gods, I was so starving.

I staggered through my room and yanked open my door, and saw Andrei sitting in front of the fireplace. He stood as he turned to me. I watched his mouth move, but I couldn't hear the words.

The only thing in my head was the demand I find that faerie bitch and drain her dry.

Fifty-Four
Sabrina

I stood in front of the mirror, eyeing my dress. I tried so hard not to cry, knowing that it would ruin my makeup. The dress Daphne had chosen was perfect. The corseted sweetheart neckline bodice accentuated my shape. On my left shoulder sat a loose skinny strap with light pink flowers sewn on. The bodice was embroidered with similar flowers, and they trailed down the A-line tulle skirt.

"Daphne," I sighed. "This is more beautiful than I could ever imagine." I turned to her and gave a warm smile.

"I am so glad you love it, dear. You look truly radiant."

I turned to my jewelry tray and my eyes went wide. "Where are my bracelets? Daphne, you know I can't go out in public without my bracelets!" Panic rose within me, and my skin grew hot. Those bracelets were key to me controlling my magic. With my emotions running high today, they were needed now more than ever.

"Now, Now," she cooed. "I am sure one of the maids took them by mistake. Take a deep breath. Have another glass of wine." She poured a glass and motioned for me to sit. I did and took the glass from her, drinking the bright pink liquid. "Let me go check with them. I will return in just a moment."

I watched as she left the room. Without my bracelets, my magic threatened to destroy this entire castle. When I was young, it had gotten out of control so many times and caused so much damage. Maybe now that I was nearly twenty-one, I had gained control of my magic. I couldn't feel it bubbling under the surface. I looked down at my hands and picked at my cuticles.

Today was the day. I was to be wed to Darius Dragomier. I thought back to the first time we had met. How rumors claimed he was a monster. How he was to destroy me and my kingdom. I learned that the true monster was his father. Darius was not going to be the destruction of my kingdom, but it's salvation.

Once we were wed, we planned to go to the golden tree immediately and cure him of his vampirism. Andrei as well, if he wished. After, I would go to war with Titus to free his people from the tyranny of their so-called king.

I felt that familiar tug on my heart. My head jerked up, and I saw Darius standing in the doorway.

"Dar, what are you doing? You know it's bad luck to see the bride in her wedding dress before the wedding." I jumped from my seat and hid behind a changing screen. I peeked my head out to look at him.

He stood in the doorway, silent. I could see his hands shaking. His eyes were a deep shade of red that I had never seen, and a pit formed in my stomach.

"Is everything ok?" I rushed towards him, taking his hands in mine. "Is it your father? Is he here?" I questioned.

In a blink, he had pounced on me and slammed me to the ground, pinning me in place. I squirmed under him. The struggle caused a side table to fall over, spilling the bright pink wine all over the white carpet.

"Darius, get off me! What are you doing?" I panicked. For the first time, I couldn't feel my magic. I was defenseless as he roughly grabbed my head and exposed my neck.

Before I could scream for help, his fangs were in my neck, and he held me tightly as he drained me dry. I tried to fight, but I felt myself getting weaker. Tears streamed down my face as soft whimpers escaped my throat. It wasn't long before the world grew fuzzy and everything faded to black.

Fifty-Five

Darius

Fuck, her blood was delicious. I couldn't stop. I did not want to. She was so sweet and intoxicating, and drank from her supple flesh until her cries went silent and there was nothing left. I pulled away from her neck and looked down at her body.

Her bright blue eyes were distant, devoid of the light I grew to love.

That's when it hit me.

What had I done?

"Sabrina?" I cried out. Tears flowed from my eyes. I lifted her and held her limp body to mine, begging her to come back to me. I laid her back down and bit into my wrist. I pressed it to her lips, hoping she would drink. "Sabrina! Please!" My tears fell onto her body as I pressed my wrist firmly into her open mouth. The blood smeared as her head turned and fell to the side. My chest felt as if it had cracked. A hollow feeling filled my soul. I heard a crash from behind me.

I turned and saw Daphne and Xander in the doorway. Looks of horror were all over their faces. Glasses were now shattered on the floor at their feet. They leaped over the broken glass and knelt beside us, and Xander pushed me out of the way.

He glared back at me as he growled, "What did you do?"

Daphne's wails filled the air as I watched a faint light form around her and then Sabrina. She screamed into the sky for the gods' help, but her calls went unanswered.

Sabrina was gone, and I was the monster everyone said I was.

Fifty-Six
Andrei

Serafina was in chaos. The citizens demanded blood. Darius felt destroyed by what he had done. I had caught him that night with a silver stake to his chest, and was able to stop him just before he could plunge it into him.

After that, he locked himself in the Serafina dungeon to keep himself from hurting anyone else. Daphne and Xander had taken over as Regents until the next queen was born. They made sure the dungeons stayed clear. Guards wielding silver weapons were posted at the entrance.

I wasn't sure if that was to protect Darius, or if that was to make him suffer for what he had done.

I traveled down into the dungeon and found Darius sitting on the floor of his cell. His hair was loose around his face, and his eyes were sunken in. He had refused to feed, even from animals. As I stood at the bars, and my heart broke for him.

Darius was not the monster he pretended to be in Titus. I had seen his heart. With what I now knew, everything made sense.

"Darius, this came for you."

He barely lifted his gaze to look at me. "Go away."

"No, Darius. Please." I forced some aggression into my tone. "Read it."

He stood and, in an instant, met me at the bars. He took the paper and unfolded it. Rage contorted his face the more he read. His green eyes shifted to red as he looked up at me once again, crumpling the letter in his fist.

"It is time we return to Titus," he said in a cold and distant voice. He grabbed the cell bars and forced them apart. Stepping out of the cell, he turned to exit the dungeon.

I followed him, as I would until the very end.

Fifty-Seven

Daphne

The Queen's death was never easy. Through the centuries, I have seen so many queens rise and fall to power. None of them I loved or cherished as much as my Sabrina.

She had been the true embodiment of good and innocence. She did not want land, wealth, or fame. She wanted to do good by the people of Serafina. By how many people attended her funeral, I would say she did not do just that, but beyond it.

Rain poured and lightning cracked across the sky. It was Vulcan that lit the pyre in her honor. One by one, each of the Elders spoke to the crowd and told stories of what a wonderful young woman Sabrina grew to be. Unaffected by the rain, the fire flared as they spoke, as if she was still with us, laughing at the stories from the beyond. For the first time in centuries, I cried. I was glad that the rain fell to wash away my tears.

Though, there was nothing I could do to wash the pain off my heart.

Xander came to my side, reaching for my hand, but I snatched it away as his fingertips barely made contact. Xander disgusted me with what he had done.

I would never forgive him and prayed that the gods would give him what he deserved. "Don't touch me," I spat. "This is all your fault."

Fifty-Eight

Draven

I sat alone in the abandoned cabin. There was something so peaceful about the silent stillness that lived within these walls. Gently rocking in the chair, I looked up at the sky through the hole in the roof.

Today was Queen Sabrina's funeral, and I wondered what kind of chaos was ensuing at the castle. I would have paid to watch the vampire prince murder the queen. Anyone who chose a vampire over her own people deserved to die.

I heard the wood creek and saw the vampire king standing in the doorway. His cane centered on the floor, and he used both hands to hold the red obsidian orb.

"It is done. Once they cross the border the God of Shadows will go mad."

"Perfect," I purred. "And the next queen is to be born in Titus?"

Dimitri let out a wicked chuckle. "Yes, the mother is already in my dungeon."

I stood and walked past him, leaving the cabin. "Perfect. Time for me to play."

Fifty-Nine

Sabrina

I tossed and turned all night. The city of Titus had been so hot this year compared to years past. Heat washed over my body as I tried to get comfortable.

Tomorrow would be my eighteenth birthday, and I had big plans. I was to meet the man that my parents had chosen for me to marry. He lived just outside the city and earned a good living as a blacksmith. I would be safe from the vampires once I moved, and I truly looked forward to it.

I heard the distant toll of the clock tower signaling it was midnight, and felt a pull on my heart as I shot up from my bed. At the foot of the bed stood the man from my nightmares. This had to be another nightmare, but something about it felt so real. His face was shrouded by shadows. All I could see were his fangs and blood-red eyes. As soon as our eyes locked, he pounced, pinning me to the bed.

I let out a scream as he sank his fangs into my neck, then everything went black.

Epilogue
Sabrina

Centuries later...

It had been a full year since I reclaimed my throne and Serafina had regained its magic. Darius had returned to Titus several months ago to rule his kingdom. I missed him endlessly. However, he had traveled back here several times to reunite with me. Those were my favorite times, but I ached whenever he had to leave.

The Vernal Equinox was upon us once again. We were still nowhere close to being able to return to the lavish balls we once held, but it did not stop us from having a small gathering between friends. In the center of the throne room ran a long rectangular table decorated with flowers, ivy, and the most beautiful butterflies made of light. Joy filled me as I saw everyone seated at the table.

Isa and Andrei were absolutely glowing. The two of them had gotten wed just a month before. Isa and I had fully repaired our relationship, and I was so glad to be best friends again.

Daphne and Ron were in the corner of the room arguing, but quickly cut it out and took their seats as I entered. Ron had a hard time adjusting to his new role of the God of Shadows, and an even harder time without his father's guidance.

Silas, Cora, and Archer had grown close as well. The fae who lived in Titus were relocated to Tasumanza and reunited with our people. The three of them had worked closely to ensure that everyone was adjusting to returning home, and the new technology that was brought from Titus.

Orlok, Morgana, Tamir, and Carlow had worked together to reconnect the people of Serafina with each other. A road system was put in place to easily connect the lost people. I opened up the castle weekly for citizens to come and voice their concerns to make sure everyone was safe and happy.

Darius approached me with a smile. "Hello, my love. Happy birthday." He pressed a gentle kiss to my cheek, took my hand, and guided me to the table. "May I have everyone's attention?" He called out. All eyes fell on him. "This year has truly been a challenge for all of us. I want to thank you for helping restore Serafina to the magnificent land it once was. Our work will never truly be done, but for tonight let us all celebrate Queen Sabrina." Everyone cheered. "Before the evening begins, I want to bestow a gift upon our beautiful queen, and ask that she bestows one to me in return." He pulled out a folded piece of parchment from his breast pocket.

I took it from him and unfolded it. I gazed down at the blueprint for a castle and looked up at him, confused.

"What is this?"

"This, my dear, is our new home. Built on the border of Serafina and Titus. May we never spend another night apart."

My eyes widened. "You..." I stuttered, "You are building us a castle?"

"It is already built and ready for you to move in whenever you wish."

"How did you build an entire castle without me knowing?"

"He had some help," Daphne chuckled. I found myself giggling in response.

"Of course, he did," I smiled, getting up on my tippy toes to kiss his cheek. "And of course, you would ask me for a gift on my birthday." I rolled my eyes and the room filled with laughter.

"It would be the greatest gift you could give me."

"What is that?" I raised my eyebrow. My heart skipped a beat as he got down on one knee and pulled out a small ring box. He opened the box and revealed my ring from all those years ago.

"Please, would you do me the honor and be my bride?"

My eyes went wide as I brought my hand to my mouth as I gasped. "Darius, where did you find that?"

"I have held onto it for centuries, for this very moment. I knew the gods would bring us together again."

"I will, but you have to make a promise to me."

"What is that?"

"Please don't kill me this time."

"Never again, my love."

That was one of the best dinners I had ever had. Not only was the food delicious, but I was surrounded by friends and family that truly loved and cared for me.

Darius and I laid in bed, with my head on his chest. He held me close. I had a secret that I had now held onto for far too long.

"Darius," I said softly as I sat up. He sat up as well and looked down at me with concern in his eyes.

"Yes? Is everything ok?"

"Oh, it's perfect..." I trailed off, looking down at the sheets. He gently grabbed my chin and lifted my gaze.

"What is it? Sabrina, tell me," he pleaded.

"I have another gift for you,"

"A gift for me?" A look of shock took over the worry that was on his face. "Sabrina, it is your birthday. You did not have to buy me anything."

"No, it's nothing like that." I was so afraid to tell him. Anxiety welled in my chest, and I just blurted it out. "I am pregnant!"

"What did you say?" He asked so softly. I couldn't tell his emotion based on the blank stare he was giving me.

"I am pregnant," I said again.

Darius quickly pulled me into his arms and held me tight. "Oh, that is the greatest thing you could have ever told me! I am so lucky not only to have the gods bless me with you as my wife, but also for you to bring us a beautiful child into this world." He kissed me hard, then pulled away. His green eyes misted over as he smiled wider than I had ever seen on anyone. "Do you know what we are having?"

"A girl," I said with a smile.

"Perfect."

The End.

Blood Equinox
A Blood Singer Short Story
Willow Asteria

The Fated

One

I awoke to the sound of a blaring horn filling the air. This was only sounded when there were official announcements by the King that were being declared. Typically those were mid-day. The fact that the sun barely kissed the sky gave me cause to worry. Never had an announcement been made this early in the morning.

I jumped out of bed, took off my night clothes, and put on a simple tunic dress. I rushed down the cottage's stairs while braiding my long, black hair.

My mother and I nearly crashed into each other as we met at the front door.

"Where is father?" I questioned.

Mother was already in perfect condition this morning. Her hair was in a neat bun atop her head, her face was perfectly made up. Her dark blue dress looked as if she was about to go meet the King himself, not one of his messengers.

"He must already be in the town square. He went into the office early this morning," she said as she glared at me. I could tell in her soft gray eyes that she was disappointed that I was not as prepared for the day as she was. She always wanted me to look perfect every second of the day. In her eyes, if your hair and face were not done, you were not presentable. My father was the mayor of this town, Anoria, she always wanted us to look our best for him. Anoria was to always see us at our best, our perfect little family.

Mother and I joined the crowded streets and headed to the town square. Father and a small, hunched-back man stood on the platform in the center of the square. Father wore a black coat with dark blue embroidery that matched the color of my mother's dress. His eyes fell on me and I swore I saw a tinge of worry in them before he looked at my mother and waved us up. We walked through the crowd who were demanding answers about what was going on. We stepped up onto the platform and stood on either side of father, and he wrapped his arms around us.

"Good morning good people of Anoria!" He announced to the crowd. "I apologize for the early morning call, but King Dimitri has sent to us an urgent message. I was told that it could not wait until a later hour." My father motioned to the messenger. He unraveled a large scroll and began to read from it.

"Citizens of Titus," he cleared his throat. "My son, Darius Edward Alexander Dragomeir, is in search of a wife. This Spring Equinox a ball will be held for him to select a bride. All women who are turning of age this year are to attend, human and vampire alike. All eligible women are to leave with the messenger immediately and be taken to the

City of Titus. Families are not to attend. Any woman turning of age who does not attend will be executed. Please note there is a theme, as this ball will be a masquerade. We look forward to meeting you, and congratulations to the lucky girl who is chosen as the Prince's bride"

The crowd fell silent. My father wrapped his arm around me tighter. I looked at him and mother and saw their eyes misted with tears.

The Prince was a deadly monster. Whoever he picked to be his bride was the most unlucky girl in the world. With my birthday falling on the equinox, I was one of those unlucky girls who were now at his mercy.

"According to our records, three girls are turning of age this year," the messenger began to speak again, and my head turned toward him. "You have thirty minutes to prepare for departure."

Two

"This will be a wonderful opportunity for the family to move up in society. Humans have not been invited to the castle in hundreds of years!" My mother said in a high-pitched tone. I could tell she was hiding her true feelings regarding this. I watched a single tear fall down her face as she zipped up my suitcase. She turned to me and gave me a weak smile. "Sabrina," she breathed, stepping closer to me. Her hands cupped my cheeks as she leaned down and planted a kiss on my forehead. "Just be your true self, and I am sure everything will be fine," she whispered.

"I will make sure to stay away from him during the ball. He cannot pick me to be his bride if we never meet."

"That is a wise plan, my dear."

She released me and turned back to the suitcase and picked it up. She walked out of the room and motioned for me to follow her. My father sat at the kitchen table and stood as we entered the room. He rushed over to me and wrapped me in a tight hug.

"Oh, pumpkin," he choked on his words.

"Father, it's ok. I will make sure to stay away from him. I will return home."

"Gods, I hope so." He pulled out of the tight embrace and held my shoulders. "If anything happens to you-"

"Don't think about that," I cut him off. Before anyone could say anything else, there was a firm knock on the door.

"It's time!" The messenger's voice called out from behind the door. I gave my parents a final hug as I picked up my suitcase.

"I will see you soon," I said over my shoulder as I headed out the door.

Annabelle and Mirabelle were horrid creatures. The twins sat across from me in the carriage gossiping and giggling the entire ride to the city. Neither of them seemed to care that we were on our way to not only one of the most dangerous places in all of Titus, but we would be right in the belly of the beast. Darius had killed hundreds of people in my lifetime. His reign of terror was well known across Titus.

He took what he wanted, and killed who he wanted.

"You should stay out of our way when we get to the city," Mirabelle sneered at me.

"Darius is going to choose one of us," Annabelle added as she twirled her blonde ringlets around her finger.

"Or both of us," Mirabelle giggled.

I rolled my eyes in response. "I plan to stay as far away from him as possible. Have at him."

"You should be more grateful for this opportunity!" Annabelle's voice was like nails on a chalkboard.

"Whoever marries Darius will be the next Queen of Titus!" Mirabelle snapped in my direction.

I looked back toward them and shook my head. I spent much of my free time in the town's library and read many books regarding the royal family. There was always a pattern with the Queen of Titus, she always died shortly after the heir to the throne was born. I always wondered if it was a vampiric trait that caused this, or if something more nefarious had occurred. Knowing the atrocities the Dragomeir family had committed, I wouldn't be surprised if it was the latter.

"No worries. If you do not take this honor seriously, it is just one less girl for us to compete with," the twins said in unison, turning up their noses at me.

Three

We arrived to Titus three days before the ball. Once we arrived we were taken to the east wing of the castle and put into private rooms. The guards informed us that we were not to leave our rooms until instructed and that everything we needed would be brought to us.

A guard stood out every bedroom door to make sure that we all stayed compliant. I felt more like a prisoner than a guest. The room was larger than I expected. A four-post bed was centered along the back wall. The walls were painted a dark gray and the wooden floors matched in darkness. The gray tones were broken up by a plush red rug and red and gold tapestries that hung on the walls. A fireplace was nestled into the right wall, a fire already going, but the room still felt cold. The left wall was filled with a built-in bookshelf filled with tomes. A mahogany dresser sat next to the bed. I sighed and began to unpack my suitcase.

I heard my door open and I spun to see who it was. A tall man stood in the open doorway, he pushed his blonde hair out of his face and looked down at me with his bright blue eyes, a look of shock overtook them as our eyes met.

"Can I help you? I thought knocking was customary," I snarled at him. He looked as if I had slapped him then cleared his throat.

"Good evening. I am here to check everyone in." He looked at me up and down, I swore I saw a flash of sadness in his eyes. "What is your name and where are you from?"

"Sabrina Delmazzi. I am from Anoria."

"Delmazzi..." his voice trailed off as he wrote on his clipboard. His eyes then rose to meet mine once again. He shut the door and stepped closer. "Do I know you from somewhere?" My heart skipped a beat. I had never spoken to a vampire, let alone been this close to one.

"Unless you have been to Anoria, I do not believe so," I whimpered.

"No, never. I don't look familiar at all to you?"

I shook my head. "Should you?"

"No," he chuckled. "I suppose not." He turned back to the door and opened it. "My name is Andrei, if you need anything please have your guard call for me."

Four

S creams awoke me from my slumber. I shot up and looked around and found that I was back in Anoria. Did the ball already happen? How did I get back here? My head was pounding and everything was so hazy.

I rushed to the window still in my nightgown. The sky was blood red and the full moon was just rising over the mountain tops. I looked down and my stomach churned as I saw the dead bodies that littered the street. I heard a crash from downstairs. Against my better judgment, I rushed downstairs to see what had happened. The front door had been ripped off the frame and it now lay in the center of the floor.

"Where is she?" I heard a rough masculine voice from the next room. His voice sounded so familiar, but I could not place where I had heard it before. Hearing it sent a chill down my spine that caused me to pause at the foot of the stairs

"I will never give her to you!" I heard my father cry out. It was then silent for a moment before I heard my father scream in agony, then a thud.

Panic filled my chest and I felt tears threaten my eyes. Like a moth drawn to a flame, I could not stop myself from continuing my way into the kitchen. My eyes went wide and I bent over and released the contents of my stomach as I saw my parents on the floor. Their lifeless eyes stared out, their skin drained of all color. Blood pooled beneath them.

I straightened and stepped forward, only to collapse to my knees before them.

"Mother? Father?" I sobbed. I shook them firmly. Their limp bodies move to reveal the bite marks on their necks. "No! No! No!" I sobbed.

I felt a firm grip on my shoulder.

"There you are, doll. I have been looking everywhere for you." It was that rough masculine voice once again. I felt his other hand grab me by my hair and yank me up. I screamed and tried to pull away, but his grip tightened and he spun me around to face him. I froze as my eyes locked with his. They were blood red and filled with hunger.

He gave me a predatory smirk and revealed his fangs, and blood dripped from the corner of his mouth.

He leaned forward and a few stands of dark hair fell in front of his face. He put his face into my neck and took a deep breath. My body stiffened as he ran his tongue over the skin.

"Let me go!" I demanded and tried again to pull away. He pulled me in closer and held me so tight I lost my breath.

"Never," he growled and sunk his fangs into my skin.

487

Five

I awoke in a cold sweat and my heart pounded in my chest. Just a dream, I kept reminding myself. I swallowed hard and wiped away the tears that flowed down my face. I got up from the bed and entered the adjoining bathroom. I turned on the sink and let the water run cold before splashing some on my face.

I could still feel his hands on my body and his fangs on my neck. The look in his eyes burned into me, and I could not shake away the feeling. Who was that man? He looks so familiar, as if I had seen his face hundreds of times. I prayed that I would never see it again. I turned off the water and dried my face with the plush black towel.

I crawled back into bed and stared up at the ceiling, trying to get the vision of his red eyes out of my mind.

Morning could not have come fast enough. As soon as I began to drift asleep I felt his fangs in my skin and I jolted away. A soft knock sounded on the door. I sat up, using the silk sheet to cover myself. I prayed it wasn't Andrei again. I did not like the look in his eyes either.

"Who is it?" I called out.

"I am your seamstress, it is time for your dress fitting." It was a soft feminine voice that spoke. I told her to come in. She opened the door and rolled in a rack with a dress hung in a linen bag, and a cart of supplies. "Good morning." She was a small woman with olive skin and short dark curly hair. Something about her presence gave me a warm and safe feeling.

"Good morning!"

"I am sorry to arrive so early. Such a busy schedule today! You, darling, are my first fitting." She moved a circular platform into the center of the room. "Please come stand on the stool so I can take your measurements." I got out of bed and got up on the platform. I looked down at her and watched as he began to take my measurements. She looked up at me and gave me a small smile. She stood and walked over to the door, opened it, and asked the guard to have a vanilla latte sent to the room. "There is no problem a good latte can not solve, Hopefully, it will assuage your nerves."

"Thank you," I said to her. Vanilla lattes were my favorite. Something deep inside me told me that I should not be surprised that she knew that about me. I wanted to question it but decided not to. Everything here was strange. A strange sense of deja vu washed over me.

She walked back to me, leaving the door open, and continued to take my measurements. "My name is Daphne by the way. You are going to love the dress that was selected for you."

"I am very excited to see it. This is the first time I have ever been to a ball, let alone a masquerade."

Daphne chuckled under her breath as she went over to the rack and began to open the linen bag and revealed a sage green tulle dress with golden flower embroidery on the bell sleeves. It was the most beautiful dress I have ever seen.

"It is already almost your size. Go ahead and slip it on and we will work on the final alterations."

Just as she said that one of the maids came in.

"Excuse me," she said softly. I looked over to her and she had a mug in her hand. "Did you request a latte?"

Daphne spun and took the mug from her. She then skipped to me and nearly shoved it in my hands.

"Drink, child," she said with a smile.

Six

I t was finally the night of the ball. The ball started at 8 pm and was to go until the early
hours of the morning. When the clock struck midnight I would be of age. This will
honestly be the most interesting birthday I would ever have. All I needed to do was avoid
the King and Prince during the ball.

Daphne came into my room with my dress just an hour before the ball was to start.
Two extremely beautiful women followed her in.

"Sabrina, meet Shay and Lana. They will get you ready for the ball." Daphne motioned
to each of them as she named them.

"Hello Lady Sabrina," they said in unison. The two of them stepped closer and Shay
picked up a piece of my hair and Lana placed a finger under my chin to lift it to get a better
look at my bone structure.

"Your hair is like silk," Shay said in shock.

"You have extremely beautifully high cheekbones! I can't wait to place some highlighter
right here," Lana said as she gently stroked her finger to the top of my cheekbones.

I blushed as they talked about how beautiful I was. They were the epitome of beauty.
Shay was very tall and had shoulder-length curly hair, her light-brown skin was so glowy
it looked as if she had stepped out of the sun, and her golden eyes were the sun itself. Lana
was about my height, had an angular bob with dark roots and teal ends, and her makeup
was flawless. The dark smokey eye and the bright red lip stood out against her fair skin.

"Beauty fit for a Queen. Don't you think?" Daphne asked them and the two women
agreed.

The three of them worked diligently to prepare me for the ball.

When they were done, they blindfolded me and guided me over to a full-length mirror.

"Are you ready?" Daphne asked.

"Oh she's not ready for this," Shay and Lana said in unison.

Gooseflesh took over my body as the anticipation built. I couldn't wait to see what I looked like. I was not allowed to see what had been done to my hair or makeup during the entire time they got me ready. The blindfold was removed and my jaw dropped. I had never seen myself so beautiful before. My hair was in a long side braid, with tiny flowers woven in, and a few pieces loose to frame my face. A delicate rouge adorned my cheeks and a rose gold sparkle sat top my cheekbones. My lips were a soft rosy nude shade. My dress was a perfect fit. I did not think I would ever wear anything so beautiful ever again. I raised my hand and gently brushed against the green iridescent butterfly wings that hung from my ears.

Daphne put her finger under my chin and lifted it to shut my mouth.

"Sabrina, dear. Stop that, or you will get flies," she chuckled.

My eyes welled with tears as I began to thank them.

"No! Stop that! You will mess up your makeup!" Lana shouted. I held back the tears from falling and hugged her, then Shay, then Daphne.

"Thank you. I never imagined how beautiful I would look!"

"Remember, child," Daphne began. "True beauty shines from within. Do not let anyone dim your light." Her face turned grave as there was a knock on the door and it opened. Andrei stood in the doorway and I caught the glare she gave him.

"Come along, Sabrina. The ball will begin soon," he said in a cold and collected voice.

"I thought I was to escort her," Daphne questioned.

"Change of plans. Sabrina, Let's go."

"Andrei, no!" Daphne cried out. I looked over at her. What was going on? Why was she so against me going with him?

"Daphne, you know I can not refuse him."

"You are a fool!" She spat. She turned to me and hugged me tight. "I will see you in another life. I love you," she whispered in my ear. She pulled away and tears were streaming down her face. I looked at her with confusion and shock. Before I could say anything she ran out the door.

"Are you ready?" Andrei questioned. I stood there wide-eyed and looked toward him. "Don't mind her. She is crazy. If she wasn't one of the best seamstresses in the kingdom the King would have executed her by now."

I said my final goodbyes to Shay and Lana and followed Andrei out the door. The hall was lined with guards who stood in front of each doorway. Every single one of them avoided looking at us.

"The other girls aren't coming?" I questioned.

Andrei chuckled. "Where I am taking you? No, absolutely not."

A lump formed in my throat. "Where are you taking me?"

He stopped and turned to me, leaning down to look me directly in the eyes. "Be quiet and come along."

I could no longer speak. I tried to force out the words, but nothing left my lips. Andrei turned back and continued to walk down the hall. I followed him even though I screamed at my body to stop. Each step caused blood to pulse in my ears. My vision tunneled, everything became so blurry and dark. I felt as if I was going to fall apart. A familiar voice snapped me out of my own head.

"Thank you, Andrei. You are dismissed. It's good to see you again, doll."

Seven

"It's..." my words jammed in my throat. My eyes locked on the man from my nightmare. At least I thought it was. He looked identical in every way, except for his eyes that shined through his black mask. They were now a bright emerald green. "It's you," I whimpered as I finally forced out the words.

I wanted to run, to scream, but something deep inside me wanted me to get closer to him. I hated to admit how handsome he was, especially in his black suit with red embroidery. The scent of pine and cinnamon washed over me, causing me to crave him.

The predatory smirk dropped from his face and his eyes widened. In a blink he was directly in front of me, causing my body to tense. "You... remember me?" His voice was soft and he raised his hand to attempt to touch my cheek. I flinched away to escape his touch.

"Don't touch me you monster!" I cried out. The man staggered back. I couldn't tell if it was anger or sadness that flashed across his features before that predatory smile returned to his features.

"Oh, doll," he chuckled. "That's no way to speak to the Prince of Titus."

My heart stopped. The man from my nightmare, the man in front of me, was the man I was to avoid at all costs during the ball. He took another step forward to close the gap between us. I was frozen as he gently held my chin and lifted it.

"Oh, Sabrina. You really cannot sit here and tell me you do not want me to touch you. I can feel your heart race." He leaned down, his lips just a hair away from brushing against mine. "Lie to me again. Your lies taste delicious," he purred.

My heart skipped a beat and I felt my core heat. Everything inside of me screamed for me to close the gap between our lips. I swallowed hard and pulled away. His arm wrapped around me and pressed into the small of my back. He took in another deep breath, as he just held me there without another word.

"What do you want with me?" I said weakly.

He laughed again, finally releasing me. "Well, what did the invitation to the ball say?"

"No," was the only word that escaped my lips. Had he already decided for me to be his bride? How could he decide that? Was that truly him in my dream?

"It is too late," he said nonchalantly. "You are already mine. I am already yours. We made that promise to each other lifetimes ago."

"What do you mean?" I raised an eyebrow at him.

"Oh don't worry your pretty little head about that. Once the clock strikes midnight, none of this will matter." Darius went over and sat in a red velvet armchair that sat in front of a roaring fire.

"Why not?"

"Gods, you are annoying. You ask too many questions. Do you see that silver dome?" He pointed over to a table where the dome sat. I nodded. "That is for you. I had it specially made. Seeing as this is your last meal, you should at least enjoy it."

"My last meal? What do you mean? Let me go!" I demanded.

Darius stood from his chair and rushed over to me. He grabbed me by my wrist and pulled me to the table, he sat in the chair and pulled me into his lap, with one arm wrapped around me to keep me in place. He removed the dome and revealed a chicken breast stuffed with what looked like broccoli and cheese with a side of mashed potatoes. I could not lie that it smelled delicious and my mouth watered at the sight of it. I watched as Darius grabbed a fork and cut into the chicken and brought a piece to my mouth.

"Open," he demanded. I obliged. He put the piece into my mouth and my taste buds flooded with the flavor. It was absolutely delicious. "Such a good girl, doing as you are told. Can you eat the rest without force?"

I nodded in response and took the fork from him. I wanted to hate being in his lap—being this close to him, but something about it felt so right. Like two puzzle pieces that fit together perfectly. Somehow during that interaction, he made me forget what he had said.

This would be my final meal, and that thought made a chill run down my spine.

I heard the door open from behind us. Both Darius and I turned our heads to look. Andrei stood in the doorway.

"Sorry to interrupt, but the King requests your presence immediately," he said.

Darius let out a groan, He gently picked me up as he stood and then placed me back into the chair.

"Finish your dinner. I will see you at the ball," he said to me before turning away and heading toward the door. He stopped right before Andrei. "Watch her, and then escort her to the ball when she is done eating."

"Yes, my Lord."

Eight

Darius

White hot rage ran through me. She was so close. She was mine. My heart tore into two as she looked me in the eyes and called me a monster. I let myself hope for just a moment that when she said 'it's you' that she remembered me— remembered us.

"You are a sick bastard!" I screamed at him as I stormed into Dimitri's study.

"Whatever do you mean? I thought you would love having a masquerade to find your bride. Isn't how you found your first one?" An evil grin grew across his face. "I heard there is a very beautiful girl from Anoria in attendance. According to reports she looks just like that faerie whore."

"She is not a whore! She is my wife and I love her. I will find a way to break this curse and rid this world of you!" I exploded. The papers and books went flying as the desk flipped into the air. Dimitri jumped from his seat and slammed me into the wall and held me by my throat. A wave of pain shot down my spine as Dimitri leaned in and looked me in the eyes.

"Enough!" He spat. "I will see you in the ballroom in fifteen minutes. I can't wait to watch you rip out her throat at midnight." He released me and in a blink, he was gone.

Nine
Sabrina

Once I finished the meal, Andrei guided me to the ballroom. It was already flooded with women from all over Titus. The only men were the King and Prince who sat on an upper level balcony. The King sat back on his throne, a satisfied look on his face.

Darius had his eyes glued to me. I froze as our eyes locked.

Go. Enjoy your night. don't just stand there and look at me all night.

I heard his voice in the back of my mind. I blinked hard. Was that really him, or a trick of my mind?

"There you are!" I heard a familiar screech. I spun and saw Annabelle and Mirabelle coming toward me. Both wore identical red satin dresses. Mirabelle wore a white mask and Annabelle a black mask.

"Isn't he handsome?" Mirabelle asked, motioning with her eyes to the Prince.

"Handsome and soon to be mine," Anabelle added.

"Ours," Mirabelle spat. "Oh! He's looking this way!" The two of them smiled up at him and curtsied.

I chuckled under my breath. I could feel his eyes on me. If only they knew what he had just told me during our encounter. Not that I wanted to be his bride— to be his.

Or wanted him to be mine.

I felt a tug on my heart. I looked up toward the balcony and Darius and the King were both gone. I heard the twins gasp, and my head spun to look at them.

"It's an honor to meet you!" They said, looking past me. I did not need to turn to see who they were talking to, as I could feel his presence from behind me. I turned to face him.

"I would be honored if you would let me have this dance," he said looking down at me, completely ignoring the twins.

Heat rose to my cheeks as he took my hand and gently kissed the back of it. I heard the twins hiss from behind me. Darius looked through his brows at them, and gods if looks could kill. The sounds of their heels hitting the floor rang in my ear as I heard them run off.

"A dance? With a girl who is going to die?"

"Humor me," he said coldly.

"Will you answer my questions?" Something stirred within me. I don't know why, but I was not afraid of death. As soon as he told me I was going to die, a part of me welcomed it. This was odd since I had never once been ready to die. I am not sure if I was ready now, but I knew I wasn't afraid.

"Yes, but we need to be quiet about it."

I allowed him to lead me into the next dance. He gently took my left hand and wrapped his arm around me to pull me close. My right hand rested on his chest. I could feel the entire room watching us.

"How do you know that I am going to die?"

"Because I am going to kill you when the clock strikes midnight."

My heart skipped a beat at his answer. His voice was so cold and distant. He pulled me in tighter. I breathed in his scent and my body set on fire.

"Why?" I whimpered after a moment of silence.

"Long ago, you were Queen of the Fae. We fell in love and I betrayed my father. I was ready to burn the world for you. He did not take kindly to that. He placed a curse on us that causes me to kill you on your eighteenth birthday, only for you to reincarnate and repeat the cycle."

"How many times?"

"This is your fourth life," he said softly, his voice cracking. "He orchestrated this entire ball just so he could watch me kill you. I will not give him that satisfaction."

I heard a large crash from behind me. I spun and saw all of the servers that had been walking around with serving trays had dropped dead. Their trays, hors d'oeuvres, and drinks were scattered on the floor. Several of the guests had also begun to fall. Darius grabbed me by the wrist and began to run, pulling me with him.

"Close the exits! The food has been poisoned!" One of the guards called out.

Andrei appeared seemingly out of nowhere. "Let's go. I cleared out the west hall."

"Did you kill all of those people?" I cried out to him.

"Yes," Darius said without a care. He continued to pull me into an empty hall. "I had to. Otherwise, I would not have been able to get you out of there."

I tried to pull from his grip, but he just held me tighter. He hit his fist against the wall and the stone pressed in, causing the wall to slide open and reveal a secret passageway.

"I will see you later, Dar. I have to do damage control," Andrei said.

"Good luck," he said as he pulled me into the secret tunnel and shut the panel leaving us in total darkness. I felt Darius' hand wrap around my body and lift me, putting me over his shoulder. "These tunnels have no light. Hold on tight and I will get us to where we are going in just a moment."

"Put me down!" I demanded, struggling against him. I was so small and weak compared to him that my fighting was no use. Even if I could get down, would I be able to navigate the darkness?

No. I stopped fighting, and let him carry me.

"I am glad you came to your senses. Such a good girl," he purred.

My body heated at the sound of him calling me a good girl. There was something inside of me that craved his praise. We walked in silence for a few moments before the light began to seep into the tunnel. Finally, we exited and he put me down. I jumped back to gain space between us. I realized we were now in a small garden, filled with red lilies, on a cliff. In the distance, you could see the Kikaro mountains. I walked over to the edge of the cliff and stood there, looking out. My heart broke as I reminded myself that I would never see my parents again.

"This is one of my favorite secret spots in Titus. I discovered it just a year after you died the first time. I spend most of my free time here," he cleared his throat and came to stand by my side. "I thought you would like the view."

"It's beautiful," I said softly.

Darius sat and let his feet hang off the edge of the cliff. He patted the ground next to him and I sat by his side. I looked down and my stomach twisted as I saw how high up we were. How far did we travel in those tunnels? I wondered how far we were from the city. Darius quickly grabbed my chin and made me look up at him.

"Eyes on me, doll. Nothing good comes from looking down." He wrapped his arm around me and pulled me in close.

"Darius," I whimpered.

"Say my name like that again and I won't be able to resist you," he growled. I swallowed hard as heat rose to my cheeks. He reached up and removed my mask. "There you are. There is that beautiful face that I miss so much."

I stared into his bright green eyes and saw into his soul. I saw the fragile broken man behind the hard façade.

"Can't I run? You do not have to kill me."

"I wish that were true. As soon as it hits midnight your blood will be the only thing I crave. I will smell you and know exactly where you are. There will be no escaping me. I need to warn you. When it is time, I will be another man. I will be cruel. I will be a monster." Tears flooded his eyes. "I don't want to hurt you. I love you." Those tears began to fall down his face. "I am sorry."

In the distance, I heard the chimes of the clock tower. My heart sank as I heard the twelfth bell toll. Darius' eyes changed to blood-red. I jumped up and backed away from the ledge.

"Darius," I whimpered. I blinked and he stood in front of me. He grabbed my wrist and yanked me to him. Fear flooded my body. I tried to yank my wrist away, but he just held tighter.

"I told you what was going to happen if you said my name like that again," he licked his lips. In an instant, he slammed me to the ground and pinned me by my wrists. His fangs sank into my neck and I let out a blood-curdling scream as my body felt as if it was on fire.

Everything then faded to black.

Acknowledgements

I want to thank everyone who made this a reality. I published Blood Singer in 2022, and did not know what to expect. I found an amazing community that is so supportive of indie authors it makes my heart happy!

Without all of you, I do not know where I would be. Thank you for making my dreams come true!

Also By

The Realms of Elswyth:
The Curse of Orilon
The Assassin of Irolyth
The Vengeance of Alari
The Sacrifice of Aeros

www.ingramcontent.com/pod-product-compliance
Lightning Source LLC
Chambersburg PA
CBHW061853310726
48972CB00004B/1001